T0129438

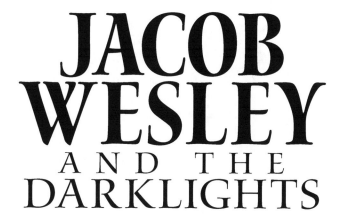

# JACOB WESLEY AND THE DARKLIGHTS

## JS MITCHELL

iUniverse

# JACOB WESLEY AND THE DARKLIGHTS

This is a work of fiction. All of the characters, names, incidents, organizations, and dialogue in this novel are either the products of the author's imagination or are used fictitiously

iUniverse books may be ordered through booksellers or by contacting:

iUniverse
1663 Liberty Drive
Bloomington, IN 47403
www.iuniverse.com
1-800-Authors (1-800-288-4677)

Because of the dynamic nature of the Internet, any web addresses or links contained in this book may have changed since publication and may no longer be valid. The views expressed in this work are solely those of the author and do not necessarily reflect the views of the publisher, and the publisher hereby disclaims any responsibility for them.

Any people depicted in stock imagery provided by Getty Images are models, and such images are being used for illustrative purposes only.
Certain stock imagery © Getty Images.

ISBN: 978-1-5320-4490-8 (sc)
ISBN: 978-1-5320-4492-2 (hc)
ISBN: 978-1-5320-4491-5 (e)

Library of Congress Control Number: 2018904073

Print information available on the last page.

iUniverse rev. date: 04/02/2018

# 1

# THE BOY WITH
# DIFFERENT EYES

"WAKE UP! You impudent rascals, wake up at once!" A screechy voice shouted like nails on a chalkboard behind the orphans' room door. "There's cleaning to be done. That hallway better be so clean I can see my face in its shine before breakfast!" Her footsteps shuffled through the hall. Following closely behind was a raspy meow that echoed throughout the room.

"Coming Ms. Larrier," spoke a short and skinny boy with black wavy hair. Standing up from the bed, he rubbed his light green eyes and looked at the hands of the clock, which had a giant crack down the middle and read seven AM. He was frustrated though; frustrated because he woke from a beautiful dream of a world far away from where he could fly around, high above the clouds. Rain fell upon Griffin, the city they lived in. Droplets pelted the ceilings throughout the orphanage like a thousand fingers tapping on a desk. In front of the barred window, the sky's gloom made Jacob realize he was far outside of his dream, and an escape was impossible.

Jacob stretched. His back was sore yet again from sleeping on his small cot, which had a mattress so thin that it could almost be mistaken for a sheet. The tiny, crowded room that held the twenty orphan boys was meant to fit only eight. Even though it was the oldest and least-kept room in the orphanage, it was the only place where Jacob could escape his sad reality. It was what he was used to, but his body still struggled to adapt to the uncomfortable bed.

Jacob continued to get dressed, putting on his stained hoodie that had a missing string and his stained jeans with holes in each knee. His shoes were faded white with missing laces. Surrounding Jacob in his claustrophobic room were twenty cots too small to sleep in. The walls had chipped paint. One of the boys opened the door, and the rest ran through. Just outside the door were several buckets filled with water. Jacob picked up a brush and began to scrub the dirty brown stairs that lead down to the living room. Water and soapy suds flooded the area. Sticky gum lined the ground where they walked, and there was a terrible musty smell that emanated from the walls.

"That's more like it, my little rodents, and if these floors don't glow like the morning sun, your little behinds will see my hand's wrath!" In front of Jacob and near the end of the hall was the disastrous director of the Kendal Drive Orphanage. Margaret Larrier was perhaps the meanest lady to ever exist in the history of our universe. She was the last person you'd ever think would believe in true happiness because she was mad every second of every day. She was a tall, wiry woman with scraggly hair, a long, pointed nose, and a giant mole placed perfectly atop her forehead. Next to Ms. Larrier was a plump puff of gray fuzz named Smaltz. Jacob thought she looked like an overgrown dust bunny with a growl that sounded like a baby whining. Smaltz used this growl to her advantage by alerting Ms. Larrier of any mischief that was taking place. Pictures of the plump ball of fur scattered throughout the dusty hall, which made it even harder to clean.

Jacob tried to ignore the dust and globs of cat hair that filled the air. He decided to focus on his dream he had woken up of. The dream was extraordinary. He was flying around a city that was different than the gloomy town he was from. This city had futuristic-styled buildings that were a mile long. Just as Jacob started to drift into a daydream again, cold, dirty water smacked him in the face and drenched his clothes, spilling in through the holes in his jeans.

"That floor gonna clean itself, Weird Eyes?"

Once Jacob was able to rub the water from his vision to see again, he saw that a redheaded, freckle-faced kid wearing denim suspenders over an orange shirt was standing hunched over him with a bucket clenched in his fat hands. Immediately, the pudgy-faced psycho in front of Jacob erupted into laughter, and the rest of the orphans followed suit.

"Thanks, Tommy." Jacob cowered back to cleaning the floor. Tommy wasn't a particular type of boy. He was the biggest of the group, and for the most part, he did Ms. Larrier's dirty work for her while she wasn't around. He loved giving the other kids wedgies and making Jacob's life extra miserable.

"Now clean the floor, you wet noodle." Tommy shoved Jacob down into the puddle of water underneath him as he passed.

Jacob's face met the puddle of water as the laughter grew louder, and Tommy winked back at the other boys. The last thing Tommy needed was more reassurance that what he put Jacob through was hilarious. Jacob struggled to get up from the dirty water, his cheeks beaming red. Jacob grabbed his cloth and brush and went back to scrubbing the floor. He was happy to be out of the way of the musty smell lingering from Tommy's unwashed armpits.

Just before he could relax, an annoying hiss came from behind him.

The plump ball of fur had made her way back into the hall, followed by the scraggly orphanage director.

"He did it," said Tommy, who pointed over at Jacob.

Jacob knew the trouble he was in now was far more severe than the embarrassing water that flooded his sneakers. When Ms. Larrier saw a mess, her hair would stand up, leaving her mole pulsating in plain sight. He was sure to get in trouble that was even deeper than the puddle underneath him. Another week in timeout, perhaps. Jacob rose to his knees and gave one final glare over at Tommy, who had stuck his fat tongue out at Jacob.

"Tommy, you're a dear, just like me. If I ever had a son - if I ever wanted a son, that is - I hope he would revere troublemakers as much as you," Ms. Larrier said. After Tommy's undeserving compliment, she turned her head creepily in Jacob's direction.

"Smaltzy, are my ears working correctly?" Ms. Larrier sloppily paced forward through the crowd of boys. The cat twirled its tail around her legs maniacally. "I believe I heard laughing, and what does Ms. Larrier say about laughter?"

In unison, the group said, "Laughter isn't polite, and not being polite is not being a person."

Ms. Larrier strode right over to where Jacob sat in his puddle of water. He trembled, the brush still in his hand.

"What are we missing here?" she grunted.

"Sorry, Ms. Larrier," Jacob mumbled.

"You'll have to speak louder. These old ears don't work like they used to," Ms. Larrier smiled and revealed dirty yellow teeth underneath her whiskers. The mole above her forehead began to pulsate. Jacob heard Smaltz hiss in his direction.

He lowered his head reluctantly. "Laughter isn't polite, and not being polite is not being a person, Ms. Larrier." Ms. Larrier's ugly snarl turned into a nasty smile. Each whisker above her upper lip gave Jacob a chill. Her mole was now calming down to normal size.

"You know, those nasty little eyes remind me of seaweed, and speaking of which, something stinks around here." Ms. Larrier spun around and headed back down the hall with her plump ball of fur dragging behind.

"Now, finish up! We have cold oatmeal and boiled eggs for breakfast, you little rodents!" Ms. Larrier screamed, pacing angrily down the stairs. Fortunately, Jacob seemed to be safe from punishment well, at least for now. Jacob knew she still wasn't thrilled with what took place first thing in the morning.

Ms. Larrier wasn't too fond of Jacob and his constant "accidents." He had gotten in trouble so much that he might soon be in the Kendal Drive Orphanage's Troublemakers Hall of Fame.

The issue had always been the differences between Jacob and the rest of the boys. For one, Jacob's eyes were unique. Most every other person he came into contact with had solid colors that centered around a pupil. However, his eyes only had a green outline around his pupils, with gray in between. Whenever he asked Ms. Larrier why his eyes were the way they were, she spat back at him in a nasty tone; I don't know, they were always ugly little things. Now go clean!

Besides his eyes, strange things happened around him. It wasn't a coincidence that Smaltz seemed to have an odd sense of smell for Jacob, and that Jacob wound up in trouble more than any other boy. Specific things just happened to him.

Once, Ms. Larrier got so sick of looking at Jacob's "ugly little eyes" (as she coined them) that she made Jacob wear these old sunglasses that looked like they were straight out of her grandmother's closet. Tommy had almost laughed his freckles off when he caught a glimpse of Jacob's new look. However, after nearly an hour, the sunglasses popped off his face and exploded in mid-air, creating a trail of fire that caught onto Ms. Larrier's dress. Once the flames had disappeared, Ms. Larrier grounded Jacob for an entire week, with no television or recess time outside with the other boys.

Another time, to Jacob's surprise, Ms. Larrier had put him on cooking duty. He was responsible for making a rosemary turkey that came out very different than the one in the beautiful cooking book he was given. Every time he got near the stove, it lit on fire and set the turkey ablaze. The taste of charcoal and rubber caused Ms. Larrier to spend a night in her bathroom regurgitating the overcooked turkey. Besides getting another week of a timeout, it was the last time Jacob was allowed with cooking anything.

The worst trouble Jacob had ever gotten into was two field trips ago when the boys were taken to the nearby roller rink. When Tommy was giving Jacob one of his regular upside-down wedgies, to his and every other boy's surprise, Jacob rose in the air while still upside-down. When he moved around the area, all of the skates near him began to explode. Finally, after a bizarre thirty minutes of floating around and spontaneously combusting roller-skates, Jacob was back in timeout, this time for two entire weeks. Ms. Larrier was charged for the damages. Jacob exclaimed his innocence every time she approached, but his punishment remained. The upside-down wedgie that Tommy had given him must have been what lifted him off the ground, he complained.

At this point, it was vastly becoming normal for Jacob to be grounded. He could count on spending time alone in his room at least once a month. As removed as he was from the rest of the group, sometimes it was for the best. He had time to dream, relax, and disappear from the torment of Ms. Larrier and the other kids.

Cleaning, cleaning, and more cleaning. Ms. Larrier always found a way to keep the boys busy cleaning her filthy home. The only boy that Ms. Larrier didn't make clean was Tommy Badton. Not only did he not have to clean, but he was entrusted with the job of making sure the rest of the orphans kept busy. This was commemorated by the toy sheriff badge that Tommy wore proudly on his right suspender. If anyone got out of line, it was Tommy's job to either whack them back into shape or tell Ms. Larrier what was going on.

After the cleaning, for the most part, Jacob and the other boys funneled down the black wooden steps and into the poor excuse for a kitchen. Dust lined the mustard yellow walls. Faded cabinets with broken knobs looked as though they hadn't been washed in ages. There wasn't just the usual dust, but also leftover clumps of hair from Smaltz walking around. Smaltz even left behind crumbs of her food that spilled out of her pink and yellow food dish. Jacob caught a hiss from the fat cat as she stared him down from atop the sink like a gargoyle. In addition to being tortured by Tommy and receiving the occasional belittling from Ms. Larrier, Smaltz made it very well known that she didn't care for Jacob's scent, either.

"Prepare the dishes for the other children, you ugly-eyed rodent," Ms. Larrier snapped in Jacob's direction.

"Yes Ms. Larrier," he grumbled. A tail swiped the white dish that Jacob had been reaching for right out of his hands, sending it smashing to the ground. Jacob and Smaltz did not get along at all. Jacob was a trigger for Smaltz's growl, and any sight of him signaled the alarm. Time after time, she would growl at Jacob after she purred around the legs of Ms. Larrier. It wasn't unusual for her to break a dish or leave a mess, and the blame would be placed on Jacob. Recently, an urn that contained the ashes of one of Ms. Larrier's relatives was knocked over by the fat gray tail of Smaltz, only to shower Jacob with the ashes, leaving him covered in them.

"Watch it, you! You're going to hurt Smaltz, or me!" Jacob shrugged and picked up the broken pieces from the plate. Tommy and the other kids giggled at him. The children sat around the middle breakfast nook as they were served their old white bowls of sloppy oatmeal.

Jacob looked down at the cold gray glop of food in his bowl. It looked like pale baby food. It smelled like a box of used crayons. Next to the bowl of oatmeal was a soft-boiled egg that smelled like one of Tommy's farts. Reluctantly, Jacob picked up a rusty fork and dug into the soft-boiled egg. The taste was like bland, dry fish, and it almost made him gag. To wash it down, he drank his cup of plain water. He had to take several gulps to remove the dry taste.

Next was the gray glop of goopy cold oatmeal. Jacob grabbed a rusty spoon next to the fork and spooned out a mouthful of the oatmeal. He closed his eyes, bracing for the cold bite.

Just as the tip of the oatmeal was about to sting his mouth, Jacob felt a tug in his hand. Fat knuckles clenched his fist, and the spoon flung the oatmeal like a catapult right into his face. Glop clung to Jacob's nose, cheeks, and lips.

"You're supposed to catch the food in your mouth, Dumb Eyes!" Tommy yelled. The rest of the orphans started giggling uncontrollably.

"Looks like you don't need the rest of that, then." Tommy grabbed the bowl of remaining old, cold oatmeal and scarfed it down like it was hot lasagna.

After wiping away the drippings of oatmeal from his face, Jacob sat back in his chair. A titanic gurgling sound came from his stomach. Jacob was okay with not being able to finish his usual breakfast. The tastes never pleased him much, and Tommy eating the rest of his meal had saved him from having to experience it yet again.

After breakfast had finished, the boys were ordered to clean up after themselves. Jacob was on rinsing duty. Each dish had gray glop stuck to the edges. The sponge looked like a brown block, and it barely erased the crud from the plates. He had to use his fingernails to dig in to get the food off.

Henry Buford III, the homeschool teacher, had assigned them homework on different types of languages. In their room full of cots, Jacob was reviewing the differences between Egyptian hieroglyphics and Sumerian symbols. The unique symbols for each word intrigued him.

Then, all of a sudden, a massive knuckled hand swatted the book from Jacob's lap. Tommy stood like a statue in front of Jacob. A few of the other bigger kids that were known to be Tommy's henchmen grabbed Jacob underneath his arms.

"Hey, Weird Eyes! Are you deaf, too? I was talking to you, Doof Face!" Tommy rubbed his giant knuckles across Jacob's scalp and then proceeded to knock on his head like he was pounding on a door.

"My bad, Tommy, I was just study-"

Tommy shoved Jacob's head under his unwashed armpit, releasing him from his henchman's hold. The musty smell from his armpit plagued Jacob's nose. He could barely breathe under there, never mind the tight grip around his neck. His head could pop off of his body at any moment. Jacob tried to speak, but choking made it difficult.

"I thought… Maybe since it wasn't due until Wednesday, I'd… I'd…" Tommy's forearm was wrapped around his neck so tightly that it cut off his circulation, only allowing Jacob to get out a few words.

"You thought what? You'd wait a little bit? Hello, Weird Eyes! Think, you little jabroni! I'm going to need at least an extra day to copy it. Crazy Buford would flip out if I turned in a sheet of paper with your ugly writing on it, dingleberry." Jacob felt the tight grip release from his neck. He coughed a few times, but before he could regain his breath, Tommy's large hands shoved him right into the two other boys that were standing behind him. Their sweaty palms went right back under his arms. His neck started to feel better, but now he had disgusting sweat dripping down his hoodie from the two other boys.

"Hey Tommy, check out this nerd's shoes. He's got no laces! Maybe he can borrow some of Ms. Larrier's shoes, huh?" One of the goons was pointing at Jacob's shoes. The rest of the boys joined in with laughter. Tommy ignored it and crept closer to Jacob, his big nose inches away from Jacob's. Jacob tried to lean back to avoid the putrid stench of Tommy's breath.

"So, what about that homework, hmm, Weird Eyes?" Tommy knocked on Jacob's head with his knuckles again. Jacob looked over at the rest of the group, looked down, and then back up at Tommy still.

"I'll get it done for you now, Tommy." He lowered his head again. The henchmen released Jacob from their sweaty grip. They shoved him away, and just as he was about to step forward, Tommy threw his foot out in front of him. Jacob crashed to the ground, his hands smacking the floor, barely breaking his fall.

"Watch where you're going, butthead! You better get some laces for those shoes, so you don't go tripping around everywhere you walk."

Tommy and the other boys laughed out loud as they raced back upstairs. Jacob gathered his books in embarrassment and started to head in the other direction. Just when he had reached the first step on the stairs, a knock came on the front door, followed by a few rings of the doorbell. Footsteps came trampling back down the stairs to see who was there. Ms. Larrier, followed by Smaltz, rushed to the entrance.

"Who is it?" croaked Ms. Larrier. Jacob huddled right behind her anxiously, trying to look through the peephole. By now, the rest of the orphans had piled back down the stairs and into the living room.

"Margaret, ta ta! It's Henry, hee-hee!" said a very goofy and jovial voice from behind the door.

"Who?!" clamored Ms. Larrier. Jacob thought that was odd because she knew exactly who it was.

"Your friendly neighbor, Henry Buford III, of course! You know who I am, tee-hee." Henry's joy made Ms. Larrier's skin crawl.

"What do you want now, Henry? I am busy!" she retorted, globs of spit hitting Jacob on top of his head.

"Margaret, today's the day we are taking all the orphanages to the Griffin Museum of Historical Artifacts, ta ta!"

Jacob heard the excitement in Henry's voice, which triggered his own.

Ms. Larrier's mole started pulsating so much that it looked like it was going to burst and send gooey mole stuff all over the house. "How could I forget?" she mumbled furiously under her breath.

Tommy folded his big arms over his chest, but Jacob and the rest of the boys had smiles on their faces. Every year, the town provided special field trips for the orphanages, to get them out of the house and enjoy different things. It was Jacob's only escape from his horrible filthy home.

Ms. Larrier stormed over to the front door, let out a scratchy sigh, turned and snarled in Jacob's direction, then unlocked the four oval locks on the front door.

A short, stout man entered through the doorway. His face was soft, pudgy, and completely covered in orange freckles. Amidst the lentigo were a pair of oval-shaped spectacles. Twirling down like twisting party streamers were orange strands of hair buried underneath a blue fedora. His neck was held together by a bright blue bowtie, which Ms. Larrier always found obnoxious. Wrapped around his body was his blue and yellow striped trench coat.

The stout man skipped lightly into the center of the room; his arms folded cleanly behind his back as he swayed through in a skating motion. He tipped his hat towards Jacob and gave him a comforting smile.

"The best day of the year! How exciting, ta ta?" He turned his attention towards Ms. Larrier, who stood still as a statue, her eyebrows furrowed, shooting a death stare in Henry's direction. "Cheer up, Margaret! You'll get to have the day to yourself, hee-hee," giggled Henry. Ms. Larrier was redder than a tomato and seemed about to burst right into tomato juice. Henry moved to his right, unaware that Smaltz's tail was next to him. His next step squashed the tail. Her meow shrilled, piercing the boys' ears. Then she ran behind Ms. Larrier, who was even more mortified than before. "Ooh, oh me, oh my, my apologies, my little furry friend, I can be quite the stepper!" Henry tried to pet Smaltz, but she just hissed again and hid further behind Ms. Larrier.

"Henry," Ms. Larrier began to compose herself slightly.

"Why, yes Margaret?" Henry inched closer to her with anticipation.

"Is this necessary? The boys and I have much to do today," Ms. Larrier replied. Jacob's head sunk down to his chest.

"I'm sorry, Margaret," Henry moved away from her. "But we already confirmed with the museum for all of their tickets, and, ta ta, we have a van waiting outside."

Henry turned towards Jacob yet again. Jacob picked his head back up off his chest and stared into the man's kind, freckly face. It was tough to see his eyes through the spectacles, but he could have sworn one of them winked at him.

"Jacob, good to see you, ta ta!" Henry jovially placed his finger atop Jacob's nose. Then, Ms. Larrier stepped in between Jacob and Henry to prevent the further niceties from being exchanged.

"This little rodent doesn't concern you, Henry. Besides, his eyes might turn you to stone." She twisted an evil grin back at Jacob before turning her attention to Henry again.

"Oh, come now, Margaret, the boy's eyes are one-of-a-kind!"

Ms. Larrier grunted at the compliment. "Henry, the boys have lots of cleaning to do today. The house needs its pick-me-up. You can appreciate a good spring cleaning, can't you?" Ms. Larrier tried to display a smile, but her yellow chicklet teeth didn't do it justice.

"Sorry to disappoint, Margaret, hee-hee," Henry chuckled. "But we've paid for all the tickets, and there's a bus waiting outside. They will only be gone a few hours, and after, they can return to tidy up this elegant castle, tee-hee." Henry then pulled out a funny looking pocket watch with four dials on it from inside his blue and yellow trench coat. "Oh my! We're already late, ta ta!"

"Henry, these trips are so childish, they are just nasty things that nasty people do, I-"

Before Ms. Larrier could finish, Henry placed his index finger firmly on her whiskered upper lip.

"Now Margaret, that's not the way to talk in front of the boys. No nasty business here! They may be childish, but these are all children, of course, ha-ha!"

Frustrated and with an angry growl, Ms. Larrier turned around and bolted up the steps towards her room. "That man will be the end of me, Smaltz, the end of me!" she yelled from the top of the stairs. Raspy meows echoed behind.

# 2

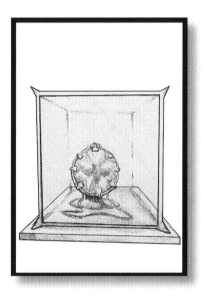

# THE JEWEL OF FUTURA

The boys piled into the old yellow bus an hour later. To Jacob's luck, he was getting time away from Ms. Larrier and her nasty feline tattletale Smaltz. Jacob walked down the aisle of the bus, trying to find an open seat. Unfortunately for him, he was one of the last kids on the bus. Walking curiously down the aisle, he quickly approached the bigger kids. Finally, he spotted a seat, and just as he was about to take it, a giant orange sneaker jumped out in front of him. He fell to the ground, smacking his head hard.

"Nice trip, freak," Tommy yelled before sitting back down in the seat across from Jacob. The bus jolted into laughter, and Tommy stood up with great pride.

One of the smaller kids helped Jacob up, and he took a spot in between two other boys. He sat scrunched in his place while Tommy's eyes fixated on him. Before Jacob could enjoy another moment of happiness, Tommy's fat head turned to face him.

"You're lucky, Ugly Eyes," Tommy whispered with his fat nose placed right on the back of the seat. "You're lucky, you little loser. If I were you, I would stay far away from me at the museum, and don't worry - when we get back, I'll find a way to get you in trouble."

Jacob knew he couldn't speak up to him, but instead, sent a thousand mental daggers soaring towards Tommy's freckled, spoiled face. "Okay, Tommy."

Tommy stuck out his gross tongue at Jacob, placed his hands above his head like antlers, and teased him for a few minutes before Jacob leaned to the right, ignoring him along with all the other kids who were giggling.

Jacob was hoping that today at the museum would be different than most days. He made himself an oath that he was going to keep to himself and keep as far away from Tommy as possible. If her were to accomplish his goal, just maybe he would even get to enjoy his time at the museum.

The bus had left the orphanage and Tommy went through a few of his regular routines for getting under Jacob's skin. He tried everything. He made fart noises with his smelly armpit and then gave another young boy next to him a few wet willies. Jacob tried his best to ignore Tommy's antics and was able to do so until Tommy started talking about superheroes.

"Batman is by far the best," he said, after nudging one of the older kids next to him.

"What about Iron Man?" said the other.

"Wolverine," said another.

"Superman is the greatest," mumbled a young boy who was sitting right next to Jacob.

"Why is that, Pea Brain, huh?!" snickered Tommy.

"He cc-can fly," the smaller boy bravely explained.

Jacob saw Tommy's face grow even fatter with an evil grin that was as wide as the wingspan of an eagle. He knew that Tommy had already decided what to do to the little boy next. Before he knew it, the little boy had his underwear pulled out from his shorts. Tommy stretched the boy's underwear so high it almost ripped right out from under his pants.

"I wish I could fly," Jacob said, after recalling his wonderful dream from the previous night. "Then I'd try to fly as far away from here as possible."

Tommy's freckles looked like they were going to burst right off of his face as he gritted his teeth at Jacob. His face grew like a bomb ready to explode. Tommy dropped the drawers of the little kid in the middle of stretching them over his head. Then he jumped into the seat in front of Jacob, knocking two other kids out of the way in the process.

"YOU CAN'T FLY, YOU IDIOT!"

Jacob looked over at the rest of the boys, who had been giggling uncontrollably. Jacob decided that being quiet was a better option than getting his undergarments strewn all over the bus. He stuck up for the other orphan, taking a verbal bullet in the chest for him. He sat silently, trying to ignore the bully with the puffed-up chest which was hanging over his seat with bated breath.

"What's the matter, dingbat? Cat got your tongue?" Tommy flicked Jacob's nose. A red hue filled Jacob's cheeks as he stared into Tommy's soulless eyes.

"Oh, you're right Tommy," Jacob mumbled. "How could I be so silly?"

Jacob's lackluster apology didn't seem to work on the witless brute.

"This little dingbat thinks he can fly!" Tommy turned around in his seat to face the other orphans. "What's next, pigs can talk?" Tommy grabbed Jacob by the hoodie and lifted him towards his fat face. Tommy's breath smelled so foul that Jacob had to hold his breath to block it out.

"All right lads, calm down, ta ta!" Henry patted both Jacob and

Tommy on the back. "We are just about there now, hee-hee." Henry turned around in a skip and strutted back to his seat.

"You're lucky, Ugly Eyes. If Mr. Bowtie wasn't here, your face would be mincemeat." Tommy released his grip on Jacob's hoodie, and Jacob roughly fell into his seat.

The bus had pulled into a gray parking lot. Rain continued to fall upon Griffin as the droplets made a staticky sound outside the bus, but the rain didn't stop the museum from being packed. In front of the parking lot was a three-story rectangular building made of white stone. There were ten giant glass windows on each level of the museum. At every level were tall cement pillars connected to each other.

At the entrance of the museum, each boy received a stamp on their hand. Inside the building were three escalators which lead to each of the main floors. The boys were enclosed by crystal white walls and marble tile. It smelled like a combination of wax, grease, and rubber, but that didn't bother Jacob. He much preferred this smell to any of Tommy's foul odors. The floors had such a beautiful shine that Jacob could see his reflection in it. Jacob walked into the front area and was simultaneously greeted by a giant statue of an Egyptian Pharaoh, and a security guard with a stomach of equally impressive size. *Maybe a future Tommy*, he thought to himself.

Jacob kept his promise to himself that day in the museum, and he kept his distance from Tommy and the other older boys as much as he could. Lucky for him, Henry stayed close to the group and kept an extra eye on any funny business that Tommy might think up. After several exhibits and a lot of walking around, the boys were treated to a free lunch of peanut butter and jelly sandwiches, with plastic cups full of soda. What a relief it was to have something tastier than the bland foods they were forced to eat back at the orphanage! After lunch, they were given tiny pudding cups for dessert. However, when Tommy demanded another pudding cup because he destroyed his within one gulp, Jacob had to settle for no dessert.

Besides the lack of pudding, Jacob was having a wonderful time. He learned about all types of old famous buildings and civilizations. He was able to hold different sports memorabilia and watch an incredibly spectacular electricity display.

About an hour after lunch, Jacob and the rest of the orphans were led by Henry down to the third floor. "Right this way boys, hee-hee, the most fun exhibit awaits you!"

Down the stairs was a backdrop of black space with tiny stars sparkling in place. In the center of the area was a 6-foot holographic image of a man in a flying pose. It was the coolest thing Jacob had ever seen. Surrounding the area were sloped golden walls with hanging globes of light attached to the sides. Near the ceiling were several cars with wings on either side, floating in place. Perhaps one of them would be a good getaway car that Jacob could take advantage of.

Behind the hologram of the flying man was a red oval-shaped vehicle inside of a spinning wheel with two wings sticking out near its sides. Jacob was mesmerized by the object, but before he could reach it, a fat fist shoved him out of the way. Barely maintaining his balance, he looked up and spotted Tommy barreling past him towards the odd spinning vehicle. "I want to ride this right now!" Tommy snapped, out of breath. Jacob caught up with the rest of the group behind Tommy.

"It's a simulator rollercoaster ride. Thrilling, fun, and you definitely can take it for a whirl," said a teenage boy with a brown museum uniform.

"Let me on, then!" Tommy yelled at the teenage boy.

Henry stepped forward and approached the young man in uniform. "How much to let the boy ride the, um…?"

"…Chaos Coaster sir, and that'll be just two dollars."

Henry paid, and Tommy entered the chamber. Jacob leaned over the ropes to get a closer look. The ball moved up and down, to the left and the right, then diagonally. Lights went on and off. It swerved around, over and over. Every boy sat frozen, tongues out of their mouths, waiting to see the enjoyment on Tommy's face. The ride came to a slow halt, followed by a loud whistle. The doors opened, and Tommy wobbled out of the coaster.

"I don't feel so good."

And just like that, Tommy let out a long streak of orange vomit all over the shiny marble floor. Jacob chuckled to himself as Tommy was hurried off by Henry towards the bathroom. Disappointed, the other boys moved on to another exhibit with giant lifelike pyramids nearby.

Jacob began to follow, but then something caught his eye. To the right of the stomach-cringing futuristic ride was a small glass case about the size of a mailbox. Inside was a silver necklace attached to a beautiful emerald green gem. Inside the gem was a silver insect with a crystal blue gear hovering around it. Jacob looked around to see if anyone else had spotted it. He confirmed he was alone, and pressed on towards the object. The description on the glass read The Jewel of Futura.

"Unique, isn't it, hmm?" whispered a voice behind Jacob. He quickly turned around to see a man in the same uniform that the teenager had been wearing, but he had overflowing puffy red curls sticking out of a baseball cap and large round goggles over his eyes.

After looking the man up and down, Jacob turned back suspiciously towards the case with the unique necklace inside.

"What is it?" Jacob asked.

"It's not from this place, you know, or from this time, hmm." The man inched closer to Jacob's side, placing his hand on top of the case. "It harnesses something very unusual, ha," the man chuckled.

Jacob pushed his face right up against the glass to get a closer look. His eyes widened, and his eyebrows rose to the top of his forehead. His curiosity shifted in the direction of the museum employee. Suspiciously missing from his shirt was a nametag. "Hey, you don't have a-"

"Do you want to hold it, hmm?" The curly-haired man interrupted Jacob before he could finish his question.

"Hh-hold it?" stammered Jacob.

"Yes! Surely you want to hold it. Don't you want to know what makes it so special? I mean I do, but you know…"

"…But what do I know?" Jacob lowered one of his eyebrows and let go of the case.

"That's not important right now. What's important is that you try it on silly, hmm, ha-ha," the mysterious man chuckled yet again. Jacob shifted his gaze back again to the shiny box in front of him. The curly-haired man suddenly snapped his fingers, and each plate of the glass slowly separated, moving in different directions. The gem with the necklace hovered in the air by itself, held up by nothing that Jacob could see. Jacob looked up at the man, anxiously waiting for a sign of what to do next. "Neat trick, huh?" the man nodded and twirled in place.

"You're not a museum worker, are you?" Jacob asked in astonishment. The man shook his head with a smile as broad as a watermelon slice.

Jacob swallowed hard and kept his eyes fixated on the man who was now softly dancing in front of the emblem and next to Jacob.

"Go ahead try it on Jacob, ha!"

Jacob stared at the man with his jaw quivering. Before he could raise his voice, the emblem started slowly hovering over towards Jacob, who took his full attention away from the suspicious man who knew his name. He stuck his index finger out timidly to touch the emblem that was now inches away from him.

"Go ahead! It won't bite, you know," the man giggled.

Jacob touched the emblem, and the cold silver chain did not bite him, just as the man had said it wouldn't. He took the necklace and placed it slowly over his head and around his neck. The moment that the gem touched his chest, a sharp pain shot through and ran into his throat, then back down through his veins of his arms. He could feel all sorts of stinging sensations, jolting like electricity from his toes to his fingertips. He then began to feel as though he was suffocating and it wouldn't stop. The sensation was worse than holding your breath beneath the water.

He opened his eyes and could see the ground far beneath his feet. He was eye-level with the white curved ceiling. He stuck out his hands to reach for anything he could find to hold on to at that moment. He was losing his breath and his life at the same time and didn't know how to save himself.

Suddenly, a blinding light overtook his vision. The throbbing pain continued back up his legs, roared through his stomach, and inched into his throat yet again. It climbed through his esophagus and into his mouth. He bellowed out the loudest scream, rivaling even a siren in volume. It was louder than Smaltz's annoying meow, more decibels than one of Ms. Larrier's angry tantrums, or even one of Tommy's cackles.

Then, just like that, everything went black.

When Jacob came to, the mysterious curly-haired employee was suspiciously missing. The emblem was no longer around his neck, and everything seemed normal. He looked towards the glass that had encased the emblem, which was now empty. As he stood up, he heard a nagging voice from behind.

"Jacob… Jacob, my good boy, ta ta, I thought we had lost you. You gave old Henry a great scare." Henry stumbled on his way over to Jacob.

"I, uh, I was just…" began Jacob, as he scratched his head.

"Never mind that now. We need to get back to the bus. It's almost dark, and the museum is closing." Henry picked Jacob up and led him forward.

Jacob climbed into the bus and Tommy's fat face was stretched into an evil smile. The orange vomit streaks that covered Tommy's shirt didn't prevent him from picking on Jacob again.

"Wait 'til Ms. Larrier hears you left the group," Tommy complained.

Jacob was the only boy who didn't join the crowd of Oooohs that rang out throughout the bus.

He decided to ignore Tommy and the other boys after he took his seat. Why should he care anyway? What just took place was the most bizarre thing that had ever happened to him, even more, odd than the exploding roller skates, the upside-down wedgies, or the blown-up sunglasses.

When the old yellow bus pulled into the rusted black gates of the Kendal Drive Orphanage, Jacob's stomach leaped. Tommy hopped over the seat, barreled through the other boys, and jolted out of the bus, screaming, "Ms. Larrier!" over and over, all the way up to the top of the stone steps.

By the time Jacob made it into the house, Ms. Larrier was sloppily pressed against the yellow striped wall. Her mole was twitching feverously. Her lips were curled, and her teeth grinded back and forth. She could barely muster any words.

"You! Room! N-Now!" she yelled, after staggering in place for a brief moment.

Later that night, Jacob sat alone in the claustrophobic, stinky room upstairs. He was huddled up on his rock-hard bed while the other boys got to watch their nightly movie. He took the opportunity to wonder what he had witnessed earlier. Was it a dream, or did it happen? Did he pass out in the middle of the museum? Admittedly, it had to have occurred, as the necklace was no longer there when he came to. But who was that man with the red curly hair, and why didn't he have a nametag? And how did he know Jacob's name? These questions raced through his mind like tiny horses around a track, over and over again.

Twelve years, twelve horrific years Jacob had lived at the Kendall Drive Orphanage, and nothing, not any of the other wacky events or field trips, had ever been like this. What if the dream he had where he was flying around in a different world had something to do with this? Did it have something to do with the burning sensation he felt when he was in the museum? What was that feeling? Maybe some powers? Or maybe this was finally Jacob's way out of the orphanage.

Jacob dreamt a lot, and when he did, it often centered around him flying away and hanging out with his birth parents, people who cared for him in the way he only ever dreamed and hoped for. His mother soars with him, and his dad watched from below, waving as he worked on a special machine. Jacob never knew what this machine was, but he knew it was only a dream. If Jacob ever dared to ask Ms. Larrier about his birth parents, she just scoffed at him and yelled at him to clean the nearest area. He hated the orphanage, even though it was the only home he ever had. He often wondered if there was a different home out there for him, a house without filthy Ms. Larrier, nasty boys, and an annoying plump cat.

And then, for a moment, Jacob realized something. It wasn't the only time he had seen the odd man at the museum. When Jacob had gone to the restroom in the roller rink, the same man with red curly hair had nodded to him. Once, when the boys were outside cleaning the yard, a man in a striped blue and yellow coat had winked at him. Ms. Larrier caught wind of this and slapped him on the back of the head, then ordered him to continue pulling weeds.

Jacob had never spoken a word to this curious gentleman. Not until earlier today, when he had stumbled across the great emblem.

Whoever he was, he seemed to be very interested in Jacob, and he didn't seem to care that Jacob looked different than most boys. Jacob Wesley was an unusual kid, and rare events happened to him, and this was definitely the most extraordinary event of his life.

He then began to drift into more profound thought when the light to the room flickered and then went out. Surrounded by darkness, Jacob suddenly heard a loud, bloodcurdling scream.

# 3

# THE GHOST SWITCH

Jacob was supposed to have a long night alone in the filthy boys' room, but the darkness that crept over the orphanage now caused him to leave his punishment behind. He jumped out of his bed when he heard the scream, and headed down the bronze stairs. At the end of the hall, he could make out a tiny glow of light. It was flying quickly, so he picked up his pace to run after it. The light zipped down and around the stairwell. Jacob followed after it, down the stairwell and towards the patchy yellow walls of the living room. Just as he met the bottom of the stairs, the light disappeared, and it was replaced with several burning candles. Holding the candelabra was one of the younger boys. He held it steady over the head of a hunched-over, scrawny woman. Jacob peeked over the heads of the shocked boys to find Ms. Larrier sprawled on the floor.

"The light flickered, she screamed and fainted on top of Smaltz," one of the other boys whispered. Ms. Larrier's stomach was sticking straight up in the air with her skinny arms spread across the wooden floor. Squeezed underneath her hardback were a fat tail and two paws. Smaltz let out a screechy, shrill meow and pushed her way out from underneath. The sound woke up Ms. Larrier instantly, and the candlelight gave the group a closer look at her. Her makeup was now smeared around her face and left large pink lines of lipstick over her cheeks and near her eyes.

"You!" she stretched her bony finger forward in Jacob's direction. The kids shifted the light towards Jacob's face like a detective about to interrogate a criminal. His eyebrows threw themselves to the top of his forehead immediately.

"Me? But Ms. Larrier, I was in-"

"What other little rodents could have possibly pulled a prank like this when you were the only one by yourself after your little stunt at the museum?" Ms. Larrier swayed forward as she got back to her feet. Tommy stood to the left of the group, laughing to himself with his elbows leaning on top of another orphan.

"You! Fat one! Get the light for me!" Surprisingly, she was addressing Tommy. He sat up and went over to flick the light switch on. The lights came back on and revealed that one of the antique lamps from the corner of the room was face-down on the floor.

"Oh, no! You selfish little troublemaker, you broke my lamp! If you pull something like this again, I swear I'll-"

Before she could finish, the lights flickered again.

"No, please don't-"

The lights shut off and then came back on again, quickly freezing Ms. Larrier in place.

"See, Ms. Larrier? I couldn't have possibly done this! They just flickered again," Jacob jumped in.

"Shhh, just keep your trap shut!" Ms. Larrier yelled and began to tiptoe over to the stairs.

The lights flickered one more time, and Ms. Larrier bolted up the stairwell. "I hate ghosts, Smaltzy! I hate them!" The plump cat and the freaked-out Ms. Larrier zipped right into her room, hiding from the flickering, eerie presence. The boys stood there for a moment in silence, unsure of what to do next. The door to her room snapped open wildly.

"OFF TO BED, ALL OF YOU RODENTS... NOW!" Ms. Larrier screamed, shutting the door again with a loud smack, smashing the hinges that struggled to hold it together. A quick meow was heard, more like a raspy mumble, as Smaltz barely made it back inside before the door closed.

Jacob and the other boys just looked at each other for a moment, and then sprinted toward Ms. Larrier's door to try and catch a sound of what was going on. They listened very intently and stuck their ears as close to the thin crack beneath the door as possible. They could barely make out what Ms. Larrier was saying, which sounded like mostly mumbles and jumbles.

"Oh, Smaltzy, not again! Not again, Smaltzy," said Ms. Larrier, whose voice was shaking feverously. "What could this be? Ghosts again? I hate ghosts. Maybe the boys are messing with me again. I'll punish them, those troublemakers."

The only thing Jacob could see were Smaltz's fat paws pouncing around the floor. Then they were gone.

"No, it can't be them. They are too stupid to figure out that I'm afraid of ghosts. Barney, is that you? Mimi, is that you?" she asked quietly. Could her ancestors be the ones playing a prank on the orphanage?

"No, they wouldn't scare me. It's nothing, Smaltzy." Ms. Larrier began to reason with herself again. "Nothing at all, probably just a few bad bulbs. I'll change them tomorrow." Ms. Larrier was talking to herself, and now Jacob had sworn he'd heard it all, but he would soon come to find out that he hadn't yet.

The following day, Ms. Larrier was still scared and trapped in her room with the door locked shut. Jacob was using one of the urinals in the upstairs bathroom. Suddenly, something foul wafted over to Jacob's nose, and it wasn't coming from any of the stalls near him.

To Jacob's right, at the entrance of the bathroom, Tommy stood holding each of his suspenders with a stupid grin on his face. He tried to wink at Jacob, but he was too dumb to understand how to close one eye instead of two. Jacob thought he would be called "Dumb Eyes," but with the inevitable twisted underwear experience that was in his future, he decided not to say anything. Behind Tommy were two of his stooges. They were both fat and lazy, but their jobs were simple - hold down the younger boys while Tommy ripped their underwear above their heads and laugh at what Tommy says, even when it's not funny which was all of the time. His jokes were the furthest thing from being funny, but they still laughed.

Jacob stood in place as Tommy and his chubby gang approached. His arms were still stretched out. It looked like he was about to hug the air.

"Well looks who the dog dragged in," Tommy said. Jacob tried to ignore his incorrect use of the phrase and flushed the urinal instead. He ran to one of the sinks, but the two thugs behind Tommy cut him off and dug their hands roughly under his armpits.

"I couldn't help but notice you had an ugly smile on your face when that coaster ride injured me," Tommy's pudgy nose was now inches away from his own. "Someone getting injured is not funny, and you know what Ms. Larrier says about laughter..." Tommy grabbed Jacob's hair and gave a maniacal cackle.

"Tommy, I didn't laugh at you," said Jacob, in a last-ditch effort to avoid the inevitable torment. With his other hand, Tommy grabbed the back of Jacob's pants, and Jacob tried to hide inside of himself, bracing for the upward pull of his underpants.

"Blah blah blah," said Tommy. Then the bathroom lights flickered. Jacob jumped back instinctively, stepping on the fatter stooge's left foot. This broke the tight wrestling hold on his arms, followed by a nasal shriek. He hopped around clutching his foot, knocking into the other stooge, who barreled down to the floor, clunking his head on the bottom of the bathroom sink.

"OUCH!" bellowed out from the smaller fat one. Tommy stumbled over the huddled boy, trying to get to Jacob, and fell to the ground face-first. Jacob took this opportunity to exit the bathroom swiftly. Jacob darted out of the bathroom and down the stairs. Yells, cries, and grumbling could be heard echoing throughout the entire house as Jacob raced back to his bed to find an escape.

That was what it was like for the next few days. He would get cornered in the kitchen, the bathroom, and the living quarters, but nothing happened. There always seemed to be bizarre light flickering right before Jacob could get caught.

A few days later, Ms. Larrier had Jacob and the other boys clean her bedroom and bathroom. The bathroom was the most disgusting; filled with her scraggly dark hair, Smaltz's gray fur, and these blotchy stains on the bathroom mirror. Those stains had to have been from her popping her ugly pimples.

"Okay, you little rodents. No one's leaving my room until it's cleaner than my teeth!" Ms. Larrier sat in her yellow and pink throne, placed right in front of her king-sized bed. She smiled to reveal her mustard-stained teeth, which gave the boys quite a confusing set of directions. Smaltz was fluffing her tail on her mini-throne next to Ms. Larrier.

"Fat one, make sure the little troublemakers keep cleaning. I'm going to take a nap!"

Tommy smiled and revealed his shiny toy sheriff's badge proudly as he stuck it in the faces of each of the children as he paced around them. Besides his far-from-official sheriff's badge, Tommy had found a long, dull stick in the yard which he was granted permission to keep. Time and time again, he would use it to smack the other boys' legs when Ms. Larrier wasn't looking - not that she'd probably mind if she'd seen it anyway.

Jacob watched Tommy pace around him while he was stuck wiping down Ms. Larrier's toilet. What kind of a nasty woman puts this boy in charge?

"You little twerp!" Ms. Larrier snapped. "You no-good troublemaking scoundrel, why are there still large clumps of dust on my dresser?" She was pointing at an old chest next to her bed.

"How's the toilet, Gross Eyes?" Tommy was now standing over Jacob with a crazed look on his face. His fat knuckles cracked as he strengthened his grip on the stick even tighter. "Maybe you need a closer look?" Tommy asked as he hit the toilet with his splintered stick. Jacob looked around the corner of the bathroom for help - not as if Ms. Larrier or anyone else would be brave enough to help him.

"C'mon Tommy, leave me alone," Jacob squeaked as he attempted to stand up.

"Aww, listen to the little pig squeal." Tommy flapped his arms, apparently trying to imitate a pig. "What's the matter? Afraid of getting your pretty hair wet?" Tommy hit the toilet with his stick again, antagonizing Jacob, and every whack made Jacob tremble. He looked down to see what he had to try and defend himself against the ugly brute. He was armed with a less-than-intimidating scrubber and yellow gloves, not much of a defense.

Loud snores temporarily distracted the orphans. They turned around to find Ms. Larrier sprawled across her throne, her whiskers fluttering with each heavy snore. Turning his attention back towards Jacob, Tommy leaned in closer.

"Okay, piggy, time to make those eyes look right!" Tommy raised his right hand, stick held high above his head. Jacob braced himself; his scrubber pointed in the air in an attempt to defend himself.

"Ugly Eyes, meet stick! Stick, meet Ugly Eyes!" Tommy shouted. But when he took one step closer to engage Jacob, the lights flickered and quickly went out. Tommy stepped his fat foot right into a muddy puddle in front of him. He slipped, twisted, and plopped his large head right into the toilet water. Loud screaming belted out, so high pitched it sounded like a fire truck siren. What Tommy had just experienced was like another horrific tail-spinning roller coaster, but no vomit this time. Jacob had the best view in the house, and boy, did he and the other boys get a kick out of sight. Laughter drowned out the horrific screams.

The scuffle awoke Ms. Larrier abruptly. She was shouting all sorts of odd things while she stumbled to turn the lights back on. "Bumbling rodents! You little twerp troublemaking nuisances! Why aren't the lights working? What are you numbskulls doing now?!"

Ms. Larrier tried several times to turn on several switches, and nothing turned on. The more chaotic the scene became, the more Jacob enjoyed it. He had an enormous grin on his face, thinking all the wedgies and groundings were worth it.

Tommy was drowning in toilet water while Ms. Larrier fumbled around in the darkness. Everything else disappeared for Jacob at that moment, as he laughed and laughed, soaking in the disaster that his two least favorite people were experiencing. Finally, the lights came back on. Ms. Larrier was on the ground, arms and legs spread out like a flattened spider, her long snout sticking straight up in the air with her puffy hair frizzled. Tommy laid underneath her, slumped over, dripping wet with toilet suds. While Jacob was laughing as hard as he could, a small gray ball of old fur padded down the hall and circled Ms. Larrier. This, of course, was followed by a ton of annoying meows. Jacob received several scratchy hisses in his direction from Smaltz, who was able to wake up Ms. Larrier with her tail.

Jacob quickly snapped out of his reverie and back into reality. The cold, damp floor beneath his feet sent a shiver up his spine. Ms. Larrier came to and sloppily shifted her gaze first in Tommy's direction, and then Jacob's. Her face turned all sorts of reds and purples, and her mole began to twitch.

"Ugly-eyed rodent! Did you- Did you do this?!" Ms. Larrier belted out after she crawled towards Tommy. "Did you shut the lights off and push the fat one into the tt-toilet?!"

Jacob raised his right eyebrow, shocked to hear that he was being blamed as the culprit behind the hilarious, but awful, scene.

"Ms. Larrier, I was over here the entire time scrubbing your toilet. Tommy tripped when the lights went out. It wasn't me," he said. "Honestly-"

"I don't care what your excuses are, boy!"

Just as she was about to punish Jacob, the lights flickered briefly again while she was standing there. Her face went from red to pasty white; all of the colors had drained away. Then it turned into a sort of greenish color, and then back to white again.

"N-N-No! No more, please!" Ms. Larrier dropped to her old knees. "I can't take anymore…" she cried, putting her palms together as if she were praying.

Escaping punishment again, Jacob looked on as Ms. Larrier sloppily sprinted towards her bed and planted herself face-down. Jacob and the other boys were fully aware of her fear of the paranormal. Jacob relished in the fact that Tommy would be deprived of giving him another punishment. His denim suspenders were full of toilet water, and there would be no retribution for the crime. Jacob was quite alright with that.

"There's no way he gets away with this Ms. Larrier, look what he did to me!" Tommy cried. Ignoring Tommy, she put the pillow over her head to try and shield her from the flickering light madness that was taking place. Then she suddenly popped up from the bed like a fresh popcorn kernel. Her eye makeup was now drooping down to her cheeks like lines of black rain. One eye seemed much bigger than the other.

"Which one of you nasties is messing with the lights?!" Ms. Larrier then threw her nose around the room and tried to sniff out the perpetrator.

"You think this is funny? Hmm? Quickly! Go to the back of the room!" Ms. Larrier barked.

The boys huddled towards the back of her room. With no light switch in sight, Ms. Larrier crept back towards the huddled boys. She was anxious as she waited for the lights to make another move. The lights gave a slight flicker, and just when Ms. Larrier began to calm down, they shut off immediately. A loud raspy scream curdled out, and when the lights came on, Tommy and his stooges were all sitting down sobbing in pain with their very large white underpants pulled over their heads. Jacob bumped fists with one of the smaller boys. What a week this had been! Tommy never embarrassed himself this much!

For the next hour, a frightened Ms. Larrier and an angry, sleep-deprived Smaltz, accompanied by all of the boys, replaced every lightbulb in the entire orphanage.

Late at night, while everyone else was sleeping, Jacob was tossing and turning. He couldn't sleep. The constant pacing around from Ms. Larrier down the hall kept him awake until finally they had ceased.

Jacob was about to dose off when suddenly, a tiny light about the size of a small fly hovered above his face. It zipped and buzzed and then fled away. Quickly, Jacob jumped out of his bed, threw on his gray pajamas, and ran after it.

The lights were off, and Ms. Larrier's nasally snores could be heard from a distance. Jacob tiptoed down the dark and dusty hall, his heart beginning to race. Then he heard something faint that sounded like a soft whistle. Right after the whistle came loud buzzes once again. Suddenly a bright flash flew down the hall. Jacob changed his pace and sped down the hall after the glint. He raced forward, the floor creaking with each step.

As he grew closer, he saw a round fluffy object darting through the light which caused him to go faster. He didn't care how loud he was. Finally, he caught up with it.

Jacob gave a great leap and caught hold of the tail of the creature. It felt scraggly and dry, and it blurted out a loud, sharp, deafening meow. Ms. Larrier burst through the open door and pointed an old flashlight directly at him. Jacob was exposed, and to his great dismay, in his tight grasp was Smaltz, trying to inch her way free. Ms. Larrier yelled in horror at the sight.

"BACK TO YOUR ROOM, RODENT!" she clamored at Jacob.

"My poor Smaltzy, are you hurt?" she nervously asked as she picked up the great fat ball of old fur. Smaltz turned from afraid to happy, and as Jacob looked back, he could have sworn the cat winked at him, basking in his punishment.

The next day, Ms. Larrier woke the boys very early. The lighting issue had gotten worse. Electricians visited and said they had never seen anything like it, and the entire house was correctly wired, nothing was wrong.

To Ms. Larrier's revolted displeasure, she even let Henry Buford III inside of her home to take a look. Henry was less than coy about the situation and confirmed Ms. Larrier's biggest fears.

"I don't know, Margaret, ha-ha! You might have a ghost on your hands. You should try-" But before he could finish, he and his obnoxious bowtie were shoved out the door and sent back to his cozy home.

As the week dragged on, so did the bipolar lights. Sunday, while Ms. Larrier was enjoying a nice warm bath, the lights shut off twice, and this time she could swear she heard low grumbles in the air. Frightened, she squeezed the soap so hard that it flew out of her hands and into her mouth with a splash and a sour taste.

The next day, the lights began to flicker even more rapidly, and no one could also get any chores done. Tommy had a few clumsy falls. Jacob was blamed and given several wedgies. While the boys dusted the dark halls blindly every few seconds, Ms. Larrier kept herself locked in her office. Hanging around the office were "ghost-repellent" garlic cloves. Apparently, she didn't know that garlic was meant to repel vampires, not ghosts. Ms. Larrier didn't stop there; she added ten locks to the front door.

"We don't need light switches, anyway," said Ms. Larrier, as an idea crept up her scrawny spine and into her silly brain. Determined, she jetted around the house and lit candles in every room. She refused to use any of the light switches.

However, when the last candle was lit, a whistling sound pierced through the hallways, blasted past the boys, and into Ms. Larrier's eardrums. She was also met with a large gust of wind, and all ten locks on the front door burst open in a rush.

Smaltz staggered and clawed her way up to Ms. Larrier's back and on top of her scraggly hair. The candles flickered, creating pitch darkness, and then, just like that, the candles were relit, and Ms. Larrier's door was shut again.

"No more, no more!" screamed Ms. Larrier. "I can't do this alone, Smaltzy. Rodents! Come out at once and come to my office, and I don't want to hear a peep!"

Ms. Larrier looked deranged, with one eye wide open, red cat scratches over both sides of her face, and strands of her frizzy hair falling off with every step. Moments later, she had the boys picking up her king-sized bed and squeezing it into their overcrowded living quarters. To accommodate her silliness, she made the boys stack their beds against the back of the room and sleep head-to-toe.

The lights had stopped turning on and off, and the noises had ceased as well. Tommy was, of course, allowed his bed, and slept peacefully next to Ms. Larrier.

Jacob stayed awake, scrunched in between a few of the other orphans and the back wall. In addition to having nothing for a sheet, he had a flat pillow to sleep on. He stared at the cracked popcorn ceiling above him and tried his best to ignore Ms. Larrier's snores and the repugnant smells from Tommy's armpits.

The following morning, Jacob and the other boys of Kendall Drive were overly tired from being woken up to patrol the halls throughout the night. Breakfast was a failure; one boy who was on the egg station was barely able to keep his eyes open. He served globs of broken egg yolks with shards of eggshells still in them. One of Tommy's stooges was in charge of the bacon and burnt it to a blackened crisp.

Ms. Larrier barreled into the kitchen with Smaltz and yelled at everyone in sight. Her beady eyes were mostly fixed on Jacob, though.

"Are you trying to get me to choke?!" she shouted. "You nasty rodents! What's wrong with you idiots?!"

"We were up all night sweeping the halls for you," Jacob said. From time to time, Jacob dared to talk back to Ms. Larrier. Mostly, it earned him either a spanking or a spot in timeout. Tommy was sure to pick up the slack. Ms. Larrier walked straight up to Jacob and stuck her crooked, pointy nose right in his face.

"That will be the last out of your ugly trap, or you will have a date with your favorite place," said Ms. Larrier, then turned around to grab a piece of bacon. Jacob cringed as she took a firm bite, and it almost cracked her tooth.

"The bacon, too!" Ms. Larrier was mad, and Jacob was sure that she was already the most insane inhabitant of gloomy Griffin, but today, her craziness was at an all-time high.

Hours later, she paced around and waited for the lights to flicker again. Her eyes were wide, her lips were dry, and she looked as though she was lost. Jacob was more alarmed by how frightful she appeared than the odd happenings that had taken place in the house.

"Ms. Larrier has lost it, hasn't she?" cried Tommy. "She doesn't even remember my name!"

Jacob lacked the empathy Tommy was looking for; Ms. Larrier had snapped at everyone that night, even Tommy. She blamed him for not keeping the boys in check. During her screaming fit, she couldn't also remember his name. "Blithering big idiot, whatever your name is!" She had said.

Jacob remained in the living quarters as darkness fell upon their home. Footsteps loomed about, followed by big cat paw steps. Finally, Ms. Larrier walked into the living quarters, a frown on her face. Then she smacked the bed with a loud thump. Smaltz jumped on the edge of the bed behind her.

"Bedtime, little troublemakers! Lights out... just go to sleep!"

Jacob knew this was his chance to investigate again. Moments later when everyone was asleep, Jacob jumped up and left the room. Tommy was too concerned with Ms. Larrier even to notice.

Outside the living quarters, the candles were barely holding their flames. Finally, after moments of searching, the small light appeared again! It was edging around the corner as Jacob caught sight of it. He hurried after it and noticed that it led right down the black stairs, through the yellow-walled living room, and underneath a creaky door behind the dusty red couch. Jacob nervously opened the door, which revealed old wooden steps that led down a dark hole. Jacob gathered his confidence and began down the steps, and with each step grew an ounce of fear inside the pit of his stomach.

The inside of the basement was eerie and creepy. It smelled strongly of burnt wood, and the floorboards creaked and cracked. Throughout the basement were old torn dolls and small brown shoeboxes. Icky cobwebs and dust surrounded the room which tickled Jacob's ankles at his every step. You could tell this place wasn't visited much.

*When's the last time someone came down here?* He wondered to himself as he crossed over each floorboard.

Gigantic drops of rain pelted the ceiling as Jacob finally reached the area where the light was flickering. It flickered again and then landed softly on a pile of dusty old clothes. Then it flickered a bit more.

Jacob slowly paced forward, trying not to alarm it. The light budged a bit, and a few of the shirts slid off the top of the pile, revealing the edge of something golden and shiny.

Droplets of rain smashed the tiny window like fists of steel. Thunder quietly growled outside the orphanage. Then the tiny light creature zipped, buzzed, and flew quickly back up the wooden steps and out of the basement.

His curiosity shifted back over to the pile of clothes. Taking one big gulp, he removed the rest of the clothes from on top of the shiny object.

Beneath the pile lay a bronze book with golden trim. A light was beaming from inside the pages with a golden glow. On top of the book, in the center of the front cover, was a familiar symbol. There was an outline of gear, and tucked inside of the gear was an image of the same insect creature; he saw inside the gem at the museum. He picked up the book and blew off the remaining dust on top of it. He turned to open the book, and suddenly, a loud knock sent a shockwave through the orphanage.

BOOM BOOM BOOM!

Jacob picked up the book and hid it under his gray hoodie. He tucked it inside and belted for the top of the basement running back up the wooden steps, dodging cracks on his way through. Just as he made it back into the boys' room, Smaltz was standing in the opening of the door like a police officer ready to cut off a criminal.

BOOM BOOM BOOM!

Again, the knocks sent shudders through the house and rattled the dust from the doorways.

Jacob ran to his bed. He slid the book underneath it and covered it with some of his clothes.

BOOM BOOM BOOM!

Ms. Larrier sprung out of bed as though she were on a trampoline. Jacob noticed a thick glob of drool lining her upper lip, trailing down to her shoulder. Along with Ms. Larrier, Jacob froze for a moment. Silence crept into the room, but then they heard it again.

BOOM BOOM BOOM!

Jacob swore the ground beneath him was going to open up and swallow him. Finally, Ms. Larrier headed for the door, and without even thinking, Jacob and the other boys followed suit.

# 4

# KENDAL DRIVE'S
# NEW TENANT

Ms. Larrier's heart raced faster than her mind. Her beady eye pressed tightly to the peephole. The darkness made it difficult for her to see. She could barely spot the two silhouettes standing in front of her door. The only noticeable difference between the two was their height.

Inside the house, it was tough to get a good view. All the orphans had scrunched together and surrounded Ms. Larrier near the door.

Jacob's perspective was constricted between the legs of Tommy's fat henchmen. Rain splashed the cement doorstep and crashed into the pillars outside.

"And who might you be?!" Ms. Larrier growled behind the door, her eye pasted to the peephole. "Why are you trespassing on my property at this time of the night?!"

"Evening Miss, hmm," said the taller figure. "Could we please come in? It's pouring out here, and we might catch a cold." The figure knocked on the door once more.

"I'm not letting you in until I get an answer, you trespassing solicitors! Who are you and your little companion, and what are you doing on my property? You're scaring the children that live here!" Ms. Larrier looked back at the crowd for reassurance. None was given.

"I'm sorry miss, are you Margaret Larrier, and is this the Kendal Drive Orphanage, hmm?"

Ms. Larrier staggered backward from the gust of panic that rushed through the door and smacked her in the chest. This forced the other boys alongside Jacob to fall back as well. She almost tripped over the plump ball of fur next to her leg. Smaltz let out an annoying meow and hissed at the bottom of the door. Jacob chuckled a bit to himself. Ms. Larrier regained her composure and approached the door again.

"Listen, you dimwit, I go by Ms. Larrier, and yes, this is an orphanage, but there are no hmms here," she said sternly.

"Splendid, Ms. Larrier, aha!" the fellow began. "My name is Nathaniel Yaakov Xavier, a representative of GDCS, and-"

"What in the blazing saddles is GDCS?" interrupted Ms. Larrier, who now stood with her skinny, crooked fingers pressed against the door.

"The GDCS is the Griffin Department of Children's Services... the foster program, Ms. Larrier. Now, may we please come in? The rain is coming down out here, hmm?"

Ms. Larrier looked down at Smaltz to get a second opinion, and the plump gray cat just hissed angrily in disagreement. Finally, despite her displeasure, her thin fingers unlocked the remaining bolted security on the door.

In walked a gentleman of average height. His face was pale and freckled, and his eyes were a yellowish brown. He had dark red curls that were dripping wet and partially hidden beneath a blue fedora. He was wearing a long gold and blue striped trench coat, along with large dark brown buckled boots that squished puddles of water all over Ms. Larrier's recently cleaned floor. He spotted her smile turning into a nasty sneer as she grabbed paper towels. She then placed them quickly on the wet tracks left by the two figures on the hardwood floor.

A small boy stood next to the odd-looking fellow. His skin was very dark, but his eyes glowed gold. He had black hair that spiked straight up in the air like a porcupine, and his clothes were painted gold with a few holes in the back. Jacob squeezed through one of the fat kid's legs to get a better look.

"Cut it out, butt-face," snapped the annoyed orphan. Jacob ignored his comment and kept on looking.

"He's got beady little eyes just like the doofus!" shouted Tommy from behind Ms. Larrier. Jacob ignored his ridiculous comment too, as did the strange visitors.

"It's nice to meet you, Ms. Larrier. Thank you for letting us in." The man extended his hand for a shake, but it was not reciprocated.

"This is Daren," he continued. "Daren Lit. He is unique. Kind, but very quiet. He doesn't say much – well, nothing at all, actually - and he's just twelve years old." Nathaniel patted Daren on the back.

"What does this rodent have to do with me and my home?" snapped Ms. Larrier. She moved back to the door and lifted her arm outwards as she opened it again. Nathaniel just ignored the gesture and continued to pace across the room.

"Well, he's here to stay with you and all of these fine young gentlemen, of course, aha!" exclaimed Nathaniel.

"Listen Mr.… whatever your name is. This home is full of plenty rodents as it is. Enough little troublemakers are running around these halls. I'm at maximum capacity here. I can't possibly fit anymore, so Daren here will have to-"

"Daren here will have a nice home with the Kendall Drive Orphanage," interrupted Nathaniel. Nathaniel got right in Ms. Larrier's face, almost nose-to-nose. Then he reached inside his gold and blue trench coat for something. Ms. Larrier darted back against the door, stepping on Smaltz, which caused another ear-piercing meow.

"H-H-He's got a gun!" shouted Tommy, who ran into the corner and hid behind his henchmen, kicking Jacob in the shoulders along the way.

The boys clamored backward trampling over Jacob, frightened of the weapon this new stranger had in his pocket.

Then a thought smacked him right in the face. This man looked eerily familiar. He unusual voice reminded him of someone he couldn't place.

Just as Jacob started to connect the dots, the man removed his hand from his trench coat pocket and revealed a brown sheet of rolled-up paper covered in smudge marks, likely from the rain they had experienced earlier.

"Nothing to be afraid of, lads, just a wet piece of paper, aha." Nathaniel's attention shifted back to Ms. Larrier, who stood braced against the door.

Jacob confirmed his thoughts when he recognized the voice and the expression the man had just used. The red curls atop the man's head shot a memory straight through Jacob's brain. He knew this man. He had seen him several times. It was the same man that he had seen at the roller rink, at the museum, and on the street. Now he was a social worker, too?

"This is a letter for you to read, Ms. Larrier. I believe you'll change your mind about allowing Daren to live here in your home, hmm."

Jacob noticed an intense tension that overtook the room. Ms. Larrier's eyes were glued to the man and his comrade. Then he and everyone else shifted their gaze to the wet letter he held out. At the bottom of the letter was a golden seal in the shape of a gear. Ms. Larrier took out her old, round, purple reading glasses.

Dear Margaret Larrier, Headmistress of the Kendall Drive Orphanage,

The City of Griffin Town Hall and the Griffin Department of Children's Services at this moment grant permission for Daren Lit, age twelve, to enter and stay with the orphanage until eighteen years of age or legal adoption.

Under no circumstances may Daren be rejected or removed from the home unless the city of Griffin or GDCS classifies him otherwise.

Sincerely,

Justice of the Town, Magistra Dayan

Ms. Larrier started to regain her composure, but not in a calm way. Jacob's attention was held by her mole, which pulsated and twitched. Her upper lip curled back. She crumpled up the letter and threw it back at Nathaniel.

"Ms. Larrier, there's no need to be rude about it, hmm," Nathaniel spoke. "Besides, Daren here is very fond of cleaning. He will fit right in."

"The last thing I need right now is a new little nasty-"

"The city has informed me that if I do not see this home as a stable fit for Daren, then I have the right to remove all of the boys and close it down," Nathaniel finished.

Jacob couldn't believe his ears. He wanted to jump and scream. His heart started to beat faster and faster. This would be his chance to leave this wretched place, begin anew, and get away from annoying fat cats and big, freckle-faced bullies.

"Nothing to, uh, to worry about Mr., uh, Nathaniel," Ms. Larrier groveled. "You'll find that this home is well fit for all the boys, and it's tidy," Ms. Larrier nervously continued.

Jacob couldn't believe the lies that spewed from Ms. Larrier's venomous mouth. His hope shrunk, and his excitement fell.

"Well then, I must be off, Ms. Larrier." Nathaniel buttoned up his coat. "It's getting late, and I have a feeling this storm is only beginning."

A bolt of lightning cracked outside, and defeat overwhelmed Jacob.

He felt sorrow as he watched the strange man pat Daren on top of his spiky head.

"Daren, you're in good hands now. As for the rest of you, good luck! Ta-ta for now!"

Jacob was disappointed by the departure of the strange man. He wanted to know more. Jacob had endless questions for him, and he needed to make his way up to the front to ask them before he left. He budged his way through the tight squeeze of the orphans and passed through the tangled web of Smaltz and a few of the younger boys. He finally made his way into the open, in front of everyone. Just as he was about to run after the coated man, a thin, wrinkled hand reached out and pulled him backward. It was Ms. Larrier, of course. After slamming the door behind the man, she proceeded to lock all ten locks.

Daren kept quiet through the night, not saying much of anything except for "Thank you" and "Okay." The other boys didn't take too kindly to the new tenant of the Kendall Drive Orphanage. Jacob was spared, though, as Tommy, of course, granted Daren a few initiating wedgies, while the others followed with their usual cruel laughter and inappropriate jokes.

Daren's eyes were different. He had no pupils, just golden globes that sat on either side of his nose. It was only a matter of time before he received a similar nickname as Jacob. He was the only other boy Jacob had ever seen with abnormal eyes, except his were gold and shined very bright.

Once the chores were complete, Jacob went near his bed and pulled out the shiny book he found earlier in the creaky basement where the light bug had led him. He smoothed his hand over the cover, feeling the firm edges and an image of a gear which popped out of the middle. It gave him a sense of joy and curiosity. He began to open the book, but before he could continue, a hand reached out and grabbed his. Looking up, he spotted Daren sitting there with his finger over his lips, shaking his head.

"Do you know what this is?" Jacob asked.

Daren nodded his head up and down.

"What is it?" Jacob went to open the book again, and Daren grabbed his arm one more time.

"Not ready yet…" his deep voice slowly let out.

"What do you mean? What would I be-"

Before Jacob could get out another word, a fat-fingered hand tore the book from Jacob's grip.

"Well, Ugly Eyes," Tommy blurted out. "Looks like there is someone else with eyes even uglier than yours. How many freaks is this place gonna take in, anyway?"

Jacob swiped at Tommy to try and grab the book back. "Give it back, Tommy! I found it first!"

"Whoa, whoa, little doof, what's got your pants so hot?" Tommy moved the book behind his back, making it impossible for Jacob to reach for it. With his other hand, he grabbed Jacob's forehead, keeping him a fair distance away. Jacob tried to remove his fat knuckles from his head with all his might, but couldn't do anything. The rest of the boys just laughed behind him.

"Sorry there, pea-brain! Finder's weepers, stronger keepers! This is mine now!"

Tommy stuck his tongue out to tease Jacob and then let out a very maniacal laugh. Jacob couldn't move, even though he was trying with all his might.

"Put him down," a deep voice behind Jacob and Tommy said. Tommy's eyebrows rose so high they might have popped off his head to reach the ceiling if they could.

Silence swept over the other boys as they stood still in anticipation. Thunder cracked right outside the window, causing everyone to flinch. The only ones who didn't flinch were Tommy, Jacob, and Daren, who now held his hand out within reach of Tommy. Jacob's eyes were fixated on Tommy, and his fat nemesis returned the same look.

"What did you say to me, No Eyes?!" growled Tommy. It didn't take long for Tommy to spew out a nickname for the new tenant.

"Put him down and give him the book," Daren softly repeated himself. Jacob was no longer flailing his arms and sat frozen under the clutch of Tommy's hand.

"Listen, Stupid Face, when I tell you to talk, you can talk. Now, what are you gonna do about it? Cry, you little crybaby?" Tommy blurted out.

Daren leaped in the air and sent his right foot into Tommy's arm. The blow spun Tommy around and caused Jacob to fall to the ground. Jacob felt the gush of wind that raced past his face from the kick. It was mighty. Tommy shook his hand, trying to alleviate the pain in his arm.

"How dare you? What do you think you are, No Eyes?" He then barreled like a bull towards Daren, who quickly moved out of the way, sending Tommy to a nearby desk. He met the desk with such force that he crashed through it.

The room was frozen. The boys were like a bunch of statues. Suddenly, one of Tommy's henchmen jumped on top of Daren from behind, but Daren clenched his right fist into a steel ball and slammed it right through the orphan's fat face. He retreated backward, clutching his nose in agony. The other henchman took a few steps back into the crowd, not even attempting to help out.

The rest of the boys couldn't help but start cheering: "Fight, fight, fight!"

Tommy charged at Daren again, who leaped over his head, splitting his legs in the thin air. He came back down to the ground, gave two sharp jabs to Tommy's abdomen, and sent another steel fist straight through Tommy's jaw. Tommy crippled to the ground in pain. Jacob had the biggest grin on his face as he jumped up and down, rooting Daren on.

Just before Jacob could relish in the defeat of his most prominent bully, the door crashed open, and Smaltz pounced into the room. Scraggly Ms. Larrier followed her, and she almost fainted at the horrible sight in front of her.

"What on earth do you think you are doing?!"

Jacob's smile turned into fright.

"You're not allowed ever to lay hands on another rodent here, you imbecile! You come into our home unwelcomed and lay your hands on someone else?" Ms. Larrier kept her beady eyes fixated on Daren, who was still in a karate styled pose.

Tommy was crying on the ground, covered in sweat and blood. Jacob could see an imprint from Daren's fist on Tommy's freckled cheek.

"Ms. Larrier, Tommy started it." Jacob spat out. "He wouldn't stop picking on us, and Daren was acting in self-defense."

"Shut your rodent mouth, this doesn't concern you," Ms. Larrier cut Jacob off. "This little nuisance put his selfish little hands on our beloved Tommy. Someone help Tommy up and get him some ice." She then threw her thin fingers at Daren's head and wrenched his earlobe, yanking him forward. "You are coming with me!"

Two more lightning bolts cracked down upon the orphanage, which made everyone jump. Ms. Larrier sped out of the room with Daren attached to her nails.

Jacob screamed after her to try and save Daren again, but Ms. Larrier ignored him and proceeded down the dark, dusty hall. Jacob quickly picked up the bronze book on the ground and put it back underneath his bed.

Later that night, an ambulance came and picked up Tommy to take him to the hospital. Jacob felt that was a bit extreme, considering he just received a few punches and a kick, but the longer Tommy was away from the orphanage, the better Jacob felt.

Jacob tossed and turned in his skinny bed, his mind racing down a track he couldn't get off. He turned over his bed and stared underneath it. The shiny bronze book sat there; untouched, unopened, mysterious, and left alone. Jacob wanted to open it. He was dying to catch a glimpse of what was inside, but he couldn't get the image of Daren telling him that he wasn't ready yet out of his mind.

Sick of waiting, Jacob reached underneath his bed and grabbed the heavy book. He looked around the room suspiciously to see if anyone else was watching him. Several boys laid stretched out on their beds in a deep sleep. He laid back down on his bed, his head against his pillow, but his eyes were fixated on the mysterious book that he held so tightly in his hands. He traced the spine of the book with his fingers and then finally touched the edge of the cover.

Closing his eyes for a brief moment, he laid there, heavy with anticipation. Then he lifted the top cover of the book to reveal what sat inside.

A shiny creature zipped out of the book like a bat out of a cave.

The tiny creature was made of light, and it hovered over his face for a brief moment. It was a dark brown, coffee color, its head was round, and it had two golden wings and a long black tail. Its eyes were those of an insect but had little lids that covered them.

The little light-fly zipped even closer to Jacob's face and sat upon his nose. Jacob just froze, unsure of what to do next. The creature winked with its left eye and then flew off his nose, leaving behind a prickling sensation. The light-fly went through the crack under the door and out of sight.

Without thinking, Jacob closed the book, jumped off of his bed, and jetted out the door. At the end of the hall sat the light-fly, buzzing in place. Not even thinking about how he could potentially wake up the rest of the orphanage, Jacob ran as fast as he could after it. Each step caused a creaking sound on the floorboards. The light from the little fly creature created a bright trail that he could follow. He hustled down each step of the black stairs, holding onto the yellow pillars on each side so he wouldn't fall.

He reached the end of the stairwell and lost sight of the creature. To his right was a beam of light that was slowly disappearing. He picked up his speed again, chasing after the light trail. It led him past the dangling chandelier in the living room, across the filthy kitchen, and right up against the chipped door that leads to the basement. He paused for a minute, but then opened the door to the familiar musty smell that he ran across the night he discovered the book.

The light trail continued through the basement and into a corner. The fly was zipping around in circles, and Jacob watched as it made a few figure eights. His eyes widened, and he looked at the bug, and then back at the floor again.

He noticed a small black knob that was oddly placed in the middle of the gray carpet.

He tugged at the knob, which lifted up a rectangular wooden door. The light creature let out a soft buzz and flew down the dark hole, revealing an old stone pathway with a ladder attached to the side. Jacob tucked the book under his arm and followed the ladder down.

The smell of murky sewer water ran up his nose, and the sounds of dripping water got even louder the further he descended. He jumped from the final ladder rung, and his socked feet met a giant puddle of filth. Slime seeped in between each of his toes. The smell was putrid.

The light creature was fizzling near his face once again. It let out a few faint buzzes and then flew forward.

This time, the pathway was covered in green filth, and it was too small to walk in. The tunnel would only allow someone to crawl through it. Jacob dug into the ground on his hands and knees reluctantly but began to crawl quickly through the underground sewer system.

There was a moment where he passed right through an area filled with the sound of enormous, raspy snores. *Must be underneath Ms. Larrier's room*, he thought to himself.

Before he could finish his thought, a dark silhouette sat down in front of him. Light began to radiate out in all directions, but the figure remained dark. Spiky hair laced the top of his head, and his eyes opened, releasing two golden rays of light.

Jacob was still. Very still. Slime dug underneath his fingernails.

It was Daren, the new orphan who made Tommy cry like a baby earlier.

Daren stared at Jacob with his golden eyes. The fly creature landed on Daren's shoulder, and its light went out. The glow from Daren's eyes was the only light remaining. The buzzing sounds from earlier had silenced, and now the only thing that could be heard was the slight drip of running water in the distance.

"Did Ms. Larrier put you down here to punish you?" Jacob asked.

"You are Jacob Wesley," Daren interrupted, in a low but very crisp voice.

"I am, but you-"

"You are the Light One," Daren whispered back.

"I'm the what?" Jacob tried again.

"You are not from this world, and you must finally return home."

Jacob stared blankly at the dark golden aura that encased the new tenant of the orphanage. Questions sliced through his mind like a thousand daggers, wanting answers.

"But this is my home," Jacob rebutted.

"This is no home for the Light One. Jacob Wesley must return home." The low voice growled louder and echoed throughout the tunnel, which sent gusts of wind past Jacob, forcing him to dig his hands deeper into the slime to maintain his grip.

"The book, do you have it?" Daren nodded in Jacob's direction. Jacob grabbed the book out from inside his hoodie. "Let me see it."

Jacob was still, clutching the book to his stomach. He looked down from Daren to the book and then back up again at the glow radiating from Daren who had now outstretched his hands in an inviting pose.

Reluctantly, Jacob handed the book over to him.

"What's in the book? Why is it so special?"

Daren's eyes suddenly closed, and the rays of light disappeared.

"You must return home… NOW!" he growled, sending a shuddering earthquake of power throughout the tunnel. Jacob fell backward from the force. Then Daren opened the book, and a very bright white light shot out, illuminating the tunnel but blinding Jacob in the process. A loud, deafening buzz like the sound of hundreds of bees penetrated Jacob's eardrums. The wind swirled all around as he struggled to keep his balance. Even the sewer slime began coursing past him like a river.

Daren slowly raised his hand and pointed it towards Jacob. Out of the book, a swarm of those light bug creatures flew towards him. Daren began to disintegrate like particles of sand in the wind, leaving behind even more.

Jacob turned around as fear took over. He tried to crawl forward to escape the terror. He hurried his pace but was not quick enough. The buzzing caught up with him, and the light-flies circled him and landed on his skin like tacks on a wall. He was covered in them, causing him to twist and turn as he tried to remove them. The rest continued to buzz and fly around him, over and over again, until he couldn't see anymore. The wet, slimy sewer disappeared right before his eyes.

He felt a tightening around his throat, the same feeling he had in the museum. It felt as though a plethora of spikes were running through his blood, coursing towards his mouth.

Just as it climbed through his body, he felt a terrible spinning sensation, like he was being whipped around in a fierce tornado. A loud scream jumped from his throat, and then a large white flash encompassed him as he heard a roar like a cannonball being shot out of a cannon.

He thought he was dying, and he couldn't hold on much longer. Wind pierced his body. He tried to open his eyes, but the bugs covered them. His vision faded, and he finally let go. The white flash in front of him faded to black.

When he finally came to, it felt like hours had passed, but it was only minutes. A soft muffled voice that sounded like it was underwater called out to Jacob.

"Jacccoobbbb, areeee ya okayyyy? Jacccoobbbb? Cannn youuu hearrrr me?"

The voice echoed softly, slowly bringing Jacob's vision back. He saw the outline of a shadowed figure. As Jacob's vision returned, the invisible voice became clearer.

"Jacob, Jacob, you okay, ta ta?"

He opened his eyes fully, and he could finally see the figure that stood - or rather, floated - before him. It was a man wearing a blue and yellow coat down past his knees and a high collar that went up to his ears. He had curly red hair sticking out of his head and yellow goggles covering his eyes. On his wrists were golden bracelets that hovered in place, not touching his arms. It was the Nathaniel guy who dropped Daren off at the orphanage.

Jacob could barely move, so he decided that sitting up was his best option.

"Where… where am I?" he spoke very softly.

The man seemed to be quite delighted to see him. A smile stretched from ear to ear as he gazed upon Jacob. Jacob, instead of feeling mutual adulation, was somewhat confused. This has to be a dream. Is this a nurse? Am I in a hospital? Jacob thought to himself. He tried rubbing his eyes to wake up from the dream, but the world remained, and the figure still stood in front of him, gleaming with his every move.

"Is this real?" Jacob asked the floating Nathaniel.

He let out a great laugh as he clutched his belly. "Tee-hee! Ha-ha! Ha-ha! Tee-hee!" laughed the strange man.

Before Jacob could speak, the curly-haired Nathaniel knelt over and extended his hand.

"Welcome home, Jacob Wesley, welcome home, hee-hee, ta ta!"

# 5

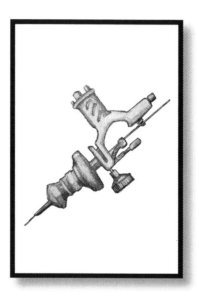

# A MALL IN THE SKY

Nathaniel leaned over and extended his hand towards Jacob. He grabbed his arm and pulled him to his feet.

Jacob stood frozen like a statue as he turned his head to get a view of his new surroundings. It felt as though he was in a subway station. Golden archways were a mile long above his head, and they twisted through clouds inside the building. The walls that enclosed the station were pearly white with bronze and gold pipes that twisted in a zig-zag pattern. Light shone in through beautifully constructed glass windows.

In the center of the station were bronze gears the size of semi-trucks that moved back and forth.

Fresh air filled his nostrils, along with the smell of cold steel. The twisting sounds of metal and steam engines roused him from his heavenly daze. Suddenly, a loud bang, like the sound of a bullet being shot from a gun, tore through his eardrums, and in front of Jacob was a bubble the size of a fist. He scrunched his eyes to try and make out what was inside of it. Then the bubble grew to twice his size, and out floated two odd-looking gentlemen wearing long coats that had collars pulled up to their ears, with different-colored metal goggles over their eyes.

"Cloudians, hmm," said Nathaniel, who was still floating above the ground.

"Cloud-whats?" Jacob caught sight of another odd-looking man as he entered one of the silver glass tubes attached to the wall. A whistle blew through the air, and clouds rushed from beneath the tube in their direction. Jacob ducked for cover, but the clouds were just clear mist.

"Your people, ta ta," Nathaniel spoke, as he reached inside his coat.

"You're the man from the museum and the man who dropped off Daren, right?" Jacob turned his attention back to his greeter.

"I haven't even shared my name yet! My name is too long to be bothered with, so everyone just calls me Nyx!" Nyx then pulled out large black boots with buckles and clasps on either side.

"I'm the watcher of the night, protector of what is most important, and for the past twelve yers, that has been you. You probably didn't recognize me from all of my clever disguises, ta ta!"

Nyx pressed a button on either side of his boots. The buckles clasped into place and tightened around his feet. Nyx then snapped two fingers in the air and whistled a soft tune. The two golden rings that hovered perfectly over each of his wrists began to shake. He nodded joyously towards Jacob.

A big rippling sound shuddered beneath Jacob's feet. It felt like a miniature earthquake. When Nyx's feet touched the ground, he pressed another oval button on the side of his right foot. A grinding metal sound came from the boots. "There, that's much better now, ha!"

"Well, nice to meet you Nyx," Jacob stuck out his small hand to shake, but Nyx clutched his forearm instead, and paused for a moment.

"Hmm?"

Jacob decided to do the same and clutched Nyx's forearm as well.

"Tee-hee, you must have stuck out amongst all the Gravits with your unique glowing eyes!"

"What's a Gravit?" asked Jacob.

"A Gravit is someone who is restricted by gravity, and walks on the ground, instead of, you know, as Gravits would call it, 'floating about.' Griffin's full of them, hee-hee. I'm sure you're glad to be away from that nasty lady Gravit! Man, did she know how to be rude! To think anyone wouldn't want to take in good old Daren, ta ta." Nyx removed the goggles from his eyes and put them on top of his head. Jacob noticed that he didn't have any pupils. His eyes were just solid blue.

"Uh, Nyx, I'm not so sure I belong in this place. I don't look like you or anyone else here." Jacob's hands trembled a bit as he spoke.

"Don't be silly, Jacob! If there's a place you belong, it's here, and besides, did you think you belonged in a place as depressing as Griffin?"

Jacob smiled, and Nyx patted him on the back lightly. "Now, let's make you an official Cloudian!" Nyx took a step forward, leaving behind a footprint in the marble cement ground. However, a second later, it dissolved, and the ground went back to normal.

"Nyx, is this snow?" Jacob noticed that the closer they got to the glass chutes against the wall, the more this white fluff fell from the ceiling. He caught a few of the pieces of it and blew it off.

"Ice-puffs? No sir, not snow. More like little clouds that fit in the palm of your hand. You should see them during Donumdans; they get quite large. It gets pretty cold during Augusta, and the flycers go into hiding too, so it's perfect for skiing around High Corner, aha."

Jacob thought of so many questions at once that his brain almost exploded. "How do I become an official Cloudian?"

Nyx stopped a few feet away from the oval glass chute. He then reached inside of his striped coat yet again before pulling out a black and gold trimmed band, which looked like it belonged to a watch. He rolled up his blue sleeve on his right arm. He slapped it over his wrist, and it twisted like a snake in the air. The metal bracelet hovered around his wrist without touching his skin.

"This lux-band is getting old." Nyx tapped on it a few times. Jacob looked on with amazement.

"Okay, now I may need to backtrack a bit, ha-ha. It's been awhile since I've seen the entry list for a Cloudian." Nyx pressed a small white button on the left side of the band. A holographic 3D image of multiple dials that were spinning popped up.

"Okay, it's ten. Well, that's good to know, hmm." Nyx then swiped his index finger over the dials and to the right. The image changed to a screen with a red outline of someone with a long beard and a golden mohawk. Over his face, there was a stamp that said New.

"Oh, Bronny, you can wait, tee-hee," Nyx giggled to himself. He swiped faster before finally arriving at a green screen that read Lists for Entry. He double-tapped the invisible screen with his index finger again, and out popped a list of several items.

"Here we go, Jacob. The Cloudian Entry list!" Nyx put his thumb and index finger close together and then separated them to make a shape of the letter L. This widened the screen and zoomed in so that Jacob could see the list as well.

LIST FOR ENTRY: CLOUDIA

All citizens of Cloudia must have the following items to join the Elemental Academy. Additionally, they must be purchased by the age of thirteen to deal with the terrain properly.

Cloudian Navus Mark

Holopic Identification

Lux-Bands (Gold, Silver, Black, and Sterling White)

Lux-Shades (Regulation Size)

Levy Boots (Buckled, not laced)

Volans Coat (Sizes available: Low, Mid, High)

Portare Bag (Orange, Blue, and Forest Green)

Alterations are allowed for Volans Coats, but not for any other item. Under the regulatory law, all equipment must pass inspection to and from Cloudia.

"Well, we can get the first few items today, but we will need to get the rest tomorrow then, aha." Nyx clicked his futuristic tech-band, and the image disappeared.

"Where am I going to get all this stuff? I have no idea what any of this is, Nyx," Jacob was blushing a bit.

"Well, good thing you have me to take care of you, ta ta!" Nyx walked over to the oval glass chute. The tubes went from the bottom of the ground all the way to the ceiling and through the clouds. They reminded Jacob of water slides because of the way they rose above the station and curved near the top.

Nyx pressed another white button on the outside of the glass chute. Jacob felt the ground quiver a bit, and from the chute, a door unlocked and swiveled upwards.

"Travel tubes, Jacob! Don't worry; they are the safest way to travel! Step inside!" Nyx motioned towards the space inside the water slide chute. Jacob tried to look up to see how far it extended, but he could barely see past the clouds about a hundred feet up, and from there, he was met with a blinding light that made his eyes water.

"Careful, there. Not going to be able to see much above the travel tubes, ha-ha. No use of trying to tell; it'll leave you without eyes if you stare long enough. Even more, reason to get you a pair of these, ta ta," Nyx giggled again as he placed the yellow goggles from atop his head tightly over his eyes. The yellowish round goggles were something like a combination of a snorkel and night-vision gear.

Jacob took a brave step inside of the tube and was met with the smell of plastic. The air seemed thin.

"This is gonna be a long ride then; I take it?" Jacob asked.

"Not that long at all actually, hmm." Nyx pressed a similar white button on the tube to the left of Jacob. There was a loud buzzing sound and another clear door opened as Nyx stepped in.

The tube doors closed. Above his head, the tube spiraled, as if he was going up a staircase. His stomach rumbled, which reminded him of Tommy's simulator coaster ride back at the museum. Jacob's memory of the orange vomit did not sit well now, though. Nyx caught his attention and pointed to the side.

"What?" Jacob searched around him.

Although Nyx spoke, Jacob couldn't hear him. The tubes made Nyx's voice sound like a muddied whisper.

"Press the button, hee-hee!" Nyx shouted.

Again, Nyx pointed towards a small object near Jacob's head. To his left was a blue rectangular button. Jacob pressed it, and the ground immediately disappeared beneath his feet. A gust of wind rushed up under his cheeks; the sky swirled, and everything was blurred in front of his eyes. Lights flashed all around him. His stomach grew queasy extremely fast, and then... nothing. The flying sensation had stopped just as soon as it started.

The glass tube door opened at the same time as Jacob's eyes. He took a step onto the brick pavement in front of him. To his left and right were large walls with beautiful blue and white crystals the size of lanterns hanging on them. Gigantic statues of cloaked figures stood above him. Fog patches of soft clouds fluttered around his feet. Lots of chatter could be heard around. Golden escalators and silver walkways stretched in front of him.

Suddenly, there was a loud splash behind him. Jacob turned around to see Nyx coming out of his travel tube.

"Fun trip, hee-hee?" Nyx said, with a big smile on his face.

"Welcome," said Nyx, "To High Corner."

The pair moved away from the tubes, and in front of Jacob was one of the most amazing spectacles he had ever seen. Nyx couldn't help but chuckle at his wonder. In front of Jacob was a three-story center with large shops on each level. Spiraling down from the golden-arched ceiling were ice puffs, like back at Pines Station. Silver walkways and golden escalators led from the platform they were standing on. Palm-sized crystal bulbs hovered in place and lit up the giant mall. Sounds of gears spinning, bells ringing, and distant whistles brought the area to life with an incredible sense of joy. It had the feel of a busy street market but smelled like freshly cooked pretzels.

"Cloudia's favorite and only mall." Nyx moved his arms in the air, presenting it to Jacob. "It's quite the experience, and will give you everything you need, aha!"

As they moved throughout the platform, Jacob tried his best to soak in the feeling of this new mall. He wished that his head could permanently spin so that he could see everything at once; the different buildings, the people, and the shops.

Jacob and Nyx passed by a red shop with a top hat above it. Several people floated past them, including a stout, chunky man who was floating quickly towards the shop. "Oh, yes! Fifty percent off, and it's not even Donumdans!"

A younger kid with orange hair parted in the middle was being dragged sideways to a shop with rings spinning around each other.

"But Mom! You promised I would get golden sky rings. I don't want the tower rings. Everyone will make fun of me at Sky School! Pleaseeee!"

Jacob let out a few giggles, even though he had no idea what they were talking about.

In front of Jacob, near a silver walkway, was a three-story shop. On the first level were all different types of goggles. The second level had those 3D bands that Nyx had used earlier. On the top level, there were holograms of different long coats and buckled shoes.

"How's that belly of yours?" Nyx tickled Jacob, which caused his stomach to let out a low gurgle.

"Well, I think that sums up how I feel." Jacob clutched his stomach.

"Halwin's Shakes, straight ahead!" They passed by a white and red striped floating stand. At the top of the shop was a blue cloud with a large red straw sticking out of it, which was bent at the tip. Jacob's stomach let out an even louder growl.

"I don't think I have had anything to eat or drink in a very long time," said Jacob, clutching his stomach again.

"Well, you're in luck, hee-hee, ta ta." Nyx let out a scream of joy.

Nyx walked up to the front of the tilted kiosk called Halwin's Shakes, and he pulled down on a large silver knob to the right of the store window. Immediately, a loud whistle sounded, and something like a crow cawing echoed throughout the mall. Jacob covered his ears from the sound that pierced his insides. He looked around to see if anyone else was bothered by the sound, but everyone was moving normally as if it never happened.

"That's gonna take some getting used to, I suppose," said Nyx. "Those ears aren't used to Cloudian frequencies, ta ta."

The window of the shake shack burst open. Glass shards flew towards Jacob, but then froze right before Jacob's face. Out came an older man who was only a few inches shorter than Jacob. He had gray hairs that spiked out from his face, a puffy hat that resembled a cloud, and eyes without pupils, but his were a faded blue.

"Great skies, Nyx, I didn't know you were back!" The two grabbed each other's forearms and smiled.

"How long has it been? I was beginning to think you were the only one in all of Cloudia that didn't like my shakes."

"No, no, Halwin, trust me, I've missed your sherbet malted puff more than you know! I've been on official PPA business for the past dozen yers," Nyx said, as he nodded back towards Jacob. Halwin looked at Nyx, and then at Jacob, and then at Nyx again, as a twinkle grew in his eye.

"Is… is this?" said Halwin, quivering. Nyx gave another nod and smiled as he turned towards Jacob.

"He's finally here, I can't believe it. The Light One has returned-"

"Shhh, tee-ta. Halwin, we have a lot to get through today. I'd rather keep his identity as quiet as possible. The last thing we need is everyone rushing him while he's just getting his feet off the ground, ta ta," said Nyx.

"Well, it is an honor to have the Light One visit my little shack of shakes here, an extreme honor!"

Jacob didn't know what to say. Halwin stared at him with tears bubbling in his eyes.

"Pick anything, anything at all, it's on the house," Halwin exclaimed.

"I guess being you has its privileges, huh, Jacob?" said Nyx with a wink.

"Thank you very much, Halwin, and it's a pleasure to meet you," Jacob said, as he approached the window and ducked under the floating glass. Halwin took off his puffy hat and revealed a shiny bald head. He scrunched his hat in his hands so tight, tearing it became inevitable.

"The pleasure is all mine, Jacob Wesley, all mine. Now, the flavors are to your left. You can combine them if you like!" Halwin began jumping around.

Jacob read down the holographic image of different flavors that had odd-looking fruits and chocolates which danced right into each other. He had never seen anything like this, but he was sure it beat having to drink old milk or dirty water every day for the past dozen yers.

These were the flavors he saw:

Chocolate Noodle Crunch
Sherbet Malted Puff
Skycreamsicle
Caramel Pieces in Vanilla Cookie

"Uh, what do you recommend?" asked a confused Jacob, who was trying to decide between all the unfamiliar flavors placed in front of him. Nyx chuckled in the background.

"How 'bout the Caramel Pieces in Vanilla Cookie? It's absolutely scrumdiddlyumptious. All the children go nuts over it, just nuts!" shouted Halwin.

"All right. Sherbet Malted Puff for your old friend, and the first-ever Caramel Pieces in Vanilla Cookie for the young man to my right," Nyx ordered for the two of them.

Halwin winked with his uncovered eye, pulled down on another chain, and finally yanked a few wheels behind the window. The noises belted out again, and steam rose from the top of the straw into the sky. Halwin came back with two short, broad, and puffy cups that had bent red straws in them.

Jacob grabbed his and gave it a suck; the flavors were sensational, tasting like a mixture between sweet caramel syrup and oreo cookies as thick liquid ran through his insides. He drank it in several gulps, which at first made Nyx and Halwin think he didn't like it, but then, after a smile, the two were reassured by his delight.

Nyx smiled and waved at Halwin, who waved back and shouted, "Good luck!" as he pressed another button on the inside of the kiosk.

Jacob saw the glass that was floating above his head dart back towards the window and back into place.

Nyx drank his shake in one big gulp. He chuckled, as usual, and patted Jacob on the back. Then he pointed to the escalator that hovered in the air. It wasn't attached to anything. Regardless, they hopped on and glided towards the top.

As the two approached, Nyx grabbed Jacob's hood. The two lunged forward to another escalator. They landed on a platform that was encased in marble, just like the museum he had been to before.

"Duck!" Nyx yelled at Jacob. A small, fluffy, winged creature with a tiny metal head covered in what looked like orange steel leaves flew right over his head and landed in front of a shop full of large brown gears that spun in place.

"Flycers! Feral creatures. You gotta watch out for them, ha-ha. One nearly just took your head off, hee-hee." Nyx motioned forward, but Jacob was distracted again. This time, loud cheers came rumbling to the right from a huge cloud dematerializing in front of a flat television screen. The screen was inside a memorabilia store named Sky Racing Stuff and Stirs with a sign on the side that read, "Boards, Bands, Books, Badges, if you like Skyracing, it's the place for you!"

A crowd of young boys and girls around Jacob's age ran in and out of the shop. One boy ran out with a bronze flat board that had silver trim and spikes that hung from the bottom. Jacob thought it was a skateboard without wheels. "Now I'm going to be just like Ezekiel Addams," said the boy.

They bought Jacob's goggles in a shop on the fourth floor called Heaven's Headwear. There were open cabinets full of goggles as shiny as a pair of new diamond earrings; golden goggles, goggles covered in sterling silver, goggles that were bronze like a penny, goggles as black as night, goggles as white as pearls, and in the back, there were old used goggles with a half-off stamp on them. Jacob tried on a pair of silver goggles with a beautiful dark green trim. Nyx chuckled when Jacob fumbled with them. He couldn't figure out how to adjust the size to fit his head.

"Here ya go, Jacob. Just pull back on the scalp loop and tighten the grip on the socket tag, ta ta!"

Jacob had no idea what Nyx just said, but he found a loop on the back of the goggles and pulled forward. When they were tight enough, he proceeded to place the goggles over his eyes. Looking through them, he could see tiny particles swirling in the air. Nyx looked like he was standing ten feet closer. All of a sudden, numbers popped up in front of him, along with a counter. The numbers spun in place extremely quickly and stopped at 275, followed by the symbol Jacob kept seeing over and over.

"What does the number mean?" Jacob asked.

"The numbers you see are amperes; little units of measurement for how in tune to the energy around them someone is, ta ta! Most Cloudians read around 150 amperes, but those of us who work for the PPA tend to be higher on the scale. Optimal selection, special people, hee-hee," said Nyx, while he flailed his arms and kicked his feet in either direction.

"What's the PPA?" questioned Jacob.

"You'll find out soon enough, aha!" Nyx leads Jacob out of the goggles shop.

"Now, it's time for the boring stuff: your Cloudian certification," Nyx giggled.

After three floating escalators and two long walkways, Nyx lead Jacob through a darker area where steam billowed out of the sides of the building as they walked. There was a light foggy mist that made it difficult to see ahead of them. The two had to dodge a few howling flycers on the last walkway.

At the end of the walkway was an old brown brick building with squiggly black ink that lined the exterior like icing on a gingerbread house. At the top of the shop was a giant bronze hand covered in ink. Clutched in hand was a small tool which resembled a cross between a water gun and the inside of a clock. Coming out of the end of the gun object and streaming through the sky were flashing letters that read, "Citizen Ink: For Fun and Entries."

The tattoo shop had an old musty smell. In the front lobby was a small black desk with a golden button in the center. Behind it was an old dark red curtain.

"Okay, press it!" Nyx nudged Jacob forward. Cautiously, Jacob's finger lightly tapped the button. A buzzing sound played from inside, and then a blue 3D screen appeared with a face imprint and a message that said, "Place your face within the sensor."

Jacob looked back at Nyx, who gave a smiling nod. Jacob placed his face within the sensor, and a red scanning line went over his cheekbones and up to the top of his head several times.

"Jacob Wesley, age twelve, complete." A silver band resembling the one Nyx had shown him earlier popped out of a slot on top of the desk.

"Take it, it's yours, ta, ta," Nyx pointed towards the band. The band clasped onto Jacob's right wrist and then expanded until it hovered around his skin. It felt like tiny electric pulses were circling his wrist.

"Whoa… cool," Jacob said with a big smile.

"There's your first lux-band!" Nyx clapped and moved Jacob forward towards the red curtain.

Behind the curtain was a brick backdrop with cracks the size of spiderwebs. In the air were eight dusty old red leather cushioned chairs. Underneath each chair was a golden glow. It reminded Jacob of the barbershops back in Griffin.

On the ground were two chairs, and in them sat a boy and a girl who appeared to be much younger than Jacob. Little men with just one spike of hair on the top of their bald heads held water gun-looking devices next to the boys. Before Jacob could see what would happen, rectangular shielded booths fell and covered the chairs.

"Push it!" Nyx nudged Jacob.

"Push what?"

"That over there! The button, ha!"

To the right of Jacob was a cracked golden button that was about the size of his head.

"This world sure does love to use buttons," Jacob said as he leaned in. When he pressed it, there was a loud and rusty noise like a door creaking open. Then a pop, like a balloon had burst, and then nothing until a chair swept Jacob off his feet from behind without warning.

It floated upward towards the ceiling and spun in place sporadically. The store and Nyx became instantly blurry. Jacob felt almost as sick as Tommy did in the simulation rollercoaster.

"Station seven!" The chair halted in the air. Then it hovered over to a station close to the back of the shop. Jacob felt a shiver slowly trickle down his spine. The chair lowered and attached itself to the ground. There was a small hunched man waiting for him. He had a tiny golden bowtie, puffy gold pants, and a single, slick spike of white hair sprouting from the top of his head.

"Greetings," he said quietly.

"Hi," said Jacob cautiously.

"Hmmm," said the man as he looked Jacob up and down, and then deep into his eyes. He was barely a few inches from Jacob's face. His breath smelled like old wheat bread.

"You're a little old to be coming into this shop, but something is unique about you. Yes, that's it - your eyes. Don't think I've seen eyes quite as green as those before," the man said.

Then the man pressed his nose to Jacob's cheek and looked even deeper into his eyes. His nose felt like greasy rubber.

"Nevertheless, as I said, you're a little old to be in this shop. What might your yers be?"

"T-T-Twelve," Jacob stuttered nervously.

"Twelve yers is too old to be getting a Navus mark. Maybe you're just trying to sneak into Cloudia," the hunched man said as he poked Jacob in the chest. "What's your business here, boy?"

Jacob's nerves grew with every moment that passed. He had no idea what to say.

"I have some identification for the boy, ta ta," shouted Nyx from behind them. He had floated towards the two. Jacob felt relieved to hear Nyx's voice.

"I think you'll want to see this." Nyx clicked a button on his right pant leg, and a bronze round spectacle materialized in front of his eyes. Nyx pressed Jacob's lux-band, and his identification shot up in a 3D image.

"Jacob Wesley? Well, why didn't you say so, boy?" The man turned back towards Jacob, who had shrunken into his seat.

"Let's keep the hubbub down, though, hee-hee, ta ta," Nyx giggled. "We're trying to keep a low profile here." Nyx patted the hunched man on the back. Then he retreated backward and out of sight. The man stuck out his frazzled forearm, and Jacob grabbed his cautiously.

"Pleasure to meet you, Jacob. My name is Techne Katab, but Cloudians around here call me Mr. Kat. Now even though you're the Light One, you're still older than the maximum yers to get a Navus mark. The only difference is, your skin has adapted to the Gravit world, so this will sting a bit. Do you have a preference of which shoulder?" Mr. Kat raised the water gun device.

"Uh, well, um, right, I guess? How much will this hurt?" Jacob asked very awkwardly.

"Well, it's just a brief sting. It will pass quickly. Your colors are green and silver. Your Navus mark will gain you entry into each of the six cities, even Shei El, although you'll probably never use it there."

Nevertheless, Mr. Kat moved towards the back of the chair. Then he pressed a bronze button. Sure enough, a buzzing sound screamed out, followed by the shielded booth that Jacob had spotted earlier.

"Here we go! Are you ready?" Mr. Kat asked with excitement.

"I think so." Jacob tensed up in the chair as Mr. Kat approached his right shoulder with the ink gun. The lights shut off. He pressed down, and a sharp sting jetted through Jacob's arm and down to his fingers. It tingled lightly, like a sting from a bumblebee. Then he felt a cold thump in that area. He opened his eyes to find that Mr. Kat had pressed what looked like a large ice block onto his shoulder where the sting had taken place.

The booth was removed, and the lights flickered on. Nyx floated over to the chair as he and Mr. Kat looked at Jacob's arm. Nyx raised an eyebrow, and Mr. Kat let out a deep breath. On Jacob's arm was a green mark. It was about four inches tall and curved like an arrow. Inside of it was a silver oval surrounded by a shine like diamonds.

"Strange," said Mr. Kat as he examined Jacob's arm closely.

"Strange indeed, ta ta," said Nyx.

Jacob thought everything he had experienced that day was strange; the glass was breaking and then fitting back together, those flycer creatures, and his number-reading goggles.

"Why is it strange?" Jacob worried.

Mr. Kat looked at Nyx, and then slowly turned his head towards Jacob.

"The symbol, Jacob," Mr. Kat began. "The symbol is very different than anything I have given before. I've never given anything but the standard Navus, but this is no Navus. It's different."

He pointed towards Nyx's mark, which was the usual Cloudian symbol of a gear with the light creature inside of it; the same shape within the emblem from the museum.

"What's mine called?" Jacob asked.

"Don't have a name for it, but I suppose it fits right in line with your uniqueness," Mr. Kat said.

Jacob grew very tense in his seat. He was already at odds from receiving a tattoo, and he felt very weary. All the uniqueness, from his eyes to his mark, now unsettled him. He was unique in his old home and unique in his new home. It didn't matter where he was; he just didn't fit in.

"Well, it's been a pleasure, but we must be going, sir, ta ta," Nyx interrupted.

Nyx grabbed Jacob and headed to the front of the shop. Jacob nodded over towards Mr. Kat as he left with a sickening feeling in his stomach.

Night crept through the clouds and light was shining above High Corner. Jacob and Nyx continued back down the floating escalators and walkways, and out into the center floor of High Corner. Darkness grew over the ceiling and clouds merged overhead.

"And here we are, ta, ta!" Nyx pointed in front of them. "Huts for Stay! You'll never want to stay in another place again."

Contrary to its name, it was a skyscraper of a hotel. Beautiful pillars out front made its presence very well known. Nyx pushed Jacob forward, and the doors to the front lobby swung upward. It was luxury with a dab of confusion. Inside, golden staircases wound up and down between different levels. The ceiling was made of beautiful blue glass, and the skylight was in the shape of a gear. Underneath the ceiling was a wide glass structure that sat about thirty feet off the ground. It flashed with fire one second, and with water the next. To the right of the lobby was a tiny bar surrounded by red velvet ropes. There was a sign that read "Spiked Trumnits" on top. Two of the Cloudians were drinking out of an hourglass-shaped cup. Two other Cloudians floated right by Jacob. They waved politely and smiled.

Then a small man with flattened gray hair and a mustache that pointed out from either side of his face waved in Nyx's direction.

Nyx nodded and tipped his hat in the man's direction.

"Who's that?" Jacob asked.

"That is the Elemental Academy's skyzing instructor, Bill Natansis, aha."

Noises of gears are twisting, and metal grinding led them to an oval door that was the size of a garage and resembled a bank vault. In the center of the door was a small silver gear. Nyx turned the gear to the right, and the oval door tore down the middle and split in two. Each piece retracted backwards and revealed a shiny golden platform. Nyx guided Jacob over to the platform and began their journey upward.

Arriving on the fifteenth floor, they were greeted with about twelve triangular bubble-shaped pockets. As he entered one of the pockets, Jacob's eyes widened. Bronze pipes traced the walls like snakes covering grass. Behind the pipes was a marble background painted black that looked like someone had just thrown it on the wall. Instead of beds, there were silver egg-shaped pod hammocks that were hovering above the ground. Jacob noticed a quiet, friendly atmosphere. It had been awhile since he had heard silence.

"Okay, Jacob," Nyx said, laying down in his pod. Pressing a button, two blue sheets unraveled and went over his stomach automatically. "Get some rest, ta ta," Nyx giggled. "To tomorrow, Jacob," Nyx said, and then fell asleep.

"Same to you I guess, Nyx," Jacob said, before pressing the silver button on the side of his pod too.

# 6

# NEW KID IN TOWN

Jacob woke early the next day. His pod was extremely comfortable, with a fluffy mattress that made him feel like he was bundled in clouds, and smooth, silky sheets that wrapped him in a wonderful cocoon which helped him get the best sleep of his life. When he pressed the silver button on the side of his sleep pod, it released the comforting sheets from over him and tucked them back into the sides of the sleep tank. Stepping out of the pod, he noticed that the room was empty.

Nyx's pod had no sign of him. He looked around for a clock, but couldn't find one of those, either.

At his feet was a small orange box with a note placed neatly on top of it. "Check your lux-band, tee-hee!" was written in squiggly letters on the top. He pressed the button on the side of his silver bracelet. A transparent blue screen popped up with a 3D image of a red blinking envelope. Remembering how Nyx used the lux-band yesterday, Jacob tapped the red envelope with his index finger slowly.

Nyx's curly-haired face came into view. "Woke up a bit early. I didn't want to wake you, ta ta, figured you were catching up on some much-needed rest. Went out to get an early morning Halwin shake. Oooh, Sherbet Malted Puff is so yummy! Meet me at the High Corner right outside Cloudian Gear for the Great! Time to get you out of those Gravit clothes, aha! Oh, and press the big button on the Portare Box!" The message ended, and Nyx's face zipped back down into Jacob's shiny lux-band.

Underneath the note was a large orange button. Jacob pressed it, and it made the sound of a zipper being pulled down fast. The box nudged and budged, turned, jumped in midair, and transformed into something that resembled a backpack. With a big smile, Jacob picked it up and placed it on his right shoulder. The bag only had one strap on it at first, but suddenly, another strap materialized like a snake gliding through grass and ran over his chest until it clicked into place at his waist.

High Corner was much louder than it had been the day before, and it seemed to be more densely populated. The big mall in the sky had tons of people in high-collared cloaks floating throughout. The commotion almost made Jacob lose his bearings. It was hard not to get lost in the gigantic sea of people. It reminded him of Times Square, a place he had read about during one of Henry Buford III's lessons back at the orphanage.

Steam rose, whistles whistled, feet pounded, and although Jacob felt incredibly out of place, it was nice to hear the sounds of this new world. Jacob looked out into the abyss of the mall. Several towers of three-tiered bronze shops stood in front of him. Floating escalators and walkways closed the distance. He moved forward but stopped before three separate escalators. Looking out onto each, he was hesitant to jump onto one.

Then, out of nowhere, a loud squawking sound pierced his ears. Ducking, he felt a powerful gust above his head. Looking up, he noticed a winged creature known as a flycer swing by his head and land atop one of the shops to his left.

"Man, these metal animals don't mess around," he mumbled to himself.

"Hey, give it back, Buster! Come on!" Jacob heard a nasally voice to his right yell out. He decided to pace slowly towards the commotion taking place outside of the shop he noticed yesterday, Skyracing Stuff and Stirs.

Beneath the sign with the skateboard looking item, and to the right of the shop, was a kid that was shorter than Jacob. He had light brown hair in a bowl-cut, with his bangs parted down the middle of his forehead. In front of his eyes were giant oval-shaped glasses with orange frames. He wore a high-collared red coat with a yellow shirt, and he had a single strap diagonally across his chest which must have been a type of suspenders.

Holding the collar of his coat with one hand was a tall, lanky boy with jet black hair that was spiked up and to the side. Behind him was a heavier boy with a shaved head and pimples all over his face who reminded Jacob of Tommy. He stood with his arms folded like he was the boy with the spiked hair's bodyguard.

"What's a little dingbat like you carrying around a rock like this for?" asked the boy with the spiked hair.

"It doesn't matter, Buster," the boy with the bowl-cut said. "It's mine, come on." The boy tried to swing his arms to grab the blue rock, but the taller kid just held it away from him with his other hand.

"Did you get this from Daddy? Did he scoop this up when he was cleaning up mammanil poop?" The two bigger kids laughed.

"Buster, what should we do with the little flybean today?" the fat boy with the shaved head smirked. "I got to be honest; I'm getting pretty tired of dunking his ugly head in toilet water."

The two kids laughed again, and the fat boy grabbed the oval glasses off his face. "Maybe we should break his gogs again," the fat boy blurted out, as he tightened the grip on the oval glasses.

"Easy now, Probus. There's no need to bruise your knuckles on a loser like Albert here." the boy with the spiked hair, known as Buster, flicked the nose of the smaller kid, who was Albert.

"I think you should back off," Jacob said.

Buster dropped Albert to the ground and turned his attention to Jacob. Jacob took a step back, immediately regretting his words.

"Well, what do we have here, Proby?" Buster and his big goon approached Jacob. "I don't think I've ever seen you before." He was now a few inches from Jacob. "What is your name?" Jacob looked at the big goon behind Buster, and then back at Buster again.

Buster shoved Jacob firmly to the ground. His hands broke his fall, but he landed hard on his butt. Buster leaned in with an evil smile plastered on his face. "I'd watch your back around here. You want to make sure you're making friends with the right people, or that ground will be the softest thing you've felt if you mess with us again."

Buster and his goon, Probus, turned and headed back in Albert's direction. Buster chucked the blue rock to the ground near Albert, who quickly snatched it up.

Buster snickered and nodded towards Probus, and the two disappeared into the fog. Jacob sat up and dusted his pants off. A small hand extended in front of his face. Looking up, he spotted Albert, who was awaiting his grip. He helped Jacob to his feet, and a smile was stuck on his face.

"I sure would love to give Buster a double-stomp-swipe right across his nose," Albert said, and flailed his legs up and sloppily over to one side, before standing in what Jacob assumed was some karate pose. Jacob giggled a bit to himself. Albert laughed, too.

"Greetings, my name is Albert Egan." The boy stuck out his forearm. Remembering the way Nyx shook his forearm the day before, Jacob reached out and grabbed Albert's forearm to return the shake. Jacob noticed that the boy was squinting through the giant glasses on his face. They were orange with oval lenses, but now those lenses had giant cracks in them.

"Nice to meet you, Albert. I'm Jacob," Jacob replied.

"So, what brings you to High Corner?" Albert breathed over his glasses and tried to wipe away the cracks.

Jacob paused for a moment, unsure how to answer the question. "Well, I'm traveling with this person. His name is Nyx, and-"

Before Jacob could finish, Albert stumbled backward. "You're... you're traveling with Nyx?" Albert tried to regain his composure, and he placed his right hand on Jacob's shoulder. "You mean the Nyx? The Watcher of Most Important Things? One of the most decorated PPA members in the history of Cloudia? I mean, Nyx is superb, he's witty, he's infamous, but why are you traveling with him?" Albert was panting, and holding onto Jacob's shoulder for dear life, it seemed.

"Well, he brought me here," Jacob said, helping Albert stand upright.

"Brought you here from where?" Albert asked, starting to regain a normal breathing pattern.

"Griffin. That's my home, and there were these light-bug creatures back at Ms. Larrier's orphanage, and Daren melted into a bunch of them. They flew towards me and stuck with me, and the next thing I knew, I woke up in that station place with the water slide tubes. Yesterday, Nyx showed me around the mall, and now I'm looking for him."

Jacob slowed his speech down since Albert was frozen like a statue in front of him. He waved his hands in front of his face, but Albert didn't budge. "You okay there, man?" Jacob loudly asked.

Albert blinked and then spoke again with his nasal voice. "You are from Griffin, and Nyx - the Watcher of Most Important Things - brought you here to Cloudia. You have Gravit clothes on, and... and your first name is Jacob. That could only mean one thing." Albert took a deep breath, his Adam's apple bobbing up and down like it was bouncing in water.

"What one thing would that be?" Jacob's eyebrows raised to the top of his forehead.

"You're Jacob Wesley, the Light One, the person that To Tomorrow was written about. This is splendid, serendipitous, and stupendous." Albert began hopping around with excitement.

"To Tomorrow. I heard that yesterday from Nyx, but it's a book, too?" Jacob leaned on Albert's shoulder.

"Yes, the most popular book in the whole wide world of Cloudia, and you, sir, are the basis of it." Albert folded his arms and calmed down a bit. "You had no idea, did you?"

Jacob shook his head. His brain was having trouble keeping up with all this.

"Well, looks like you have a lot to find out, then. I can't believe I met the Light One, and he stood up for me, too!" Albert started dancing around in a circle with his arms and legs moving about in frivolous motions. "You said you were meeting Nyx here. Where did he say he'd be?" Albert stopped spinning.

"Cloudian Gear for the Great?" Jacob replied.

Albert led Jacob to a second-floor shop with a sign that had a big brown barrel and a metal gear slicing through the middle of it. In the middle of the doorway was one of those angry flycers.

"Permission to dress for the best," Albert said firmly.

"Permission granted," bellowed the flycer, in a shrill voice. The doors swung upwards, revealing the entrance to the shop. Several young men and woman were fitted in small cylindrical rooms that had the shape of wooden barrels. The barrels covered their bodies from their ankles to their foreheads, leaving only the tops of their heads and their feet exposed. Bordering the brick walls were bronze and gold gears in between several steam chutes that went up to the ceiling. All around were different coats and shoes, making whistling and buzzing noises. They glided on invisible strings from the barrels.

"Well, I already got my digs earlier, so I'm going to check out a new pair of gogs," Albert said, holding out his broken oval glasses.

Jacob nodded and nervously approached one of the empty barrels in front of him. He edged closer, but then a blonde, freckle-faced girl about his age grabbed his arm.

"Hi!" said the girl. "Getting another Volans?"

"It's my first, actually," said Jacob.

"You're a little old to be getting your first Volans coat, and I bet your first Levy boots too, then?" she asked. Jacob never heard a voice so angelic before, like music to his ears. It was different than anything he had ever heard before, although, he only had Ms. Larrier's raspy scream and Smaltz's annoying meow to compare with it. Jacob silently nodded but couldn't muster any words to say.

"Oh, well, make sure you pick the right ones. There are so many colors. I have to make sure I fit in. My friends already got theirs, and they got the prettiest colors: rosy red and canary yellow!" The girl was twirling her hair. She jumped as another girl left one of the cylinder barrels. This girl was wearing a slim-fit velvet coat around her body. The end of it barely touched the tops of her knees.

"And now she just got pride of violet. That's the one I wanted!" She seemed to be very bothered by others' selections of outfits.

"You get your lux-band yet?" the girl asked.

"Yeah. Yesterday. Pretty neat looking stuff" said Jacob.

"Say, I have never seen eyes like yours before. That emerald green color is unique. They're pretty. You never really see unique eyes nowadays. Everyone in Cloudia usually has golden or blue eyes. Yeah, I've never seen that color before." She twirled her hair again.

Jacob blushed bright red. He had never been complimented by a girl before. The only comments anyone ever made about his eyes before were the nasty insults made by Tommy and Ms. Larrier.

"Well, I'm up! Nice to meet ya! My name's Anna Friendly." She winked and ran off to her barrel.

Jacob couldn't get out his name before she took her barrel. Then, before Jacob could move any further, a pain shot right up his back. He turned around to face a flycer. With its face on his back, it edged him forward with a loud grunt.

"Ouch! Alright, alright, I'm going."

Jacob stepped forward after the angry push. The brown barrel in front of him opened into three pieces. Inside the barrel were eight 3D images of what were called Volans coats. Beneath each image was a silver knob.

"Make your selection," a robotic voice announced. The third image was a dark green coat with silver trim. He pressed the shiny knob, and his clothes were ripped from his body, leaving him only in his underwear. Before he could reach for his clothes, a tight, silky fabric wrapped around his arms, belly and legs. The coat materialized around him as well, the collar stretched around his neck and ended just under his ears; a perfect fit.

The barrel spun around again. This time, the holograms displayed black boots, brown boots, red boots, silver boots, and even green boots. Jacob picked the dark green boots with silver buckles to match his coat. This time, the ground opened beneath him, and another huge gust of wind blew over his body. The barrel flew in the air, and Jacob levitated in place. His old shoes and socks were thrown off his feet. They were replaced with the selection he made, and the buckles clicked into place on their own.

Then the barrel lowered back to the ground. The holograms disappeared, and the buttons retracted into the wood of the barrel. A screen located in the center of the barrel revealed his new look, which immediately put a smile on Jacob's face. He gripped the edges of his coat and stepped out of the barrel.

Meanwhile, with his new gogs, Albert was moving around in circles again. He was throwing odd kicks and flailing his arms in different directions. Nearby, Cloudians were dodging his arms like they were running from a rainstorm. Jacob cleared his throat to get Albert's attention.

"So, do I look like a Cloudian now?" Albert stopped his sporadic movements and lit up when he saw Jacob's new outfit.

"Whoa, Jacob! It's a perfect fit." Albert started measuring Jacob's arms and his waist with his fingertips. "Sixteen long and forty-one wide, I presume. Great pick!"

As the two exited the shop, Jacob noticed the girl he had seen earlier with her new orange outfit. She smiled and waved in his direction, causing Jacob to blush. Nervously, he stuck his hand out and waved back, while she trotted off with two older Cloudians, probably her parents.

"Well, look who no longer has Gravit written all over him, ta ta!"

Nyx had floated over in their direction as though he were ice-skating. Excitedly, Jacob ran up to Nyx and shook his forearm.

"Where have you been, Nyx?" Jacob asked breathlessly. "I woke up and got your note, but I couldn't find you when I got here. Luckily, I ran into Albert here." Jacob turned to face Albert, who was frozen in place; like a perfect nerd statue standing in the middle of High Corner. "Albert!" Jacob yelled, knocking him on the head. Arising from his star-struck coma, Albert slowly stepped forward in Nyx's direction.

"I'm-I'm your biggest fan, Mr., uh, Mr. Nyx. I-I-I have a holo of you, and I studied all about your early PPA days." Albert was trembling, with his forearm stretched out like a slippery noodle in Nyx's direction. Jacob cocked an eyebrow and turned curiously towards Nyx.

"Well, my boy, it's a pleasure to meet you! Nice to see that Jacob is making friends already, aha!" Nyx shook Albert's forearm, and Jacob practically had to hold him up to keep him from fainting.

"So, getting used to this world? Gotta love the atmosphere, ha-ha!" Nyx exclaimed.

"Yeah, it's starting to grow on me. I still feel really odd, but it sure beats the orphanage." Jacob let go of Albert, who was back to normal by now.

"Nyx, would it be okay if Jacob stayed the night at my house?" Albert croaked behind Jacob, who looked at him, and then back at Nyx for approval.

"Hey, no problem here, ta ta! Have fun with your new friend! Just be sure to meet me at Pines Station first thing in the morning, hee-hee! We have to get to the Airz taxi."

Jacob smiled and turned to Albert, who was smiling too.

"Rad!" Jacob fist-bumped Albert.

Beautiful orange and pink clouds sifted through the air in front of them, leaving behind a peaceful trail of mist. Jacob stood with his new Levy boots in a muddy area in the middle of the bright green tall grass, in front of a beautiful lake.

"We're here! Home, sweet home." Albert ran sloppily forward, and Jacob followed behind. In front of Jacob, and behind a retreating mist, was a beautiful navy-blue house made of bricks. It sat on top of a steel structure with four beams that went into the ground. It looked like as though it had once been a bird cage that held only the gigantic creatures. The windows wrapped around the doors like tiny glass shields. Above the house were three dark blue clouds that materialized into the shape of the numbers six, eight, and four, and then disappeared for a few seconds before reappearing again. This repeated over and over.

Albert led Jacob to a green rectangular pallet on the ground. Albert pressed a green button near its side, and they began to rise into the air. A circular glass door held in a bronze frame led them up from the ground about ten feet high.

"We prefer to stay as far away from the center as possible, which is about 37.43 miles away," said Albert.

"Wow, that's far, Albert," said Jacob, only half-serious, thinking of how far he was from the Kendal Drive Orphanage.

Albert waved his hand in front of the framed circle. The circle separated into six pieces and retracted into the walls that surrounded it. Jacob stood with his mouth open in amazement.

"My sources aren't home right now, but it's cool. They let me stay here alone," Albert said, as he took a step inside.

"Your sources?" Jacob paused for a moment.

"Right, silly me. I refer to my parents as my sources. Cool, right?" Albert ducked under a low-hanging glass chandelier.

"Yeah, that's pretty neat, I guess." Jacob followed behind him. The living room was wide, with high, vaulted ceilings. It reminded Jacob of the Griffin Museum's submarine exhibit. Albert went to the far side of the room, and after pressing a button brought up a 3D movie theater-sized screen. Surrounding Jacob was a ton of golden pipes and other odd structures that looked like clocks. There was a red and brown tile that looked like a chess board. To his left was a big board of disks floating around books. There was a sign with a 3D image floating in the center that read, "Travels and Research, Don't Touch!"

"Collection of his research while he's away. Dad works for the PPA and does scientific studies on gemstones and such. He's never really home. He spends all his time out there." Albert waved his hand near the bottom of the screen and a red box popped up.

"Looks like one of my sources left a message for me." Albert picked up a round black pad with different buttons on it. He pressed one towards the edge, and a beautiful face with a pinkish hue and wavy blonde hair that twisted up like a pretzel took up the entire screen.

"Good evening, Mother," said Albert, in an elated, high-pitched voice.

"Albert, it's nearly six, and this is the first holo-call I've received from you all day," said Albert's mother, in a concerned yet soft spoken voice.

"Sorry, Mom. I had an eventful day at High Corner, and I made a new friend today. I just kinda got carried away with things." Albert's voice turned a bit low, and his head cowered.

"You made a friend? That's wonderful, dear. What's his name?" Albert's Mom's voice grew with excitement.

"Well, he's right behind me." Albert turned towards Jacob, who was still marveling at the living room. "His name is Jacob."

Jacob headed over to the screen and waved. Albert had a big, goofy smile on his face.

"Well, hello there, Jacob," she said softly. "It's a pleasure to meet you. You have unique eyes, I must say."

"Thank you, uh, Mrs.-"

"Wendy Egan, but you can call me Mrs. Egan," she smiled. "And I assume you're going to the Elemental Academy too, then?"

Jacob didn't know how to respond. He stared blankly at Albert.

"Yeah, he's going too, Mom. He's super excited. Right, Jacob?" Albert nodded towards him.

"Yeah, just a bit nervous, I guess," said Jacob.

"Oh, not to worry," she assured Jacob. "It's a cakewalk. Just listen to all of your instructors, and study hard; very hard. In fact, studying is the most important thing you can do to succeed. I'm sure you'll have no trouble with your assessments. If you stick with Albert, you'll do just fine. He's a bright young boy, just like you. I'm sure of it." She pointed through the screen in the direction of Albert.

"Thanks, Mrs. Egan. I'll be sure to follow Albert around as much as possible," Jacob said and nodded back towards Albert.

"Okay, sweetie, I need to get going. There are a few patients that I need to carry out a check up on right now. Don't forget to water the Plantae, wash your clothes, and clean the moat, and call me in the morning, first thing, before your trip to Gordonclyff." Her voice escalated to a higher pitch after each chore she listed.

"I won't forget, Mom, I have calculated that each task should take me an hour to complete," Albert said, winking over at Jacob.

"Okay, good night and good luck! Nice meeting you, Jacob."

"Nice to meet you too, Mrs. Egan."

The screen clicked off and disappeared back into the black pad Albert was holding.

"Okay, it's time to purify the moat," Albert announced. "Clear, clearer, and clearest, that's what the sources want the water to look like; It shouldn't have a single lick of green."

Albert led Jacob outside again, and back down the elevator pallet. Albert raced over to the edge of the water just behind the house. The grass was fine, very green, and tall. Jacob liked the way it felt on his hand. It wasn't itchy if you rolled in it like the grass back home. It was smooth and felt like ribbons.

The water was a gorgeous blue, it already looked plenty clear to him, and for a moment, he could see a few creatures about the size of bass fish, but they had three pearly whitetails that were flowing away from their bodies. They looked like miniature mermaids as they swam back and forth in the moat.

"Tripoles," Albert said. "They are hydro creatures from H-Twenty. Dad rescued a few while he was out there last Maii, brought them back here, and we cared for them ever since. There are only 524 left in existence. They sing underwater and move at incredible speeds because of their water tails." One of the tripoles scattered under the water, which sent several bubbles to the surface. "They get scared easily, too."

"I've only ever seen fish before, back in Griffin. They have these cool fins and swim too," said Jacob.

Albert had a bizarre look on his face with an eyebrow raised. "Fish, that's an interesting name. Alright, so now I have to change the sulfuric chemical of the water so that it's twenty degrees diluted." Jacob nodded slowly as if he understood what Albert was saying. Albert brought out a silver tube with blue and gray buttons all over it. He pressed every button that Jacob could see and held the object with both hands tightly. He nodded over at Jacob, instigating his curiosity. A blue, jelly-like chemical oozed out of the object like slime and dove into the water that surrounded them.

"Don't worry; it won't hurt the tripoles." Albert clicked the buttons, and the slime stopped pouring out. "They really enjoy it."

Soon the water was covered with thick blue foam. "There we go, just like magic!" Albert placed the tube back in his pocket. "Just a few more tics and the water will be back to clear, clear, clear."

Albert was right, and soon enough, the foam disappeared, and any hint of green was gone. Beautiful clear blue water surrounded the house.

Jacob noticed that the sky was beginning to turn from blue to orange. The clouds that were nearby started to float away into the distance.

"Come on, Jacob, let's head back in before nightfall."

Back inside the submarine-like home, Albert led Jacob up through a silver chute that winded up to the ceiling. Without thinking, Jacob jumped into the familiar-looking tube. It reminded him of the Pines Station travel tubes.

Stepping out of the tube, they reached a circular door with a frozen holographic that said "Hydro's Greatest." Jacob stepped in and was hit with the smell of sea salt. The room reminded Jacob of the inside of a boat. The walls were faded gray and sky blue. One of the walls to the left of Albert's tiny pod bed was a clear holographic with images of dark-cloaked figures trying to kick one another.

In the corner of the room, right under two silver compass devices that said "Directional Holos" above them, was what looked like the base of a trophy. It was gold and had blue trim. There were about twenty of them lined up in a row. Jacob picked up the one in front of him, on which was printed "Nyx" in very fancy blue letters. Jacob pressed a blue button on the side of the object, and a very familiar holographic 3D image jumped up. It was Nyx, with his red curls and faded blue fedora. His hands were behind his back, and his legs moved like he was skating.

"Nyx is awesome," Albert began. "While he's not the strongest, he's very peculiar and smart. He was given the coolest responsibility, too - watching over you. That's the first Holo I ever got. I got it a few yers back for Donumdans."

"Neat," said Jacob, admiring the object.

At the back of the room, hidden under a few slim-fit outfits, was a five-foot tank that glowed turquoise and was decked out in miniature Christmas lights. A plump orange pig with a metal looking mouse's tail was sitting in the middle of it, on top of a rock. It let out a loud sound that sounded like a belch.

"Don't mind him, he just ate." Albert turned towards the creature and tapped on the glass with his finger. "Where're your manners, Keery?" It snorted back at him as Albert reached into the tank and ran his hand over its snout.

Albert made room on a nearby red leather chair for Jacob to sit in, then laid down in his pod bed, slouching over. "What do you think?"

"It's incredible, Albert, truly incredible." Jacob was grinning as he sat down in the chair. "I've never seen anything like this. It's the coolest house ever."

Albert's glasses fogged up as he smiled back at Jacob.

"What a night," Jacob could hear Albert mumbling to himself. "I finally have a friend, Keery. Well, besides you, of course."

Jacob smiled in his chair, feeling the same way about Albert.

# 7

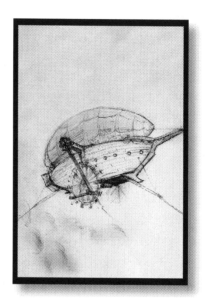

# CLOUDIA IS HOME

$J$acob awoke the next morning to the sounds of metal grinding and steam chutes. His hair looked like a wave about to be surfed, dark rings were under his eyes, and globs of drool hung like icicles from his bottom lip. The ruffled quilt that he clung to throughout the night was in a bundle on the floor, barely covering his feet. Trying to rouse from his groggy daze, he scratched his head a few times, and then slipped on his new Cloudian outfit. He headed down the pallet elevator to greet Albert, who was in the kitchen

"Morning, Jacob," Albert croaked. "We better get a move on if we are going to catch the Airz taxi. It arrives at nine and leaves at nine-fifteen."

Jacob yawned, and Albert handed him a flat bubbly stick. Jacob took a bite, and the taste of golden yolk and crispy honey ran through his gullet.

"What is that?!" Jacob's grogginess immediately subsided, and he reached for more from a nearby plate on the counter, stuffing his face repeatedly.

"Becon," Albert replied. "It's a mixture of bacon, eggs, and honey. Only fifty calories and plenty of nutritious vitamins."

"This is the most delicious thing I have ever tasted!" Jacob smiled as he chomped on another piece of becon.

"Wait 'till you see what the Airz taxi has." Albert threw Jacob his orange backpack. Jacob struggled to catch it, barely keeping it from smacking the checkerboard tile in the living room. "Put on your Portare bag. You got your lux-band?" Albert motioned towards Jacob's wrist. Jacob clicked it on and nodded back towards him.

They reached Pines Station about an hour later. Albert clicked a button on his lux-band to check the time. Spinning dials populated on a transparent blue screen before landing on eight-thirty. Albert sloppily pointed forward, as his hand began to tremble nervously. Skating in the air in their direction was the bubbly, stripe-coated Nyx.

"Well, I'm going to head over to the taxi. It looks like Nyx wants to have a few words with you."

Albert was right about that because while Nyx was still skating joyously in the air, his smile wasn't as big as it usually was.

"I'll catch you later, Jacob. I'm glad I got to meet you." Albert shook Jacob's forearm.

"See you soon, Al." Jacob blurted out a nickname for Albert without thinking.

Albert smiled and nodded. "My nickname? It was from the Light One too. So cool," he mumbled to himself as he ran away.

"Jacob, tee-hee, did you have a good night with your new friend?" Nyx cracked his knuckles and then anxiously put them under his chin with that half-smile again.

"Yeah, it was pretty cool. I got to meet a tripole and a pig-looking animal. Oh yeah, and becon! It's amazing!" Jacob exclaimed. "What's wrong, Nyx?" Jacob noticed that Nyx was trembling a bit as he sat in the air.

"This new world to you, Cloudia, is where you are now, but Griffin is the home you are familiar with, hmm." Nyx clicked his Levy boots and descended to the ground. "You were brought here to stay. You're welcome to visit Griffin from time to time, but ultimately, Cloudia will be your home now. You'll be in Cloudia, training at the Elemental Academy at Gordonclyff for the next six cycles." Nyx leaned backward, bracing for impact.

"What are cycles?" Jacob asked cautiously.

Nyx inched forward again. "There are twelve cycles every yer, and they have 30 dis." Jacob looked at Nyx very oddly. "They are like your Gravit months."

Jacob nodded. "A training academy seems cool. What do I do there?"

Nyx started to smile. "It's an incredible academy, ta ta! You'll learn such amazing things there, and you'll get to join an elemental line, ha-ha! As I was saying, this is the part where you decide. You have your Navus mark, but it can easily be undone if you want to return to Griffin. Once we take the Airz taxi, there's no going back," Nyx said anxiously.

"I've really enjoyed myself so far, but I probably don't fit in here anymore than I fit in back home. I'm a Gravit, or I was a Gravit, but at least I was with other Gravits. I hadn't really thought about anything until now." Nyx lowered his head. "But, I do know that not fitting in here is a cakewalk compared to dealing with wedgies from a fat kid and insults from scraggly Ms. Larrier. I want to stay!" Jacob raised his voice.

Nyx danced and spun in place. "Well, let's get you to Gordonclyff, then, ta ta!" Nyx grabbed Jacob and bolted forward.

Soon after, the two reached the area in front of the sky-high tunnels at Pines Station. Nyx skipped in the air, delight, and excitement beaming from his face. Thinking that the best was yet to come, Jacob smiled as well.

Jacob raised an eyebrow as Nyx reached deep inside his coat and revealed a sharp yellow object which resembled a compass. He clicked the side of the device, and a hologram flashed before them. Dials spun in place between twelve points. Starting from left to right, the dials read numbers from one to sixty, one to twelve, and AM and PM. The dials stopped and landed just to the right of eight-forty-five AM. The combination of the three flashed several times.

"Oooh, holowatch says eight-forty-five, ta ta!" Nyx smiled, clicked the button to close the image, and put the device back in his coat. "We need to move, aha!"

"We aren't taking those big-traveling water slide things?" The two now moved past the travel tunnels they had taken to High Corner.

"Don't be silly, Jacob. Those are only for inside Pines Station. We need to be in town, and to do so, we have to take the Airz Taxi," replied Nyx, hurrying forward.

Jacob's arm was almost ripped off by Nyx, who floated quickly past other people who had been scurrying in the same direction.

"Come on; they are tough to come by so soon! Everyone is traveling in and out of Cloudia all the time, and the only means is the Airz Taxi. Cloudia is too far to walk to, and the Airz Taxi only fits about fifty Cloudians at a time." Nyx continued forward and waved Jacob ahead.

Jacob's heart beat faster and faster with anticipation for an Airz Taxi ride. A taxi that fit fifty people? He had never heard of that. Maybe a bus, but not a taxi.

Soon enough, they reached what looked like a docking port. There was a large line of people in front of them, most of which were floating in the air. Only a few were standing on the ground. "Ha-ha, you'll learn how to skyze soon enough, ta ta," Nyx giggled.

Above the crowd was a thin cloud, which began forming words in the sky: "Next Airz Taxi arriving in a few whistles."

Jacob wondered if "whistles" meant "minutes" here. They probably did. He wasn't used to Cloudian terminology, and the more he heard, the odder it sounded.

"Here it is," Nyx shouted as he waved. The crowd let out a loud piercing sound that nearly deafened Jacob. He covered his ears and looked up. Approaching them was a beautiful golden boat with a large white football-shaped top. It reminded Jacob of the blimps back in Griffin. On the sides of the golden frame were golden gears the size of airplane wings spinning in a forward motion. Beneath the vessel were three flagpole-sized spikes that moved in different directions as it circled near the dock, which caused large clouds of smoke to bellow out from beneath. The smoke caused massive ripples in the sky above the crowd. A click was heard as the boat slid right next to the dock. Along the sides were pearly white framed windows trapped between each of the giant gears. The gears came to a rest and then retracted upward, revealing the inside of the taxi.

"Stand still and wait for the arrivals to unload," said a deep voice from the loudspeakers.

Passengers filtered out in a hurry, skyzing in different directions like ants on a hill. One boy with long golden hair got onto one of those hoverboards Jacob saw at High Corner and raced out from the Airz Taxi, nearly slicing through Jacob's head.

"Look out, peeps, I'm coming through!" the boy shouted.

Jacob looked back, his eyes following the boy as he sped away. "That hoverboard thing looks really cool," he said to Nyx, who wasn't paying any attention to him. Then Jacob took a nudge to the shoulder, which caught him off-balance, sending him crashing into Nyx. Jacob looked up and noticed the lanky bully from the day before trotting towards him with a smile.

"Let's go, Jacob, don't want to miss your first Airz Taxi ride, ta ta!" Nyx chuckled, as he grabbed Jacob's arm again.

There wasn't any connecting platform from the dock to the Airz Taxi. He swallowed and braced for a leap, but they just passed through an invisible bubble and found themselves inside the Airz Taxi. Inside, there were blue bubbles the size of train compartments on each side. With each step on the transparent glass floor, Jacob could see the beautiful golden engines moving in a clockwise direction. Above his head was a translucent glass ceiling. At the back of the row was a bronze gear with the light-bug symbol placed in the middle of it. Whistles and the sound of a boiling teapot could be heard every few seconds. The smell reminded Jacob of a candy store.

Jacob passed a younger child with green hair sticking out from his head like porcupine spikes who screamed, "But I wanted to sit in the top tier!"

"Well, the top tier is too packed," shouted the man who sat next to him.

They passed another bubble of people on his right, and he noticed a few kids huddled around a device with a hologram that projected outward. There were mirror images of them, and as they moved, the holograms moved in place. It looked like some video game.

"You can't beat my score! You're only on Z File Eight," shouted the boy, as he tried to knock the other off-balance.

"Cut it out, fly bean," yelled the other, as he staggered backward.

Jacob and Nyx continued through the Airz Taxi until they reached the back, where a few empty bubble pockets remained.

"Hmmm, looks like she's too full for both of us to share the same pocket. Here, you join those lads over there, and I'll grab a seat back here, tee-hee," Nyx giggled.

Each compartment had red leather seats. A glass window in a golden frame was in the middle, on top of a bronze box that resembled a bank safe.

Inside was a boy and a girl who looked identical, except for their genders. They both had plump faces and sterling silver braces on their teeth. The boy had blue hair that spiked off to the left side of his head. The girl had short purple hair that spiked off to the right side of her head.

Looking back, Jacob saw Nyx just gliding through his pocket

compartment. As Jacob entered his pocket, he was met with an odd sensation, like a large wad of bubble gum momentarily sticking to his skin. He plopped down in one of the empty red leather seats, putting his orange pack on the seat next to him. The sticky feeling had disappeared.

"Mornin'!" said the blue-haired boy.

"Heya!" said the purple-haired girl.

"Hello," mumbled Jacob.

"The name's Colby," continued the blue-haired boy, "and this is my sister, Brandy. Our last name is Johnston."

"Nice to meet you. I'm Jacob. Jacob Wesley." Jacob extended his hand as the two froze in place, turned slowly towards each other, and then glanced back at Jacob.

"J-J-Jacob?" Colby said, with a gulp.

"W-W-Wesley?" Brandy followed.

"Yeah, that's me," replied Jacob, and his eyebrows curiously rose. The two sat gawking over at Jacob. To avoid the awkward silence, he edged over by the window.

An incredibly loud horn blared. As the Airz taxi left, Jacob could see tons of different-colored clouds fly past. The outside glass shell of High Corner quickly reduced to the size of a peanut. Excitement swelled like a balloon inside Jacob's stomach.

"So, you're the Light One, then? The one To Tomorrow speaks about?" Colby interrupted.

"He's the one that's supposed to… to…" said Brandy, turning to face Colby.

"Apparently," Jacob retorted.

The twins mumbled in unison, "Whoa."

They stared at Jacob, which made him feel even more uncomfortable than when the girl in Gear for the Great told him his eyes were pretty. Jacob turned backward to see if he could get Nyx to save him from this awkward conversation, but he was fastened inside his bubble compartment and out of sight.

"So, how do you like it here?" Jacob changed the subject.

"Um, we like it, yeah," Colby broke free from his star-struck daze.

"Well, besides Mom and Dad hounding us to study all the time. And having a curfew sucks, too. Outside of that, though, it's wicked cool."

"What is it like being the Light One?" Brandy interrupted.

"I don't know," said Jacob. "I don't even really believe it, to be honest. I mean, it doesn't really feel like anything. Honestly, I just found out yesterday."

Jacob saw the twins gulp again as they intently listened to him.

"Just found out yesterday?" Colby's left eyebrow jumped up on his forehead.

"You mean to tell me the Light One of Cloudia has no idea what he needs to do?" Brandy followed.

Colby turned to Brandy, confused, and whispered something in her ear. Jacob could still clearly hear him, though.

"You sure it's Jacob Wesley? He could be lying."

"I doubt it, Colbs; he's got green eyes. No one's ever had green eyes before," Brandy whispered back.

"Not convinced, B." Colby turned back towards Jacob. "Prove it," snapped Colby, and he stuck his nose up at Jacob. Jacob knew they wouldn't back down, and there weren't any seats left in any other pockets on the Airz Taxi. He even wished he was next to the annoying kid who dragged his dad to the second floor. But instead of resisting, Jacob lowered the Volans sleeve over his right shoulder.

"Well, I was told that everyone has the same tattoo... uh... Navus thingy, but mine is different. No one else has this, so I guess that makes me... me?" Jacob said cautiously.

The two siblings snuck a closer look at the Navus mark and then sat back in their seats with a thump. Then the two began to talk to each other again.

"Come on, Colbs," Brandy began. "Green eyes, different Navus, who else could he be? He certainly isn't Follcane."

"Definitely not Follcane," replied Colby.

Jacob rolled his sleeve back over his shoulder quickly.

"So, what brings you two aboard this Airz taxi?" Jacob continued.

"Well, we're going to the Elemental Academy at Gordonclyff, and we hope we get Metallum. We live in the Upper East zone of Cloudia, and a lot of our relatives have been Metallum, including both our parents. Mom and dad both think we're destined for it. I don't know though. Stranger things have happened. At Skyschool, our instructors said we were probably destined for Timber, but Brandy and I want Metallum."

Jacob had no idea what Colby was talking about, but before he could ask them what Metallum or Timber was, he heard an angelic voice speeding towards him through the Airz Taxi.

"Whatever, I saw him first, and your coat looks ugly!"

"Not as ugly as yours!"

"Well, at least mine's unique."

Anna Friendly hurried up to the pocket with her purple backpack in her hand, and her face was red with frustration. She came to a sudden halt right in front of the bubble pocket that Jacob and the twins sat in. She made her way through and gave Jacob a sweet look. "Excuse me… you're the boy with pretty green eyes, right? Is this seat taken?"

Jacob's color went from pale white to rosy red as he was hit with a shy blush again. He shook his head and grabbed his orange backpack, leaving the seat empty for her.

"Thank you," she said politely.

The twins chuckled. She glanced right at Jacob, and Jacob looked back at her, but then looked away.

"You know, he's Jacob Wesley," Brandy said, nudging her brother in the arm.

"You're Jacob Wesley?!" Anna shot back, staring at Jacob, and covering her mouth with her right hand.

Jacob gave the Johnstons an annoyed look. The blush finally left his cheeks, and he nodded at Anna.

"Which means you're really here to save us?" Anna asked curiously.

Jacob pulled his sleeve down to reveal his Navus mark once again. She leaned over and traced the outline with her fingers. The blush returned to Jacob's face, which elicited a few giggles from the siblings.

"Well, that explains your eyes, then. You sure are one-of-a-kind," said Anna.

"Yep," Jacob replied bashfully.

"Wow. So, are you going to the Elemental Academy too?" Anna continued.

"Sounds like it, yeah, but I'm not too sure what it's going to be like. It's my first time in Cloudia." Jacob tried to shake the blush from his cheeks again. "So, you're going to this academy thing to learn stuff too?" Jacob asked.

"Yes, definitely, and I can't wait!" Anna leaped up from her seat. "I have tried to get ahead of the curb and begin skyzing." Anna was focused hard on the ground, her feet balancing in the center. "At the Academy, we have to be focused, and if I focus hard enough, I can rise with the best." She lifted off the ground for a brief moment, then fell back into her seat.

"Whoa, that was really cool!" Jacob exclaimed.

"So, if ya not from Cloudia, then ya must be from Griffin, right?" Colby shifted his attention back over to Jacob.

"Yeah, and I guess that means I'm a Gravit." Jacob was a bit embarrassed saying it out loud.

"What was that like?" Brandy followed.

"Different. They aren't as nice as all of you. Back home, there was this boy, freaking Tommy, he picked on all the kids, and Ms. Larrier, she was the worst," Jacob said.

"What a weird name Freaking Tommy is," Colby said.

"Yeah, and Jacob probably hasn't met Buster yet," Brandy said in a high-pitched voice. "At least you didn't have to put up with Skyschool."

"What's Skyschool?" Jacob moved closer to the twins.

"It's school, dude. The place where ya go to learn boring things like history and stuff" said, Brandy.

"Wicked boring, Jake," said Colby. "School only lasts until ya twelve. Once ya finish, ya move on to the academy to be trained and placed in your elemental line after that."

"I think I could be Electro," said Anna. Anna crossed her legs and smiled in Jacob's direction.

"Yeah right, only one of us gets selected to Electro, and I doubt it will be you!" yelled Colby.

"Well, it won't be you either!" Anna folded her arms and turned her attention outside the window. Jacob looked over in that direction, too. As far as he could see, there were clouds of all shapes and sizes. What really stuck out to him were the different colors. Pink clouds, purple clouds, and even orange clouds flew past the Airz Taxi.

"Beautiful, isn't it?" Anna pointed out a light purple cloud with a blue outline.

Jacob smiled and nodded. The Airz taxi curved around beautiful green mountains with water caverns running down the sides. "Never seen anything like it," Jacob mumbled. "Back home it rain all the time. The sun barely crept through the clouds, and the clouds were all gray."

"Back home. Ya mean Griffin?" Colby asked from across the pocket, spoiling the moment.

"And who'd ya live with?" asked Brandy, with a lowered left eyebrow.

"Her name was Ms. Larrier. She's… well, she was… never mind, she's not worth mentioning." Jacob had enough of living by her rules and being reminded of the horrible lifestyle he lived before falling into the world of freedom and beauty that he was experiencing now. Up until this moment, he had barely even thought of the orphanage. It was hard to believe that only a few days ago, he was whisked away by that bizarre child full of those firefly bugs.

Just as Jacob was brushing away the thoughts of his crooked-nosed caregiver and her loud, pesky cat, a ringing sound ripped through the Airz taxi. It was so loud that he was forced to cover his ears in a desperate attempt to shield them from the noise. The other children in the bubble pocket didn't even flinch.

"You okay?" Anna asked, confused by his reaction.

"I don't think I'm used to the sound difference. The same thing happened back in Pines Station. I think it's something with the frequencies, maybe," Jacob replied.

The noise finally disappeared. Suddenly, from the top of the bubble, huge cords dropped down right in front of them. A black round tray materialized on top of their knees. The same thing happened in all the other pockets, too.

"Food," Colby explained. "Ya order food. Press the button on top of the z-tray."

Colby pointed at the top of the disk that hovered in front of Jacob. After he pressed the button, a large transparent hologram of a menu with many different food items appeared.

"They offer you a free meal when you ride the Airz Taxi from Pines Station to Cloudia," Anna explained with a smile, through her hologram.

"Yeah, but ya only get one. It's all delicious, except for grizzly squash. It's gross. It tastes like rubber and tree sap," Brandy said, puckering her lips like she tasted something funny.

Anything was better than cold oatmeal and runny eggs, or any of the other concoctions that Ms. Larrier had the boys cooked up.

The curved blue screen had different items, and Jacob swiped through them with his index finger. A golden, crispy sandwich that sparkled called a Cinnabutter Jellywich, a hot dog that had cheese inside of it, surrounded by a fried bun with French fries called a Curly Dog of Cheese, a bowl with what looked like white, yellow, and orange cheese oozing out of ravioli called Cheesypasta Nibs, and the last item he swiped through were different grilled chicken shapes surrounded by crusty and creamy mashed potatoes called Chicken Mash Hearts and Potato Stars. Although it was the strangest food item he'd ever seen, it definitely sounded the most delicious at the same time. He decided to go with Chicken Mash Hearts and Potato Stars.

The black disk spun several times before a crazy blonde chef in a white Volans coat appeared on the hologram. He gave Jacob what looked like a salute with one hand. Then the hologram disappeared along with the disk and was replaced with a golden plate filled with sliced up-meat which looked like chicken in the shapes of hearts and stars, with a creamy brown sauce drizzled over each piece, encrusted by creamy mashed potatoes. Then a silver object crashed onto his plate. It had two prongs on top, and it was curved near the bottom, sort of like a fork on one end and a spoon on the other.

"That's what ya eat with." Colby stuck his silver utensil into his bowl of hot cheesy pasta balls.

"How do I use it?" Jacob lifted his awkwardly.

"It's called a churk." Brandy raised her churk full of pasta balls to her mouth. "Ya pick it up by the bottom and stick it in the middle, see?"

She stuffed four different large cheesy pastas into her mouth. Anna took a giant bite of her golden sandwich and purple jelly and creamy peanut butter oozed out of it. Colby stuffed five large cheesy pastas into his mouth. Before he finished chewing, he took yet another large bite and swallowed it all down. Jacob gulped nervously.

"Go on, it won't bite back, ya know," Brandy said, wiping her mouth with her sleeve.

He poked the chicken meat with his churk and then closed his eyes. Bracing himself for the mystery taste, he raised the meat very timidly to his mouth. He was about to take a nibble so that he could tiptoe into the taste, but Colby and Brandy were laughing and leaning back in their seats.

"What do ya call that? Huh? Our baby cousin takes bites bigger than that!" Brandy clutched her stomach, seemingly trying to prevent a laugh monster from ripping out of it.

His food smelled like smoky brown sugar and tangy garlic from the mashed potatoes. He leaned in and took a big bite. The flavors of chicken and honey tickled his tongue. Immediately, he finished the meat off, licking the last remnants of hot chicken and fluffy mashed potato crust off his lips.

"There ya go, ya finally had a Cloudian meal," Colby mumbled, with a mouth full of his macaroni, and cheese strings sticking to his lips.

"How was it?" asked Anna, after she wiped the sides of her mouth with her sleeve.

"Unbelievable! It was so delicious! Best thing I've ever tasted!" Jacob shouted, leaning back in his chair. He was full. "Back home, we had to cut tiny pieces of food and eat it very slowly to make it last, so this is super bizarre."

"How do they cut with their churks?" Colby asked.

"And how long do they take?" Brandy followed.

"Well, they have forks, spoons, and knives. They use them to cut their food. This, uh, churk looks like a combination of them. And I don't know, everyone's different, so maybe it takes them a few minutes to an hour or so," said Jacob.

"A few what?" Anna asked.

"Never mind," he replied. He was already feeling embarrassed about having to explain something as unimportant as silverware.

Another whistle sounded, and a cup shaped like an hourglass flew down to each of the pods in the pocket. The others picked theirs up and drank the beverage in one gulp. Jacob held the cup to his mouth and tried to mimic the others.

"Here," Anna said, as she pressed the button on the side of his cup. The top swirled downward, and a line of thick liquid ran down his throat and into his belly. It tasted like a thick, fizzy soda.

"Thanks." Jacob started to blush again. "What are those called?"

"Trumnits!" Brandy shouted, and downed hers, too. "They come in different flavors, but Nerry is the best. Latochoc is sweet, too, and you get them for free on Airz Taxis!"

"Oh, well, that's good to know." Even though the food and drinks were delicious, Jacob still felt uncomfortable. He was in a land he knew nothing about. It was like being born again and walking for the first time. All of the words sounded like they were gibberish that was just made up on the spot. Even the ways that Cloudians ate and drank were different than what he was used to. He had felt out of place at the orphanage, but here, he felt he was living in an alternate universe. *At least they speak the same language as me*, he thought to himself.

The pocket opened, and Nyx floated in. He had a big smile on his face as he skyzed over to the children.

"Nyx!" Jacob shouted, excited that a familiar face had come to break the awkward thoughts he was having.

"Oh, I see you had your first trumnit, hee-hee. Shame they don't have Tars-Flerry on Airz Taxis. It's my most favorite, ta ta!" Nyx clapped his hands together. "Hello, lads. Better get your things ready, Jacob. We are arriving in a few whistles. Check out the view, and I'll be back soon, tee-hee!"

Nyx giggled as he left the pocket, and a nervous knot twisted up the insides of Jacob's stomach.

"Wicked!" Brandy bumped Colby's shoulder with her fist. "Nyx just showed his face in our pocket, and said hello!"

"He looked at me first, Brandy." Colby shoved his sister back.

"No way, Colby, he looked at me first," Brandy retorted, with another shove.

"Well, I thought he winked at me." Anna crossed her legs and smirked. "Besides, he only wanted to speak to Jacob-"

Before Anna could finish, another person squeezed into their pocket. Only this time, it wasn't Nyx. It was another boy.

"Greetings, mates. How's your ride been?" asked a boy with a familiar nasally voice and orange oval glasses.

"Fine," said Brandy and Colby, in unison.

"Heya Albert, how's your ride been, man?" Jacob scooted over to make room for him. Jacob and Albert bumped each other's forearms. Colby and Brandy gave each other looks of disgust.

"It's been fun, as per usual. Did you know these Airz Taxis run at fifteen-hundred revolutions per whistle, and the gears are made out of solid silver? And the food is so good; I wish I could have more to eat. What did you eat?" Albert's excitement was palpable.

"Look, little dude, this pocket is full. We're almost there, too. I'm sure ya have a seat ya can go back to," Colby rudely interrupted.

"The Chicken Mash Hearts and Potato Stars were unreal, man. I'd put it right up there with your becon." Jacob could still taste the food he just had.

"I'm Anna." Anna extended her forearm out to shake, and Albert accepted it.

"Nice to meet you, Anna, my name's Albert Egan."

Meanwhile, the twins sat with their arms folded and glared death stares in Albert's direction.

"These quiet fly-babies are Colby and Brandy Johnston," said Anna, as she kicked Colby in the leg. Jacob smirked, and the twins extended their forearms reluctantly. "It sounds like you've met Jacob before, too!"

"Yeah, Albert was kind enough to help get me acquainted with High Corner, and his house is fascinating." Jacob gave Albert another forearm bump.

"Are all of you on the way to Cloudia to begin training?" Albert asked. He still had as much energy as when he first entered the bubble.

"We're all going to the academy, so we will be going through initiation. You as well, I take it?" Anna asked.

"Oh, splendid! Yes, me as well. I can't wait. I've been reading everything about the Hydro line. Ever since father got back from H-Twenty, I've been very fixated on water. Lum Wallabee, Rufus Scord, even Bulton Shawn are all famous Hydros, and I hope to join them, too! I heard it takes a full cycle before you can even control water. Electro is the most difficult, but Timber would be fun, too. Well, anyways, I must return to my pocket. Pleasure meeting all of you. Say, Jacob, maybe we will get in the same line together. That would be a hoot!" Albert left, and Jacob heard the twins crumble with laughter.

"Like that flybean will make it through Hydro training," Colby nudged Brandy.

"I sure hope I don't get stuck in line with him," Brandy replied and nudged him back.

"He seemed to know a lot more than you two," Anna jumped to Albert's defense.

"Hey, what's that patch on your shoulder?" Jacob pointed at a bright red circle with a stitched image of three silver spikes on Colby's right shoulder.

"Oh, dude, it's only the most wicked sport of all, Skyracing!" Colby pressed his red lux-band over his wrist, and a holographic image of an older boy with spiky red hair, a chiseled chin, and a long red and silver Volans coat popped up. His hologram was rotating, and the name Ezekial Addams hovered around it.

"Who is he?" asked Jacob.

"Ya don't know who Ezekial Addams is?" croaked Colby. "Okay, okay, look at this." Colby tapped on the image, and Ezekial's hologram jumped on a hoverboard, then started swaying back and forth. Underneath him were the words:

EZEKIAL ADDAMS

RANKED #1 SKYRACER

Agile, tough, and known for his speed, Ezekial is believed to be the greatest performer in Skyracing history. He is unbeaten in 25 qualifying matchups and 8 Annual Great Skyraces.

To the right of the description were several numbers:

5'8" 155 lbs
25-0 (5-0)
Screeching Twist, 35.8 mph

"Whoa." Jacob's mouth was hanging open.

"Well, he will need to watch out for Darlene this yer!" Anna shouted in Colby's direction.

"Yeah!" Brandy backed her up.

"Ha-ha, she doesn't stand a chance. Ezekial isn't slowing down for nobody." Colby pressed his lux-band and the image disappeared.

Jacob had never seen anything like Skyracing before, and he loved sports. Anytime the boys at the Kendall Drive Orphanage were allowed to watch fifteen minutes of television; he was always the most excited to watch the Griffin Gourd or the Griffin City Canes, the town's baseball and football teams.

"Darlene almost had him last cycle, and you know it!" Brandy jumped up into a challenging stance. "She had the lead for several laps, too."

"Ya know as well as I do that Zeke was toyin' with her. Come on, sis, ya better than that." Colby waved her off.

"That 180 Air Spinner move near the last leg was unbelievable," Brandy yelled, as she sat back down.

"Nobody's got nothing on him, he's wicked B.A.," Colby belted.

"This all sounds amazing! Do we get to watch it at all?" Jacob chimed in.

A loud noise suddenly blared through the Airz taxi.

"We're here!" Anna shouted excitedly. Outside the window, they were slowly approaching tall green mountains surrounded by purple and orange clouds. It looked beautiful.

"Well how about we all get together tonight for the open they have at Skyracing stadium? Say, Jacob, what do ya think?" asked Colby. Jacob nodded his head without even thinking.

"Count me in, too," said Anna.

"Meet us at Center City at about six tonight." Colby picked up his Portare bag and headed outside the pocket.

"Yeah! To Tomorrow, Jake," said Brandy.

"Bye, Green Eyes," said Anna.

"To Tomorrow, and nice meeting all of you!" Jacob said as he shook each of their forearms. After the group left the pocket, Nyx floated up right behind Jacob.

"Enjoy your travels, hee-hee?" Nyx giggled. "I see you've already made some friends, and some plans, by the sound of things."

The group waved at Jacob as they exited the Airz Taxi. Jacob waved back and yelled one last time, "Nice to meet you! To Tomorrow!"

"To Tomorrow, Jacob!" They yelled back, in unison. Jacob also saw Albert, who squeezed his way through the crowd after he departed from the Airz Taxi.

Jacob finally made it through the docks; above him was a number 7 surrounded by thin clouds that dusted through the middle of the number. Ahead of him were tall, gorgeous, gold and silver gates that were placed on the platform.

"Welcome to the heart of Cloudia, Jacob. Your home truly awaits you now, ta ta!" Nyx said and continued onward.

A floating escalator led from the ground up towards the top of the gate.

"Watch your step, ta ta!" Nyx grabbed Jacob and once again hopped onto the escalator. Several escalators climbed from the bottom of the platform and curled towards the top of the gold and silver gate. Flattening at the top, the escalators came to a halt. With each step, Jacob felt more nervous as he awaited his grand new home.

"Here's where the fun starts, hee-hee," whispered Nyx.

After a loud whistle sounded, the gates began to open slowly.

# 8

# ELEMENTAL SELECTION

Jacob and Nyx jumped off as soon as reached the top of the escalators. People were scattering in all different directions, some of them off to the right towards a building made of marble bricks. Above the door, a wide block was inscribed with the words Cloudian Town Hall. Twenty-foot tall golden gates with bus wheel sized gears that spun clockwise stood at the top of the white escalators.

As the gates opened, they revealed a city surrounded by golden walls that arched over the outer edges about fifty feet high. The city was draped in a bright mist that swept across the ground. Clouds filled the streets; in, out, and above. Directly after the gates was a waterway surrounded by two rows of green grass. In the far distance, two giant white towers curved inward towards each other. Off to the left and right were very modern looking white buildings. Throughout the city were light bulbs that hovered in place. Jacob could hear the commotion of everyone running around and bells ringing off in the distance. The mist is clear and dense, and he felt like he could almost grab hold of it as he passed through. In the center of the city was a deep void of land surrounded by water and trees. It was a mystery to Jacob what was inside of it.

"Greetings, Nyx," said a deep voice. Standing in front of Jacob was a muscular man with a golden sleeveless Volans coat. He had a huge smile. One ear was covered with a golden contraption, and his hair was in a mohawk.

"This must be the Light One. I remember carrying you around through Pines Station and five different portals to escape Follcane and his guard. Back then, you could fit in the palm of my hand, and now, you're almost as big as my belly!" He let out a loud chuckle. Jacob didn't recognize him at all, but the huge man seemed to know Jacob very well.

"Jacob, hee-hee, this is Bron Brutus, ta ta! He was the one that carried you to the orphanage in the orange Portare bag you're carrying right now." Nyx let out a chuckle.

"Hey, Bron, very nice to meet you, and thanks for, uh, saving my life." Bron just stood there, shocked. Jacob thought he might have offended him with his words, but then Bron regained his composure.

"My, my! Well, my boy, honestly, I am sure you'll return the favor one day." Bron winked at Jacob. Nyx clapped and approached him.

"Well, this is where we part ways, Jacob. I must be off to check in with the PPA, ta ta!" Nyx said joyfully.

"But Nyx, you're leaving already? I barely even got to see you." Jacob was confused.

"Don't you worry; Bron will be your chauffeur throughout Cloudia.

We will see each other again real soon, I'm sure, ha-ha." Nyx shook Jacob's forearm, and Jacob reluctantly smiled.

"Well, thank you for everything, Nyx. It's been a pleasure." As Jacob spoke, Nyx started to skyze away.

"To Tomorrow, Jacob, hee-hee, ta ta!"

Just like that, Nyx was skating through the air and off into the distance. Jacob turned back towards Bron. Bron's feet were making giant cracks in the street with each step he took in his hulky levy-boots, and the mist disappeared around him. However, when Jacob looked at them, he noticed that the cracks were going back to normal after they passed.

"I prefer to walk. Skyzing gets old after a while. Bet you didn't know I'm originally from Griffin myself. I lived most of my life between Cloudia and H-Twenty though. It was my idea to stash ya at Griffin with the other Gravits all those yers ago. Let me tell you; I've had some nasty battles working for the PPA over in H-Twenty." Bron motioned towards his golden ear. "I'm sure you are wondering why Nyx is leaving you with me."

Jacob nodded.

"You're probably wondering a lot, I imagine."

Jacob nodded again.

"Well, we need to act fast. Usually, children don't join their respective elemental line until they are thirteen, but since your borndi isn't until a few dis from now, we have to bend the rules just a bit." Bron winked over at Jacob.

"I'll be joining one of those elemental line thingies?" Jacob suddenly got excited and nervous at the same time.

"Yes. Well, not right away. You go through a test of sorts, along with the others, before you are chosen." Bron started to quicken his pace.

Jacob remembered the kids from the Airz taxi bragging about the different lines they wanted to join.

"How many others are there?" Jacob ran to keep up.

"Seran says that the Elemental Academy is set to initiate around forty new Cloudians into their elemental lines this yer. I sure hope no one gets Incendiary. Follcane has been snatching them left and right."

Jacob noticed a loud bell ringing again, similar to the one he heard at Pines Station. The bells caused people to change direction suddenly. It wasn't as loud as before, Jacob thought. Maybe he was finally getting used to the different noises.

Suddenly, Bron stopped in his tracks. He knelt over the ground and felt around for something that Jacob couldn't see.

"So, this is Cloudia?" Jacob turned his head as he tried to everything new that he passed, whether it was a family skyzing by or a holographic image of a trumnit.

Ignoring Jacob, Bron pulled out the object he'd been searching for, which was a golden tube with a silver stick attached to the top of it. He placed it against his arm, and the stick wrapped around his wrist like a snake coiling around its prey. He pressed a bronze oval button near the bottom of his wrist. A hologram projected of a small woman with a wild purple and green coat. Purple rose petals stuck out of the top of her head, and her hair spiraled upwards like a wedding cake.

"How can I help you, Bron?" The lady patted the top of her head anxiously.

"Well, Magistra Dayan, I have one last Cloudian reporting for elemental selection. It's crucial that we delay until he arrives." Bron nodded over towards Jacob.

"That's fine, Bron, there shouldn't be an issue... and surely, a holocall wasn't necessary for that," replied the woman.

"Well, that's not all. He's twelve. He won't be thirteen until the thirteenth. Seran has given me orders to expedite his selection."

"Very unusual, Bron. What is the boy's name, then? I'll have to put in an official order to move him forward. I trust that he has his Navus mark?" The lady pulled out a piece of parchment and wrote with her fingertip.

"Indeed, Magistra." Bron lifted Jacob's Volans coat from his shoulder to check. He raised an eyebrow, and Jacob knew he was confused by what he saw. Bron decided to proceed anyway.

"His name is Jacob. Jacob Wesley."

Magistra Dayan stopped immediately at the sound of his name.

"H-H-He's here," she mumbled to herself. Looking back at Bron, Magistra Dayan continued. "He's here in Cloudia? That's him?"

Bron nodded and revealed a shy Jacob next to him, still confused by what was going on.

"Great skies! Surely, I can make room for him. Not a problem at all, Bron. I was wondering why Seran would be involved in elemental selection. This makes sense now." Turning towards Jacob, the woman waved. "Hello."

"Hi," Jacob replied bashfully. "Nice to meet you, Magistra...?" Jacob waved at the hologram.

"Magistra Alexandria Dayan is my official name, and it's a pleasure to meet you, too, Mr. Wesley. I look forward to seeing which elemental line you're selected into. It's so exciting. Very, very exciting." She clapped and waved very excitedly at them.

"Well, thank you, Magistra Dayan. We will be there in just a few whistles." Bron came back into the frame. "Thank you for making the exception for him."

Jacob could see her blush in the hologram.

"Anything, anything at all for the Light One, of course. See you soon, Bron, and Mr. Wesley, too!"

The two waved as Bron clicked off the hologram and placed the golden tube back beneath the ground.

"Well, now that that's settled, do you have all your stuff in your Portare bag?" Bron pointed at the big orange carrying pack over Jacob's shoulder.

"If you mean the rings that go around your wrists and the goggles that go over your head, then yeah, I believe so." Jacob rummaged around in his pack to find the zipper.

"No need to prove it, Jacob. Just wanted to make sure, since Nyx can sometimes be a dullard. To be honest, I'm kinda surprised he got everything that's required of ya," Bron chuckled to himself.

Bron patted him on the back and pressed forward. As they passed through the silver streets covered in a bright mist of white clouds, Jacob felt a sense of eagerness to be selected for his elemental line.

They approached a very tall building which was held up by two gigantic female statues. The structure curved upwards and had a bizarre contortion in the middle. It reminded Jacob of a frozen tornado. On the ground were large fields of beautiful green grass.

In front of the building were four men with their lux-shades on, and dark robes covered their Volans coats. They also had neatly groomed, jet-black hair that wasn't spiked like the rest of the Cloudians Jacob had met. Their lux-shades were different, too; sleeker, and no band was attached to their heads. Instead, large ovals were placed in front of their eyes. The men stood in front of a gorgeous sterling silver door that was covered in objects that looked like gears.

The cloaked men reached out their hands and halted Jacob and Bron in front of the entrance. The man nearest to them stepped forward.

"One on the left?" he muttered.

Jacob looked over at Bron nervously. He suddenly felt like a criminal caught in the middle of a robbery. Bron leaned over and whispered, "Just relax. Security check to make sure we are Cloudians."

The man closest to the door clicked something on the side of his lux-shades. "475 amperes. Must be in the PPA."

"On the right?"

"Odd."

"Report?"

The man stepped forward and whispered in the other's ear. He removed his lux-shades to stare deeply at Jacob. *This is it,* Jacob thought. *Something is wrong, and I'm going to be taken away. I'll be locked in Cloudia's form of the hole; a disgusting dungeon that has loose pieces and mad birds with little heads pecking at me all the time. How can I get out? How can I—*

Before Jacob could make a run for it, a third cloaked security guard stepped in front of the pair.

"Cloudian Registration," the man without his lux-shades demanded.

Bron eased off the right sleeve of his Volans coat. He revealed a Cloudian symbol with a bright red scar through the middle. The man raised an eyebrow that could be barely seen over his lux-shades; then he raised a thin, black gun. It emanated a red light that traced the symbol all around.

"Brutus, Bron. Accepted."

Then he turned his attention towards Jacob and approached with the scanning object. Jacob stood there frozen, unsure how to proceed. His mark was different than everyone else's. He was sure he would be captured and tortured because of who he was.

"Navus mark?" the man asked after he raised his scanner. Jacob stepped backward in concern but revealed his unique symbol. The man turned his head back towards the one that seemed in charge. He nodded and granted permission to proceed. The red light traced Jacob's Navus mark. When the scan was complete, the man put the device back into his cloak.

"Wesley, Jacob." The man spoke firmly. "Accepted."

"All right, let's go, Jacob. Close one, eh?" Bron let out a chuckle as Jacob followed him forward.

The doors swung upwards. Inside was a stark interior with marble casing throughout. It reminded Jacob of the museum. Walls reached higher for what seemed like miles and miles. Giant golden gears moved throughout the building in a clockwise direction. In front of them was a desk, and sitting behind it was a beautiful woman with long curly golden hair. She let out a bright and wide smile as she winked at Bron.

"Welcome to Gordonclyff Tower, home of the Elemental Academy," she greeted.

"Thank you," Bron said, curtly.

Bron took Jacob and moved past the woman onto a round silver platform to the right.

"Which floor?" The woman asked, and twirled her hair with her fingers.

"77, please." Bron looked down at Jacob. "Hold onto me tight."

"Enjoy your stay," the woman said, as she pressed something from behind the desk.

Suddenly, the platform jolted upward, spiraling into place. Jacob could barely make out the marble, which now just looked like a white and silver blur. The wind passed over his cheeks and spiraled down past him.

Finally, the platform came to a halt, and a bunch of kids his age were huddled in front of him. He noticed the Johnston siblings off to the right, playing some game that involved holding your shoe in one hand while hopping over the other.

Bron remained on the platform with his arm held out.

"You're leaving?" Jacob asked nervously.

"Just for a little while. You need to find your elemental line, and then I'll be back. You still have yet to meet the rest of the PPA." Bron walked back towards the center of the platform.

"But what do I do? I don't even know what I'm doing." Jacob anxiously stood in front of Bron.

"Don't worry, little guy. You'll fit in. The Elemental Academy will show you the way. Besides, Magistra Dayan already knows who you are, and she's expecting you. To Tomorrow, Jacob." Bron extended his arm towards Jacob.

"To Tomorrow, Bron."

The two exchanged a Cloudian farewell, and Bron zipped back down. Small remnants flashed behind him.

"Better late than never, I'd say." Magistra Dayan had sidled up right behind Jacob.

"I'm sorry, Magistra Dayan, I had no idea-"

"Don't be foolish. We're just glad you're finally here. We've been waiting for yers. What're a few more whistles? Hmm," she chuckled. "All right, join the others. The elemental selection is about to begin."

"Thank you, Magistra Dayan." Jacob turned around to face an auditorium with golden seats rotating around a marble stage. Behind the platform was a 3D screen made of glass. The ceiling was made of glass as well, with bronze gears attached to the top. The room smelled like a mixture of wood and fresh paint.

"Jakezilla, what's happening?" Colby blurted out.

"We didn't think you were gonna show," Brandy said.

"Yeah, what took you so long, Green Eyes?"

Jacob turned around and spotted Anna in front of him, just as beautiful as ever.

"Uh, well, Brutus, uh, Br-"

"Bron Brutus?" Colby jabbered. "You got to see Bron Brutus?"

"He's my hero. I have so many holos of him at home!" Brandy yelled.

"You know him?" Jacob asked.

"Know him?" Colby gulped. "Jake, he's like the most famous Metallum ever."

"He reads like 500 amperes, I've heard," Brandy jumped up and down as she spoke.

"Being you has its perks, huh?" Anna nudged Jacob.

"I guess. I'm still kind of overwhelmed with it all," Jacob replied, feeling anxious.

"Take your seats, young elementals." Magistra Dayan hovered in place. Scrambling like eggs in a pan, the rest of the children filed into the nearby seats surrounding the center of the room. Jacob scattered forward, trying to locate a seat. Lucky for him, Anna grabbed his hand and yanked him to the left just in time to catch two empty spots.

Jacob was stunned at sight before him. A barely-lit platform stood in the middle of hovering benches that were circling the room. He felt like he was in a planetarium, only much more relaxed and neater.

"Greetings, greetings, young Cloudians, and future masters of elemental control. My name is Alexandria Dayan, and I am the Magistra for the Elemental Academy of Gordonclyff Tower."

Loud cheers erupted from everyone. She skyzed over the crowd towards the front of the room.

"As you know, you are here today to go through a selection test to see which elemental line you will find yourselves in. This will begin your journey into elemental control and Cloudian supremacy. Now, for the exciting part. There are five Cloudian elements."

The lights went out, and darkness overtook the room. Jacob's excitement reverted to nerves again. Being in the dark was something Jacob was unfortunately used to, but did not favor. Memories of being grounded started to spread through his brain.

"Hydro; the use of liquid elements," Magistra continued.

A big holographic image of a figure with a crystal blue outline appeared in front of the bright glass screen. Water jetted out from the palms of his hands. Then he made the water swish around into a ball, and it dropped to splash over the audience.

Cheers roared again from the group.

"Timber; the use of wood."

This time, there was a hologram of a figure with a dark brown outline. As he raised his hands, pieces of wood came together to build a small plank in front of him. Then he punched through it, and the pieces flew over the audience and quickly disintegrated. Cheers sounded again, and this time, Colby let out a loud whistle. Jacob smiled as his nerves grew into excitement.

"Metallum; the use of solid steel and other metals."

A figure with a silver outline appeared. Pieces of metal spiraled in front of him. He raised his left hand; the metal flew together and clung to him like armor. He raced forward and dove into the audience, but disintegrated as he fell. Louder cheers roared, and Brandy jumped up and down over and over again.

Just as Jacob was laughing and enjoying himself, he suddenly caught eyes with Buster Nalum, the annoying bully from High Corner. The two locked eyes and stared at each other for a brief moment.

"Incendiary; the use of fire."

Buster winked at Jacob and turned to face the front again. A chill raced down Jacob's spine. Hopefully, he won't get placed into Incendiary, he thought.

Behind the stage, the glass screen illuminated. A figure appeared, outlined in a dark crimson red. He stood still, as fire surrounded him. As he moved his hands in a circle, the crowd anxiously awaited what came next. Then, the figure pushed a stream of fire forward and into the audience. The flames went out before they could light the crowd ablaze, and Jacob shielded himself.

"It's just a holo, Jake. Relax, dude," Colby giggled.

A few cheers were heard, but not as much as the other lines.

"Finally, Electro; the use of electricity and wind. This is the most sacred line out of all the elements; only one of you will enter into Electro."

"Here we go," said Colby.

A figure appeared with an emerald green outline. He levitated above the ground, took a step back, and stood in a concentrating pose. As he raised his right fist upward, the crowd grew silent. Then the figure let out a screeching yell and opened his fist. A large yellow ring with small lightning sparks protruded from his hand, and a big gust of wind encased the whole room.

The loudest cheers and applause took place. Everyone whistled and screamed. It was obvious to Jacob that this was the most popular line.

The figure disappeared, and the lights turned back on. This time, Magistra Alexandria Dayan wasn't alone. Behind her were eight figures in cloaks with collars up to their ears, and each wore the colors of the different lines. Over their eyes were lux-shades.

"Everyone go to the back of the room, please. We will be calling you by name and administering your Elemental Aptitude Tests."

When Magistra Dayan finished, kids scurried towards the back. Jacob was still frozen in place, amazed at the spectacle that had happened. He then felt a mighty tug and found Anna, who dragged him behind her. The two went to the back of the room and joined the Johnston siblings.

Jacob never thought he would be in such a bizarre but exciting world. A city that somehow remained suspended in the clouds and didn't fall to the ground. Never mind the floating escalators and reverse water slide tubes. Now he stared at a brightly lit hall shaped like a circle. Around the room were all sorts of bronze and black objects that hovered in place. Towards the ceiling was a gear that spun and moved through tiny clouds.

Jacob was in the middle, towards the back. He was a bit shorter than the rest of the teens, so he had to stand on his toes to see forward. Magistra Dayan stood still, her hands clasped together.

Anna whispered to Jacob, "Magistra Dayan is a Timber. Best Timber in all of Cloudia."

She seemed to be very confident, but mysterious at the same time.

One of the eight figures stepped forward. Magistra Dayan pressed a button on the sides of all the figures, activating them. She then brought out a solid, pearly white structure with a stand that stretched out from the bottom, like a scale. She pressed a button on the scale and out came a piece of metal with a band around it.

This was something Jacob saw back at the museum. It would be interesting to see Tommy try this out. What a great laugh it would give Jacob to see him barf in front of everyone.

The others around him were fixated on the structure, not taking their eyes away from it.

"You were read as you entered Gordonclyff earlier, but it was not a completely accurate reading. For us to judge if you are the proper fit for each line, we must know your ampere reading. However, it must be precise, and to do that; you will need to be centered in Cloudia. In front of you is a centering scale known as the Selector. Don't be alarmed; it's just to keep your internal energy precise."

Magistra went over and pulled out a large electronic device which looked like small television, seemingly with everyone's names written on it. Five of the figures went to the side of the room, where five doors began to materialize. They stood in place in front of each door. The doors were outlined with the colors of the different lines: brown for Timber, blue for Hydro, silver for Metallum, red for Incendiary, and green for Electro.

Everyone stood silently, anxiously waiting to see who would be called first.

Jacob looked rather weary. He'd had enough of odd gadgets, Navus marks, and bizarre ampere measuring throughout his journey here. He wondered when it would stop, and now, he had to be read in front of everyone. Jacob didn't feel courage, and he no longer felt excited. Instead, he felt tired and nervous. When people heard his name, what would happen?

"Brian Saunders!"

A heavy boy with purple dreadlocks popped out from the back. He stepped onto the Selector. A figure approached him and placed the band around his waist. A figure to the side of him clicked on his lux-band. Everyone waited for the reading.

"142 amperes," announced the figure.

Another figure approached and placed five different bags on the centering scale in front of him. The bags flipped violently in place, twirled, twisted, and became blurry to see. The audience shrieked.

When the bags stopped in place, four of the five bags stayed at the same height, and one bag was lowered. A figure approached the bag and loosened it. A piece of wood was revealed.

"TIMBER!" shouted all eight figures at once. Each figure raised their hand and motioned towards the dark brown door. A few of the people in the audience applauded as the boy wiggled his way over.

Magistra Dayan smiled and continued.

"Lindsey Goodman."

A girl with blue hair in the shape of an ocean wave skipped forward towards the Selector.

"137 amperes." All the bags fell again except for one, and the figures announced: "HYDRO." The applause continued as the girl skipped over to the crystal blue door.

Andy Addams went to Hydro, and his brother, Shard Addams, was the first inducted into Metallum. Many more cheers and applause took place this time.

Probus Sniffelton, Buster's sidekick, was up next. He had an evil grin on his face. "152 amperes," the figure called out; the highest number so far. "Incendiary." Stomps were heard this time in the audience, and loud barking sounds. Jacob could tell it wasn't the most desired line.

"Anna Friendly!"

Anna darted to the scale and put the band around her waist, then waited excitedly for the decision. The Johnston siblings laughed and waved over in Jacob's direction.

"143." The second bag leveled. "HYDRO!" Anna let out a big smile and joined the others by the crystal blue door.

"Brandy Johnston."

"142," followed by, "Metallum."

"Colby Johnston." Colby patted Jacob on the back and ran up to the centering scale.

"All right, Colbs!" shouted his sister Brandy, who stood along with the other Metallum that had been chosen.

"142," followed by, "Metallum." Colby joined his sister with an air five and a Cloudian shake.

Jacob started to grow even more nervous than before. This was supposed to be exciting and joyous, but he couldn't help but feel his insides twist like the gears that spun above his head. What if he showed Incendiary, and the Follcane guy came to take him away? What if he didn't have a reading at all, and that's why the men out front were whispering about him?

Albert Egan, his first friend was next. He had a big smile on his face. He was so tiny that they had to stop in the middle of the service and adjust the scale to fit the band around his waist. "129," followed by, "Hydro!" Albert jolted his arm in the air to celebrate and almost took the scale with him as he bounced off the platform with the belt still attached.

Just as Jacob had guessed, Buster Nalum was announced into Incendiary and drew an ampere reading of 151. He and Probus locked arms and clunked their heads together. Jacob was convinced that Tommy had somehow followed him into this world and took over Buster's body.

"JACOB WESLEY." All of the cheers suddenly stopped, and everyone looked in Jacob's direction. He quietly stepped forward as everyone's eyes locked on his every movement. Conversations began to erupt all over the room.

"He's here?"

"In our selection process?"

"What will he be?"

"Metallum? No way."

"Timber, maybe?"

Jacob approached the scale, and one of the cloaked figures strapped the band around him. He could feel the figure's hands tremble as he did it. The other figure scanned him, but murmurs started to erupt from the audience.

"What is he?!"

"Yeah, come on! What's taking so long?!"

"Shut up!" barked Colby at the out-of-control kids.

Jacob noticed the figure did not say anything. One of the mysterious figures in front of him even pressed the button next to his lux-shades twice. A reset, perhaps? Great, he thought. Here we go. His worst fear took over. He wasn't going to get a reading. He didn't belong here.

"I've never seen this before," he heard one of the figures whisper into Magistra Dayan's ear.

"He can't be, though. He's not of age," she replied. She turned towards one of the cloaked figures by the Electro door. He nodded towards her.

This time, Magistra Dayan walked forward to announce to the group, "777."

All of the murmurings stopped at once. Jacob couldn't believe his ears, and it seemed like the rest of the room couldn't, either. He had yet to hear an ampere reading that high, but he had never even used any powers at all or had any idea what to do with them. Maybe someone had spiked the trumnit he drank earlier.

"No way!" shouted Buster. "The scale must be broken." Jacob couldn't help but agree with Buster.

"I assure you, Mr. Nalum, we have run over the reading several times, and it is accurate," Magistra Dayan shot back.

"Well, what line is he?" shouted Brandy.

Jacob, along with everyone else, noticed that all the bags weighed the same. Finally, one bag dropped to the floor, through the scale, and smashed the ground. The figure hesitantly opened the bag and revealed a gust of wind and an electric spark that spiraled towards the ceiling.

"Electro!" the figures shouted. The band released from Jacob's waist. The bags shuffled back onto their platforms. Everyone continued their silence as he headed cautiously over to the door outlined in a bright green light. The figure in front of the door nodded his way.

"All right, Jake!" shouted Colby excitedly.

"Way to go, Jacob!" Anna followed.

"The Light One belongs to Electro! Rightful fit!" yelled Albert.

Everyone else finally joined in with cheers and applause. Buster and the rest of Incendiary refused to join in; instead, they had evil eyes and smug looks and kept their arms folded.

The remaining boys and girls were selected into their elemental lines. No one eclipsed the ampere score that Jacob read. In fact, the highest score next to him was Probus' 152. Even Bron's reading hadn't touched 500, and he was a fully grown PPA member.

The lines were set with 10 in Timber, 14 in Metallum, 8 in Hydro, and 7 in Incendiary, but Jacob was the only one who stood silently next to Electro, like a kid waiting to be selected for schoolyard dodgeball. The difference was that according to his selection, he would be the most popular kid in school.

He smiled as Magistra Dayan ordered the scale to be lifted and carried out. She then approached the front of the room again and gazed at every young academy student with a smile and a twinkle in her eye. She bowed to them, showing great respect for what they would now enter into. Then Jacob noticed that she bowed her head, moving her arms upward, and flexed with her fingers outstretched.

"Greetings again, Timbers, Metallums, Hydros, Incendiaries, and even Electros," she winked at Jacob. "You now join some of the most historic Cloudians on your journey to learning to control the elements of our realm, and using this power to protect and defend our world." Magistra Dayan flicked her head forward, and out of nowhere, the wood started to materialize from her hands. Hundreds of small pieces of splintered wood spiraled above her hands. She leaned forward and threw her arms in front of her. The wood flew towards the teenagers and then abruptly stopped in mid-air.

"You will need focus, attention, and much practice to control your elements. You must never stray from your mind's ability to work with your body," she continued. She started to sway her arms back and forth, and the wood joined together to make a round table with chairs, enough for all of them. Jacob was absolutely amazed at what he was seeing take place. He couldn't believe that such wonder existed in this world.

"You never know what beauty can come from your imagination, and how useful your powers can be," she smiled, dropped her arms, and completed the high chairs around her. "Enjoy tonight, for tomorrow begins your journey towards elemental control. Enjoy, and To Tomorrow to all!"

"To Tomorrow!" shouted the rest of them. Magistra Dayan turned around and swished her Volans coat behind her. She left puzzled looks on all of the students' faces. Jacob flinched, as right next to him, the cloaked figures corresponding to each elemental line approached the new students and raised their arms in the process. They scanned them with their own gloved hands and then stopped. Slim-fit suits with colors coordinated to their elemental lines materialized in front of all the elemental students.

In the middle of each suit were the symbols for each line. Timber was represented by an oval with a rectangle outline inside of a brown gear. Hydro was represented by a light blue symbol of a crystal blue gear. Metallum was represented by a black gear with a smaller metal gear inside of it. Incendiary was represented with an orange gear surrounded by a red flame. Electro had two giant white lines curved by a bright yellow gear with six green and silver circles inside.

The cloaked figures then passed out the suits to the elemental students. The figures then motioned slowly in unison towards the tables. They began a routine of waving about. They then raised their arms towards the plates. The Johnstons jumped back in surprise, Anna clapped her hands feverously with excitement, and Jacob's eyebrows rose so high they could have jumped off his head and darted over to the table. All sorts of food and drinks started to materialize in front of them.

And at last, in unison, the figures spoke in dark voices, "Dine."

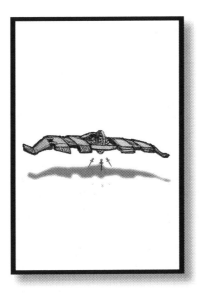

# 9

# SKYRACING

Hours later, pulling his Portare bag over his shoulder, Jacob hurried past the stone walkway through the lighted vaulted walls. Cheers, laughter, and applause started to echo louder as he approached. Excitement blew up in his stomach like fireworks, and a smile grew from ear to ear. Moments later, he found himself standing in front of massive white walls which covered what looked like a huge football stadium. Its dome shape had a beautiful gold checkered pattern lining its walls.

"Quite a sight, huh?" A familiar nasally voice stole Jacob's awe from his face. Jacob turned to meet Albert, who was wearing a slim-fit red suit with a patch covering his shoulder which showed the face of a spiky-haired racer. "There's a skyrace once every month, and they never get old. Ezekial Addams hasn't been beaten yet. He's the best, number one skyracer in all of Cloudia, and he's only sixteen," he tried to yell over the cheers that were almost deafening. All sorts of crazy-haired, long-coated Cloudians were pouring into the stadium.

"Hey, Jacob!" The Johnston twins and Anna ran up to them. The group exchanged forearm shakes and headed towards the entrance.

"Where we sittin', Colbs?" Brandy tried to grab the tickets he had in his hand.

"Near the top, unfortunately, but there isn't a bad seat in the house."

The golden platforms were chock full of other Cloudians, which moved to different levels depending on the button pressed. At each level sat sterling silver bleachers that were somehow suspended in the air. Colby lead the group to the fourth platform, which read Section 212.

Jacob was nudged to an empty area on the fifth bleacher, in between Colby and Albert. Jacob's view was good, but they were high up; maybe 50 feet off the ground.

They were on the left end of the flat rubber track. Blue strobe lights were twisting in and out of the black charcoal ground and morphed into a shape of the number eight. There were beautiful patches of tall green grass inside the track. At the center of the track was a giant empty space with a beautiful holographic screen illuminating 3D images of several spiky-haired skyracers with their boards next to them. Then, the screen shifted to a commercial for trumnits, with a big golden banner of the drink that read, "Sherry's Sour Trumnits; one gulp and you'll lose your lips!"

"So, what do you think, Jake?" Colby jumped in. "Isn't it sick?!"

"Like nothing I've ever seen. I've never even been to a basketball game," said Jacob, in awe.

"What's basketball?" asked Brandy.

"It's nothing," Jacob muttered.

Albert, meanwhile, had his orange lux-shades over his eyes and was shaking his head in a clockwise direction. "Whoa!" he said, tapping the side of his lux-band. "I can see Zander Steed right there!" Albert pointed towards the back of the track, where a silver awning bent over a tunnel. Inside was a blue-haired boy in a black Volans coat, twisting his board in his hand.

"There's Darlene Flight! She's right there!" Anna sprung to her feet excitedly after noticing the blonde girl stretching next to Zander. Jacob unzipped his Portare bag and fumbled with his lux-shades until Albert helped him put them on. He clicked the button and saw the skyracers starting to form a line near the edge of the dark tunnel.

"Where's Ezekial? Where is he?" Colby was panting heavily as he paced around to find him.

"Relax, Colbs. He'll be here," said Brandy, patting him on the back.

The sky turned a gorgeous orange hue, and within the next five whistles, the stadium was filled entirely with Cloudians.

"What do you get when you combine two Johnstons and a couple of flybeans?"

The group turned to face the slender boy with black hair that Jacob first witnessed back in High Corner: Buster Nalum. He was accompanied by the more significant boy, Probus, as well. His face was scrunched up like he had just chewed a bumblebee.

"A pile of hot garbage," said Buster, with his hand on the bigger kid's back. They both erupted into maniacal laughter.

"You again! The new dweebit. What's your stupid name?" Buster was pointing in Jacob's direction. His dark eyes traced Jacob like a metal detector looking for something to go off so he could attack.

"Do you know who you're talking to?" Albert squeaked out. Buster's eyes didn't leave Jacob's. "This is Jacob Wesley!" he shouted, with a mean look on his face.

Jacob turned his head slowly towards Albert. "Al, shut up, man," said Jacob.

"Well... how nice," said Buster, with a twisted grin. "The almighty Light One finally here?" Buster leaned in closely. His nose was only a few inches away from Jacob's. His eyes squinted into two little beady daggers. Jacob knew exactly what was coming next. Tommy would shove his fat nose into Jacob's face and then turn his underwear inside-out afterward. Jacob started to lean backward and brace for impact.

But instead, Buster just said, "I'll be seeing you around, Jacob. Having the right friends in a place like Cloudia is very important." He nodded in his direction and continued down the row to where his seats were.

Then, a sound like a truck horn blared through the stadium three times. Shockwaves filled the stadium, and everyone started shuffling their feet. The noises were incredible, and gave Jacob chills all the way down his spine.

"Cloudians," spoke a voice that was coming from the center of the arena. In front of Jacob now stood a hologram of two older Cloudians with gold and velvet Volans coats, twisty mustaches, and gray hair that parted down the middle.

"Bard Dine and Harold Porter! They've announced every single skyrace match ever," Albert whispered to Jacob.

"Boys, Girls, Men, Women, it is time for the 16th cycled skyrace match!" shouted Harold. The fans shuffled their feet, and a thousand whistles filled the arena. The hologram disappeared for a moment and showed a skyracer zip through a hurdle.

"We have five skyracers taking the track tonight. Are you ready?!" followed Bard. The fans stood from their seats. Colby and Brandy clapped feverously. Unsure what to do, Jacob joined, as well.

"You are ready, so let's goooo!"

Screams and shouts polluted the stadium.

"Introducing the challengers: representing the East and West quadrants of Cloudia; Xander Steed, Horace Green, and Elizabeth Owens; and, representing the South quadrant, she is a two-time champion of the South, stands at 5'3" tall, she broke the record for the quickest jump out of the gate, Darleeeeeeeene Flight!"

Anna and Brandy jumped in the air. Brandy reached across the row and bumped fists with Anna. "Woooooo! Go, Darlene!" Anna shouted.

The racers jumped on their sky speeders and zipped around the center of the track. Darlene gave a thumbs-up to the crowd.

"And now, introducing the champion; he stands at 5'7" tall, he is undefeated in the Great Skyrace, and currently holds a record of sixteen wins, zero losses. He is the reigning, defending, Skyrace Champion of the world, Ezekiaaaaaaaal Addams!"

Suddenly, a rocket full of red flares came spiraling into the stadium. It lapped the other racers, leaving waves of red around the track. The crowd roared exceptionally loudly. The waves spun throughout the crowd, filling the stands with excitement and awe.

"There he is! It's him," Colby mumbled, frozen in place.

Turning his lux-shades towards the bottom of the track, Jacob spotted the ball of red light turning into a boy with a red mohawk and a shiny red slim-fit suit. Ezekial Addams was tall, skinny, and dark-skinned, with a sharp jawline and thick eyebrows. He looked like a sculpted statue from the museum Jacob had been to.

"Managing the action tonight will be Dominus Fugam." A silver-cloaked person stood on a glowing purple skyspeeder in the center of the track. A shiny velvet hood covered the mysterious Dominus's face. Then suddenly, Dominus's left arm raised into the air. Everyone in the stands became so quiet that even an ice puff falling to the ground could be heard.

Jacob looked to his left and right, confused. Out from beneath the hole at the center of the track floated a black orb the size of a cannonball that was electrified with yellow sparks. With a sharp gesture from Dominus's other hand, the orb sped to the right side of the track.

"Aye Hover!" she said. The racers leaped into the air, leaving dust spiraling beneath them. Jacob looked around again, and then between his friends, searching for any sort of response. The group leaned forward silently. Jacob followed suit.

The black orb turned a crystal blue, and before Jacob could blink, five different-colored streaks replaced the area where the racers were.

"And... here... they GO!" Bard screamed into his microphone. "Xander off to the early lead, followed by Darlene, Horace, Ezekial, and Elizabeth. Look out, Ezekial is speeding up, quickly passing Horace around the corner!"

Jacob tried to keep up, but the action was too fast. He was pressing the button on his lux-shades harder, tightening them around his head. He kept seeing numbers go up and down like a radar detector, followed by a rainbow tail that represented the racers. The tails of color sped quickly through the figure-eight track and approached their second lap furiously.

Then the crowd screamed in unison: "Ooooh!"

Jacob noticed the blue tail start to slide off to the right of the others and spiral into the ground.

"DOWN GOES HORACE!" Bard shouted.

"Ezekial caused the distraction, Bard, and Elizabeth took advantage."

"He had no chance with that holoboulder, Harold."

When the color disappeared, a skyracer with wavy brown hair was rolling on the ground. To his right was a big gray rock tumbling furiously towards him. Jacob shifted his attention back towards the track and the remaining blurred tails. The red tail, which he assumed was Ezekial, covered the yellowtail on the second lap. Jacob looked at the giant holo-screen in the center of the stadium, which showed a view of the racers. All sorts of weird objects were forming and then shooting out at the racers as they went by.

"Oooh, a close one for Elizabeth there. Barely dodged the alphashells."

"You're telling me, Harold. I thought for sure she was going to be knocked into H-Twenty."

Jacob turned his head wildly in Colby's direction. "What is going on?"

"Shhh, dude, I'm trying to watch." Colby waved Jacob off.

Frustrated, he turned his attention to Albert. "Al, who's winning?"

"Right now, Darlene and Xander are neck-and-neck. Elizabeth and Ezekial are trading flips out on the track. Did you know that Elizabeth Owens once performed the swipe-flip 47 times in a single match? 47 times! It's statistically impossible." Albert smiled and then turned his attention back to the colorful tails spiraling through the track.

Even more frustrated than before, Jacob sat back down in his seat as the racers continued. At least now he knew who was in the lead. The skyracers moved so fast and so seamlessly through the track. Their movements were so quick that they appeared to be traveling at the speed of light.

Harold and Bard were still trading announcements back and forth.

"Elizabeth spins again!"

"Ezekial passes Darlene!"

"Xander is losing his lead!"

And within ticks, the lead had changed yet again. Darlene passed Ezekial and roared through what Jacob could tell was the fourth lap. Boots stomped, and Jacob felt like the bleachers were going to collapse underneath him.

The race somehow became even faster and more challenging to keep up with for Jacob. Ezekial and Darlene's colors combined and created a large blob of orange. Lightning bolts started shooting out from the sky and onto the track. Jacob ducked and shielded his eyes with his hands. When he opened his eyes again, he saw that no one else had done that. It's as if they expected it to happen.

"Ezekial out in front on an incredible front-flip," said Bard.

"How did he do that?" roared Harold.

The red light disappeared from the yellow light, and cheers erupted from the floor. Jacob began to feel dizzy; lost in action. Then suddenly, the cheers turned into gasps. The purple light and the brown light faded, and Elizabeth and Xander plummeted towards the ground so fast that it looked as though they were debris falling from a fire. Jacob could barely keep up with their rapid descent.

"They're going to crash! Is anyone going to do anything?" Jacob jumped from his seat. The rest of his friends remained still, facing the action. Colby grabbed Jacob's shoulder and moved him back into his seat. Just before the inevitable crash, a clear net shot out of the ground like a spiderweb and caught them just in time.

"Don't worry, Jacob," Anna shouted from down the row. "The stadium has built-in damage protectors, just in case!" Jacob had been pale and frozen to his chair, but after Anna reassured him, he came out of his horrorstruck coma and shook his head to get refocused. He put his lux-shades back over his eyes and leaned forward to see the action again.

"Now, we enter the second-to-last lap. Just two skyracers remaining, folks," said Harold, on the edge of his seat.

"Ezekial looking to keep his record intact here, and what better racer than the fabulous Darlene Flight?" followed Bard.

The two blazing colors spiraled in and out, heading toward the middle part of the track. The red light was inching in front of the yellow light. The holo-screen briefly showed a slowed-down version of the race, and finally, Jacob could catch a piece of it. Several of those gray boulders were pouring down the tracks. As if they were weightless, Darlene and Ezekial dodged each one of them. They must have a sixth sense, Jacob thought to himself. They moved so effortlessly through the air that it was like they were attached to strings being controlled by a puppeteer.

When the boulders stopped rolling, Ezekial was seen hovering high above Darlene, taunting her by moving up and down like a chopping block. He was using this as a distraction while Darlene was trying to navigate the rest of the course, anticipating the next obstacle in front of her. Cheers cut in and out, feet stomped, and the crowd clapped. Darlene spun in and out of the holo-boulders with her skyspeeder again, the spikes turning with each spin through the air. Anna and Brandy rose to their feet again with their fists clenched under their chins. Ezekial was lunging forward with his board spread out, like a surfer.

"He's toying with her!" said Bard, sounding more excited than nervous for her.

"He's the most strategic skyracer we've ever seen, Bard," said Harold emphatically.

"And unless things change, I don't see Darlene escaping this terror from above."

"You don't give her enough credit, Bard. She's more focused than we've ever seen. And now, the final lap!" As Harold finished speaking, the jets of light circled through the figure-eight track one more time.

"Ezekial flies past Darlene, who then flies right past Ezekial, and this is getting close, folks. Yes, this may be the closest to losing we have ever seen Ezekial come." Bard was standing.

"It's going to be an incredible finish. I can't believe the speed they are showing today!" Harold rose from his chair, too.

"Darlene inching closer to supremacy!"

"I don't know if I can watch, Bard!"

"Ezekial! Darlene! Ezekial! Darlene again! Now Ezekial once more! Darlene! Ezekial! They are nearing the final corner, Harold!" The two lights were blurring again into an orange blob as they turned at full-speed, weaving in and out of each other's colorful streaks.

"He's got this. Come on, Zeke!" Colby shouted, and stood up from his seat. "You can't lose today!" The crowd seemed to agree with Colby, as they all rose from their seats. It looked like a sea of red and yellow colors building a wave in the ocean.

The two racers dodged an obstacle of more alphashells ripping past them. It looked like they were dodging a meteor shower. Jacob had no idea who was winning, or what was going on, for that matter. The screen had stopped showing the slow-motion replay.

"It's too close to call. Statistically, I can't keep up with it!" shouted Albert.

"Let's go, Darlene! Take out Ezekial!" Anna jumped up again.

"I second that!" Brandy yelled.

The two lights crossed the finish line and fluttered to a stop. It sounded someone braking on ice. There were leftover red and yellow trails from their skyspeeders just beginning to vanish from the edge of the track.

"And, by a hair… just… like… that… it's all over! Ezekial keeps his record alive," Bard announced.

"He did it, Bard! Ezekial Addams' 17th skyrace victory in a row," Harold added.

Ezekial Addams stood on his skyspeeder ten feet above the ground with his red Volans coat twisting in the wind. Beads of sweat poured down his forehead like a water faucet.

"WOOHOO!" Colby was dancing in the row. Jacob was in a whirlwind; everything happened too fast. Brandy and Anna sat in their seats with their heads buried in their hands. Albert was standing and applauding the victor.

The holo-screen in the middle showed three numbers next to Ezekial's name: 14:52:03, and three numbers next to Darlene's name: 14:52:04.

Slowly, the crowd started stomping their feet. The ground started to shake like a volcano opening up. Chants of 'Greatest Ever' were bellowing throughout the stadium.

"Wow, he kicked you-know-what today," Colby said, leaning forward in a surfing pose as the group trickled through a path of Cloudians trying to battle their way through the crowd. "He's unstoppable! Nobody can beat him."

"He's definitely the best I've ever seen." Albert caught up with Colby and tried the same surfer pose. Brandy and Anna had their heads held low and their arms firmly folded, still sour from Darlene Flight's loss.

Jacob just nodded in response, still unsure of the spectacle he had just witnessed. In the background, chants were still echoing, and songs were being sung beautifully. The atmosphere was incredible, but the race was confusing, to say the least.

Jacob shook his friends' forearms, and after a few "To Tomorrows," he began to head out of the stadium.

Then, out of nowhere, a hand grabbed his shoulder. Chills shuddered down his spine, all the way to the tips of his toes. Nervously and slowly, he turned and was met with one of the cloaked figures from the selection ceremony. It raised a crooked gloved finger in front of its face, which Jacob took as a sign to remain quiet. He then waved his other hand in front of Jacob. A dark brown door with a bronze gear in the center suddenly materialized in front of them.

Jacob felt the figure's arm tighten his grip firmly on his shoulder. The door opened, and Jacob was pulled through like a rabbit out of a hat. Everything briefly turned black. His skin felt like a thousand ants were crawling all over it. He struggled to breathe. Invisible balloons were popping in his chest. The sinking feeling he had at the museum returned, and then...

The feeling stopped. He came up for air as if he had been drowning in a pool. He panted for a few moments with his hands on his knees, until he realized the magnificent skyracing stadium had vanished. He and the figure were now standing in what appeared to be a beautiful hallway inside of a building. Jacob's comprehension finally set in. He realized that he had teleported again.

# 10

# THE PROPHECY
# PROTECTION AGENCY

Despite the fact he had just spent the last few hours in a whirlwind of confusion, trying to understand the sport of skyracing, Jacob now felt more lost and afraid than he ever had before. His sense of unfamiliarity, the new world he had lived in for only a few days, and the darkness of his kidnapper started to creep into his mind like a timid spider.

"Are you okay, Jacob?" asked the figure, turning his head towards him attentively. "Transport is not as easy as it looks."

"Who are you?" asked Jacob, holding his head up delicately. It felt as though it had almost popped off from the teleportation. "Where did you take me?"

The figure turned its head and slowly removed its hood. "My name is Seran Keerinus." The man was middle-aged, judging by his thin black and silver hair, which was tightly slicked back over his head. He had silver stubble and a scary red scar which ran over his right eye through his dented cheek, which looked like it had been hit several times.

"And you are in the Hall of Entry," he announced and threw off his large black cloak to reveal a long brown Volans coat that swept beneath his knees, with a high-necked collar and two silver strings that hung down past his chest.

"What do you want with me?" Jacob asked with terror in his eyes.

Seran turned back towards Jacob with a look of shock on his face. His lips curled into a smile before he let out a few laughs. Jacob's panic turned to confusion again. He placed his hands on either side of Jacob's head.

"Trust me when I say, Jacob, I'm definitely on your side. You have no need to fear me. I am the one in charge here. Nyx and Bron work for me." He patted Jacob on the back, winked with his scarred eye, and turned away.

Relief washed over Jacob in a calming wave.

Ahead of them was a long gray hallway with multiple oval-shaped doors. In between the doors were beautiful pearly white bricks. On the ceiling was a row of lights that radiated a heavenly feel. In between the lights were black lines tracing the ceiling like vines.

"So, tell me, Jacob," said Seran. "What do you think?"

Jacob raised his hand instinctively to his head and scratched it.

"I… well… this place is like nothing I've ever seen," he said. "It's a lot to take in, though. I'm not really used to everything. I'm sure you can tell."

He looked up at Seran and noticed a very pleased expression on his face.

"I can only imagine," said Seran. "You've finally returned home, you've come back to Cloudia, and you're still reeling from being a Gravit your entire life."

"Nyx said the same thing; that this place is my home, but it doesn't feel like it," said Jacob, who was still struggling to comprehend it. Seran was walking at a slow pace, and it felt like where they were headed was a mile away. In the distance, Jacob could see a faded object.

"So, what is this place exactly?" Jacob passed another oval door with a small gear in front of it.

"The Hall of Entry leads to many places. All of these doors you see here are ways to transport through Cloudia without being detected."

"Sounds secretive," said Jacob.

"It is," said Seran. "Not many have seen this place, or even know it exists, for that matter. Only members of the PPA get a chance to walk through it."

"What's the PPA?"

"Oh, you'll find out in a few moments," said Seran mysteriously. "Straight ahead, Jacob."

They proceeded through the bright hallway. Lights flickered towards the end of it. A cold feeling started to seep into Jacob's veins. Jacob looked backward, but couldn't see anything now. It felt like they were in a never-ending maze.

"Why didn't you just get me when I originally arrived at Cloudia?" Jacob cautiously asked.

"Because I wanted you to be with your friends, and for me to get to witness your selection myself," said Seran. "Besides, my level of knowledge dictates that I should keep a low profile. In any event, if I exposed myself to you, I could put you in more danger. It will be difficult to contain your celebrity status, but the longer we can, the better."

"My celebrity status?" Jacob hustled to keep up with Seran.

Seran glanced down briefly. "Soon. Be patient."

The faded object in front of them started to become bigger. Jacob wondered why Seran had quickened his pace, but he had too many other thoughts that kept his mind busy.

"So, this Electro element. I'm going to learn how to do the funky lightning stuff with it?"

"Accurate," said Seran, now quickening his pace a bit more.

"Who's going to teach me?" Jacob continued. "I mean, is it like a school-type place? My friends mentioned it a few times on the Airz taxi, and…"

"The Elemental Academy in Gordonclyff Tower will be your new place for learning. There, you will be trained and taught by several instructors who will guide you through elemental control."

"Do you teach as well?" asked Jacob.

"I never was much of a trainer," said Seran. "I'm more of a leader. Besides, I couldn't keep up with Soriun. He is a master of his craft, and he will know how to handle a thirteen yer old with 700 amperes much better than I could think to do so."

"Who?" Jacob asked abruptly.

"Soriun Athene. You'll meet him," Seran smiled briefly.

"I don't understand how I have so many of those ampere thingies. I've never lived here before, right?"

"Well, that's why you're special, Jacob. The most special Cloudian to have ever lived. Being an Electro has its privileges."

"You were an Electro, too?" Jacob's excitement grew with each response from Seran, even if some of his questions weren't fully answered. There was something palpable about Seran, something that made him stick out. Then, to top it all off, he was an Electro, too.

"I was in your shoes a long time ago," Seran continued. The two headed down the hallway full of different-colored doors and past a bunch of lights that flashed on and off.

"This is where I'll be staying?" Jacob was bewildered because there weren't any beds in sight.

"Not right here, no." Seran stopped. "To Tomorrow, Thornswapple." Seran turned his attention to the object that became clearer in front of them. The object was a tiny man in a gray and white Volans coat. He had a few white hairs on his head, and was, at most, four feet tall. He had a long nose and pink bumps all over his face.

"To Tomorrow, Sir Seran," he said in an old raspy voice. It was even raspier than Smaltz's meow, Jacob thought.

"To Tomorrow, Tomorrow To. Allow us access to protect the many and the few," Seran spoke quietly and firmly.

The man turned, still in the seated pose, and pushed the small gear behind him. The gear wiggled and budged, then began to lengthen. It grew so massive that it took up the entire back side of the room.

"And To Tomorrow, Jacob Wesley." Thornswapple pressed the center of the gear door.

Before Jacob could return the greeting, the door vanished like it was sucked into a black hole. Powerful gusts of wind knocked into Jacob and Seran with hurricane strength. Seran latched onto Jacob's arm and moved forward.

The darkness disappeared to reveal a room that had one wall which curved around a center console full of different figures who looked like high-tech security guards, waving their arms in front of a transparent glass screen. The screen had all sorts of images on it, and radars with blinking red lasers. The security team was moving so quickly that it was difficult for Jacob to keep up. The room smelled like the inside of a tunnel. The figures sat in white leather chairs that lifted them off the ground every few whistles. Rotating around the figures were curved plates of glass, which sporadically blocked them from Jacob's view.

"Whoa." Jacob couldn't help but drop his jaw in awe.

"Amazing, isn't it?" Seran lead Jacob down a set of metal stairs to their right.

"What are they doing?" Jacob turned back towards Seran.

"Protecting us, and making sure that Cloudia rests peacefully in the night." Seran headed over to one of the male security guards and pointed towards the screen. Jacob saw a bunch of red dots light up, but he was still confused.

Seran waved over to Jacob. "You see, Jacob, it's one thing to believe in the prophecy; to protect it and fight for it, but it's another thing to see it; see you are what we've been waiting for. That's what PPA stands for, Prophecy Protection Agency."

Jacob stood blankly in front of him. "I'm not sure I understand, Seran."

Before Seran could respond, a faint whistle was heard in the distance.

"Jacob! Hee-hee!" Nyx shouted as he skyze-skated towards them.

Joy flushed through Jacob as he gripped Nyx's forearm. "Nyx, it's great to see you!"

"And you as well. Are the rumors true, aha? You'll be joining Electro? And a 700 amperes score! I'm not sure we've ever heard of such a score from a boy your age. Well, looks like the Light One has arrived… and in style, too, ta ta!" Nyx clapped.

All the men and women that were stationed at each computer ceased what they were doing and turned to face Jacob as Nyx spoke aloud. Then, they turned their attention towards Seran. He waved his arms in a patting motion, which triggered the rest of the workers to get back to what they were doing.

"Nyx, no need to embarrass our new tenant on his first day. I trust you're up to speed on watching High Corner? No sights on Follcane?" Seran asked after he removed his lux-shades.

"Right you are, Seran. No one out of the ordinary in sight," Nyx responded, and saluted Seran. "However, I did see a flycer nudge a funny-looking woman with a tall, flowered hat right in the bottom, hee-hee. It almost made me turn upside-down on the spot."

Seran didn't look amused, but Jacob couldn't help but let out a few giggles.

Each of security team had yellow Volans coats on, too. Jacob also noticed that they wore golden fingerless gloves, and they had silver patches placed on their fingertips.

At the top of the clear glass plates were numbers and letters littered all about, and they changed from one side to the other, along with turquoise shapes, which formed and moved as well. Several of the team members waved their arms and directed the patterns to materialize and then disappear. The movement was controlled by their hands.

"Sir, Gordonclyff is clear, Cloudia's gates are on the rise, and the streets are emptying," bellowed one of the agents in front. He had wavy orange hair, and on his right arm was a big crest of the emblem that Jacob kept seeing everywhere.

"Thank you. How about Pines Station at High Corner? Any travelers?" Seran was firm now.

"Checking now… stand by," said the figure.

Seran winked over at Jacob as the team continued to move their arms about. Jacob saw three turquoise shapes converge into one. Then the screen displayed the message: "Clear."

"Looks like we're clear there, too, Sir Seran."

"Fantastic. Jacob, follow me, and you too, Nyx." Seran left the center console and pressed a button on the side of the curved wall in front of him. The wall broke apart and revealed a beautiful white hallway with black dots sprinkled underneath golden pipes.

"Jacob, I want you to know something," Seran began. "I know this is a lot to take in, and you've been introduced to it all very quickly. I want you to have faith that this is all necessary. It's not my intention to rush you, only to prepare you." Seran picked up his pace. Jacob rushed to keep up, along with a bumbling Nyx.

In the hallway, there was a certain emptiness that filled Jacob's stomach. At the back of the hallway was another glass case, similar to the one in the museum, resting beautifully upon a marble pillar. The light was beaming away from it, illuminating the ceiling above them.

"Do you know why you are here?" Seran asked. "Why I- we have brought you back to Cloudia?"

"Not a clue. I was hoping you could tell me, sir," Jacob responded, with a gulp that felt like a bowling ball in his throat.

"You are different, Jacob." Seran stopped in the middle of the hallway, halting them. Nyx jumped. "Very different. Ever notice why your eyes were different than the other Gravits back in Griffin?"

"Yes, sir. I used to get teased for my eyes. I wished they were like everyone else's." Jacob lowered his head, and Nyx frowned.

Seran's finger lifted his head back up to meet his eyes. "You're not just different in Griffin. You're also different in Cloudia. As you see, my eyes are different than yours. They're blue, with pupils so small you can barely see them. Your eyes are light green with rings around the outside, and pupils like the Gravits have." Seran let go, and Jacob let his head fall again. Nyx looked up towards Seran, anxious for him to get to the point.

Seran paced towards the shiny case and waved his arms slightly in the air above it as if moving imaginary waves. He was mumbling something under his breath that Jacob couldn't make out from his distance.

"Because you're different in Griffin and different in Cloudia, that makes you special. You're the most special being that either of our worlds has ever known. Your uniqueness is interesting, to say the least." Seran turned around to face Jacob with his hands held tightly behind his back. "We know very little of your actual parents. Your mother was a normal woman, and any history of her wiped away yers ago, but she was a Cloudian. We never met your father, but we do know he was born in Griffin, from your former world."

Nyx stared bug-eyed in Jacob's direction, waiting for a reaction.

"I-I-I don't know what to say. I mean, it makes sense that my mom is from Cloudia, and my dad... I guess he... but why would he leave me? Why did I have to put up with Ms. Larrier and Tommy, and live as an orphan? Where is he? Is my mom dead? Where is she?"

"Unfortunately, I don't know the answers to those questions. It's quite a mystery. We assumed that your dad passed away, and your mother's whereabouts are unknown. The only thing we know about your history is written here." Seran revealed a crystal frame surrounding a beautiful golden piece of paper with silver lettering on the page. He handed it to Jacob. It read:

To Tomorrow.

As it writes, for it cites, for he gives us solace and life in the light.

To Tomorrow, there will be a time. One will be born on the fourth cycle's night.

There will be a child of kin to save us from horrible darkness. He shall be different than all who surround him, born of their world and ours.

But on that day, we will rejoice, for a hero is created to match the power of the darkest foe.

Do not be mistaken; he will have to make a choice, but take heed and listen to his voice.

He will look different than those around him, and will not find a home until time has bound him.

Only then he will save us and breathe life into tomorrow.

Look forward to his return when he starts to conquer the ash and burn. To Tomorrow, we wait and yearn.

Jacob read the plaque with his right eyebrow at the top of his forehead. He looked at Seran and Nyx, who eagerly awaited his response.

"This prophecy… it's about me?" Jacob asked.

"Do you know of another boy who was born in our fourth cycle?" Seran joked.

"What's your fourth cycle?" Jacob asked.

"Abreel."

Jacob heard Nyx giggle behind him, and Seran shot another death stare at him.

"Where did you guys find the book? How did it arrive? How did this writer know about me?" Jacob had a lot of questions. He didn't understand how his future could be predicted like this.

"Hmm, good questions. All good questions. I suppose I'd be asking the same if I were in your shoes." Seran scratched his beard. "The book was brought to us well before you were born. It was created from the ash of Mount Incipiens, which is a volcanic mountain in the city of Shei El. It erupts once every cycle, and one cycle long ago, this book was created. On an expedition, Robert Wesley found it. He was supposed to be your guardian until he fell." Seran took the plaque back to its case.

"Who is my darkest foe, then?" Jacob called out to Seran, who stopped for a moment.

"Well, it's getting late," Seran began. "I suppose it's time to visit your quarters, where you'll be staying. It's not much, but it will do for now. Oh, and I'm sure you'll appreciate your bunkmate."

"Bunkmate?" Jacob looked up at Seran, wondering who he would be sleeping alongside. He secretly hoped it was Anna.

"We're not going to leave you by yourself, now," Seran responded.

Just as they spoke, a door opened at the end of the hall, and with half of his face laced with shaving cream, and his golden ear bobbing up and down, Bron stuck his huge head out. "Welcome back, little guy."

"Bron! Good to see you again!" Jacob was thrilled to see Bron again, even though he had only briefly met him before. His legend had boosted his perception of Bron significantly after what the others had been saying about him.

"I trust you're in good hands. That will be all for now. Come on, Nyx." Seran turned to walk away. "Oh, and Jacob…"

"Yes, Seran?" Jacob replied.

"Welcome back home again. It's great to finally have you here," Seran responded.

"It's great to finally be here, sir."

Jacob followed Bron into the room, which had two large bunk beds strapped together in the middle. To the right was a mirror and a silver bowl full of golden trimmings; from Bron, of course. Next to the bed were all sorts of lux-bands.

"I'm sure you're tired, little guy. I'll let you hit the hay."

Jacob was about to speak up and ask Bron about the lux-bands but instead decided to crawl into his bed. He was exhausted from the day; a day in which he learned even more about the home, he never knew about before.

While he was sleeping, he went into a dream. It was odd. He was swimming in a pool with a dark figure, while cloaked figures poured fire into him. A shark, breathing flames, circled him, and Seran hung from the top of the roof. Jacob yelled for help and tried to blast back at the shark and the other figures, but nothing came out of his hands. Buster was in the background and had jets of fire streams, as well. He burst into laughter at the sight of Jacob. Ms. Larrier was there with fat-faced Tommy, who pointed and laughed at Jacob, as well.

Just before the fire reached him, he woke up. He trembled, sweat pouring down his forehead. He looked over at Bron, who snored as loud as could be, making a ruffling noise with his lips and then a whistling noise with his nostrils.

Jacob smiled and turned over again to fall back to sleep.

# 11

# MOVEMENTS

"I can't believe it's him."

"Who? I don't see him."

"Yeah, black hair with a silver strand, green eyes, in front of the freckled-face chick."

"You ever see green eyes before?"

"No, I never have. Especially not green ones like those. Definitely not."

"700 amperes. He must have cheated."

"Or he must be it."

Mumbling conversations followed Jacob all morning long, from when he left the PPA to when he arrived at his first day of training. Almost every single person talked about him, his ampere reading, or his green eyes. Some people were creative, and they made up incredible tales.

"I heard he flew here."

"I heard he wrestled a flycer with one arm when he was shopping for his Volans coat."

Several of his fellow elemental pals approached him and asked if he was able to regrow limbs. Jacob just smiled and shook his head in response as he boarded the platform.

At Gordonclyff Tower, there were all different types of platforms. There were platforms of gold and silver, thick and thin, curvy and straight, some that swiveled and others that rotated, ones that made all sorts of grinding noises and others that were so quiet that if you closed your eyes, you wouldn't know you were moving at all.

Besides the classrooms, secret rooms existed, too! Some of them shouted at you if you approached them the wrong way. Jacob accidentally got on the wrong platform that morning and ended up near the sixth floor, in front of a glass case that held a mysterious looking room bordered with silver gears. A hologram of a short, plump man with a large spiky beard pointed his finger sharply at him.

"Stand back! Not allowed! Not even for you!" the man yelled.

Luckily for Jacob, Albert Egan had run into the same troubles and dealt with the same furious holo, too.

"Hello, you dingbat! Take your friend and scram, I said!"

Before Jacob could manage to turn around, a silver-gloved hand tightened on his right shoulder. He looked over towards Albert and noticed a silver-gloved hand upon Albert's left shoulder, too.

"Going somewhere, you two?" A man with a long beard and no hair stood behind them.

"We were lost, uh, sir, I mean, we're reporting for, uh, Elemental Academy!" Albert exclaimed, trembling and twitching.

Jacob and Albert returned to the first floor, where the beautiful blonde secretary stared at them. Selena Tee was a thin, ageless woman with rosy red cheeks and long, golden blonde hair. Selena was more familiar with Gordonclyff and its patrons than anyone else in the building. Being the front desk greeter for over 25 yers, she had learned quite a few things about its history and purpose. Some of the Cloudians believed her to be a secret agent for the PPA, and a handful of others thought her to be a spy working for Follcane.

As the boys stood there, unsure how to proceed, Selena stood from her desk and whistled over at them. She used her purple glittery-polished index fingernail to point them over to the right platform.

"Thank you," they said in unison, embarrassed.

She winked and smiled at them. "Have a nice day, boys."

They jetted upward, towards the 77th floor of Gordonclyff Tower, finally on their way.

There were several different training classes for the elementals. The training classes proved to be very difficult for Jacob. It wasn't just something you found inside of a textbook. You couldn't wave your arms and magically produce your powers, either. Unfortunately, Cloudia was no different than Griffin when it came to homework. Phrase recitals and studying were required here, too. Each class had different studying techniques.

Five times a week, they went out to the skyzing rink on the 8th floor of Gordonclyff, where an old, scraggly little man known as Mr. Natansis taught them how to levitate and begin to skyze around. Mr. Natansis was very different. He had a sort of tick where he constantly twitched his eye. You'd think he winked at you every time he twitched. He was all business, though.

As soon as they entered the skyzing rink, Mr. Natansis darted into the air with a snap and a whistle. "The Navus mark isn't what makes you a Cloudian," he said. "Any jolly old fellow or young buck can stride into our city and show off an ink stamp claiming they belong here." He scooted through the air, right in front of Albert and Anna. "What separates us from the rest of our universe is our ability to skyze. We cannot be ruled by the physics of our realm."

He continued over to Buster and sized him up and down. Jacob let out a quiet giggle. The Johnston siblings did, too. "To skyze is an art, and I shall let you know that; each one of you will grow to appreciate it throughout your training," Mr. Natansis stated. "If you don't, then you have no place in my class." At once, he did a backflip and skyzed over to the center of the rink.

The rink was made of solid ice, with sloping walls that hung over, just like the streets of Cloudia. After Mr. Natansis gave them instructions, immediately he signaled each person to give it a try. "On the count of three, focus your core, snap, whistle, and dust off."

Jacob focused, snapped, gave a poor excuse for a whistle, and slipped, smacking the ice hard with his backside. He opened his eyes, bracing for embarrassment, but all 20 of the new elementals had collapsed like a deck of cards on the outer rink, too.

"I said snap, Brian, not clap!" Mr. Natansis yelled, and a vein looked like it was going to burst from his forehead. By the end of the training class, only some of the students were able to levitate for a few seconds. Brian was getting so frustrated that his skin grew a shade of purple that even his hair couldn't match.

Jacob enjoyed Cloudian History, even though the others complained that it was boring. It was instructed by Magistra Dayan herself, and as Jacob saw, she took great pride in speaking of the lineage and origins of their beautiful world. Magistra would project cool holographic videos of how Gordonclyff Tower was constructed. The elemental control enabled them to build things without the need of the tractors or other construction vehicles that Jacob was used to in Griffin.

Joan Chambers, the weapons trainer, had a unique Volans coat which wrapped around her body like a mummy. There were rumors of Joan being in the Battle of H-Twenty, and that she was so impressive that she snapped 30 necks with one swing of her silver stick.

Behind her were bright bronze gears that spun, and the famous silver stick was tied to her back. When Colby asked to hear how Joan Chambers was able to snap 30 necks with one swing of her blade, Jacob and the rest were disappointed, as she stayed silent with her eyes closed, in a very calm trance. Colby waved his hand in front of her face to see if she was asleep. Instantly, she flung the object from behind her back and waved it through the air. The sword split through the air, separated in two, and then came back together. It was so fast that Jacob could have sworn he saw 50 swords at once!

Jacob was still struggling to adapt to the new world. He wasn't doing too good in his classes, but a lot of the new elementals found it difficult also. Only Albert Egan, Anna Friendly, and Buster Nalum were among the few that were excelling. Everyone else was on the same level as Jacob.

A few days later, inside the skyzing rink, Brandy tumbled right into two nearby male elementals. They let out a few chuckles and bashfully waved in her direction. She hawked a loogy at the ground in return. The boys turned around immediately, and Colby bashed her for it.

At lunchtime every day, the different elemental lines got to meet up with their friends and discuss the day's events.

"When do we get to check out skyracing?" Colby asked. "I heard they let us practice in the race track, but nothing has been brought up yet."

"Getting ya hopes up for the lucky entry this yer, Colbs?" Brandy downed a trumnit and scarfed her sandwich in two bites. It might have been the most disgusting food item that Jacob had ever seen, but Brandy seemed to enjoy it.

"I don't need hope, Brandy, I'm getting in by pure skill. I've been practicing, too, ever since dad got me a Roar 2.0 skyspeeder for Donumdans." Colby paused and turned towards Jacob. "Which is the same one Ezekial Addams uses." Colby lunged forward from his seat, planted his legs in a surfing stance, and motioned with his arms as if he was flying.

"You wish, ha! He'll fall off his skyspeeder just like he did at the local race rink," Brandy poked fun at Colby.

"What's Donumdans?" Jacob turned blankly to Brandy.

Albert hopped over Brandy on the table to face Jacob, but before he could explain, Brandy stuck her arm out in front of Albert.

"Let him find out faw himself, dude," she said, before returning to her four big cheesy pasta balls.

"You hang up clouds, and your parents drop gifts in each of them," said Anna.

Anna smiled at Jacob. "So, are you boys ready for Movements?"

"You have no idea!" they said, in unison.

Albert jumped up, ready to show off the fighting skills he had displayed yesterday for the group.

"Relax, little guy; we already know ya looking forward to it," Colby joked. Albert sat back down in his chair bashfully.

"Anyways, who do ya think is training us?" Brandy asked, breaking the awkward silence.

"I don't know; I hope it's Bron. He should be able to free up some time from the PPA," Colby replied.

"Yeah. Jake, ya have any idea if the big guy's showing up?" Brandy said.

"He didn't mention anything yesterday, so I'm not sure, to be honest," Jacob said.

"Ya saw him yester…"

Brandy's excitement was silenced as a cloaked figure approached. A dark glove revealed a crumpled piece of paper with silver lettering on it. The figure left it between Albert's plate and Anna's trumnit. It was addressed to Jacob. In sparkly silver ink, it read:

> Have fun today. Take it slow, and don't try too hard in Movements; it will come naturally. Focus and pay attention to everything Athene says. We'll chat afterward. To tomorrow. –S.K.

Seran had sent him the note, and it brought a smile to Jacob's face. For the remainder of lunch, the group tried to solve the puzzle of this Athene character, and Jacob's excitement started to bubble up.

Soon, Jacob and the rest of the elementals found themselves staring blankly at each other in a dimly lit room as they stood on a padded floor. It was much warmer here than anywhere else in the school. Beads of sweat had already started to drip down Jacob's forehead. Lights swung from the ceiling, illuminating one half of the room, and then the other. It reminded Jacob of the school gym back home. Surrounding him were old-looking rows of bronze floating seats.

"It smells like my grandpa's feet," Albert whispered to Jacob.

Jacob nodded in agreement as he browsed the ceiling, which was shaped like an ocean wave. Suddenly, Jacob was distracted by a whistling noise in the distance that grew louder and louder. "Do you hear that?" he whispered to Albert.

"Hear what?" Albert responded as the noise grew louder in an area that was sectioned off by red curtains.

Then, the curtains swung open, and a black cast iron door exploded, sending pieces of wood everywhere. All of the elementals braced themselves as a figure dove out, fist-first. He proceeded to flip down the middle of the room before landing in a fighting pose.

The man was of average height. He had hair that stuck out at the sides and came together in a widow's peak. He was much older, and he had pointy eyebrows and two strands of salt-and-pepper hair that hung down from his mustache. His eyes had dark black rings around them, and they were void of any sign of life. His skin was a rough, pasty white, with old scars in several areas. He wore slim-fit armor that was similar to the elementals', and a beige Volans coat with gold trim.

He raised one arm and waved it around quickly. All of the elementals ducked as if he had aimed at them. The splintered pieces of the broken wooden door flew back into place and closed off the room.

He began to pace with his arms folded behind his back, eyeing each of the elementals as he passed. Jacob suddenly felt as though he was back at Kendal Drive, in front of a Cloudian version of Ms. Larrier.

"That's the same guy from earlier when we were on the wrong floor," Albert whispered.

"I know. Quiet, man," Jacob returned, trying to avoid getting called out.

"Soriun Athene is my name," he spoke softly. "For the next few cycles, I will be instructing you in the art of Movement." The room was quiet enough to hear a pin drop. "You are here to learn ways to defend yourself, and make no mistake; the battle is imminent." His voice was deep and had a sense of dark passion to it, and the elementals remained focused on his every word. "Unfortunately for all of you, the hour you have with me doesn't include your little abilities to focus on throwing pieces of metal around or blowing water at your friend's face." The group sighed in unison, and Colby snickered in Brandy's direction. "Silence!" Jacob and Anna gave each other wide-eyed, worried looks.

"I can assure you that what you learn with me will not only prepare you for what's out there, but might wind up saving your life, or someone else's. While I can't rely on you to see the inevitable future of your furious fists at this moment, I can expect you to obey my every command. Watch, listen, be patient, and learn from each of my words. Don't give up on yourself, and I won't give up on you." Albert was so googly-eyed that he had practically left puddles of drool on Jacob's boots.

Athene stopped pacing right in front of Brian Saunders, who shivered with such fear that he might as well have exploded. Jacob was worried about him.

"You, what's your name?"

"Buh-Buh-Brian, sir Athene." Brian Saunders' legs were wobbling so much that they looked like they were about to snap.

"And Buh-Buh-Brian, do you know how to perform a dust-wrench kick?"

Albert jumped out of line and threw his hand in the air, volunteering to try. Athene ignored him, with his eyes seemingly fixated straight through to Brian's soul.

"N-N-No, I don't, s-s-sir Athene." Brian tried to hide his face with his hands.

"Would you like to learn?" Quickly, Soriun Athene took a step back with his left leg, and then threw his right leg up and over Brian's head, grazing the purple hairs on the edge of his dreads. Brian fainted backward after nearly parting ways with his head.

Athene curled his lip into a snarky smile. He paced again until he stopped right in front of Lindsey Goodman, who had a few tears bubbling up in her eyes from fear. Jacob couldn't believe the spell their new trainer had fixated on all the elementals. He was in complete awe of Athene's abilities.

"And you, Miss?"

"Lindsey Goodman, sir," the blonde girl responded.

"Ever tried the famous angle-step punch?"

Again, Albert jumped out of the line. He was desperate to participate. Jacob tried to shush him so that Lindsey could speak, but she just shook her head instead. Athene ignored Albert again, Jacob breathed out a sigh of relief, and with lightning speed, Athene leaped with his right foot angled back, throwing his right fist inches from Lindsey's ear. He hammered forward with enough force to send a wave of air towards the back of the room. The elementals stumbled after being the wind harshly flew by. Athene then proceeded to do backflips from his position until he landed right in front of Jacob.

Athene stood there silently, glaring up and down at Jacob. He seemed to scan Jacob for information which Jacob didn't think he had.

"And I presume you'd be the so-called Light One. Tell me, Mr. Wesley…" Athene shoved his face inches away from Jacob's. Jacob's heart started to pound. "Ever used those two little fists?" Jacob stood there silently with his legs beginning to quiver. "I didn't think so. Well, now's your chance to prove your worth. Show everyone why you have so many amperes. I want you to try and hit me as hard as you can."

Jacob was fixated on Athene's eyes, his legs feeling like slippery noodles and sweat beginning to trickle down his forehead. Athene postured in front of Jacob with his hands behind his back as he anxiously awaited Jacob's approach. Jacob looked over at Colby and Brandy, who both nodded simultaneously at him.

"How could someone so pathetic get selected into Electro? Are you truly the Light One, or did you rig the selection ceremony? What do you have, Mr. Wesley? Come on!" Athene antagonized Jacob beyond all measure until Jacob started to clench his fists in anger. Athene noticed, and sent another smile his way, trying to bait him. His efforts were resembling Tommy at this point. "Well, are you going to continue wasting all of our time, or are you going to do something with those little fists, Mr. Wesley?"

Jacob had enough. He sloppily lunged forward with his right arm towards Athene. Athene caught his fist like a frog catching a fly. Jacob felt his feet go out from under him; he spun until he landed roughly on his back. He opened his eyes slowly and was met with giant scarred knuckles clenched into a fist. Then, Athene's hand opened, and Jacob looked up and saw a smile on his face.

"Don't worry, Mr. Wesley. There will be plenty of learning ahead of you." He picked Jacob up off the ground and dusted his back before he shoved him back into the line. "Maybe one day, you'll use that brave fist of yours." Athene winked at Jacob and continued to address the rest of the group.

"Not everything you learn in here will be to attack your opponent. Sure, you will all be professionals in the art of swift kicks, speed punches, skyze flies, and lightning grabs, but perhaps it's most important to learn how to stop what's coming at you. You will be tested, you will be tried, and you will feel like you want to quit. I'll push you harder than you want to be pushed. You will feel like snapping, but we all must be trees: bend but don't break. Now, split into two lines on either side of the room."

Everyone stood still, solidly in place, as they took in what had just happened. Athene stopped pacing. "NOW PAIR UP!" Instantly, all of them scurried to find places. Brandy stood in front of Colby. Albert landed in front of Brian. Buster was in front of Probus, and oddly enough, Jacob found himself directly across from Anna. He felt himself blush when she waved at him. Suddenly, two fingers snapped in front of his face and woke him up. Athene's, of course.

"The first sessions with me will be about defense and counter." He gestured to the large red and blue pads that were piled behind him. "Your main objective is to stop your opponent from connecting with you. I can't go and have each of you getting hurt and being sent back to mommy and daddy crying, so I have placed stabilizing pads in front of you so that you can't feel the force of a punch or a kick if it connects. Put them on."

Things got interesting from there. It felt like a military boot camp. Before they even started, Soriun Athene had them go through these odd stretches and do push-ups. Jacob had never worked out before, and his arms began to feel like Jell-O. Athene snapped at anyone who got out of line or slacked. He was brutal and kept being cruel to each of the elementals, whether they were a boy or a girl. Colby and Brandy were continually being smacked on the head every time they tangled up in battle. Athene gave them one last whack as they finished.

"Continue this ruckus, curlies, and you'll get booted out of the room." The class laughed at their new nicknames.

From time to time, Jacob would glance around at the others to see if they were picking up on the difficult lessons. He wondered to himself how Ms. Larrier would do in this class. She probably would run into her bathroom and cower with her Smaltzy.

Albert followed Athene's instructions very well, and correctly blocked all of Brian's moves. Athene smiled at him and then continued down the line. Buster and Probus blocked each other's moves until Probus got a punch to the gut from Buster. Buster smiled, and Athene didn't look too pleased. "Easy there, tough guy." Athene placed a pad back over Probus.

Jacob had difficulty and wasn't able to block all of Anna's attempts, but it was probably because of his affection for her, and also, he didn't want to hurt a girl so he claimed.

"Come on, what do you got? You gotta be better than that, Green Eyes." Anna had thrown the dust-wrench kick they just learned to Jacob's abdomen. He blocked it and pushed her to the ground accidentally.

"Sorry!" He went to grab her to pull her up, but she locked onto his head with her feet and sent him tumbling past her.

"Good work, Freckles." Athene created another nickname. Everyone continued through the rest of the lesson, throwing blocks, kicks, and punches. They had to repeat the same moves over and over again, until the end.

"What a day! So much fun! I felt like a superhero in there," Albert bragged. Jacob felt so sore that he could barely keep up.

"Yeah, we get it Al, ya like listening to Professor Brutal." Colby rubbed his head. He had taken too many smacks to the back of it from Athene.

"What? You making up nicknames now, too?" Brandy joked as the group headed out onto the first-floor platform.

"I think you two took the biggest beatings out of everyone, and you gave 'em to each other," Jacob said, and the rest of the group laughed with him.

After leaving Gordonclyff, and the others retreated to their dorms, Jacob found himself outside the giant tower in the middle of the green fields that were covered in small ice clouds which fell like snow from the sky. Dusting himself off, he leaned against a small structure in front of a beautiful blue waterfall.

"Hey there, stranger!"

Jacob leaped in shock and turned quickly to face Anna, who was right behind him.

"Oh… hey," he said breathlessly. His cheeks began to turn red. "I didn't see you come up behind me. I thought you guys were supposed to be in your dorms. Early start tomorrow, right?"

Anna rolled her eyes and stepped closer to him.

"Well, I was kind of bored, I guess." She leaned against the waterfall structure beside him. "It gets pretty out here at night."

Jacob nodded, embarrassed. Now that it was just him and Anna, he was out of conversation starters.

"You did well in Movements today." Anna nudged his shoulder with her own.

"Yeah," said Jacob. "For someone who was your punching bag." Anna let out a loud giggle. Jacob smiled, relieved that his joke went over well.

"So, do you like Cloudia so far?" she asked.

"It's cool," said Jacob. "It's tough getting used to it, but everyone is nice here." Jacob looked over at Anna. She was starting to turn red too, he noticed.

"Well, we all…" she looked down for a moment. "We all like having you here. You're a lot cooler than we expected."

"Thanks," Jacob said. His insides twisted so quickly that he felt as though they might turn into a pretzel. Anna just called him cool, and at that moment, he felt like he was the king of Cloudia. Maybe I should try to kiss her, he thought to himself, but then that thought was washed away on a wave of nerves.

"I had no idea what was going on during that skyracing match." Jacob returned to being a bit nervous and didn't know what else to say.

"We could all tell," she laughed. "Well, if you need help with anything, like-"

Anna didn't get to finish her sentence. Approaching them from a distance was a shadowy figure wearing a large cloak.

"Sounds like fun," the figure said, then removed his hood to reveal a smiling Seran. Jacob's panic was washed away with a sigh of relief at the sight of him. "I hope I wasn't interrupting anything," Seran added.

"Oh, hey Seran." Jacob was slightly disappointed that the conversation he and Anna were having had been interrupted. "This is Seran Keerinus. And Seran, this is Anna."

Anna stood like a statue in front of the two.

"I think she knows who I am, Jacob, but thank you. It's nice to meet you, Anna." She nodded her head at Seran slowly. "How was your first day of Movements?" he asked.

"Athene is tough," Jacob blurted out.

"Oh, I remember when I was in Soriun's training class for Movements. It was one of his first, too. I was more worried about my safety than the rest of the elementals." Jacob and Anna's mouths hung open. "Let me guess; he asked you to try and hit him as hard as you could?" Seran smiled.

Jacob closed his mouth again. "Yeah. How'd you know?"

"Well, how'd you do?" Seran asked, ignoring his question.

"Not too well," Jacob said bashfully.

"He got flipped on his bottom!" Anna yelled.

Seran let out a great laugh. "I can't say I blame old Soriun for trying that on the Light One. I might have, too." Anna laughed, while Jacob kept a serious face. "Well anyway, there's a reason why I asked you to meet me, Jacob. I'm glad you have a friend here, too."

Jacob felt fear grow in the pit of his stomach again. He hated feeling uncomfortable. What could it be now? He was tired of surprises.

"Today is your thirteenth borndi!" Seran said, and from out of nowhere, Bron was suddenly standing there with a half-smile on his face. Nyx skate-skyzed over wearing a large silly hat with spiral strings that stuck out from the top. Albert, Colby, and Brandy ran up, too. Bron played an instrument that looked like a cross between a trumpet and an accordion. All of his friends jumped in, and together, the group sang to him.

"A borndi for you, for you and your next, we celebrate this life's step. Oh, to be a Cloudian, To Tomorrow, a borndi, you win!"

"Why didn't ya tell me, Jake?" Colby yelled.

Jacob had forgotten about his birthday, or borndi, as they called it. He never celebrated it with Ms. Larrier or the orphans, and with all the hype of training and transporting to another world, it hadn't crossed his mind, but since he learned a new way to say it, it was okay with him.

An eventful week was capped off with a great finish as the group continued the birthday celebration and sung more songs.

# 12

# LEARNING TO FLY

The next month of Maii, which was similar to May back in Griffin, came very quickly, and the ice puffs were melting as they touched the ground. Sunlight spun a beautiful web upon Cloudia. The sunshine wasn't enough to keep half of the Cloudian History class awake, though. The elementals were bored while Magistra Dayan was explaining how the city was painted when it was first built.

"The only thing maw boring than watching paint dry," whispered

Brandy, "is hearing about it." Colby didn't hear her because he had been snoozing on top of his books with a glob of drool hanging from the side of his mouth. "Are ya excited for skyracing lessons today, little guy?" Brandy turned towards Albert, who ignored her as well, his eyes locked and fixated on every single word that came from Magistra Dayan's mouth about the acrylic styles that were used to bring out the intricate ceiling of Gordonclyff Tower.

"Brandy, I had almost forgotten it was today," Anna leaned in to acknowledge her.

"Maybe I should skip it?" Jacob suggested as nerves spilled out of him. Jacob had forgotten and was more nervous about this skyracing sport than facing an angry Ms. Larrier after spilling something on her dusty hallways.

"You'll be fine, Green Eyes," said Anna convincingly. "All of us are learning for the first time, and it doesn't matter if you struggle at first. Eventually, you'll pick it up!"

All week, the group had been bragging about skyracing and how fun it was. They kept impersonating race moves like they were professional surfers and running around Cloudia Center as if they were racing each other. Colby was the worst; he couldn't stop talking about how much he practiced at home and spent all of their vacations from Sky School racing his sister behind their house. Albert chimed in often, but it was mostly with knowledge about the great Ezekial Adams and his statistical performances in the Great Skyrace. He rivaled Magistra Dayan's lessons with almost equally as boring tips about dodging tricks that he had read in a skyracing game plan novel that his cousin had given him.

Skyracing's more popular than the Superbowl, Jacob thought to himself. All the elementals discussed it in almost every conversation.

Brian Saunders had never touched a skyspeeder. He was equally as nervous as Jacob was, but for different reasons. He tripped over his own two feet everywhere he went, so how was he going to navigate a board in the air?

The bell sounded, and Brandy smacked Colby clean in the back of the head to wake him up. Outside the platform, the group was putting their books back into their floating lockers. Jacob moved to put his inside, but a large fist crashed into his chest, sending him up against the cabinet.

Probus sneered in his direction as Buster took advantage of the distraction to shove Jacob's Cloudian History book to the ground, along with the notes he had been taking.

"You see that, Wesley?" Jacob was trying to ignore him and grab his book off the floor. "That's gonna be you today at the rink. You're gonna be glued to the ground, and I recommend you stay there."

Picking on Jacob and even Albert had become a ritual for Buster and Probus. One time, while in the Gordonclyff Tower bathrooms, the two had occupied a couple of stalls. Buster and Probus wet all the toilet paper rolls in each stall and removed the soap from the dispensers, as well. Jacob and Albert had to use the notebook paper from their bags to clean up.

This time Anna stood up tall to face Buster on Jacob's behalf, ready to fight. Jacob was half-embarrassed and half-happy that someone was coming to his defense.

"Oh, look, Probus! The dweebit's girlfriend has to fight his battles, too." Buster leaned in close to Anna. "I'd be careful if I was you, blondie. Don't think for a minute I wouldn't toss you to the ground, too." With an evil eye, Buster turned towards Jacob and then strutted back towards the end of the hallway. Probus kicked Jacob's notebook against the locker and left in a huff, too.

An hour later, they were standing in an arena that was on the very top floor of Gordonclyff Tower. There were marble walls that curved over to protect them from falling off the roof. In the center was a small green patch of grass surrounded by a circular black track with small white blocks just above it. It reminded Jacob of what the streets looked like back in Griffin, only the white lines were in the air. It smelled like a mixture between freshly mowed lawn and the rubber from brand new tires. It was a beautiful, bright, and windy day. Walls stretched as far as the tops of the clouds and wound down into a corkscrew in the middle. The grounds sloped into levels, and each level had a platform that rotated clockwise underneath.

In a pile in front of the group were bland skyspeeders painted with a single stripe in the middle.

"Well," said Albert nervously, "here's where we find out who's good off their feet. The track is 421 feet in length… 321 feet too many."

"Don't worry, Al, it's just a bit faster than what you're used to!" Anna attempted to calm his nerves.

"Besides, even Mr. Light One over here hasn't touched a skyspeeder." Colby pointed in Jacob's direction.

"Way to make me feel great, Colbs," Jacob replied.

"It won't matter anyway, especially now that Buster and his crew all have top-of-the-line Roar Epic speeders." Brandy nudged the group in Buster and Probus' direction; the two bullies were menacingly holding their skyspeeders under their armpits while cracking their knuckles.

"Eat your heart out, Darlene!" Anna shouted as she jumped a few times in the air.

"Easy there, Anna," Colby said. "Ya got cycles to go before ya can touch the air she flies through." Jacob couldn't help but smirk, but Anna ignored him with an annoyed look on her face.

Per usual, Albert was giving them tips about skyracing that he had learned from his parents. "My sources tell me that you need to bend your knees. Don't lean too forward, and tilt your head slightly to the right or left when attempting to turn."

Even though Brandy and Colby laughed at the demonstration, Jacob kept his attention glued to Albert's quirky movements.

"And also, my sources say to grip the speeder with your heels, keep your hands at your waist, and think of fast things." Albert demonstrated this stance for the crowd to see.

Jacob felt Buster Nalum's presence nearby, and he quickly tensed up.

"Probus, check out the dingbat trying out for the town circus!"

Probus and the other Incendiaries laughed loudly.

"Save it for the track, Buster!" Anna shouted as she shielded Albert. The group then walked over to the pile of bland speeders. Brian was already standing in front of them cautiously.

"My older brother told me that these speeders are crap. The ones that Gordonclyff provides are old 'S speeders' that came used from retired skyrace veterans. He said some of them have off-balance spikes and sway back and forth while you ride them."

The group was huddled around the speeders when an alarm sounded and drew their attention to the middle of the track. The ground opened up with a whistling noise, accompanied by a dark-skinned woman who had a red mohawk and silver lux-shades. She landed on her skyspeeder in front of the group. The ground shook like an earthquake beneath Jacob's feet.

She flew by once and then turned around to fly by again. The elementals cheered in amazement. The only groups that didn't seem to be fazed were Buster and the rest of the Incendiaries. She did a front-flip midair and then spiraled into a backflip. Briefly, she left the board, and then caught it with her hand as she touched down a few inches before the ground. Afterward, she took off her lux-shades and gave a cool wink towards the front.

"Aye, the name's Dominus Fugam. I've been a skyracer for over twenty yers now, and while it's certainly dangerous, it's the most fun I've ever had." She combed her Mohawk with her hands and picked up the bottom of the board, revealing spinning spikes underneath. The rest of the group were frozen like statues, in awe of Dominus.

"I don't suppose I'm here to just enter a staring contest with all of ya," she snapped. "Those of ya who don't have a speeder, grab one from the pile."

The group rushed forward and grabbed speeders left and right. Some were gray, others were brown, some had splinters coming off the board, and others had a few fewer spikes than the rest. Jacob was one of the last to grab a speeder. His speeder had a few chips in the corner and said "Property of Gordonclyff" in smudged, faded letters on the side.

"Now, reach down and press the oval button underneath the speeder," called Dominus Fugam, who stood in the middle of the group. "And stand about a foot back from your speeder. Careful of the spikes; they move at the shift of your weight."

Everyone pressed the button, and their boards quickly lifted about two feet off the ground. Anna's speeder was perfectly balanced in place.

Albert's wobbled back and forth, and Brian's spun wildly in front of him. Luckily, Jacob's stayed perfectly still in front of him.

A bit of luck, he thought to himself. Going last finally paid off.

Dominus Fugam showed them how to strap into their speeders without toppling over; making sure each elemental was fastened tightly to the straps.

Jacob, Colby, and Brandy were amused after they witnessed Probus accidentally knock into Buster, bumping their heads together.

"Now, when I wave my hand in the air, you thrust your head forward quickly," said Dominus Fugam. "Keep your balance still, don't waver, tuck your shoulders under your neck, and keep your fists out forward. Don't go more than five feet in front of you. Ready? And… here… we… go!"

The group aimed forward, and several of them hovered into the air. Jacob's board was a tad shaky, but he seemed to get the hang of it almost immediately. He swayed forward and then spun around to approach the group. Anna was slow to start but wiggled her way forward. Albert was too timid, and couldn't get the head bobbing motion right. Of course, Buster showed off, circling each member of the group. Brandy and Colby constantly got tangled up with each other before they figured out how to do a smooth transition.

"All right, very good. Very good, most of you. Others, you'll need some practice." Dominus Fugam hovered in the middle of pack, while she guided a few of those who had struggled back to their original spots. "That's okay. In front of you is what we call a race trail. It's used for skyrace trials and amateur practice. We are going to practice hovering around the trails in a single-file line. I don't want any of you going faster than the person in front of you. I'll lead in front, followed by Ms. Lindsey Goodman, and Mr. Andy Addams. The rest of you stay close. No funny business." Jacob noticed Dominus shoot a glare over in Colby's direction.

The elementals hovered over to the start of the trail and got in line. Jacob was to follow Lindsey Goodman, but Buster Nalum nudged him out of the way and took his place.

"You're in my spot, Light One."

Jacob gritted his teeth but retreated behind him. Once everyone had filed into a line safely, Dominus went up and down the line to confirm their position.

"Normally, there's a blue light that falls to the surface to initiate the race, but since we are only practicing, you will wait for my arm motion again. Wait for three ticks for your fellow elemental to go before you lean forward. When we turn, make sure to arch your hands in the direction you are turning."

Dominus waved her arm in the air. Lindsey Goodman and the first few elementals easily dusted off. Jacob felt a ball of excitement knock around in his stomach like a pinball machine. Eventually, it was his turn, and he lunged forward towards the beginning of the pack. The group remained in fine form as they circled throughout the trail. Jacob checked on Albert, who swayed clumsily back and forth as he moved. Many others were having a tough time keeping in line, but even though they were shaky, they still made their way around. They took turns, but it proved difficult for most. They had to shift their entire weight, but mostly, their fists had to be angled correctly to the sides of their skyspeeders. The spikes beneath the board caused it to sway in a motion that helped them turn. If they moved too quickly, the board pushed back out from under their feet.

Colby and Brandy got the hang of it and swerved in and out, while Brian Saunders was right behind them, looking dizzy. Jacob noticed Brian lose steam and struggle to keep up with the others. His face was pale white, and his legs were wobbling like noodles.

Dominus circled back to attend to him. "Are you okay, lad?"

Brian couldn't hold back anymore and let out orange vomit all over Dominus Fugam's face. She fell off her board and tumbled to the ground, taking others with her like dominos.

Suddenly, Jacob was nicked by Probus from behind. After he raced past Jacob, he knocked into Anna, which sent her off her speeder and onto the ground as well.

"Keep your eyes on the trail, sweetie pie!" Probus yelled as he whizzed by.

Probus then caught up to Buster, who hovered near the edge of the trail. Buster burst into laughter at the elementals who tumbled to the ground. "Nice work, Barf Face!" he shouted down at Brian.

The other elementals that were still hovering got closer to Dominus Fugam, who was unconscious under the pile as the class began to get out of control.

"Shut up, Buster! Why do you always have to be so mean?" Lindsey Goodman yelled from below the pile.

"Oh, look at the little princess, sticking up for Barf Face." Buster clutched his stomach and continued to circle in front of Jacob.

"Come on, Light One! Want to put those amperes to the test? What's the matter, Wesley? Too chicken to dance?"

Jacob had no idea what Buster meant but knew it was probably something bad because Probus was laughing. Buster and Probus kept antagonizing Jacob, flying in figure-eights around him.

"What do you say, flybean?" Buster high-fived Probus. The two proceeded to race around the trail.

Jacob didn't let his nerves and his inexperience get in the way of stopping Buster.

"Don't do it, Jacob!" Anna yelled from below, stepping over the pile of elementals and boards. "Once Dominus wakes up and sees you…"

Jacob had already taken off and chased Buster and Probus. His heart beat so fast that it felt like it was going to jump up into his head. He stood angled on the speeder, and lunged forward, up through the air around the track, his cheeks flapping furiously as the wind gusted into them, his Volans coat pointing straight up. Even though his heart raced, he noticed that he was good at something he didn't have to think about; it came naturally and was beyond fun.

The fallen group below burst into cheers as he flew near Buster and Probus, who were already flying at amazing speeds for thirteen-yer-olds. Buster caught wind of Jacob's approach and took a sharp corner, then turned around in mid-air to face Jacob directly. He looked shocked to see him on his tail.

"What's the matter, Buster? Not as fast as you thought you were?" Jacob stabbed. "Or is it that all my amperes are too much for you?"

Buster, although obviously worried, motioned towards Probus.

Probus already had an evil grin on his face, and he lunged backward in a flip towards Jacob. The two were naturals with their skyspeeders, as if they'd had a ton of training beforehand. Although Probus now glided towards Jacob with furious speed, Jacob didn't budge. Then he did something that even he didn't anticipate.

Jacob swiveled in a clockwise direction as Probus lunged at him. He missed Jacob and spiraled towards the track wall. He clunked his head against the wall and fell to the ground. Buster sat stunned on his speeder.

Albert and the Johnstons jumped for joy below, and the others joined in with a few whistles and cheers.

"What will you do now, Buster? Probus just ate dirt, and now it's just you." Jacob grew even more confident, standing up to a bully for the first time in his life.

Buster seemed to have already had this thought, as he whipped back around. "Let's see what you're made of, Wesley." Buster's head shot forward, and so did his speeder. Jacob followed suit. With incredible speed, they both dashed through the track and sped around the corners. Blurred images of the crowd below surrounded them. Although the speeders traveled faster than anyone could see, Jacob felt as though things moved at a slow pace. His blood felt cool, but his heart felt warm, and his sight was focused. He felt as though he was flying freely, with no board below him. He was one with the trail.

He took the fourth corner. Jacob was inches behind Buster, and he felt the breeze of his power brush past his face. Buster turned and couldn't see Jacob, who suddenly leaped over Buster. Jacob was showing off to Buster, teasing him with his hands behind his back like there was no effort involved. Just as Jacob turned around to cross the finish line, he was met with a red-gloved palm halting him in place.

"WHAT ARE YOU DOING?!" Dominus Fugam now stood with her hair frizzed outwards as if she had been electrocuted. Her Volans coat was covered in Brian's puke, but she was more concerned with the rule-breaking elemental who was celebrating in front of her.

Jacob's feelings of joy quickly washed away, and now panic set in.

"Who gave the two of you permission to use the track for childish fun?!" Dominus Fugam raced furiously towards the two.

"You could have gotten hurt! Or, worse you could have destroyed the track." Dominus Fugam grabbed hold of Jacob's and Buster's ears and dragged them forward. Jacob was nervous that the static from her hair might shock him.

"It was all Buster's doing, Jacob didn't—"

"Quiet, Miss Goodman," Dominus interrupted.

"But Probus and Buster—

"Aye, Mr. Egan, I can grab two ears with one hand, you know."

Albert's missile, intended to save Jacob, fell short as well.

Jacob could barely see as his left ear was dragging him and Buster was being dragged to his right. This was probably the end of his training as he knew it. If he were lucky, he'd be scrubbing toilets for the PPA. Or even worse, maybe this would confirm he wasn't special at all, and he'd be back scrubbing toilets for Ms. Larrier and getting chased by Smaltz. Tommy would be waiting for him with one of his classic wedgies.

Dominus quickly marched through the spiraling gears and under the moving platforms. As they moved with lightning speed, Jacob had to take double-steps for each step she took. Dominus was mumbling things to herself in a language he couldn't understand. Finally, they barged through bronze doors, and a purple Volans coat swished around to face them.

"Dominus, why are you in my— what happened to your coat?"

Magistra Dayan put down a shiny silver pen.

They had all forgotten about Brian throwing up on her in the wake of the heated race between the two boys who she had clenched by the ears.

"These two… these miscreants were abusing training time and sped through the course unauthorized." Dominus waved her hands in the air and looked extremely crazy.

Magistra Dayan looked a bit puzzled as she eyed the two guilty elementals. Now Jacob was in for it. The Magistra herself was going to kick both he and Buster out. The only redeeming thing about this situation was that Buster would be expelled, too.

"It was all his idea, Magistra. Jacob wanted to race. He wanted to prove he was the Light One in front of everyone. I was forced into it. I swear."

Jacob couldn't believe his ears as Buster threw the blame on him for the trouble they were in. His hopes of equal punishment quickly evaporated from his mind.

"And how exactly were they racing unauthorized, Dominus?" Magistra Dayan had shifted focus from Buster to Dominus. "I assumed they were in your sky trail training."

The only person more stunned than Jacob at that moment was Dominus Fugam herself. She was lost for a rebuttal as her eyes grew wide.

"I-I-I was unconscious; I woke up just in time to-"

"And why were you unconscious?" Magistra Dayan was only focused on Dominus. Jacob couldn't believe his ears.

"I-I-I, the boy, uh, he threw up, and it-"

"I can only presume that's the reason for your unconsciousness," Magistra Dayan interrupted Dominus. "This silly mess of a situation doesn't look too good for your training career. Now, I'm going to excuse the manner in which you brought these gentlemen here by force, and we'll keep it between the four of us. For you two, this will be the last I'll hear of free-racing during your lessons. They are for learning, not playtime unless Dominus Fugam says otherwise. Understood?"

The boys nodded their heads and Dominus gave a reluctant, "Aye." The three turned to leave, and Jacob felt like he just escaped a death sentence.

"Jacob, please stay behind for a few moments."

Jacob slowly turned back around to face Magistra.

"Have a seat, Jacob." Jacob sat down in the cold bronze chair. His nerves crept back up his stomach and into his throat.

"Who won?" Magistra asked with a smirk.

"I'm sorry, Magistra?"

"I'm interested to know who won the race. I can only presume it was you, by the flush on Mr. Nalum's face." She smiled and began to twirl her pen in her hands. Jacob nodded, and couldn't help but smile at the same time.

"I thought so. Keep training and stay focused, Jacob. I think Ezekiel Addams may finally have a worthy opponent."

Jacob's eyes widened in shock. Magistra Dayan had just compared him to the greatest skyracer in their world!

*Wait 'til the others hear about this!* He thought to himself.

"Seems you are natural, and I'll be running it by Seran to get you extra training time. That'll be all, Jacob."

Jacob smiled and moved out of her office.

At lunchtime, Albert relived the brilliant race between Jacob and Buster, which was being talked about throughout the academy. He surfed on the table and imitated the "great leap," as it was being called. Brandy was too busy to pay attention as she stuffed her face with chili-butter sandwiches and drank everyone's flerry trumnits. Anna smiled and blushed as she watched Albert's uncoordinated version of the race.

"And that's when he said, 'Take that, Probus!' Probus tumbled to the ground like a furious tornado." Albert announced, too. "Down goes Probus, down goes Probus. Now it's just Buster and Jacob, Jacob and Buster. The two spiraling speeders raced towards ultimate supremacy." Jacob mouthed the same words back in Colby's direction. Colby gave him a thumbs-up. Albert jumped off the table to imitate the great leap, and everyone gave a loud chuckle.

"Ya know, I don't remember it like that. I remember you barely passing Buster at the end, and getting ya ear caught by Dominus," Colby brashly replied.

"You were just jealous because you watched me take your place in the Great Skyrace." Jacob shoved Colby slightly.

"Oh, Mr. Big Shot now, huh?" Colby elbowed Jacob.

"Magistra Dayan seems to think so. She said I might be a worthy opponent for Ezekial Addams."

In unison, the group patted Jacob on the back.

"Well, looks like we have to get you a speeder now, don't we—"

Before Anna could finish, an ear-piercing noise buzzed throughout the room. Everyone covered their heads and ears instantly.

"What's that noise?" Anna asked.

Suddenly, a blast crushed the wall to the right of the group. The elementals ducked, and four cloaked figures stood up.

From underneath a few pieces of rubble, Jacob looked up. The cloaked figures were angled towards the blast zone. Arms began to rise, and fear took over.

Jacob felt a solid feeling inside of him that he had only felt once before. It took him back to the feeling he had in the museum when his heart pounded, and he felt as though he was going to throw up his entire soul. His head pulsated with pain, and his blood rushed through his whole body with an amazing heat. He could barely hear Anna's voice as she called to him.

"Jacob, can you hear me? We need to leave! Jacob?"

Jacob tried to focus on her words, but he couldn't help but be swayed by the overwhelming amount of energy that coursed through his veins. The cloaked figures in front of him fell off as fire jetted into the room. Elementals fled the scene, but a masked individual with a dark coat came into his vision. A searing pain shot through his body, and the figure turned its head in his direction.

Then the dark crimson figure disappeared as darkness crept over his vision.

# 13

# ELECTRO TRAINING

Jacob's eyes fluttered open. He couldn't hear too well, but he could see his surroundings. About ten elementals were laying in levitating beds with plush blankets wrapped around them. The room was dimly lit and had a newborn smell to it. Women in pearly white gowns were skyzing over to each bed. Jacob tried to move, but couldn't. Suddenly, his forehead was met with a throbbing headache right above his right eye.

"Jacob, you okay?" He heard Anna's voice faintly in his right ear. Standing next to his bed were Anna and Albert.

"Well, I can tell this isn't a skyracing match, and I'm not celebrating," Jacob replied.

"Excuse me, my dears." A beautiful brunette nurse skyzed over to Jacob's left side. With her right hand, she pressed a cold block to his forehead and then squeezed something that looked similar to a Navus mark gun against his temple, which was warm. Jacob tensed, but felt his headache subside almost instantly.

Colby and Brandy then skipped up behind the rest of the group. Colby's arm and head had silver cotton patches on them, covering his injuries.

"That was quite the end of our conversation, huh?" said Colby grimly, jumping up on Jacob's bed near his feet and causing Jacob to jump, too.

"Yeah. Follcane was in and out, just like that," said Brandy.

"He blew past security with ease, man. Fire just shooting out in every direction," said Colby.

"There was fire?" asked Jacob, looking up.

"Yeah, dude! It was wicked," said Colby excitedly. "Like, legit flames coming out of his arms, man! Just spiraling past everyone, and that wall exploding! Woo! Crazy! But anyway, how ya holding up, bro?"

He patted Jacob on his left leg, which made him tense up again.

"What exactly happened?"

Jacob sat up in his bed, not just to avoid another slap from Colby, but to ease into the conversation, too. He glanced around at each of them: Colby, then Brandy, over at Anna, and then at Albert.

"Well, Silas Follcane - you know, your counterpart," Anna began. "He showed up and blasted right through the wall. A couple of Gordonclyff security guards tried to fight back, but they were no match. He lit up the area with fire to distract everyone, and then you fainted. That's when he snatched Jasper Collins and Taylor Jane."

"Snatched?" Jacob echoed, shocked.

"Kidnapped them, and bolted." Albert jumped into the conversation now. "They were Incendiaries, too. 145 and 147 amperes."

"I can't believe he was here," said Jacob, who kept turning cold at the thought of what would have happened if he tried to fight Follcane.

There was a loud sneeze in the distance. Then, Nyx and Bron appeared at the edge of the bed. Nyx was pale and hunching over the side of the bed. He was saying very little, choosing not to be included in the conversation, and merely stood at the edge of the bed, eyes alight and frightened.

"Does Seran know?" Jacob asked Bron.

"He was here yesterday, visiting you — he's back at the scene of the explosion, trying to make sense of how Follcane got into Gordonclyff Tower."

"So, Follcane's here now?" Colby quietly asked.

"Yes," said Bron. He didn't even stutter, or try to hide the fact that the greatest feared villain was now inside of Cloudia. "And I fear he may not be leaving anytime soon."

"How would he be able to sneak into Cloudia with the PPA guarding every entrance?" Anna spoke up.

"No idea," said Bron, frowning.

"You don't think he knows someone here in Cloudia, do you?" Anna let go of Jacob's hand and faced Bron for the answer.

"I don't think so," said Bron. "But anything could be possible at this point. If you're smart, you'll leave all the answers to us to figure out." Bron looked towards Jacob with hopeful eyes. "Good to see you're okay, kiddo."

Nyx nodded and blew his nose into his yellow handkerchief again as the two left.

"I don't know, guys," said Brandy.

"It's hard to believe the PPA would miss someone as lethal as him," said Anna darkly.

"He could be coming back for more. The odds are in his favor," said Albert.

"Or he could be coming back fa Jake," said Colby. "I mean, if ya think about it, Jake's the only one standing in his way of getting to all of us, right?"

"I don't know if I'm the one you guys should be counting on." Jacob tried to get out of the bed, but the nurse near his side lightly pressed on his chest so he would stay put. "I couldn't even beat Buster in a skyrace. How could I defeat someone who just obliterated Gordonclyff's security?"

"You'll figure that out soon enough, my dear," Magistra Dayan appeared by the bed. "And that will be tomorrow. You begin your elemental training tomorrow." She winked towards the group and then strutted away.

The following day, after fifth-period Cloudian History had finished, Jacob left Gordonclyff's eighteenth floor and took a platform down to the study hall that Magistra had directed him to attend. The cloaked figure in front of him approached the yellow door that had a big prophecy symbol on it. He waved his right arm, and the door disintegrated in front of them. Jacob followed through and set off into the darkness. There were flashes of light and all sorts of grunts and shouts. The environment had an eerie tone to it.

Then he turned around and whispered towards Jacob, "Forgetting something?"

The figure then placed Jacob's lux-shades over his eyes. Immediately, yellow and green lights surrounded him. About five other elementals that were about a foot taller were dressed in Volans coats with their arms stretched out, skyzing around the room. In the center, to Jacob's surprise, was Soriun Athene, the Movements teacher, who was keeping watch of every move that took place.

The room itself was huge. The walls were eggshell white with a green lining that went down different sides of the walls. At every corner were red targets with varying values of a point in the center. They reminded Jacob of the target boards that Gravits would throw darts at.

Just as Jacob started to approach, the cloaked figure in front of him waved an arm. He removed his hood to reveal a smiling Seran.

"Don't get down on yourself for Follcane showing up. You aren't ready to face him, and I would have never put you in that position."

"But—" Jacob tried to speak, but Seran signaled with his fingers for him not to.

"I wanted to expedite your training, but I didn't want the other elementals to feel left out."

"But—" Jacob tried again but had no luck.

"As I told you before, pay attention to Athene. He knows what he's doing. To Tomorrow, Jacob."

And before Jacob could say anything, Seran skyzed out of the room.

"To Tomorrow…" Jacob turned to face the other elementals, and the righthand corner of his lux-shades started to run numbers very quickly. 320, 275, 400. Ampere numbers were flashing before him like lightning bolts during a storm. As delighted as he was to see the bigger numbers, it was getting in the way of his vision. He clicked an oval button to the side of his lux-shades, which turned the ampere readings off.

"Mr. Wesley, nice of you to join us."

Jacob turned his head cautiously in Athene's direction. Athene stood before him with his hands folded behind his back.

"Sorry I was late, Mr. Athene," said Jacob.

"Punctuality is not the Light One's strongest attribute, I can tell. It's okay; we will need to catch you up, then. You won't be training in here just yet. We will need to ease you into your Electro skills. Seran wants your training rushed, but if we do that, you won't be able to defeat him."

"Right," said Jacob, trying to sound as though he wasn't frightened and trembling at the thought of fighting Follcane.

"So…" Athene led Jacob over to the front of the room where there were three jars filled with the firefly creatures that Jacob remembered from the orphanage. They were buzzing inside.

"So," said Athene. "Electro refers to the use of your internal electrical energy. Every Cloudian has special potential energy harnessed deep down inside. We call it your light."

"My light," Jacob repeated, as Soriun Athene paced towards the three jars on the table.

"Your light," Athene continued," is measured in amperes, and yours, well… you know where you stand."

Jacob nodded, and Athene proceeded to pick up the rusty yellow jar to his right.

"However, even someone with your natural ampere reading can't just use them. It takes a jump start."

"Oh, like a car?" Jacob mumbled.

"What's a car?" Athene asked, and Jacob just shook it off.

"It needs something to cause your element to become active, and that's where they come in."

"What are they?" Jacob eyed the jars very curiously. Suddenly, he felt déjà vu.

"We call them darklights," Athene said. "They have the perfect balance of darkness and light, and their little wings flutter so fast that they can initiate an energy spike that allows your element to be used. A darklight's spark lasts for quite a while."

"These little creatures surrounded me when I left Griffin," Jacob said. Athene nodded, then pointed towards Jacob's arm. Athene let them out, and the small winged creatures surrounded his arm, latching on like tape. Light traced his veins like water going down a pipe.

"The command I am going to try and teach you is a good start to your journey, Jacob. It will impress your enemies. It's called a light spark."

"How does it work?" Jacob nervously asked.

"When it's executed correctly, it generates a small energy ball in the palm of your hand," said Athene. "It's like a mini explosion emitted from your hand. It can destroy most things on contact, but it can only severely weaken your enemy."

Jacob pictured himself closing his eyes and bracing for the impact of a giant wave of electricity to take him over. Soriun Athene continued, "The light spark blast takes a command from the darklights to get you going."

Athene opened his fist and revealed a small sphere of bright white light, surrounded by green and yellow bolts of electricity.

"Whoa," Jacob said with his mouth open. It reminded Jacob of a crystal ball, but with static lightning bolts sticking out in different directions. "So, what do you do with it once it's in your hand?" Jacob leaned in.

Athene let a smile crawl up his lips and pushed Jacob to the side with his other arm. Athene's eyes flickered.

"Light spark!"

After the words left Athene's mouth, yellow sparks of light climbed up his arm and traced the vein through the darklights. He raised his fist, opened the palm of his hand, and revealed a green sphere. The sphere blasted one of the targets and sent splintered pieces of broken redwood in different directions.

"Wow... You're going to teach me how to do that?" Jacob's mouth still hung open.

"At some point, I won't have to teach you. It will come naturally to you, like a Gravit walking on cement. The darklights have a language called Lignua, and that's how we communicate with them. Each phrase enables you to use your light in the ways you want to. It acts as a signal, commanding them. Every elemental line has its unique phrases to communicate in a way that will manipulate one's element." Athene retracted his arm back towards the jar.

"Retidum tells them to return to their previous place." As Soriun Athene pointed towards the rusty yellow jar, the darklights fluttered and spiraled back through the top.

"Too much information?" Athene spoke with his back turned towards Jacob, who just stared in shock.

"I think I got it. We have a light inside of us, which is measured by amperes. The darklights help us use it to be able to send it where we want by talking in their language, uh... lin..."

"Lignua, but very good." Athene grabbed Jacob's shoulder and nodded, showing that he approved of his understanding of the Cloudian ability that he would partake in learning.

"How do we capture the darklight?" Jacob asked, afraid of his question.

"Hmm, that's a fair question, I suppose. Futura is home to the darklights. It's where their species lives. They were dying when their source of food and energy was going out, so they ventured to our home. In exchange for giving them a home, they have agreed to generate power for us." Athene lifted the jars and showed them to Jacob.

"I see." Jacob felt better about his answer.

"There takes a certain amount of meditation to have full control of your light. Besides being able to control your light, you need to learn the ability to control the darklights and command them as well. It takes time, and unfortunately, we don't have much of it. Your sessions will be accelerated and must be conducted multiple times a week. Any questions?"

Jacob had so many that he didn't know where to begin. Just as he was about to speak up, Athene cut him off.

"Good. Today, you will be learning phrases, and then you will be required to practice them after you leave." Jacob sighed. Soriun Athene had just politely said he had homework.

"We will first practice with meditation." He brought Jacob into a smaller room, where a small white pillow sat in the center, and four candles were brightly lit in each corner of the room. "Do you have your lux-bands?" Jacob pulled out the silver bracelets he received back at High Corner. Athene placed them over Jacob's wrists and clasped them together. They hovered over his wrists and didn't touch his skin.

"What do these do?" Jacob curiously asked as he waved his hands up and down to admire the lux bands.

"Until you are used to the energy pulses, you need lux-bands to control the light inside of you," Athene explained. Jacob waved them around and tried to see how they worked. They felt heavy.

"Kind of like training wheels?" Jacob asked.

"Sounds about right," Athene replied.

Athene blew out the candles and instructed Jacob in different exercises, which ranged from opening and shutting his eyes to floating a few inches off the ground for minutes at a time. Jacob was able to internally focus on his energy and lift his feet off the ground for a solid five minutes. The lux-bands circled around his wrist, and small bolts of electricity flowed through him. He was calm but ecstatic about his control. Athene was very impressed with Jacob's quick learning.

"We'll make a Light One out of you yet," said Athene proudly. "The light spark is a very effective blast. In normal Electro training, it's one of the simplest, but for someone of your yers, it may be too advanced."

"How long does it take to learn?" Jacob curiously asked.

"We don't have much time to wait; today should be enough."

"I'm going to learn that today?"

"The darklights initiate the energy spike, and your lux-bands centralize it, but it's up to you and your concentration to make the blast effective, and to grow it. You need to empty everything out of your mind. You must be completely clear to send it. Focus on something first."

Jacob tried his best to void his mind of thoughts. Somehow, Tommy's wedgies and Ms. Larrier's mole were entering his mind. Finally, he managed to get his mind clear.

"Right," he said, trying to focus on the emptiness in his mind.

"Again, this command is known as…" Soriun cleared his throat. "Light spark!"

"Light spark," Jacob mumbled to himself. "Light spark."

The darklights fluttered from the open jar to his arm, latching onto his skin like a wad of gum. They felt icky, but he kept his focus. He opened one of his eyes and noticed the rings hovering over his wrists had started to move and a bright light emitted from them. The palm of his right hand, where the darklights were, started to heat up. A small ball of light suddenly formed. It looked like a marble covered in tiny lightning bolts.

"Whoa! Do you see this?" Jacob excitedly asked. "I'm doing this!"

"Incredible," said Soriun, awestruck. "Right, then… hold it steady."

"Yes," Jacob said, closing his eyes again tightly. Athene gently moved his lux-shades back over his eyes.

"You can open your eyes again, but keep focus. Don't lose it." Athene clicked a button on a silver gear near the end of the room, and a beige mannequin was illuminated in front of Jacob. He tried with all his might to focus on the object.

"Raise your arm slightly now." Athene's words were smoothly projecting around him. Jacob did his best to clear his mind, but thoughts of Follcane's cloak kept entering in. Any moment now, he would be blasting through the room and kidnapping Athene, or even worse, Jacob. He couldn't let it happen. He was supposed to be the Light One.

The mannequin's face started to change suddenly. A burnt hollow face took over, and a cloak rose slowly in place around it. The manikin's rubber hand turned into slimy fingers and started to reach out towards him menacingly. The lights turned into darkness, except for the shadowy aura around the mannequin, which was now alive. Jacob, gasping for air, stood frozen. A wave of terrifying fear swept over him...

"Light...spark!" Jacob panicked. "Light spark blast!" He tried again, but nothing. The mannequin inched closer, his slimy fingers almost around Jacob's neck. "Spark light spark..."

Jacob braced, closed his eyes, and cringed. But when he opened his eyes again, he noticed the marble sparks was no longer in the palm of his hand, and the mannequin was just a mannequin, standing in place. He brushed off his lux-shades and looked up at Soriun with anxious eyes. He was speechless.

"I messed up," he mumbled, wiping the puddle of sweat away from his drenched forehead.

"You saw him, didn't you?" Athene was still smiling.

"Yes. How did you know?" Jacob scratched his head.

"Here..." Soriun handed him a can full of a thick watery liquid. "Rehydrate yourself before you give it another shot. Electro is not for the fainthearted. Your worst fears can trickle into your mind when you clear it. I was stunned that you even conjured up the blast in the first place. I might have fainted if you performed the command correctly. You are very close, though."

"That was scary," Jacob muttered, downing the beverage in one gulp. "It felt so real. Follcane... he was... right there."

"Jacob," Soriun said, reaching for Jacob's lux-bands. "We can continue another time if you like–"

"No!" said Jacob fiercely, crunching the can with his fist and tossing it to the side. "I've got to be the Light One! I'm tired of being the kid who can't do it. I want to be the one who can do it. I need to do this for all of you, and for me."

"That's real Light One talk..." said Athene. "Now, remember, you need to stay focused. It helps to try and focus on the pit of your stomach. If you centralize your mind, instead of just emptying it, you can concentrate."

Jacob closed his eyes and narrowed his eyebrows. He put his lux-shades back on and clicked the button himself this time. He took a deep breath and tried to focus his mind down his throat and into his stomach.

"Again," said Athene, removing the lid from the jar of darklights.

"You can do this," said Jacob, focusing on the pit of his stomach. His mind was clear as he raised his arm. The lights engaged on his lux-bands and the darklights stuck back onto his right arm.

"Focus!" said Athene, pressing the button on the gear again. The room went dark immediately, and the aura grew around the mannequin. Jacob opened his eyes to see the shadowed figure standing before him.

"Light spark!" Jacob yelled, and the marble with lightning bolts grew to about the size of a bowling ball.

"LIGHT SPARK!" he yelled again, although this time, his voice thundered. The green bowling ball with lightning bolts shot out of his hand like a cannon. It smacked the creepy mannequin right in the face, sending it spiraling backward against the wall. The power caused Jacob to spring back and fall to the ground behind him. He pulled off his lux-bands excitedly and saw the hologram disappear back into the gear. The wall had a small dent and tiny cracks from the impact of the blasted mannequin.

"Amazing!" roared Athene, lunging forward. He picked Jacob up by his Volans collar. Jacob stumbled a bit, feeling exhausted and faint as if he had just skyraced for twenty-four hours without a break. His legs felt wobbly. The darklights quietly zipped back into the rusty jar.

"You did it, Jacob!" Athene said, grabbing a nearby leather chair for Jacob to fall down into. "I've never seen anything like that!"

"That felt amazing." Jacob wiped the sweat from his brow again as he drank another gulp of the cold drink.

"I'd say that's enough for your first day." Athene removed Jacob's lux-bands for him. "You will need to practice that phrase though." Athene skyzed over to Jacob. "You keep trailing off at the end."

"Yes sir," said Jacob. He took another drink. Athene waved the lights back on now that the darklights were resting in the jars.

"Sir Athene," he said. "Have you ever faced Follcane?"

Athene stood frozen with the jar of darklights in his right hand.

"I did once," he said coldly.

"What was he like?"

Athene turned quickly to face Jacob.

"He's not someone you take a skyracing match," he said curtly. "But it's getting late, and you need to return to the PPA, or Seran will make me look like that mannequin."

Jacob shook his forearm with a "To Tomorrow" and paced near the edge of the dojo, and then around the corner to the elevator platform hovering in place. He entered the platform and leaned against the side, still feeling a bit queasy from the blast.

Athene was apparently not too keen on discussing Jacob's future enemy. Jacob's thoughts ran back to the terrifying villain who had started out as just a mannequin. He felt alone for a moment, thinking about how much this new world was depending on him. Visions of Follcane walking eerily through Gordonclyff raced through his mind, and voices of his fellow elementals screaming in fear weren't far behind.

"They are all depending on me," he told himself sternly. "You're too deep in this world. Why can't you do it? You can. You can beat this monster. You have to!"

The platform reached the lobby and he dusted off his Volans coat.

"Hey, Green Eyes," said a buttery voice.

Anna's flowing locks of gold appeared beside him, and Jacob's heart stopped.

"So, how was it?"

"Oh, fine," he shrugged. "Well, actually, really cool. How was it in Hydro training?"

"Unlike anything I've ever experienced before," said Anna. "I might have made Albert's ears fill up with water," she said bashfully.

"He probably needed a good cleaning anyway," Jacob joked. Anna giggled.

"I thought maybe you'd like to go for a walk?"

Jacob nodded, and they went outside. The air was thin and cold, but the night sky was beautiful. Anna skipped down the long walkway of Gordonclyff's tower. Ice puffs trickled down from golden strings.

"It was most impressive watching you race against Buster. I never got the chance to tell you that," she said, giggling and skipping. She looked charming at that moment, and Jacob struggled to keep his composure. "Did you…?"

"Did I what?"

"Well, never mind," said Anna. She was twirling her hair with her right index finger. It was very cute.

"It was the most fun I've ever had in my life," Jacob said confidently. "If only I had taken him down, though."

"You were close," she answered slowly. "You didn't do so hot against Follcane, though!"

Jacob's smile turned to an embarrassed frown. Anna coyly smacked him on the shoulder. "Only joking, Green Eyes… none of us were ready for it. Think he's coming after us?"

Jacob searched for an answer. "I'm not sure… Seran might believe so. He's expediting our training."

"I don't know," said Anna, biting her lip. "Maybe Seran is trying to prepare you for when he attacks again?" She stared across the green fields and clouds to their right, apparently lost in thought, not even noticing Jacob's sweat dripping down his brow. "How's your head, anyway?"

"Much better," said Jacob, and he told her all about the bizarre healing that Seran had made him go through. He started rubbing his head when something bizarre caught his eye. It was a red crystal sticking out of the stone beneath his feet. It was encased in gold.

"Well, good, you're going to need it!" said Anna, before she noticed he wasn't answering her. "What are you looking at?"

"I have no idea," Jacob said, still caught up in the golden sparkle of the crystal. He saw several of them in a row, leading beneath the walkway.

"It's beautiful, but suspiciously, it doesn't look like it belongs here." Anna crouched down next to Jacob.

"Should we touch it?" Jacob croaked. "It's not, like, poison ivy or anything, right?" breathed Jacob.

"What's poison ivy?" Anna curiously asked.

"Nothing…" He lowered his hand to touch it cautiously.

"Don't touch that grailum!" A deep voice called out from behind them. Bron grabbed Jacob's hand just in the nick of time. "Jacob, come with me," the bulky man demanded. Jacob waved at Anna, and the two sped off.

# 14

# TRIALS

Nyx stayed in a small oval apartment near the outer edge of Cloudia, right in front of the docking station for the Airz Taxi. A bed of blue flowers and a yellow umbrella were hovering just outside his front door.

"Nyx keeps to himself in Cloudia. Surprising, huh?" Bron chuckled and pressed the silver button on his lux-band. An angelic tune sounded, like a peaceful alarm, followed by a bizarre cross between a deep bark and a metal clanging sound.

"Oh shhh, Mr. Hops. It's just a couple of visitors," Nyx said from behind the door. A golden tube stretched from the middle of the door, ending inches away from Jacob's face. It then moved like a snake, twisting and slithering around Bron's big nose. After a moment, it retracted back into the door.

"See, Mr. Hops," Nyx said. "It's Bron and Jacob, tee-hee!"

The door swung up, revealing a cheery, curly-haired Nyx holding a dog-looking creature with a metal snout, ears, and legs.

The room was very similar to PPA dorms. Plates of glass with all sorts of funky radar screens were hovering around the room, including holograms of Volans coats, and beautiful green vines traced the walls. Floating in the middle of the room was a blue and yellow striped leather couch that Nyx directed the two to sit on.

"Have a seat, ta ta!" said Nyx, petting his metal dog in between its ears. The dog smiled, revealing sharp steel teeth, and wagged its curly metal tail.

"Hope we aren't catching you at a bad time," Bron said, before plopping down on the couch. It immediately fell to the ground like a ton of bricks. Bron waved over at Jacob.

"Not at all, hee-hee," said Nyx, winking over at Jacob. "Can I get you a trumnit or some buttered pastry tarts?" Nyx opened a glass case holding golden, flaky, square-shaped biscuits that had red filling oozing out of them.

Bron grabbed the biscuits and quickly scarfed one down before handing one to Jacob. He took a bite and a delicious strawberry taste cooled his throat.

"There's a reason we're here," Bron said. "We were wondering if you have seen any intruders? Jacob and Anna found this outside of Gordonclyff Tower." Bron clicked his lux-band and again, and a holographic image of the grailum substance outside Gordonclyff materialized.

"Oh dear, hmm," Nyx squinted over the image. "I haven't seen grailum since Jacob was transported all those yers ago, ta ta."

Nyx skyzed over to the large glass screen that was against his back wall. He waved his hands around and a live feed of dust rolling through trees appeared.

The screen read: "OUTSKIRTS (CLOUDIA)."

"There is no unusual activity outside of Cloudia, Bronny. It's a bit odd that the grailum showed up around Gordonclyff, though." Nyx turned his attention towards Jacob. "Did you see it anywhere else, hee-hee?"

"This is the first time I've noticed it." Jacob reclined into the couch.

"Has anyone else besides the girl seen it?" Bron asked. Jacob shook his head.

"What is grailum?" Jacob returned. Both Nyx and Bron looked at him for a moment, and then back at each other, ignoring the question. The two went back to discussing their theories on what it meant.

Jacob stood up from the couch and headed over to the glass screen, searching for anything that might show up. It was like a satellite feed, and the camera was shifting constantly. Jacob remembered that Nyx was the Watcher of Most Important Things, which likely meant that he was watching Cloudia, now that Jacob was back.

After Nyx waved them off and Mr. Hops gave Jacob a sloppy, metallic lick, Jacob and Bron walked back to the PPA. Jacob was still wrestling with the strange sighting of this substance called grailum. Even with all the training taking place, and the upcoming skyrace prelims, all Jacob could think about was the grailum.

"You can't speak a word of this to anyone," Bron said as he climbed into his bed, the thump hitting the room like an earthquake. "You leave the detective work to the adults. The only reason I brought you along was to help Nyx understand what to look out for."

Jacob nodded reluctantly and turned over to go to sleep.

The following day, as the sun rose in the clear sky, Jacob left the PPA and strolled through the empty fields of grass on his way to the top floor of Gordonclyff Tower. The beautiful marble stadium with grass fields was straight ahead. It was odd to see it so empty, so Jacob pictured it filled with thousands of screaming fans, chanting his name over and over. Anna sat to his right, beaming, while Albert and the Johnstons jumped up and down. He felt very free in that moment. What a feeling – to be the true hero this world thought he would become. The sweet pine from the grass refreshed him until a very loud whistle broke through his fantasy.

"Wesley! Aye, back to reality you go!"

Dominus was right next to him, snapping her fingers with one hand and holding a shiny silver whistle in the other. To her right was a plain wooden skyspeeder with rusty spikes underneath.

"You studied your rules, I presume, eh?" said Dominus, her eyes looking very beady. Jacob gave her a blank stare. "Figured as much. Not even Magistra Dayan gave you a heads-up?" Jacob shook his head. "Well, then let's get going with the basics."

She trotted over to the middle rectangular platform, which stuck out of the ground like a cement well. She kicked the side of it and out poured a giant hologram of a cement boulder.

"Skyracing," said Dominus, "isn't just about flying around a track eight times. There's more to it. There's a physical element to the race that not many account for." She kicked the left side of the platform and the giant boulder shot out and tumbled down the track with the force of an earthquake.

"Six-to-eight racers at a time, eight total laps around what we call the trail."

"The trail, okay, got it," Jacob repeated. Dominus pressed a silver button attached to the end of the center platform. Another holographic object that looked like a turtle's shell jumped out.

"This is the alphashell," said Dominus. "Throughout the race, you receive different objects to slow down or stun your opponent. The alphashell can knock you right off your speeder! Get it?"

"You race around the trail and you get items to knock other skyracers down," Jacob recited. "It reminds me of this video game the arcade back in Griffin had called TrooperKart."

"Arcade?" said Dominus curiously.

"It's nothing," said Jacob, waving her off.

"Now, there's not just the different objects from the fellow racers that you have to dodge. As you saw over there, the center platform puts obstacles in your path every lap. This was the boulder. Sometimes, mini boulders shoot out of the platform. Even though they may be holographic, they can still hit you on the trail, but you can't feel pain due to the safety traps." Dominus pointed out a gray, almost invisible net that hovered just above the ground.

"Boulders, alphashells, eight laps, trail," said Jacob, who was counting with his fingers. "And you have to dodge them and the other racers." Jacob gave Dominus a thumbs-up, and she squinted at the gesture.

"I'm going to show you how to move now," said Dominus. "Line up over there."

She pointed to a spot near the edge of the black trail.

"I'm going to show you what the alphashells feel like," Dominus said. "You need to be prepared for the impact so that you can recover quickly."

She brought the plain skyspeeder over to him. It had splinters poking out of its sides. Jacob noticed that it seemed so old it was almost about to snap in two.

"Duck your head, tuck your arms, and move!" Dominus yelled towards Jacob. She blew the whistle and Jacob jumped off the ground quickly.

He moved with incredible speed as the trail became blurred in the distance.

"Here it comes!" he faintly heard Dominus yell behind him.

At once, the red turtle shell made a buzzing sound like a bee. Jacob ducked, dodging the shell, which was indeed on track to take his head off. He looked back at Dominus for approval. She smiled. Jacob turned his head back towards the trail just before something big smacked him right in the chest.

It felt as though fifty fists had just punched him. His feet felt weightless, and just before his body collided with the ground, the invisible net pressed against his back lightly. The speeder went flying to the ground and broke down the middle.

"Never turn your back on an alphashell, Wesley." Dominus caught the shell as it spun back into her hand like a Frisbee. "These things are relentless, and once they're locked on, they will follow you until they hit you. You'll need to either send it into someone else or make it collide with the track."

"Alright, dodge the boulders, dodge the alphashells. Any other weapons or obstacles that I should be aware of?" Jacob got up from the net, rubbing his head.

"That should sum it up," said Dominus.

"Has anyone ever died in a skyracing match?" Jacob asked, hoping Dominus would laugh at his question.

"Not in an elemental skyrace, but out at the Great Skyrace, there have been freak accidents, aye. Now, you showed some incredible flare in your little race the other day from what I heard, but there's one last thing I will show you."

Dominus spun around and shot forward like a missile being launched from a ship. Jacob put his lux-shades back over his eyes and bolted behind her. She stopped about fifteen feet before the floating holographic finish line.

"I call this," said Dominus, "the twisty flip, and it's a move that will not only save you in a race, but get your opponent to potentially smack into the track. It's only good in certain pockets, and I only recommend using it near the end of the lap. Here's why. You see that bright glow coming into the corner there, right next to the finish line?"

Jacob saw a small crack of light from the center platform falling onto the stands in a straight line.

"It's a blind spot, and it can be exposed when used right. You lead your opponent to that area, and just before crossing the line, perform the twisty flip. They will be blinded; they'll miss you, and could potentially smack right into the side of the trail there. Here, watch this."

Dominus hovered over to the area where the light was. Once she was close enough to the side of the trail, the light momentarily disappeared. "You see, aye," she said. Then she suddenly swung her legs to the side, as if riding an invisible railing, before spiraling into a backflip, revealing the light again. This time, it directly blinded Jacob where he stood.

"Whoa!" Jacob had his mouth open. He knew that it was going to move like this that would get him to the top of his class, and take down the likes of Buster and Probus.

The two spent the next few hours rehearsing the twisty flip over and over until Jacob had mastered it. Additionally, Dominus showed him how to take different angles and turns around the corners of the trails so that he could capitalize on his speed. Several times, she would stop to admire his speed, and then praise him before whistling for him to rehearse again.

"Well, looks like we have a pro skyracer in the making, I'd say," said Dominus, leading Jacob back down to the green patch of grass in the middle of the trail.

"You showed some serious promise out there, Wesley. We just need to keep you focused, and maybe even Ezekial Addams will finally be beaten." She patted Jacob on the back and headed out as the sky was turning dark orange.

Jacob was getting so many lessons that his head was spinning. Between skyracing practice, Electro training several nights a week, and his other elemental courses, the days - or dis, as they called them – had started to fly by. It had been four cycles since he first saw Daren disintegrate into darklights, and spun himself into Pines Station with Nyx. He finally was starting to get the hang of this new world.

Hours later, Gordonclyff Tower was very still and quiet. Jacob still felt a beam of confidence shining through his body in the cold air of the tower. Most of the elementals had already gone out to get late-night trumnits, or to hang around the Center City of Cloudia, but Jacob was strolling by himself after his lessons.

"Yo, Jacob!"

He turned, halfway down the lobby and passing the flirty blonde receptionist, when he saw Colby and Brandy throwing a small object back and forth.

"Hey, what are you two up to?" Jacob curiously asked. "Why aren't you in Center City?"

"Well dude, we were thinking," started Colby, with a nudge to Brandy.

"Yeah, Jacob, we thought we would have a little bit of fun with Buster." Brandy and Colby threw their arms around his shoulders and led him out of Gordonclyff Tower with wide smiles plastered on their faces.

"Buster has been driving us nuts," Brandy continued.

"Yeah, dude, and we know he's getting to you, too." Colby patted Jacob on the chest and gave him a convincing wink.

They stopped outside Gordonclyff Tower. The weather was a little cold, and golden particles began to float down from the sky. Brandy showed Jacob the item that the two had been tossing around earlier. It was a small, round, green ball that unraveled in a few layers.

Jacob, confused, just shrugged his shoulders. "So, what is it, then?"

"Well, to the naked eye, it looks like a plain old onion." Brandy tossed the onion back to Colby after juggling it for a bit.

"What are you going to do with a plain old onion, then?" Jacob asked. Colby laughed and looked at Brandy as if Jacob was speaking a foreign language.

"Well, ya see, bro, it's no plain old onion." Colby took it and unraveled its layers in front of Jacob's eyes.

Brandy took it back from Colby quickly. "It's called a chamenion." She spun it around on her index finger like a basketball.

"And... what is a chamenion, exactly?" Jacob was a bit suspicious.

"Ya ever try food before, and it was so disgusting that your stomach was wrenching for weeks?" Instantly, Colby brought Jacob back to the horrible cooking that made his insides twist at the Kendal Drive Orphanage. Shaking it off and clutching his stomach, he nodded his head grimly.

"A chamenion," Brandy continued, "is a super sour food. Tastes like rotten onions mixed with sour berries. It's gross. Wicked gross." She took a fake bite and did her best imitation of throwing up over the side of the walkway of Gordonclyff Tower.

Colby snorted and grabbed the chamenion back from her. "This little guy was mailed to us from Uncle James. He's a jokester. He always gets us weird little gifts. A chamenion blends in as whatever food item ya want it to be. It could be a delicious Curly Dawg of Cheese." Colby twisted the bottom layer of the chamenion, and at once, the layers of the chamenion straightened up like flower petals. They spun, twisted, and crisscrossed. Then the spinning stopped, and the petals revealed a scrumptious-looking crispy corn dog with dripping Cheesypasta noodles and French fries falling off the sides. Jacob's eyes widened at the Airz Taxi food reappearing before him.

"Or maybe ya fancy a Cinnabutter Jellywich?" Brandy twisted the bottom of the Curly Dog of Cheese. Cheesypasta flung into the air like darts and then spun into a golden crispy chicken sandwich with jelly oozing out of its sides.

"That looks pretty good, huh, bro? But what about a trumnit? Are ya thirsty?" The chamenion spun again and turned into a refreshing trumnit just waiting to be gulped down.

"Whoa! It looks amazing," Jacob said. He heard his stomach gurgle and realized he hadn't eaten in hours. "Is it edible?" He licked his lips at the tasty-looking chamenion.

"It is," Brandy smiled widely. "But trust me, it's nothing ya wanna eat." She grabbed it back and twisted the bottom layer again, sending the chamenion into the fan-like flurry before revealing itself as a candy apple with an oreo creme drizzle.

"Why not? It looks delicious to me." Jacob tried to grab the chamenion, which was quickly snatched out of his reach.

"Even though it appears as a dessert in front of ya, it still holds in its oniony sour taste, man," said Colby.

Brandy handed the surreal item over to Jacob to hold and look at. It was remarkable. It felt like a candied dessert. It even smelled like sweet creme and cookies. It was almost hypnotizing Jacob as he closed his eyes and just stood in a frozen state.

"It looks so real. Smells so real." He turned it over to see the bottom of the shapeshifting onion and noticed a very tiny dot that barely stuck out underneath. It was a knob about the size of a peanut. Jacob looked from the knob back up to the Johnston twins. "What do you plan on doing to Buster?"

"Ever since Uncle James sent us the chamenion, we've been hanging around the Incendiaries and following Buster and Probus throughout Cloudia. It's been tough, dude, I'm not gonna lie, but we were able not to get caught." Colby smiled maniacally over his devious plan.

"We did have a close call once, though, after Movements class, near the skyzing rink. Probus saw Colby's curly hair sticking out of a bush and almost yanked him right out!" Brandy laughed as she shoved Colby's right shoulder.

"Well, we still didn't get caught, did we, B?" Colby shoved her right back. "Anyways, one night, we followed them right into the food court and saw him order one of these oreo candy apples, dude. He was drooling just at the sight of it!" Colby elbowed Jacob as the idea started to seep into his brain.

"That's when it hit us! Send good ol' Buster a gift from his rich daddy an early Donumdans gift. A whole box of 'em!" Brandy tossed the chamenion in the air again.

"He will take one bite and never accept any gifts from anyone ever again, dude!" Colby took it back and twisted the knob again. It turned back into a boring old onion and he stuffed it in Jacob's hands.

"Why are you giving it to me?" Jacob stared blankly at the siblings as a nervous, lightheaded feeling took over.

"Jacob, Jake, Jakey, come on, dude," Colby said with his arm around his neck. "Brandy and I have been pulling pranks forever, but it will feel even better if the Light One is the one to do it."

"Thank you, Uncle James! Thank you for the best prank ever!" Brandy was looking to the sky, waving her hand in a praising fashion.

"Guys, this is a bit much. I mean, I don't even know how to get this over to him, even if I wanted to." Jacob looked down at the chamenion sitting in his hands.

"We will take care of the distraction; you just have to plant it!" Colby shouted. "Just don't forget to wash your hands. It's now or never, dude, come on!" Brandy and Colby grabbed Jacob by his elbows and dashed forward.

Whistles later, Jacob found himself huddled up outside of Sugarhaven, a small sweets-and-treats hut a few blocks away from Gordonclyff Tower. Colby gave a coy wink, and he and Brandy shuffled off into the shop. Jacob looked both ways and around the center to see if anyone was watching. After confirming he was clear, he slowly stepped into the shop after the two.

Sugarhaven was so packed with elementals that the three of them passed by without even being noticed. The shop looked like a futuristic diner, with red velvet stools floating around, and tables upon tables of groups of friends laughing and eating all sorts of scrumptious candied snacks. Each table had a bowl of golden popcorn. The other snacks and ice cream treats were being sent on strings from behind the bar, crashing into the tables and being unhooked by the customers. Jacob had to duck a few times to avoid flying chocolate-covered lollipops.

Small holographic images of gears were on top of the tables, and were labeled "Sounds of Skyrock". As the groups turned the gears, music came from each of the tables. One table to his right was playing "Water and Fire Does it for Me", which was a catchy, fast-paced melody with crunching metal sounds.

It was a very lively atmosphere, and Jacob wished he was there to hang out instead of to sabotage Buster. He noticed that the walls were laced with different candied fruits. There were caramel oranges, hot fudge apples, marshmallow strawberries, and chewy grape gumballs. He took one of these off the wall and bit into it. Fruity juice poured down his throat and left little-exploding sugar crystals behind to chew. As he bit down on them, they formed into blueberry chewing gum.

"Whoa," Jacob whispered.

Then, in the far reach of the room, he noticed Colby pointing to his right. Probus was holding an elemental upside-down in the air by his shoes. Buster was crouched down face-to-face with the victim.

"We can sit here all day hanging around if you want to, flybean. Probus, we have nothing to do, right?"

Probus snickered.

"As I said, I need more money for my favorite treat. You wouldn't want to rob Buster of his favorite treat now, would you?"

Buster suddenly caught sight of the Johnstons. His lips curled into an evil grin.

"Well, what brings the Johnstons down here, hmm?"

Buster nodded towards Probus, who dropped the small elemental. He scurried away, and Buster looked back in Colby's direction.

"You actually need money to hang out here, you know? I heard your family spent all their savings on your teeth. Not sure why. You're still ugly."

Just as Colby's fists clenched, Jacob came around the corner holding the chamenion.

"Whoa! Hold up, Light One." Buster quickly caught Jacob by the tip of his Volans coat. "Where did a nitwit like you get something so tasty?" Buster snatched the Oreo candy apple right from Jacob's hands.

"We were just discussing your pal Colby here," Buster said to Jacob. "Just talking about his disgusting face, and then a dingus like you strolls on by." Buster stared madly at the chamenion like a crazed scientist for a brief moment. Then, he took a huge bite. Cookie crumbs rolled off the side of his face as he licked the remaining pieces. "Thanks for the snack, Wesley! It looks like you are bound to be a hero, after all, a hero of my hunger..."

Buster's head jerked forward as a sickening sensation took over his body. Beads of sweat started to pour from his forehead.

Colby and Brandy staggered a bit, and had to hold onto each other for balance, they were laughing so hard. Probus went to catch Buster, who almost fell forward.

"What's the matter, Buster? The candy go sour?" Colby asked with tremendous confidence.

"What did you put in this, Wes..."

Buster could barely get out the words before vomit jumped out of his mouth like water from a firehose. Probus' eyes widened, and he couldn't take it either, as the sight of the vomit caused him to throw up his lunch, too. His bulging muscles were no use for the slippery ground now. He tried to catch part of the table, but it was too late. Probus blundered forward, arms outstretched like a zombie's. He tumbled down like a ton of bricks and fell to the ground with a thump.

Meanwhile, Buster couldn't stop throwing up in the same spot. The rest of the elementals, completely disgusted at sight, started spilling out of Sugarhaven as fast as they could. Probus and Buster were both sliding around in their own vomit like penguins, unable to control themselves.

"Remember that the next time ya try to take someone's food!"

Brandy laughed. The chamenion had turned back to its original form lying on the ground.

"Alright, let's get outta here!" Colby grabbed the chamenion and the three headed out of Sugarhaven with delight. Following the crowd, Colby dumped the chamenion in a nearby trashcan that was floating around. The group landed outside the shop on the stone walkway and erupted into laughter.

"Dude, that was wicked awesome!" Colby patted Jacob on the back. "Did ya see the look on his face when he realized something was wrong?"

"It was priceless! Oh, I'll never be able to get the image of Probus falling down like a big baby outta my head." Brandy grabbed hold of Jacob's shoulder.

"That was pretty cool," Jacob said, with a big smile on his face. "It felt good to get revenge on a bully like Buster finally."

The trio then headed off into the distance, skip-skyzing through Center City before they could be caught at the scene of the crime.

The week went by, and lessons with Dominus took up the forefront of his mind, along with the pranks that the Johnstons had included him in, the sparkling grailum, and the impending doom that Follcane had promised would fall upon Cloudia. Still, Jacob could not stop himself from dwelling on his skyracing lessons with Dominus. It was the most exciting training he was getting, and he was enjoying it more than the slow-paced Electro lessons with Athene. He wished very much that he could practice every day if possible, but it was only limited to once a week.

"Again, Wesley!" A couple of weeks after his initial training, Jacob was found circling the skyracing trail of Gordonclyff Tower, trying to keep up with Dominus weaving through the black track. He had just been coached, yet again, to chase her through the trail with two alphashells flying at their backs. Fleeing these alphashells was even harder than fleeing Tommy's wedgies back at the orphanage.

Jacob was finally able to catch up to Dominus after a spinning side-flip on the tail end of the trail, right near the center platform.

"Got you!" he screamed. Dominus turned to look at him, and her eyes widened. Quickly turning, the alphashell smacked Jacob right in the gut like a solid brick. After hitting the safety net below, Dominus picked him up by his hand.

"Aye, the last move there," said Dominus. "What was that?"

"I don't know," said Jacob, getting wearily to his feet after the fall. He was finding it increasingly difficult to stay focused on both the trail and racing fast while still accounting for the homing-missile alphashells and the holographic obstacles from the center. "You mean the one where I flipped over you in the quickest flash you had ever seen?" Jacob confidently asked.

"No," said Dominus softly. "I mean when you blurted out 'Got you!' after you had finally caught up to me." Dominus's eyes quickly turned to beads of disappointment.

"Isn't that good?" Jacob asked.

Dominus shifted her eyes from Jacob and towards the center marble platform. She hopped off her skyspeeder and twisted it in her hands with her head down. "How do you expect to be the hero while you're caught up in your own head?" Dominus asked.

"I was just trying to..." Jacob began, looking everywhere but at Dominus. "Just trying to win, you know?"

"Aye, to win," repeated Dominus. There was a pause during which Jacob stared at the alphashell squirming under Dominus's right arm. It was trying to wiggle free and smack Jacob in the chest again. "You do know why you are here, don't you Jacob Wesley?" Dominus asked, in a low, disappointed voice. "You do know why I am giving up my after-hours for this unwarranted lesson?"

"Yes," said Jacob stiffly.

"Then remind me, aye, why are we here, Wesley?"

"So that I can learn skyracing," said Jacob, now glaring at the fresh turf under his feet.

"Correct, Wesley, and, short as you may be..." Jacob looked back at Dominus now, annoyed. "I wouldn't have thought you'd be doing this well only after a few short weeks of training. You have the gift; you move quick, aye, but you are so caught up in winning that you are taking your eyes off the race. Were you fixated on the finish line or on beating me?"

"The finish line," lied Jacob.

"Perhaps," said Dominus, her red mohawk looking as if it might pierce through Jacob's soul. "Perhaps you'd enjoy beating Buster Nalum more than you'd enjoy winning the skyracing match? Does it make you more of a hero if you beat Nalum? If you beat Follcane?"

"No, it doesn't," said Jacob, his jaw locking a bit tighter and his fingers clenched into a fist.

"That's not why you are here, Jacob Wesley," said Dominus firmly. "You are here to save Cloudia. You are here to win the race, and it far outweighs any personal battles that you have with either of your enemies."

Jacob released the surprisingly strong grip on his fist. He knew she was right. He was finally really good at something, and he was getting the hang of this new world, but he was letting it all go to his head. It had become more important to put someone down than to excel at something.

Dominus' expression turned from anger to satisfaction as she saw Jacob's realization. "Yes, Jacob," she said, her eyes soft now. "You will be the Light One, but for now, you are stuck here with me. Aye, now if your ego can handle it, let's start again…"

Dominus kicked off the ground aboard her skyspeeder. She waved over in his direction and flung the alphashell from beneath her arm. "Aye, hover!"

Jacob lunged forward, swooping through the holographic boulder obstacles that now poured from the center platform. He was racing, his face frozen in concentration, each boulder missing him by inches. He could barely make out the tail of red light from behind Dominus's quick skyspeeder. He stopped looking at her and the boulders became bigger and brighter, growing into giant silhouettes. Dominus' tail became fainter, and in that, moment Jacob could see so clearly. What would usually be blurred visions of light and pieces of the trail now seemed to sweep past his face in slow-motion.

Near the edge of his right side, a swiveling shell came hurtling in his direction. He looked to try and see Dominus, but her tail of red light could not be found. Jacob hesitated, caught in a trance-like state as the shell was spinning inevitably towards his chest.

"LOOK OUT!" Dominus shouted from a distance. Jacob saw a second alphashell spiraling towards him. The force of the wind pushed him a few paces back. Jacob turned pale. Then he closed his eyes, relaxed his muscles, and exhaled a deep breath. His Volans coat was heating up. It felt like his arms were on fire, but it felt good. The color returned to his face as he opened his eyes quickly. In one move, Jacob backflipped in the air, smacking the first alphashell dead on, sending a tidal wave of wind crashing behind it. The alphashell went jetting in the opposite direction. It smacked a corner of the arching walls with a thunderous impact before falling to the ground.

The second shell was now behind Jacob and zeroing in on him. He twisted his skyspeeder in a spin with his arms folded in a relaxed pose. The edge of his skyspeeder cracked the shell like a baseball bat hitting a home run.

"Magnificent!" screamed Dominus at the other end of the track. "Well, Wesley… that was sensational…" Dominus's upper lip curled into a smirk. "I don't know if your direction was to take the fight to the alphashells themselves… but that was most effective…" Then, with a similar backflip, she shot back into the air like a missile and was off.

Jacob didn't say a word; he felt that his actions spoke louder than any word he could say. He was confident that he had just gained a clarity that he had never experienced before, and now, he could focus solely on winning. He felt a thrill of excitement and confidence at the same time.

Jacob kicked off the ground with his skyspeeder too, weaving in and out of the holoboulders again. This time, he patted some of them as they passed by, giving them dismissive touches as if they did not faze him at all. He was hurling along the trails toward Dominus' red flash, past the stone arches of the stadium, past the obstacles rolling by him. The beautiful black track was curling behind his speed; he was moving so fast that he was feeling one with the track.

He was feet from Dominus, and he could see her lunge forward with her arms angled in. He swiveled back and forth before finally deciding to ignore her. His eyes grew wide and he zeroed in on the edge of the track in front of him. The flash of red light was missing, and he lunged.

"WESLEY!"

Jacob came to a halt. He was frozen in mid-air as his semi-blurred vision returned to normal.

"Aye, you did it!" said Dominus, circling him and applauding loudly.

# 15

# DONUMDANS

The Augustum Cycle had arrived, which was the eighth cycle in Cloudia's yer. Soft white clouds clustered around the city and buildings appeared as though they had marshmallows melting on top of them. The sky was an eggshell color. Gold snowflakes of light fell downward. Bron said it was because they were so close to the sky, and when it reached Augustum, the light froze into strands of gold onto the ground.

The twenty-first of Augustum was quickly approaching, and that meant Jacob's first celebration of Donumdans. With all the recent events, Jacob would have forgotten about the highly-anticipated holiday, but Albert made it a point to count down the days with a song every morning.

"Which do I get, which do I get, cloud in my pocket, mom, and dad, don't you forget!"

Colby and Brandy would chime in every now and then. Anna joined in as well, but Jacob felt out of place.

"One cloud, two clouds, six for all! What will I get this yer? Maybe a skyball?"

He wasn't familiar with any of the routines or traditional songs. He hummed along with his friends so that he wouldn't feel so out of place.

Movements class was a bit different. The walls were lined with lights, and the paint had been changed to gold and blue. For Donumdans, the Cloudians got to wear costumes, and it was a tradition to dress like someone else. Albert was wearing a Volans coat that looked like Athene's, and he had a thin black line drawn under his nose to resemble Athene's mustache. Athene didn't care for the outfit.

Colby and Brandy dressed like one another by switching Volans coats and colors. They even slicked and dyed their hair to match. It was hard to tell them apart.

Anna dressed up like Darlene Flight. She wore rosy red gloves and orange lux-shades.

Buster mocked Jacob with his lack of a costume, and hummed to a Donumdans tune of his own: "Lame one, lame two, six lames for the Light One, someone takes this dingbat to High Corner."

Jacob didn't find it funny, but the rest of the Incendiary crew giggled behind Buster.

Besides the PPA decorations of parcels, lights, and blue clouds covering the building, most of Cloudia was decorated with large bushy leaves and twigs, with what looked like gift-wrapping paper on the roofs.

Magistra Dayan had taken names for Airz Taxi passes and confirmed who would travel home since they'd be getting a break from their classes. Jacob didn't receive a ticket, and despite what Magistra Dayan thought, he was delighted not to be traveling home. Ms. Larrier would scoff at giving any gifts, and probably would have Smaltz leave presents of smelly coal in his clouds.

Albert was staying too because his father and mother were called away to H-Twenty to collect more aquatic samples which were thought to sustain the darklights' light for even longer.

Following Movements, they found a large group of elementals huddling around the middle of the lobby outside of Gordonclyff tower. Magistra Dayan outstretched her arms and handed out large, silver-trimmed papers.

"Move it, Loser Face!" came Buster's raspy shriek from behind them as he nudged through. After receiving his silver pass, he turned towards Jacob and the group with arrogance. "No point to you being here, Albert. We know daddy is collecting darklight feces and mommy is giving smelly baths to old people. Maybe Probus will let you clean his bottom for your sixth gift this yer."

Albert started to go after Buster, but Jacob jumped in front of him to prevent a fight. Since Probus was lingering in the background, Jacob thought it would be best to avoid a brawl in front of Magistra Dayan.

"Not worth it, Al, he's a joke anyway." Jacob pushed Albert forward to avoid Buster. Buster shoved his way into the crowd and stretched his arm forward for his Airz Taxi pass. Jacob and Albert took the next platform back down into the Gordonclyff Tower Lobby.

"He's lucky," said Albert, flushed red and still fuming over Buster's comments. "You held me back from delivering a swipe-stomp combo to his fat neck!"

"Yeah, Buster and Probus have it coming," said Jacob. "Losing in a skyrace is the least of their worries."

"Cheer up, ta ta, Donumdans is right around the corner." An overly excited Nyx skyze-skated right behind them, wearing the goofiest of smiles. "Speaking of which, here's your first cloud!" Nyx held out two tiny green objects that looked like eggs from the grocery store.

"Donumdans gifts already?" Albert jumped for joy.

"Never too early to celebrate, hee-hee! Press them in the center," Nyx giggled.

Albert and Jacob grabbed the objects and quickly pressed them. The objects let out a buzzing sound, and bright sparks spiraled into the air like mini fireworks before growing a few inches bigger. The objects cracked open, and out popped two green bracelets with silver thread spiraling around them.

"Whoa! Jacob, these are amplets." While Albert was distracted from the gifts, the trio of Brandy, Colby, and Anna had just run up behind them.

"Well, try it on Jake," Colby said.

Jacob lifted the bracelet and put it on. Instantly, a holographic image of numbers started rotating around like the hands of a clock. The numbers fell upon 783, and the group stood silent. "So, it's kind of like a scale, then?" Jacob asked while admiring the ampere reading bracelet.

"You have even more amperes now. Training with Athene is paying off, tee-hee!" Nyx was clapping and jumping up and down. Jacob clicked off the amplet.

"Whoa, Jake! Maybe it's broken." Colby patted him on the back.

"You're just jealous, Colby. Your amperes just don't match up to the Light One's." Anna inched forward and grabbed Jacob's arm, making his cheeks turn from pasty white to rosy red.

"I'm only at 162. Rats." Albert clicked off his amplet in disappointment.

"Don't worry Al, that's much better than you were at the elemental selection, remember?" Jacob was optimistic, and it helped, as a smile returned to Albert's face.

"Well, it's the first gift of six to come, hee-hee," said Nyx, giggling uncontrollably. "And there's a special one yet to be given, ta ta!" Nyx disappeared and left the group in a state of wonder.

"Well, that was odd." Jacob scratched his head.

"What do ya think the special gift might be, Jake?" Colby asked.

"Maybe it's an upgrade to your skyspeeder!" Albert yelled as he jumped into a skyracing stance.

"Maybe it's a lifetime supply of trumnits," Brandy said, as she gulped down the one she had in her hands. "I could always use some more, too, if ya get sick of 'em."

For the rest of the evening, the group discussed the unique gift and the grailum they had been spotting in several odd places. The following day, when Jacob arose, he did indeed receive trumnits from Bron, but nothing to the tune of a lifetime supply. Brandy was disappointed to learn there were only five.

At the docking port, Jacob and Albert saw their friends off as they boarded the large Airz Taxi. "You have to let me know what your gift is, Jake!" Colby yelled as he went through the invisible bubble pocket.

"Yeah, it better be a wicked awesome one! If there are more trumnits, save 'em for me, dude!" Brandy followed.

"Al, send me a holo-message with what it is!" Anna screamed as she waved from one of the inside pockets.

Throughout Donumdans, Albert and Jacob had a blast. From ice puff throwing contests to pranking Mr. Natansis and filling their bellies up with as many different Halwin's shakes as they could, they had almost forgotten about the special gift that Nyx had promised them.

Seran had let Albert stay with Jacob at the PPA in his room. Bron was sent on a top-secret mission, so his bed was available.

On the fourth night, the two went to town for sweet mellow creams, pudding dumpling pops, orange cara-corn treats, and tall, sticky licorice called Cloudsuckers that got stuck on their tongue when they tried to eat them in one bite.

The two stayed up real late, ate all of the sweets, and practiced Movements strikes. Jacob taught Albert a double-swipe, a round-stomp, and a kick-up move, which Albert practiced until he mastered it. They swore they were masters of the art, especially Albert, who was able to successfully dismount the pillow off the chair post in the room an astounding eight times.

On the final day of Donumdans, Jacob awoke very early to find a few gifts wrapped at the edge of his bed.

"Diddy Donumdans, Jacob." Albert stretched and yawned very loudly.

"Diddy Donumdans?" Jacob looked puzzled.

"Yeah, it's like, 'Welcome to Donumdans!' Dad always used to say it on the final day."

"Well, Diddy Donumdans to you, too, Al."

Jacob got out of bed and leaned over his pile of gifts. Next, to him, Albert had quite a few that were mailed to him from his parents. Jacob's top gift was wrapped in beautiful blue tinsel and was stamped with the PPA's symbol. A paper tacked to it read "From Dominus." Inside were a bunch of holodisks which read, "Great Skyrace Collection."

The next package was a bit bigger. This one was from Magistra Dayan. It was a green gadget with a small button on the bottom. When Jacob pressed it, two holo figures popped up and shouted Electro sayings while they released fake darklights into the air and all around. The object reminded Jacob of the snow globes back in Griffin.

"Whoa," said Albert, as he peeked over Jacob's shoulder. "Wicked awesome, Jake! You got a Diashow! They're super rare."

"Really?" Jacob replied, and hit the button to see how they used their energy again. The two cloaked figures jumped in the air and shot yellow beams at each other. "What did you get over there, Al?" Jacob inched closer to Albert to take a look himself.

Albert held a stone with a crystal blue streak and another orange rock with a crystalized darklight trapped inside. "They're from my parents," Albert said, holding up the stone. "This one's from H Twenty, from my Dad. He loves sending me the rocks and stones from that world because it's covered in water. It's very rare to come across something solid."

"That's cool. Looks great, Al!"

Albert tossed it to Jacob to play around with. "Hey, there's a note under the Diashow at the bottom of your pile, Jake." Albert pointed at a crinkled-up parchment with a large red blob at the top.

Jacob opened up the parchment, which read, "There's one more gift for you. It's too important to just leave by your bedside. I'll see you soon." The signature at the bottom was S.K.

"Do you think that's from…" Albert jumped up in excitement. "It's Seran. It has to be!"

Before Jacob could open his mouth, Nyx burst into the room. "Hey lads, tee-hee, nice gifts! Let's get some grub, though!" Nyx skyze-skated out of the room, and the two followed as they levitated barely above the floor.

In the center of the PPA, surrounded by glass on all sides, were another ten individuals wearing PPA Volans coats and tall gold hats with blue trim.

"Here, take a Donumdans top," a nearby PPA member nudged Jacob. He leaned over and handed Jacob one of the other Donumdans hats so that he could fit in.

It was one of the most special and fun dinners that Jacob had ever been part of. Juicy butter-chili sandwiches and hundreds of trumnits materialized and floated above the table. Brandy would have been jealous.

At the end of the dinner, two of the PPA members led the group in a traditional dance where they stretched their arms out and stood on their tiptoes while chanting, "Diddy dum Donumdans, dum diddy, dum diddy." Despite looking ridiculous, Jacob appreciated the tradition and the togetherness that he felt during the holiday. It felt good. Different, but good. This was the first holiday he had ever experienced where he felt welcomed.

In the background, Seran had his silvery lux-shades over the top of his head, and his lips were curling together into a smile as Nyx performed a ceremonial silly skyzing dance of his creation. More and more trumnits followed, and the sticky cara-taffy was the hit of the night.

After the miraculous feast that had ensued, Jacob had pockets full of choco-crunchy sticks and handfuls of gummy star sweets. The day had been one of the best in his life. Even if it wasn't something, he was used to, finally celebrating a holiday the right way brought incredible glee to his face.

But on his way towards the bathroom, a hand cupped over his mouth out of nowhere.

Jacob's eyes shot open like two white bullets speeding out of a shotgun. Seran was standing over him with his index finger from his other hand hovering tightly to his mouth. He then waved Jacob on, who cautiously followed, anticipating the discovery of his final gift. The two quickly skyzed past the Hall of Entry, and into a third hall that glistened in the darkness. Small green lights fluttered in the air. Jacob couldn't make out what they were. Seran led them with a little ball of light that he emitted from his left hand. After several sharp turns and fast-paced, disorienting movement, Jacob had utterly lost his sense of direction.

Seran came to a halt after the whirlwind of their late-night adventure. A skinny brown door which could barely fit a broom mysteriously appeared in front of them. Seran raised his right arm, rolled up his Volans sleeve, and Jacob could hear him mumble under his breath, "Tractum Tu Separate." The door stretched wider and wider. Jacob was holding his breath in amazement. Seran leads Jacob through the darkness of the door and into a room.

It took a few moments for Jacob to realize where he was. It looked like an old rusty museum floor. Cream-colored sheets covered different statue-sized objects, and piles of ancient artifacts were mounted on top of pillars. Red velvet ropes laid on the ground, covered in dust.

Seran left Jacob's side and headed towards the middle of the room, where a white cloth clung to a gumball machine-sized object. Jacob followed Seran closer to the mysterious object. Seran threw off the sheet, and after the dust had scattered away, a beautiful crystal case on top of a bronze peg was revealed.

"I believe this looks familiar to you, Jacob," Seran said, as he dusted off his hands on his Volans coat. He waved Jacob over to the case. Atop the case was a passage written in letters that Jacob couldn't understand.

"These symbols are from the darklights' language. I believe Athene told you about it. 'Hicc Mandeciun hoad prionde gamme de salvotorias.'" Jacob remained intrigued as Seran spoke.

"What's it mean?" Jacob curiously traced the symbols with his finger.

"'Here lies the Jewel of Futura.'" Seran's eyes were closed in deep thought and focus.

Jacob's heart beat faster and faster as he anticipated the meaning of the object. He leaned in closer to the beautiful case, but could not see anything. Suddenly, a dark charcoal fog swirled about inside the case. Seran winked and glided his hand from side to side atop the case, then wiggled each of his fingers. As the fog settled, Jacob gulped. His heart continued to speed up, beating at incredible speeds. He wanted to scream but thought better of it with Seran inches away. The emerald green jewel with the darklight symbol appeared before his eyes. A black chain was tethered to it.

"You remember the emblem; I take it?" Seran picked up the jewel and handed it over to Jacob. Jacob nodded his head and gulped again.

"This belongs to you, Jacob. It always has and always will. Your final gift of Donumdans is the Jewel of Futura."

Cautiously, Jacob placed the emblem slowly over his skinny neck and onto his chest. The jewel settled in the middle of his chest and clung to him like a shard of metal to a magnet. Immediately, a rush of blood filled his body, and what felt like insects crawled through his veins and into his throat. He let out a bloodcurdling scream, and light powered through in his body. He could barely make out the voice that called to him. It sounded as though he was underwater.

"Control it, Jacob. Use your focus. Focus on the light inside of you." Jacob not only felt like he was going to die, but also like his muscles and organs were going to explode right out of his body.

"Feel it rise through you. Accept its power. Accept its power, Jacob." As Seran spoke, Jacob did his best to follow the light and harness it inside. He tried to remember what Athene had worked on with him.

Seran's voice became clearer and more transparent. It was working; Jacob controlled the power inside of him. His vision came back slowly, and he could see in front of him again. Everything had a golden tint, including Seran, and all sorts of sparkling strands surrounded Seran and the other objects in the room. Jacob could even see Seran's heart beating inside of him. It was like Jacob's eyes performed an X-Ray. Golden arches covered the room, and as Jacob looked down towards his chest, a giant green light shot out from him.

"How does it feel, Light One?" Seran smiled from ear to ear, both of his eyes fixated on Jacob.

"It's like nothing I've ever felt in my life. It's unique, it's beautiful, and I see gold everywhere. I can see through your body. I can almost, almost…"

"Almost what?"

"I think I see your amperes. There's little gold…" Before Jacob could finish, his vision turned black. He had fainted from the energy. It was too much for him.

When he came to, and his eyes opened, the gold and the amperes had disappeared from his vision. Seran sat in a dusty leather chair across from him. He waved in Jacob's direction.

He felt an incredible headache take over, and he could feel a large lump on the back of his skull.

"So… how does it feel?"

All Jacob could feel was a giant hammer that pounded the back of his head. "Well, it feels like my head's killing me right now," Jacob returned.

"You bumped your head after you fainted on that pile of armor over there," said Seran. Jacob noticed that the emblem was gone from his chest. "So," said Seran, standing up from the chair and kneeling beside Jacob. "You have now felt the true power of the Jewel of Futura."

"Nyx showed me something similar back in Griffin, and I felt like I was going to die." Jacob tried to balance himself, as he was still a little dizzy from his fall.

"The power of the Light One is unique, Jacob, and no one can fathom what its true energy could be like," Seran continued.

"What is it, exactly? It's unlike any necklace I've ever seen." Jacob rubbed the lump on the back of his head.

"It's not an ordinary necklace, Jacob. It's a jewel from the land of Futura, home of the darklights. When they were being depleted of their resources, their chief took all their remaining amperes and forged it inside one of their volcanoes."

"Has anyone else tried it on before?" Jacob asked.

"Many have tried, and many have fallen because of its great power. It's too much for a normal Cloudian. Only someone with many amperes could bear such a power." Seran held the jewel in the palm of his hand.

"I don't follow, Seran, I mean, sir."

Seran chuckled at Jacob. "You were born with an increased amount of amperes. Your parents created you under unique circumstances. Circumstances that you aren't ready to hear just yet, but know that this gave you a great amount of potential." Jacob lowered his head. Seran's words just rolled off him. Jacob's mind was still fixated on his history. "In due time, you will learn everything about your history. For now, the history of your final gift shall suffice."

After Seran finished, Jacob slowly asked, "What makes me any different?"

Seran smiled again and continued. "Your birthright… its power is only an enhancer, not true power itself. Many have searched for its origins and tried to recreate it, and have fallen and failed. Only one has gotten close. Unfortunately, you are not the only one who can control it. Silas Follcane has the right amount of amperes to bear the emblem too, and I fear that he seeks it."

Jacob stared at him. He grew nervous at the sound of Silas' name. "Who will protect it from him?"

"You will, Jacob. It has always belonged to you, but now you get to hold onto it. The emblem will remain in its case though, Jacob, and I ask that you do not try to figure out how to remove it. I trust you with its security, and it must remain far out of Follcane's reach. If he were to have it in his possession, then we would stand no chance."

Seran helped Jacob up, and the two turned to head out of the room.

"Uh, sir, I mean, Seran, have you ever tried it on?"

Seran stopped in his tracks and turned towards Jacob, now no longer smiling. "Once…"

He then continued out of the room, a curious Jacob following behind.

Donumdans was finally over, and Jacob's final gift was the most important one of all. Albert and Anna sent holo messages to each other about the news. Jacob turned over in his bed and pondered what had happened to Seran. At least, he thought, it didn't kill him.

Maybe he shouldn't have asked.

# 16

## SKY SPIES

Seran left quite an impression on Jacob when he asked him to guard the Jewel of Futura, and for the time being, the jewel stayed tucked away in the crystal case under the floorboards in Jacob's room. Jacob hoped to forget about the amazing sensations he felt when he wore the emblem, but he couldn't. He started to have visions of himself floating above the ground with his arms stretched out with a yellow flash bursting from his chest.

"Snap out of it, Jake! Ya look hypnotized," said Colby.

It was lunchtime, and Jacob had been daydreaming. Anna, who had been biting her nails ever since she received Albert's holo-message, was desperate to hear what was going on. However, Jacob could see the look of disappointment begin to set in once she realized there were no answers in sight.

"Maybe if you tell us, the visions will go away?" Anna said, batting her eyes. Jacob chose not to respond.

After Donumdans had ended, the group was sent back into rigorous and intensive training. Each elemental line got even more exposure to their specific training. Jacob had it the roughest of them all, only because Electro was more challenging to grasp at his age.

Athene was on top of the Electros that day. Storms took over, and the crack of lightning could be heard pushing through the clouds, but nothing was louder than the energy blasts that the Electros emitted.

Some of the Electros had to take breaks because the constant routine of trying to control the energy waves was exhausting them. Several elementals became very ill and had to excuse themselves from training.

Then, during one particularly grueling training session, Athene had the Electros split into teams of two. He had just let the darklights out of their jars who were now stuck to each elemental's right arm. Jacob, who was sweating puddles, turned his attention to his partner across the room: Horace Elm, a sixteen-yer-old with frosted blue hair. The current exercise was to try and deflect their opponents' light blasts.

"Right side, yell Digitus Flenta as you extend your index finger!" Athene switched over to the left side next, and raised his arm. "Left side, try to block by crossing your arms in front of your face and yelling Ne, ne!"

Jacob stood as Horace charged at him. "Ne, ne!" he called out, and successfully defended the attack. The light bounced off Jacob's forearm like a pinball before disintegrating into nothingness. "I did it," Jacob whispered to himself.

"Nice work, Mr. Wesley." Athene nodded his head reverently in Jacob's direction. "Remember: defense is just as important as your attack. Counterattacks will be your best friend if you can master the art of repelling your opponent's energy." Despite the grueling hours of training, Jacob enjoyed learning everything that Athene threw at them. "Use your focus. Don't let your mind slip. Feel the energy building within you." Athene was correcting a few of the other elementals' stance to make them more proper. "Now, switch!"

The elementals swapped, and it was Jacob's turn to be on the offense. A smile started to creep over his lips. He raised his right hand, gripping his wrist with his left hand. The two were interlocked in a staring competition, prepared to duel. Jacob had his arm stretched out, ready to fire, and Horace was still as a statue with both arms tucked tightly to his sides.

"Let's see what you got, Jacob!" Horace shouted as he began to raise his arms over his face. The darklights attached to Jacob's right arm sending jolts of electricity through his veins. His lux-bands wiggled intensely and sent a thousand tiny vibrations from his fingertips to his shoulder.

"Digitus…" Jacob waited patiently to see Horace's next move.

"Ne, ne!" Horace reacted too soon.

"…Flenta!" Jacob found his opportunity and the light sprung from the tip of his index finger like a firework, smacking Horace right on the shoulder. The attack made Horace spin out of control before he collapsed and fell to the ground.

Horace got to his feet slowly, dusting his shoulders off on the way up. Athene whipped his head around to face Jacob, who lowered his finger, nervous that he did something wrong. Athene rushed over to where Jacob stood. He scanned Horace up and down with his lux-shades. Athene didn't look pleased.

"I thought I was supposed-" Jacob began.

"You correctly emitted the Digitus Flenta blast, but your aim was off. Concentrate on the chest or inner shoulder blade, not the outside of the shoulder." Athene turned away paced the other way.

Jacob was relieved that he wasn't in trouble, but he also wanted to confirm that he was performing the blast correctly. *Follcane won't hesitate to capitalize on poor aim, he* thought. For the rest of the class,

Jacob focused on executing the Digitus Flenta blast, coming very close to the chest, but he still needed a lot of work to perfect it.

During lunchtime, Jacob found Albert, Anna, and both Johnston siblings huddled together near a window playing a game of Guess That Holo. Guess that Holo was a game where four players took turns pressing a button on what's called a holoboard, which showed famous Cloudians, and the players had to guess who they were. Each correct guess was worth one point, and the player with the most points at the end of the game won.

As Jacob approached, it was Albert's turn. A hologram appeared of a skyzing man dressed in a funny white Volans coat with curly hair poking out of his hat.

"Oooh, that's tricky," Albert said, as he twirled his finger through an imaginary beard under his chin.

"Tricky?" Colby replied. "I think we all know who that is."

"Shut it, Colbs, let him guess!" Brandy yelled. She was only down a few points.

"Timer's down to five ticks," Anna said.

"Lars Hane?" Albert sat back with a smirk. Anna shook her head, and the Johnston siblings laughed very loudly.

"Al, it's obviously Nyx," Colby said. The yellow light at the bottom of the holoboard turned green, and the laughter turned to silence.

"Your turn, I believe, Brandy." Albert had his arms folded and was grinning boastfully at Jacob.

"Who's winning?" Jacob asked after he took a seat next to Anna.

"Naturally, Al is, with thirteen points, but Brandy is close with ten," Anna replied.

"How was that not Nyx?!" Colby shouted.

"Lars Hane is his great uncle, and the difference is his hair, which is two inches shorter than Nyx's, and his Volans coat is pure white."

"Yaw unreal, Al," Brandy said, shaking her head in disappointment.

Jacob laughed but was quickly shushed by Brandy. Brandy pressed the silver button on the holoboard and out popped a woman with green flowering spikes growing out of the top of her hat. "This has gotta be Rachel Stevens." A bead of sweat trickled down Brandy's forehead, and a red light came from the bottom of the holoboard as she guessed incorrectly. "Come on, man!" Brandy buried her face in her hands in frustration. "How did I get some green-haired chick? No one knows who that is."

"Brandy, it's Gwendelin Hampshire," Colby chimed in. "The first lady to join Metallum. You should know that, sis."

"How'd Electro training go, Jake?" Anna asked as she shifted the group's attention to Jacob. He filled them in on the difficult Digitus Flenta blast he couldn't master, and the blocking techniques that Athene showed the team.

"You say Ne, ne, too?" Colby asked.

"That's our blocking phrase," Brandy followed.

"It's a universal elemental phrase used to block," Albert explained. "There are many universal phrases, like-"

"Well, looks like ya just had to confirm it, Mr. Know-It-All," Brandy blurted out in frustration.

"Hey, Jacob!" The group looked up to see Brian's purple dreadlocks clumsily bobbing over in their direction. As he began to wave, a giant pale and hairy leg shot out in front of him.

Brian stumbled and then fell forward, and would have faceplanted on the ground if it wasn't for Jacob catching his arm on the way down.

Buster Nalum laughed as Probus retracted his leg from in front of the table.

"Not funny, Buster. Keep your legs to yourself or else," Anna snapped.

"Or else what, blondie, huh? You gonna have your boyfriend use some of his hero magic?" Jacob grew a sneer as Buster and Probus laughed. Apparently, Buster was all the better after his chamenion experience. "Don't forget I play with fire, Light One. You better watch your back on the track tomorrow; could be a bit smoky around your speeder." Buster and Probus shoved their way through the group and headed back down a platform to the lobby.

"Are you okay, Brian?" Anna helped Brian up. He moved his dreads behind his head.

"Yeah, Jacob caught me." He turned his attention to Jacob, whose teeth were grinding so hard that they would have snapped out of his mouth if Albert didn't calm him down. "You are the Light One! You just saved me!" Brian smiled from ear to ear.

"I'm getting sick of Buster and his antics," Brandy said, clenching her fists.

"You'd think the chamenion would have taught him a lesson," said Colby.

"Think we ought to go to Magistra Dayan?" Anna asked.

"No, then he will make up some dumb excuse that Brian shoved him first." Colby was making a fist too.

Brian looked down, thinking he was the laughingstock of the lunchroom.

"Hey don't fret," Jacob said. "Buster's just mad that he's stuck trying to control fire, and he can't even ignite his skyspeeder to win a skyrace." Jacob patted Brian on the back, and it seemed to work, as a smile started to inch up his cheeks again.

"Thanks, Jake. So, are you ready for the trials or what? I can't wait to see what you're capable of."

Jacob looked a bit flustered, and this time, Buster had nothing to do with it.

"Honestly, I completely forgot about it," Jacob said. "I didn't get any more time on the trails this week with Dominus."

The next morning, in Movements, Jacob was paired with Albert. While he performed a triple-swipe-twist against Albert, they discussed the power of the emblem and what it might help Jacob do. Not until Albert mentioned being able to fly around Cloudia did Jacob remember the upcoming skyrace trials.

"I have to focus on the match first," he told Albert, after ducking his triple-swipe-twist. "The odds are against me big time. If I can pull off second place, I'll be happy."

"Second place? No. The Light One gets first, always," Albert said after he connected with a twist and sent Jacob buckling to the ground. Jacob couldn't help but applaud Albert's efforts. Athene was impressed with Albert as well; nodding in his direction as he passed the two. They went back to focusing on their moves the rest of the training session instead of discussing the Jewel of Futura.

After class, Jacob headed off. "Going to clear my head for a bit guys. I'll catch you later."

Jacob went up the bronze platform and onto the track. Maybe if he saw the field, it would help calm him down. After he stepped off the platform, he moved through the silver tunnel that lead out to the track. He didn't make it far before someone leaning against the wall caught his eye. The person had polished the bottom of a sleek speeder. The skyspeeder had green and silver stripes on each side, with a dark symbol of the prophecy on the top. Emerald green spikes were painted on the ends of the board.

Dominus Fugam turned her head to face Jacob. "Dreading the race, lad?" She smiled. Jacob nodded and scratched his head. The two had built a much better rapport since the vomit incident on the first day of class. "Aye, don't fear it. Nerves are good. They make you become a true skyracer." Dominus' words soothed Jacob's fears for the moment.

"That board looks cool, and it's got the prophecy emblem on it." Jacob was looking the speeder up and down. On the bottom of the speeder was a number 11 and the word AIR.

"You like it then; I take it." Dominus twisted the speeder in her hands before giving it over to Jacob. "It's yours. Seran dropped by to give it to you, but you were out with your lads. I figured I'd polish it up for you before the big race."

Dominus winked, and Jacob, overflowing with joy, grabbed the speeder and blasted off, flying around the track and doing spirals like never before. He felt like he was flying. The speeder moved so nimbly that he barely had to think about it.

Later in the evening, Jacob found his friends and showed off his new skyracing board.

"An AIR Eleven?!" Colby yelled when he spotted the number.

"No way! How'd ya score that?!" Brandy shoved her way forward and picked up the speeder, examining its unique features.

Jacob caught them up to speed on Seran's gift.

"Well, now you're a shoe-in for your group," Albert said, jumping up and down. "No way you lose to those nimrods."

Jacob smiled and enjoyed the speeder with the rest of the group into the evening. He went to bed trembling with excitement; his head ringing with thoughts about how the race would go. Bron's growling bear snores weren't the reason for Jacob's lack of sleep that night. Nothing could take the thoughts of tomorrow's trials away. Rest was needed; his first official skyrace was just around sunrise - or elevation, as they called it - but the anticipation was hard to block out.

The next day, with only a few hours or waves of sleep, Jacob headed up the very crowded bronze platform, onto the deck of the arena. The stands were packed, and others formed on the field to complete their practice routine. The seats for the fans were silver benches that floated in the air and gave a great view of the track. Holos of the track materialized in front of each set of three benches so that they could view the race up-close. The fans were mostly made up of Cloudian citizens who had bought tickets a few cycles before the new training class was announced.

In the center pit, in the middle of the race track, were just six benches, and the first few seats were occupied by Nyx and Bron. Bron chose to wear an emerald green ear cover to match Jacob's speeder. Nyx was wearing a ridiculously tall hat with Jacob's face on it and a PPA symbol stamped underneath.

Down below, just outside the arena tunnel, Jacob and the others got ready in their slim-fit elemental armor.

Dominus Fugam stood firm in front of each group. She hovered on her speeder. "Aye, lads and ladies," she said. "This is your first go at skyracing, and I'm very excited for all of you." Dominus pointed a look in Jacob's direction. "Remember: heads low, knees bent, and arms forward. Race clean, and no knocking below the waist. Now, speed off!" This was Dominus' signature calling to get the class in the air and ready to practice. Jacob's legs wobbled, and he barely made it onto his board to strap himself on. "The first group will be Group 1."

Brandy got to lead the group. Speeders hovered just behind her as the anticipation of the first race took over.

Dominus Fugam spoke again, this time addressing all the speeders in the crowd. "There will be eight laps around the track. The top two spots from each group move on to the next round to face the others. No hitting below the waist or above the neck, but everything above the waist and below the neck is legal."

Jacob glanced at the crowd and noticed that Nyx had skyzed up and down with his hat pointed in Jacob's direction as he waved. His heartbeat increased. Confidence and nerves battled it out. The first group headed over to the starting line, which was a hologram of a bunch of blue dashes.

"Aye, hover!" Dominus cried. Six skyspeeders dusted off the ground as they hovered a few feet above the track. In the first group, Albert and Brandy were joined by Buster Nalum, Nancy Stills, Duncan Reynolds, and Alice Zip. "Aye, ready… ready…" Dominus Fugam checked with each elemental to confirm they were ready. In front of the first skyspeeder, which was Alice Zip, there was a glass ball which contained a swishing fire inside of it. "When the fire turns blue, speed off!" Dominus yelled.

The surrounding crowd gave a preliminary roar. Jacob's nerves grew into excitement. The blue fire lit and the six speeders lunged forward, fists held outward. The lead was immediately grabbed by Brandy, who held her right arm forward and hinged her left arm tucked neatly under her chest. Behind her were Alice, Albert, Buster, and the rest. The first obstacle materialized on the trail twenty yards ahead of Brandy. Two horizontal doors slowly closed on each other and then opened quickly. Brandy's speeder squeezed through, followed by Alice. The rest had to slow down and wait for the doors to open again. After the rest got through, the standings shifted a bit, and now Buster and Albert were trading places. The two passed Alice, but Duncan was hot on their tail. Buster looked back at Duncan, and the two smirked at each other. Just as they took the corner in the final round of lap one, a tube of water dropped in, and Buster stopped short. Duncan shoved Albert right into the container of water, and puddles splashed over the crowd. Brandy turned her head and noticed Albert tumbling to the ground, covered in water. Albert was taken out of the race, and now it was down to five.

"Hey, they are cheating!" Anna shouted at Dominus Fugam.

"Above the waist is fair, Ms. Friendly." Dominus turned back towards the race, and Anna folded her arms, upset.

"Nice try, Albert!" Jacob belted out, trying to make up for the blunder.

On lap three, Buster and Duncan seemed to be working nicely as a team, as they sent Alice off a ramp and spiraling towards the crowd. They weren't penalized because they sandwiched her shoulders between them. On lap five, Buster shifted his weight, and an overly aggressive Nancy hurdled over him, losing her balance, eating an alphashell from Duncan, and crashing face-first into the dirt surrounding the track.

"Ooooh," the crowd sighed in awe.

Colby started to grow concerned for his sister after he watched the destruction that Buster and Duncan had caused on the track.

"It's only a matter of time. These two are bullying everyone," Anna complained.

"She's still in it. She's been leading the whole time." Jacob tried to calm his fears and keep his faith alive.

The final lap approached, and Brandy held onto the lead, dodged several floating balls and alphashells that were sent hurling from the other two. Around the second corner, Buster's speeder caught up to Brandy's, edging it off the track.

"Step off, Buster! Play fair!" she shouted, trying to keep the race even.

"Keep your head forward, Johnston! Your lead's dwindling!" Duncan yelled.

Brandy noticed Duncan on her opposite side. She was stuck right in the middle of the two bullies. She tried to keep her focus on the track, but two whizzing alphashells nearly missed her, and the sight of Buster and Duncan on either side of her distracted her long enough for the final obstacle - a leash that threw snow balls - to pummel her firmly across the face.

Covered in wet snow, Brandy struggled to see in front of her. Buster took the opportunity to lean forward and shoulder Brandy off the trail. She tumbled into the crowd. Nyx covered his eyes, bracing for the impact. Luckily, the safety net caught her, and the crowd dodged a face full of spiraling elemental.

Buster and Duncan fist-bumped in mid-air, crossing the finish line and representing group one in the next race. The two returned to the inner circle of the other racers as the fans cheered.

Colby went over to attend to his sister, and Anna comforted Albert, but Jacob's shoulder was banged into by Buster's left arm as the two passed each other. Jacob stood firm, but then he noticed Buster's body language berating him. He gulped.

"I'd worry about your race, Wesley. Probus probably won't even let you get to face me."

The second group was a very close race. Only two elementals were disqualified. Randal Hop couldn't dodge the freezing area. He turned into a block of ice on lap two. Cassandra Green took five small rocks known as pelters to the stomach before tumbling face-first into a ramp on lap seven. Andy Addams easily took first place, but Anna was able to edge out the others to claim second place. When she crossed the line, Jacob, Colby, Brandy, and Albert jumped in the air. Nyx tried to get a closer look and jump-skyzed nearby. Bron had to grab him by his leg and pull him back down to the bleachers to avoid embarrassment.

The final whistle blew, and Dominus Fugam motioned towards Jacob and five others to join her at the beginning of the sky trail. Jacob's stomach leaped with nerves; thousands of tiny butterflies spun around inside.

"Aye, Hover!" Dominus shouted. Jacob and the others leaned forward and levitated above the trail. Jacob was set to start in the fifth position, and Probus turned to face him, smiling maliciously. Jacob put his lux-shades over his eyes and got into his racing stance. The blue flame covered the orb, and the speeders lunged forward.

Right at the light, Probus shoulder-charged an elemental clean off his speeder. Zander must have flown a good fifty feet from the trail. The medical team on standby quickly went over to make sure he was okay after catching the safety net. Relief poured over the crowd as the young elemental gave a thumbs-up being carried off the trail.

After the early takedown, the remaining five edged forward, passing the first obstacle: a swinging ball and chain. Probus used his power to bump the orange bowling ball off his chest. Eliza Chance lead the pack, nearing the final corner of lap one, followed by Probus, Lindsey Goodman, Jacob, and Brian Saunders. Jacob and Brian used each other's momentum to move forward, swerving in between each other, which created a speed bubble. The creative teamwork allowed the two to quickly pass their competitors and take over the first and second place.

A few laps later, Jacob and Brian held strong as the top two. Probus sent Lindsey Goodman flying into a pond of yellow goo by sending an alphashell right to the bottom of her skyspeeder. The Incendiaries at the bottom cheered. Buster let out a few hoots and clapped feverously.

Colby whispered to Brandy, "The Flames sound like a bunch of owls."

Before Brandy could laugh, she spotted something in the corner of her eye. Buster raised his fist upward and opened his hand, showing a small flame swishing in his palm.

"Hey, look at Buster! What's he got in his hand?" Brandy asked.

The little flame shot a flash of light towards the racers. The light blinded Jacob and proceeded to send his speeder spinning. Brian could barely avoid Jacob's spinning speeder and almost tumbled off his board. He was forced to pass him. Taking over the lead, Eliza Chance and Probus easily passed him by. Jacob was spinning so fast that the world turned into a tornado of colors.

"I can't look, ta ta!" Nyx covered his eyes. He couldn't watch the mayhem that was about to happen.

"He'll be all right," Bron calmly assured him.

However, his friends felt differently. Anna and Colby leaned back as they braced for Jacob's fall.

Spiraling to his ultimate doom, Jacob meditated to let calm take over. "You're in control, you're in control," he mumbled to himself. The fans stood in silence, anticipating his fall.

Suddenly, his speeder stopped spinning, and just in time to dodge the lap's obstacle of thunderclouds and lightning bolts, he regained composure and stood still. Then he tucked his arm and boosting forward.

The crowd erupted in a deafening cheer. Bron took Nyx's trembling hands from his eyes to reveal Jacob's safety. Anna and the others joined in a group hug and fist bumps.

Jacob had dodged a bullet, much to Buster's dismay, but he was still considerably behind. It took another lap and more boulder-dodging to catch up to Eliza Chance. Rounding a corner on lap four, Eliza was too focused on keeping her third-place lead, and she lunged for Jacob's arms. With an unbelievable mid-air hop, he was able to leave his AIR board, sending her diving straight into a puddle of mud. He reconnected with his speeder and was off again. Jacob was now in third place, and only the top two would move on to the final race.

"That was close," Albert said. He leaped and mimicked the same movement that Jacob had just made.

"I can't believe Brian is still in this thing," Colby exclaimed.

"Yeah, he's gotten much better since the vomit incident," said Brandy.

"I just hope Jacob can overtake them. He's still a bit behind." Anna grew nervous as the three speeders veered towards the final lap.

Probus and Brian were neck-and-neck, taking each corner extremely quickly, swapping places, and dodging more air boulders and a hologram of a thousand knives. Jacob's speeder was just a few feet behind them as they rounded the final corner. Probus and Brian were the clear favorites to finish, but Jacob was closing in quickly.

"He's not gonna make it," Brandy said pessimistically.

"He's gonna make it," Colby countered.

"It's too close! I can't look, no, no," Nyx again covered his eyes after a quick peek.

The finish line approached. Probus passed it. Jacob, in a last-ditch effort, lunged for the line, the edge of his lux-shades just beating out Brian's purple hair. In a miraculous comeback, Jacob overtook second place to stay alive.

Nyx jumped for joy, and Bron clapped. The crowd roared, followed by chants of "JACOB! JACOB! JACOB!"

Jacob was met with a group hug after giving Brian a forearm shake after such a close match.

"You'll get 'em next time, Brian!" Jacob shouted over the crowd.

Buster pouted on the side and angrily sneered over at Jacob. His blinding light trick didn't work. All it had done was keep Probus at the top spot.

After Jacob's impressive skyracing display, the final group of eight competed and finished their trial, as well. The off-season training seemed to pay off for Colby, as he easily crushed his competition, almost lapping everyone and using a few alphashells to knock out close-by competitors.

After the final race, Dominus Fugam hovered in the middle of the field on her skyspeeder to make an announcement. "Aye, so we have had tough competition today, ladies and gents. Physical toughness," Dominus looked towards Buster and Probus. "Swift, fast speeding," she glanced in Colby's direction. "And incredible comebacks," she turned her head towards Jacob and reverently nodded. "This final Sky Trial race will take place between the fierce eight before you: Buster Nalum." There were mixed cheers and boos from the crowd. "Duncan Reynolds." The boos continued to get louder. "Anna Friendly." Cheers overtook the boos as she stood blushing. Jacob applauded very loudly for her, too. "Andy Addams." Andy was met with loud cheers as well, overpowering Anna's. "Probus Sniffleton." Some boos crossed over. "Jacob Wesley." Cheers thundered again. "And finally, Colby Johnston, followed by Trudy Stein." The cheers continued, and Brandy winked over at Colby. "Speeders, drink your trumnits and get ready for the final trial!"

The racers had a brief intermission to get their refreshments and fix the wear and tear on their skyspeeders.

Albert and Brandy gave each of their friend's pats on the back. Buster, Probus, and Duncan huddled up nearby and strategized for their illegal plays. Across the way stood the group of friends with Brandy in the middle.

"Don't worry. I'll keep an eye on the Incendiaries and make sure no funny business takes place this time," Brandy assured her pals as she stepped away.

"Yeah, and I'll put them in their place with a

double-stomp-slip-and-swipe if they try to test Brandy." Albert performed his classic Movements demonstration as the two headed back towards the crowd.

The final eight lined up at the front line as softening clouds moved past their feet and through the spikes on their boards. Colby and Buster led in the top two positions, followed by Probus, Trudy, Jacob, Andy, Anna, and Duncan.

"The final trial will be shown on the two large holos at each end of the trail, and will also be announced by Cloudia's official skyrace commentators, Bard Dine and Harold Porter." As Dominus' words faded into the background, two gentlemen were shown on one of the larger Holo Screens. They were wearing Volans coats with double-bowties on, and both had their hair parted in the middle. They smiled and waved at the screen as they took their new places at the announcer's booth which hovered in front of the middle bleacher section. The crowd went crazy, cheering and clapping for the two.

Then, the blue flame took over the orb again, and the speeders flew off.

"Colby and Buster off to an early lead here," Harold chimed in.

"Don't be surprised if you see Buster and Probus use teamwork to take some of the others out," Bard replied. "All racers will have to keep their heads up and their eyes on the trail if they want to take home a spot in the Great Skyrace this yer."

Harold was flashing his pen towards the screen. "Well, I know Ezekial would be excited to face off against his younger brother Andy."

Bard turned to Harold. "Don't forget that Trudy is a distant relative of Darlene Flight."

"Good point, Bard." Harold and Bard nodded and turned back towards the race at hand.

Buster was out in front, dipping and dodging. Probus and Colby were neck-and-neck for second place, followed by the rest. Andy and Anna were swapping places as they rounded the final corner of lap two. Obstacles were not affecting the group as they sped around the track. Suddenly, Duncan rammed a hard right, sending Trudy up a ramp and through a few dark clouds as Probus sent an alphashell to smack her back and send her spiraling into a nearby mud pit.

"Ooooh, that's gotta hurt, Harold." Bard let out a heavy sigh. "Well, looks like Darlene will be the only Flight to compete this yer."

The fans cheered as Trudy took a tumble and the rest of the speeders kept going forward. Rounding lap three, Jacob leaned his arm back and grabbed Anna, sending her forward to catch up with the top spots. Anna smiled at him and headed towards the front. No one noticed, but Buster and Probus were right behind Colby, heading into the air boulder obstacle. Anna was swiveling forward, trying to catch up with them when she noticed they were planning an attack. Colby was able to dodge a shoulder charge from Probus but was met with an alphashell right between the legs, sending him backflipping into a mud pit as well.

"Oooohs" and "ahhhs" surrounded the track. Andy tried to imitate Probus by diving for a charge at Jacob, but Jacob hopped out of the way just in time, sending Andy crashing right into Duncan Reynolds. The pair went spiraling down, getting caught by two gigantic gray boulders that threw them out of the competition.

"The younger Addams and Duncan take large boulders to the face!" Harold was so excited that he almost leaped out of his seat.

"Might want to ask the older brother for a few tips, eh, Harold?" Bard and Harold's belly laughed.

There were four sky speeders left, gracefully moving towards lap five: Buster, Probus, Anna, and Jacob. Buster and Probus were swaying in and out, trying to create a great distance between the others. Jacob was buying time by hovering behind Anna as they neared the other two racers. Dark clouds and lightning bolts did no damage as the four easily finished lap five.

During lap six, Buster and Probus moved through a few dark clouds, obscuring them from the crowd, and they took the opportunity to let out a few flames. Anna got caught up in the smoke and had difficulty balancing on her speeder. Once the two were out of the clouds, she was met with an alphashell to her chest, sending her off her board. Anna was spiraling downward very quickly, about to meet the ground face-first.

Brandy and Albert screamed when they noticed, and Nyx shielded his eyes once again. The crowd stood up to see what had happened. Hearts were beating fast, anticipating where she would land as the net didn't budge to save her.

"Is she okay?!" Nyx screamed.

"It doesn't look too good for her. I can't see anything," Bron stammered back.

As mist began to crawl back from the cloud, the remaining crowd wiped their eyes to try and see what happened. Mist spiraled forward as Jacob emerged, holding Anna in his arms.

"He saved her!" Albert shouted when he noticed.

"How did he do that?!" Bron screamed, jolting a fist in the air.

Nyx just smiled as Jacob dropped Anna onto the ground and sped back into the race. The crowd roared as he sped past the dark clouds again, zooming towards Buster and Probus. They turned around to see what had happened, then moved forward, trying to ignore it.

"I don't know how the boy did that, but Jacob just pulled off a miracle there, Bard."

"I'd have to agree, Harold. Lightning speed, quick hands, and a touch of compassion just pulled off one of the most amazing things I've ever witnessed in a skyrace."

Buster and Probus slowed down in shock, which gave Jacob an opportunity to close some of the distance, and he was able to catch up as he neared the final lap.

"Well, here we go, folks, the Light One is doing everything he can to try and catch up here," Bard said.

"I think the distance might have been too much, and the bash brothers have made it impossible for anyone to pass them," replied Harold.

Everyone left their seats as the final lap approached, and Jacob was flying in between both Buster and Probus. Just like sharks surrounding their prey, the two started to dive in and out near Jacob's speeder. Jacob kept his head tucked, and his attention focused.

"Déjà vu, Wesley. This time, we'll make sure you hit the ground," Buster smirked as they glided forward. In the distance, Jacob could see large bubbles being shot from a giant gun.

"For your sake, I'd pay attention, Jacob. We all remember what happened last time." Probus dove towards Jacob to give him a shoulder charge once again, but this time, Jacob backflipped, and Probus missed him by inches. A large bubble shot from the giant gun, caught hold of him and caused him to float in the air. Jacob had been hiding a secret alphashell behind his back, which he threw with all his might, slamming Probus right in the stomach, out of the bubble, and into a mud pit. Upset, Probus smashed his fists into the gloppy mud.

"And then there were two!" Bard exclaimed.

The crowd roared, and Bron and Nyx exchanged a few fist bumps. The ground was rumbling, and the fans were clapping in anticipation of the finale.

Jacob and Buster were moving back and forth between first and second place as the obstacles were left in their dust.

"They're up to incredible speeds!" Harold shouted excitedly.

"That's it, Wesley. You're mine." In a flash, Buster lunged forward with his arm held outright, yelling, "ARDEREEEEEE VIIIIITIDIS!"

A line of fire shot from the palm of Buster's hand and went screaming towards Jacob. Jacob threw his arms in the air and aimed his speeder sideways, blocking the fire and sending it hurtling back towards Buster, who had to move out of the way. However, the blind spot Dominus showed him in an earlier session had crept into view. Buster couldn't see in front of him, Jacob too advantage with another alphashell clean to his chest.

Jacob's speeder felt incredibly light. So light that he felt like he was racing on pillows and fluffy clouds. Passing the finish line, he lunged forward and erupted in a big scream of joy.

To his surprise, there weren't any cheers, just stunned faces.

Coming to a halt, he looked out and noticed over a thousand jaws hanging open. He saw that everyone was looking beneath him. He followed the path of their eyes and noticed that he was about one hundred yards off the ground, his speeder broken into two pieces, one underneath each foot, and he was standing in place.

"I don't believe it, Bard." Harold was still in shock.

"Me neither, Harold, he's… he's just hovering."

Jacob realized where he was, and upon his realization, started spiraling down towards the ground.

"Oh, no!" Albert was running towards the spot that Jacob was falling towards, but before he could hit the ground, Bron stood up, and with his arm extending forward, caught Jacob.

Everyone cheered again, and Nyx skyze-skated right over to him, leaping up and down. The crowd surrounded him, drowning Jacob in cheers.

"He's done it! He's done it! The Light One, Jacob Wesley, has won! He will be the Elemental Academy's representation in next yer's Great Skyrace!" Bard was dancing in his booth.

"I've never seen anything like this, Bard. I can't wait to see what the kid has up his sleeve next."

The flames surrounding Buster had to be extinguished by a few Hydros as Jacob celebrated.

"Aye, Mr. Nalum! You're in big trouble for using elemental abilities in a skyrace!" Dominus pulled him away from the group by his ear.

It was the most significant day of Jacob's life, and as he celebrated later on with his friends, he thought to himself that he had never been so loved by a group of people before.

Albert was off to the side mimicking Jacob's skills and making everyone laugh as they downed their trumnits. "You were flying! Actually flying in the air!"

"No one has ever flown before! It was amazing!" Anna said, dancing around.

"I could have had ya if I hadn't had to dodge Probus and an alphashell at the same time," Colby said bashfully.

"That's all right, Colby. I'll make sure to represent you in the race," Jacob replied.

The group cheered and laughed as Jacob left them, heading towards the exit.

Jacob walked out through the tunnel of the stadium alone, heading back to the PPA to get some much-needed rest. This had to eclipse the happiest memory of his life. The orphanage started to disappear from his memory and was now replaced with happy memories of feeling welcomed and liked.

The clouds that rolled over the grounds never looked so bright, and the sky was so beautiful with its reddish pink light. Jacob reached the platform of Gordonclyff Tower, leaving the celebration behind. Winning the skyrace trials guaranteed him a spot in the Great Skyrace the following yer. He would get to compete against the biggest star in skyracing history, Ezekiel Addams.

The platform elevator came to a screeching halt. A red light gripped his vision near the walls. Jacob stared into the dark distance, searching for whatever caused the platform elevators to stop. Suddenly, a flash of light sped quickly towards him. He quickly ducked down to dodge the light. Looking up, though, it wasn't near him. About ten feet in front of him, he noticed a shadowy silhouette and a trail of fire speeding down a nearby hallway.

Jacob stepped onto the cold ground of the sixth floor. His curiosity hypnotized him. Jacob's victory quickly disappeared from his mind as the mysterious firelight took over. As Jacob grew closer, he could see the crimson-cloaked figure moving forward. Jacob chased after him down the hallway.

What was happening? Who was this figure? Was it one of the racers from the trials?

Jacob chased the figure all the way down the stony hall before finally reaching a room made of glass. He jumped behind a post next to one of the stone walls and hid.

The figure inside of the glass room turned as if it had heard something but then continued to a wall near the back. In front of the outer wall, he began waving his hands in the air. A circle of flames started to form a six-foot ring around the wall.

Jacob moved closer to get a better look, hiding behind another pillar to his left as silently as he could. He edged his face closer to see what was happening, his nose pressing softly against the glass. He thought better than to enter unannounced.

The circle of flames popped off the wall, and the figure went through it as he joined another figure in a dark orange Volans coat.

Jacob couldn't see the face of either figure, but he could hear their muffled voices echo through the hall.

"How long did it take you, Jasper?" one of the muffled voices said.

"Only about fifteen ticks, to be exact, Taylor," said the voice that was already on the wall.

"I got held up when the hero boy finished the race early."

Jacob was trying his to make out what the two were doing. The crimson-cloaked figure pointed in Jacob's direction. Jacob ducked underneath the bottom of the door to avoid being caught. Silence and nerves spilled into Jacob's chest, and his heart felt like it was about to leap right out.

"Did you find what we came for?" continued one of the voices.

"No, Taylor, I didn't. I searched Magistra's entire office, and nothing. I don't know where it could be," said the other.

"We should get going. Follcane will not be pleased with this information."

"Let's hope, for both our sakes; he's not in one of his moods."

Jacob couldn't hear anymore voices, so he leaned upwards to peek back into the room. He saw the figures start to huddle down the tunnel through the ring when a hand grabbed Jacob's shoulder. Jacob leaped and screamed in fright.

Athene stood in front of him, arms folded, and one eyebrow raised. "Winning a race doesn't give you permission to scour the building and trespass on floors."

"But, sir, there were two of, um, Follcane's men right here. Taylor and Jasper. They were sitting right in that tunnel talking about searching Magistra's office." Jacob turned back around to show Athene, but the two were gone, and even worse, the ring of fire was nowhere to be seen.

"It looks like the room is empty, Wesley. I'll tell you what. You head back to the PPA, and we will keep this little late-night stroll between the two of us."

Jacob nodded, still in disbelief over what he had just witnessed.

Albert, Anna, Colby, and Brandy were all waiting in the lobby, still caught up in the heat of the race.

"Where ya been, Jake?" Colby rushed him as soon as he got in.

"Wicked race, Jake," Brandy said.

"Not so bad, Green Eyes. You were incredible." Anna was hugging his side. Albert was again reliving Jacob's moves towards the end of the race, and imitating the fight with Buster.

"Yeah, yeah, it was a blast, but..." Jacob grew silent as he thought to himself, still concerned with the two former Incendiaries that had been doing Follcane's bidding.

"Whoa, what could be more important than that?" Colby rebutted.

"How about spotting two of Follcane's men sneaking into Gordonclyff? And even worse, it's Taylor Jane and Jasper Collins." Jacob scratched his head.

"You mean the two Incendiaries that were kidnapped?" Brandy asked impatiently.

"Why were they in Gordonclyff?" Anna followed.

"They were after something. One of them, Taylor, said he couldn't find it in Magistra's office. It sounds like Follcane has them running through the walls, and that's how they are getting into Cloudia," Jacob said.

"You gotta tell Seran," Albert chimed in.

Jacob looked very intense as he turned his attention away from Albert and just stared at the cold ground. "Athene caught me, and the evidence of the fire ring is gone. I think this is something we have to investigate on our own."

# 17

# ELECTRO BLAST

"Shut the door behind you, Wesley."

Jacob did so very cautiously, fear creeping down his spine. The dimly lit, cold gym was empty, except for him and Athene. When he turned back around, Athene was waving over a wooden target painted with a red dot in the center on the opposite side of the room.

"Walk over to the blue line," Athene said softly, with his back still facing Jacob. Jacob paced over to a thin blue line on the floor about twenty feet away from the target that Athene had just moved over. With a quick step, Athene spun around to face Jacob. Darkness filled every crack in his face.

"Where is everyone today, sir?" Jacob asked quietly.

"Well, Wesley, tonight is a special night," Athene said. "Tonight, I teach you a move that will bring you closer to achieving the Light One status."

"What's that sir?" asked Jacob inquisitively.

"This is no ordinary move, Jacob," said Athene. He grabbed Jacob by the shoulders tightly. "But if you are successful in learning it, you will stand somewhat of a chance against your enemy."

"Understood," said Jacob.

"Now, the electro blast, as you will soon find out, is a type of electro energy blast that requires more mind control than physical force."

"Will I need it soon?" asked Jacob, staring nervously into Athene's eyes, afraid of the answer that would come next.

Athene's grip tightened, and then he smiled scornfully. "In due time, Wesley. The Dark One you so sheepishly call Follcane is a skilled Incendiary. A very skilled Incendiary."

"Does he know this move, sir?" asked Jacob.

"I'm sure he knows a different form of this move when it comes to fire, but I don't know, to be certain." Athene eased his grip on Jacob's shoulders. He thought for sure they would crumble into dust upon their release.

Athene began to pace with his hands secured behind his back. "The mind is a potent tool. So powerful that it controls any action which comes from the body. With intense focus and meditation, it can do anything. There is no limit to the true strength of its power. Those who have mastered any elemental move have mastered the ability to clear the mind. For them, it's as easy as tying a Gravit's shoe. Seran, for instance, can shut his mind down in the blink of an eye, and fix his thoughts immediately, even when he's on the move."

"How long will it take me to be able to do that?" Jacob asked.

"Usually, elementals become masters of their element by the age of 30." Athene's words felt like a shock, electrocuting Jacob's insides with worry. "Yes, it's true," Athene said, noticing Jacob's surprise. "Ordinarily, someone like you would stand an incredible distance away from grasping the abilities of a Seran or the Dark One," continued Athene. "Unfortunately, we don't have the time to wait for you to age."

Jacob shrunk down and rubbed his arm, panic crawling through him. "Well, how am I supposed to be the Light One, then? I'm only thirteen. This is a waste of time."

Athene halted his steps and turned firmly towards Jacob with his hand softly scratching underneath his chin. "When has ordinary ever applied to you, Wesley? No one has ever had your ampere count at this age before. In fact, few even come to possess the number of amperes you have in their entire lifetime. Seran believes that there is so much potential inside of you, that when the time is right, you won't need your lux-bands, you won't even need the darklights. You will be able to defeat the Dark One with your natural ability alone. This is why your elemental training has become private lessons with me. Seran wants me to teach you how to harness your abilities at this young age." Jacob began to feel very warm, and his heartbeat began to quicken. Athene approached him once more, this time softly placing his hand upon Jacob's head. This time, when he spoke, the words left his mouth as though he weighed each of them carefully. "From our initial lessons, it appears as though you do contain that potential. The only time that raw, natural power at this age has been seen was the Dark One. Luckily for us, he is unaware of the abilities that you possess. That is to our advantage, but today, you will be learning something far more difficult and powerful than you could ever imagine."

"Will it destroy Follcane?"

"The Dark One is extremely powerful, and one blast will not destroy him," Athene spoke quietly. He looked into Jacob's eyes as if searching for something deep within them to respond. "However, maybe a few of them would," Athene smirked, as he began to pace in the dimly lit gym yet again. "Although the electro blast possesses much force, its true power is to weaken your opponent, making him vulnerable," Athene confidently explained. "Your first encounter with the Dark One was laughable. You fainted in front of him." Athene rolled up one of the sleeves of his Volans coat.

"I don't know what came over me. It was too much," said Jacob urgently.

"Nevertheless, he knows you're weak. He knows you aren't ready for him," said Athene. "This is good. He isn't expecting you to have this much training or knowledge in your craft, and we need to expose that. Blasts such as the electro blast will shock him."

Athene unraveled a jar of glowing darklights from inside a nearby locker and placed it quickly on the ground in front of Jacob.

"Ready?" Athene twisted the golden top slowly off the jar. The buzzing began to fill the room. Jacob nodded enthusiastically. "Now, get into the correct fighting pose."

Jacob swung his arms in a circular motion before letting them land softly at his sides. He then bent his knees to crouch like a gargoyle. "Put your lux-bands on, Wesley."

Jacob closed the clasps on each of his lux-bands. The silver bands spun as fast as car tires before lighting up like a street lamp. "Good," Athene spoke softly.

The darklights fluttered out of the jar and latched onto Jacob's skin, tracing his veins down to his forearms. Jacob was positioned in front of a narrow target with his lux-bands fully charged.

"I want you to focus on the target. Clear your mind, but keep your eyes closed," said Athene.

"Eyes closed?" Jacob asked, eyeing Athene's arm, which was now raised firmly next to his.

"I'm merely here as a precaution," said Athene. "In case you can't control it. Since we have already worked on a few different types of elemental phrases, you should be familiar with the extent of the power that releases from your hand, and while similar strength is needed for this, your mind is most important, yet again. You will need extreme focus and concentration. Any distraction will sway you from the target."

"I'm ready." Jacob shut his eyes quickly, and darkness took over. The dimly lit gym vanished, heat began to rise throughout his arm.

"Concentrate." Athene's voice was barely audible, sounding like a distant echo down the hall. Jacob held his hand straight out and slowly brought his other hand close together. His palms pressed tightly together. His fingers were outstretched, and a bead of sweat dripped down the side of his face. He felt a tingling sensation run through his forearms down to his hands.

"Now!"

Jacob felt the tingling sensation overtake the palms of his hands. His knees wobbled, but he fought to stay still, and then…

"ELECTRO BLAST!" Jacob screamed, and the ground fell away beneath him. His head collided with a pad against the wall before he landed roughly on the floor.

When Jacob opened his eyes, he saw a smirking Athene with his arms folded behind his back.

"Again," said Athene coolly.

Jacob staggered to his feet and again got back into his fighting pose. He closed his eyes, concentrated, put both of his hands together, stuck out his fingers, and braced. He felt the electricity crawling through his veins and accepted the tingling sensation.

"ELECTRO BLAST!" Repeating the same experience, Jacob flung backward like a slingshot against the back wall. His head began to hurt, and sweat was pouring down his eyebrows now.

"Are you giving up?" asked Athene scornfully. Jacob shook his head and rose to his feet. "Didn't think so," said Athene. "You aren't concentrating hard enough, and you're trying to emit the blast before you are ready."

"I feel this tingling feeling through my arms. My mind is clear." Jacob rubbed the back of his head, and then braced for another attempt.

"Well, you aren't doing terribly for your first attempt at this, but you could be doing better," said Athene, raising his arm yet again.

Jacob threw an annoyed look in his direction but closed his eyes yet again.

"Again!" Athene yelled.

Jacob found himself against the back wall and on the ground again. His legs felt like they were glued to the ground with a bunch of elementals trying to pin him down.

"Again!" said Athene sharply. "You aren't trying at all. You are losing your grip on your energy too easily. What will you do when the Dark One is firing at you, and you can't even fight back?"

Jacob stood up again, his heart and stomach feeling like they were about to fall out of his body, or maybe as he had just received another wedgie from Tommy. Athene was silent, his back turned to Jacob in frustration, but he wasn't as frustrated as Jacob was as he continued failing to produce something even remotely close to an electro blast.

"I… am… giving… it… all… I… got," he said, through clenched teeth.

"I told you to clear your mind and focus!"

"I can't do this! I'm not ready," Jacob sighed.

"Then you shall become another victim for the Dark One!" said Athene savagely. "You are fooling yourself if you think that you're giving it your all. Just because you are a child doesn't mean that you aren't ready for this. You need to free your mind and focus on the objective ahead completely. You can do this, you just simply won't. Something is holding you back, making you weak, making you incapable of defeating him and saving all of us. Maybe you aren't the Light One; maybe you're just a boy."

"I am not weak," said Jacob in a low voice, anger now bubbling up in his body like a teapot boiling over. He was ready to fight Athene at any moment.

"Then show me! Get rid of whatever it is that's holding you back!" shouted Athene. "Free your mind. Believe in yourself. Again!" Athene stood behind him this time. "Now, this time, when you feel that tingling sensation, pause for a minute and hold it. Let it build into something bigger, and more magnificent. You will know when it feels right."

Jacob remained focused. Athene's words were drowned out. A softness took over his body. He could feel only the static electricity coursing through his veins. He was firm as he faced his target one more time. The sensation began building like a fire rising in the night. Jacob remained focused, his hands held together with the ends touching like two sharp rocks, his fingers outstretched. The tingling sensation broke through, but he stayed focused. He waited this time, mentally concentrated as the light started to appear in his vision, forming the shape of the target.

"ELECTRO BLAST!" he screamed, louder than ever. Jacob didn't fly backward this time, but he did stagger a bit. He opened his eyes, and there were tiny blue sparks against the wall in front of them, but they had not reached the target.

"Close. Much better, but still not good enough." Jacob hung his head at Athene's cold words. "Do not hang your head, Mr. Wesley," said Athene, warmly this time.

Jacob didn't respond. He still felt as though he couldn't defeat this incredible villain that everyone kept talking about. He couldn't make a simple energy move, yet he was supposed to beat someone who had bested the likes of Seran and Bron. He may have been very good at skyracing, but that wouldn't be enough to stop the Dark One.

"What if I fail?" Jacob asked.

"What if you fail?" Athene asked quickly, arms folded, playing with his beard.

Jacob was staring at the speckled ground in front of him, unsure how to respond to Athene's question. He paused and then looked up into Athene's beady eyes. "I'll let all of you down. I won't beat him, and then he'll take over and possibly kill everyone."

Athene glared at Jacob for a moment, his eyebrow twitching. Then he turned back towards the jars that the darklights came from. "There are many reasons to be afraid in this world, Mr. Wesley, a few of which you have yet to experience, and the rest, which you are probably experiencing now. Being the Light One comes with facing the Dark One, as we have discussed, and this is no simple task, but I will let you in on a little secret."

"Yes?" Jacob said, picking his head up to listen to Athene more intently.

Athene placed his index finger firmly against Jacob's temple. "It's all in your mind, and once you master true control of your fear, you will master true control of your energy."

"Do you believe I can?" asked Jacob. Tears started to form in the corners of his eyes.

"I know you can." Athene turned back around towards the jars and started navigating the darklights back into them safely. "We will meet again later this week to finish your lessons on the electro blast."

"Will do, sir," Jacob said, gathering his things and moving towards the exit.

"And Mr. Wesley, you need to work on emptying your mind of any thoughts that pour in. If you can do that, you will be one step closer to believing in yourself."

"Got it." Jacob quickly opened the big swiveling doors to the gym before giving one last look in Athene's direction. Athene was effortlessly controlling the darklights in waves. Impressed, and with a bit more confidence, Jacob shut the door behind him.

Later, he found Anna near the entrance to Gordonclyff Tower. She was sitting by the beautiful fountain encased in spinning gears. There were only a few other elementals nearby, all of them playing in the grass, or skyzing around while throwing ice puffs at each other as the sky turned into navy-blue dawn. Then his vision was completely obscured by long, flowing blonde hair.

"Hey, stranger!" Anna had thrown herself at him in a hug that nearly knocked him on the ground. "How was training? Are you alright? Did you learn anything today? I got to learn something elegant. All sorts of Hydro phrases! This one called Hydro Freeze allows you to turn water into ice.

"That sounds cool, Anna," said Jacob. He noticed she had folded her hands and a blush started to rise on her cheeks.

"What about you? What did you learn, Green Eyes?" Anna inched a bit closer, and he started to blush, too.

"Yeah," said Jacob, nerves bubbling up in his stomach. "I almost learned a phrase, sort of a glowing thingy. It's tough, to be honest. I almost got it, though."

"What's it called?" Anna had a look of curiosity on her face, which was kind of cute. It seemed like an answer given by Jacob would be the most exciting answer in her world.

"Electro blast," Jacob smirked.

"Maybe you could show it to me?" Anna blinked very sweetly in his direction.

"Alright," Jacob replied. "Well, you hold your fists out like this." Jacob placed her in the right stance with her palms spread outwards. He didn't know who was more impressed with himself at that moment, him or Anna. "Now, when the electricity fills your veins..."

Anna nodded, awaiting his instructions.

"ELECTRO BLAST!" a nasally voice called from behind them. Jacob whipped around to find Albert mimicking the pose, and then sending mimed versions of the blast towards the different elementals playing nearby.

"Albert, you spoiled it!" Anna shouted in his direction, followed by a playful smack on the back of his head. She glared at him, still breathing deeply, then turned away from him, pacing up and down. Jacob couldn't help but laugh at the exchange. "Oh, you think this is funny, Green Eyes?" Anna jumped him and started whaling slaps upon the back of his head, too. They felt more like he was being tickled than getting walloped. Albert joined in, and the three wrestled on the ground for a while, playing in the cold night.

"Wait!" Albert stopped. The other two glanced over, tangled up like a pretzel on the floor. A light trail was glistening in the night with a golden sparkle.

"Grailum, out here, in the middle of Center City?" Anna leaned over Albert's shoulder to get a closer look.

"There's much more than we saw last time," said Jacob, who moved his finger to touch it.

"Approximately 52 grailum, that is." Albert smacked Jacob's hand away. "I wouldn't do that if I were you."

"Well?" he demanded, looking at Albert deeply. "What do we do, then?"

"We tell the PPA about this, that's what we do." Anna stood up and folded her arms with a toughness that Jacob found to be admirable. "But we do it tomorrow," Anna continued. "All the elementals are going back to Gordonclyff. It's past when we are supposed to be outside."

"Are you going to pass on your chance to tell the PPA?" Albert asked.

The night was spread with charcoal clouds dusting over the grounds of the city. Just outside the tall, marble building was a shiny Volans coat swishing in the wind.

"Look," said Albert. "It's Seran!"

"What do you think he's doing out at night?" Jacob asked, huddling up behind Albert several yards away.

"He's knocking on the ground. That's kinda weird." Anna shifted to get a better look.

Suddenly, the ground opened up. A patch of what looked like fake stone popped off the ground. A muscular man with a golden beard was lifting it up.

"There's Bron too, now," Albert said, stepping forward.

Jacob quickly grabbed him and stepped in front of Albert. "Careful, dude," Jacob said, noticing Seran looking around to see if anyone was aware of his actions. Then Seran stood up and walked forward, disappearing into the ground.

"Let's go." Anna had already left the two and headed in the direction of where Seran had been.

"Go where?" Jacob cautiously asked.

"Don't you want to know where they are going, what the grailum is, and where it leads to?" Anna replied.

"I do!" Albert released Jacob's grip on his arm and ran behind Anna. Regretfully, Jacob continued after the others.

The group continued through the secret door in the ground, and Jacob's heartbeat began to speed up. It was cold, freezing, and a weird leaking sound reminded Jacob of the nasty hole in the ground at Ms. Larrier's. It was dimly lit by the retreating fire that Seran or Bron had started.

Then, a sound like walls were breaking apart rang through their ears before a giant black spiraling staircase positioned itself at the edge of their feet.

"Well, here we go," Anna said, taking a step onto the hard brick. "Come on!" She led Albert and Jacob down the staircase, its steps magically materializing in front of them. The walls were brick, painted beige, and red sparkles glittered like diamonds on every inch of the wall.

"Look," Jacob said. "It's grailum. Boatloads of it."

"What's a boat?" Anna asked, after waving her hands in front of the grailum-covered walls.

"Nothing," Jacob said, as he kept his pace forward.

A brisk wind sifted through their hair as they descended into the unknown. "We should probably keep close; the lights get dimmer the further apart we are from each other." Albert hurried his pace behind Anna. "There's so much of this glitter stuff on the walls. It's nuts; kinda scary." Albert leaped forward to keep up the pace. Just then, they noticed the lights start to disappear. Complete darkness was in their future.

"Crud, it's getting darker, guys!" Anna started to run as the materializing steps were disappearing under their feet. Albert was close behind, but Jacob was struggling to keep up. His foot barely caught the next step, and he tripped, about to tumble into eternal darkness when a gloved hand snatched him just in the nick of time.

"Igneri," a raspy voice called out, and a spiraling light fluttered throughout the staircase to reveal Bron's muscular arm holding on to Jacob's.

Seran was standing next to him with the sort of look your parents give you when you do something wrong. "What are you three doing down here?"

"Sorry, sir, we were sort of curious about the grailum we keep seeing. It's everywhere, and it was leading to the grassy area you were standing." Anna tried to speak for the group, as Jacob's head was hanging in embarrassment. Albert was stargazing at Bron, as per usual.

"You should have never followed us down here; you know that. Well, we might as well continue down now. The staircase won't be coming back anytime soon. Hurry." Seran and Bron continued forward, and the group huddled anxiously behind them.

"What if whatever was creating the grailum is down there?" Jacob asked, using the wall beside him for balance.

"We've been down here every night since Follcane's attack, and no such figure has shown its face, but something is down here now, I can sense it." Seran began to slow his pace cautiously.

Anna was getting antsy. "It's cold down here."

"Yeah. How much further?" Albert asked, shivering.

"Just a few more steps. Now, if any of you spot anything, shout immediately." Seran lead Jacob and the rest of the gang forward into the darkness.

"Why would we need to shout?" Anna asked, shivering as well.

The staircase ended, and the five of them finally reached a walkway. The hall was wide, much more extensive than the staircase itself. It had taken them so long to get there that Jacob felt like they had walked down about ten thousand steps.

Seran repeated the phrase "Igneri" twice with his right arm raised, and two streams of light flooded the hallway from his hand.

"Maybe it's the darklights. Don't they leave behind a sort of grailum?" Jacob asked.

"Good guess, but no. Darklights are too small, and their bodies are unique. They don't leave behind any grailum," said Seran coolly.

The group passed several reservoirs with running water funneling upward. Spots of grailum were scattered throughout the walls, and the water was an odd purple hue.

"The water's purple?" Albert asked, eyeing the bizarre color.

"That's not what I think it is, is it?" Anna covered her mouth to keep from gasping.

"Our drinking and bathing supply? It is. This is where it runs from. It streams from H-Twenty and into these ducts, which climb up to our irrigation system. Nifty, if you ask me," Seran smiled.

"But if the water's purple, isn't it contaminated?" Anna asked nervously. Jacob was curious to know, too.

"We've tested it, and it's fine. The water has changed colors before; it's just a color, nothing to do with what's on the inside. What it does tell us, though, is that someone has been messing with the oceans on H-Twenty…"

Seran trailed off, his eyes darting off into the distance, then widening in alarm. "STOP!" Seran called out.

A shadowy figure was speeding right past the group.

Seran stopped in the middle of the tunnel and created a barrier with his arms in front of the others. Mini footsteps could be heard scurrying from a distance.

"You heard that too?!" Albert shouted.

"Shhhh," Anna and Jacob both said.

Seran was spying around to see if he could spot where the noise was coming from, but the sounds retreated. "Something is down here," Seran murmured. "Someone, I should say."

"Follcane?" Jacob suggested.

"Those footsteps were too small to be Follcane's, and he wouldn't be that obvious," Seran said confidently. "Let's keep going, but keep your eyes and ears open. Bron, take the rear, but remain close."

The group paced forward slowly, sticking their necks out to catch the faintest sound. Suddenly, a shadow streaked by ahead. Something was there.

"Reveal yourself!" Seran shouted. "There's five of us and one of you."

The shadow ran by again, but this time Albert spotted him. "There, he's over there." Albert pointed out a limping young man with an orange and red spiked mohawk who was hurrying forward.

Seran chased after him at a quick pace, followed by the rest of the group. "LIGHT BLAST!" Seran shouted, raising his hands. A globe of white light spat out from his hands, smacking the back of the runner. The light disappeared, and a touch of smoke evaporated from the figure who was now lying flat on the ground. Jacob was amazed.

"Incredible," Albert said, catching up to the rest of the group, who was also admiring the blast that came from Seran. "Suppose that's why he's the best," Albert said to Jacob. "How did you do that?" Albert asked Seran, imitating the blast from his arm.

Although amazed at the performance, Jacob was more interested in the man behind the mystery. Bron turned the body over to reveal a young face with freckles. The boy began to cough wildly.

"He must have been, like, fifty yards away at least," Albert whispered.

"Silence!" Seran yelled at the group.

"Who is he?" Jacob asked.

"Meet Caden Lewis, a former Incendiary who graduated from the Elemental Academy three yers ago. Follcane kidnaped him during one of his attacks, and, as you can see, forced him into his guard," said Seran.

"What's his guard?" Anna asked.

"The guard is what Follcane refers to his army as. He has built a big alliance with former Incendiaries ever since the war." Seran moved Caden onto his side and ripped off the shoulder area of his cloak. On Caden's right shoulder, there was a burn scar in the shape of a symbol. It looked like a flame through the prophecy symbol, but they couldn't quite make it out.

Caden budged a bit and tried to speak. He had a wheezing, raspy voice. "The almighty Seran. I should feel honored."

"What were you doing going through the Underportal, Caden?" Seran asked, holding his wrist firmly.

Anna whispered to Jacob, "Underportal?" Finally, someone else was confused about something in Cloudia besides Jacob.

"Worried your security isn't so tight, huh?" Caden coughed a few times, struggling to speak. He tried to roll over and get up, but Bron stepped on his arm, restraining him. "Kill me; I don't care." Caden coughed again. "Follcane would kill me if he knew I failed anyway."

"Failed what? Why are you here?!" Jacob couldn't contain himself. He shouted as he stepped forward. Bron held him back with his other strong arm.

"Wild, Green Eyes," Caden began to cough a bit. "You must be Jacob Wesley, the precious Light One. You should be afraid. He's coming for you."

"I'm not afraid." Jacob struggled to move forward.

"You will be. The night is just beginning," Caden stated.

"Don't listen to him, Jacob!" Seran yelled.

"What are you saying? What does he mean?" Jacob couldn't help but ask.

"Calm down, Green Eyes. He's just trying to get in your head." Anna was trying to calm him, but not even she could convince Jacob to back off. The fear of letting his people down was getting to him.

"The night is just beginning," Caden said again.

"When is he coming? Where is he, Caden?" Jacob demanded. Caden stayed silent.

Seran moved in front of Jacob, blocking his sight. "Your buddies, Jasper Collins and Taylor Jane, are they here too?"

Caden let out a few more coughs. "Oh, they are long gone. They've already completed their mission, ha ha ha."

"And what mission would that be, Caden?" Seran was not joking. This time, he knelt down and put his charged-up hand close to Caden's face. Jacob wished he was the one doing it, instead.

"You think you scare me? Oh, great sir Seran, master of the elementals and protector of the Light One. You have nothing to scare me with." Caden was mocking Seran.

"I can think of something, Caden."

"STOP CALLING ME CADEN!" Caden screamed.

"Then what should I call you?" Seran softly asked.

"Zar Ignitus." Caden gave them a sinister smile that sent chills down Albert and Anna's spines.

"Well, Zar Ignitus, you are back in Cloudia… for good." Seran punched him square in the face, knocking him out instantly. The coughing stopped, as well as the obnoxious talking. Jacob settled down, wrestling Bron's arm off him.

"Jacob, you okay?" Albert asked.

"Yeah. I'm fine," he returned.

"He's changing them completely," Seran said. "Caden was such a sweet kid. Now he's clouded by the darkness of Follcane. He's building quite the army, Bron." The two exchanged worried looks.

"How many do you think there are?" asked Albert.

"All we know is that he's kidnapping Incendiaries. I wouldn't be surprised if there are creatures he's got under his control, too." Seran paused, turning his head towards the darkness with a pale demeanor.

"Do you think more are coming?" Anna asked.

"I wouldn't be surprised, Anna," Seran replied. "Well, now we know who's been spreading the grailum. Follcane's guard has been traveling in and out through the Underportal."

Bron held the limp Caden in his hands, and the group moved forward. Jacob kept looking around, anxiously awaiting more of Follcane's guard to show their nasty heads.

"So, what it is the Underportal?" Albert asked.

"That," Seran said, "is the Underportal."

The group had reached a dark black mass that was surrounded by clear gears that were spinning at incredible speeds. On top of the contraption were metal bars that held the black mass in place.

"This, as I said, is the Underportal," explained Seran. "This is the last resort means of travel outside of Cloudia. Until now, it was only known by a select few PPA members. It's not the most pleasant experience to use the Underportal, but it gives safe and secret passage. Unfortunately, it looks as though we aren't the only ones aware of it."

The contraption was spiraling over and over, covering the black mass. Jacob looked deep into the Underportal, expecting another figure to emerge or another one of Follcane's guard to pass through at any moment.

Seran approached the cycling sphere with clear gears and looked back. "We need to staff security here all day, every day, to make sure no one goes through. We also need to close it." Near the bottom of the big spinning device, Seran pressed a button. The sound that shot out of the contraption was like a steam engine whistle, and it pierced their ears. The gears stopped moving and slowly locked into place, covering up the Underportal like a tight suit of armor.

"What was that?" Anna yelled, still covering her ears.

"It was the sound of the machine turning off. Skipping through worlds isn't a quiet experience," Seran grinned, shutting down a few gadgets on the side of the Underportal. The black mass was reduced to a small crystal suspended in mid-air. He then knocked on the crystal, as if it was a door. "There, it's shut off. Now, unfortunately, we are putting all our eggs in one basket, but it will be our best chance to make sure Follcane and his army can only get in one way."

"What about floor six? Jasper and Taylor were able to get through to our city by the tunnel-"

"This is what's behind floor six," Seran cut Jacob off before he could continue. "The Underportal was what they were using. The tunnel leads here from inside the room just outside the lobby." Seran pointed where they stood. Sure enough, there was a hole about the size of a pothole sticking out from the ceiling with bright red and orange rings circling throughout. "This will all rest on our preparation now, Jacob. The Underportal has been closed, and our Elemental Academy has ceased its training. This is exactly what Follcane has planned for the entire time."

"Mathematically, the odds don't look too good for us, then," Albert said, holding his head down.

Anna put her head on Jacob's shoulder and sighed. Seran stood tall, and with his finger under the bottom of her chin, he picked her head up.

"Do you know the one thing he doesn't have, and we do, Anna?" Seran pointed at Jacob and smiled. "We have the Light One who is supposed to stop Follcane, the one who was prophesied to end the destruction and the darkness that hovers on the outskirts of Cloudia. We have him, the ultimate Cloudian, the hero, Jacob Wesley."

Jacob felt a glimmer of hope at Seran's brief speech. He felt important again, and suddenly, all the bad things he had done and the trouble he had gotten his newfound home into started to wash away, replaced with excitement.

They made their way back through the hall and up the spiraling staircase towards Gordonclyff Tower. Everyone was silent as the floorboards materialized underneath their feet, tracing their footsteps.

"But Seran…" Jacob began.

Before Jacob could finish, Bron jumped in. His voice was heartfelt and low. His speech was muffled. "You think the fate of Cloudia and the power you possess rests entirely on some emblem? As important as this jewel is - and don't get me wrong, it is important - Jacob Wesley, you don't have as many amperes as you do simply because of this emblem."

Bron paused and knelt next to Jacob with glee in his eyes. "You are special, little dude, beyond special. You are the Light One." He pointed at Jacob's chest. "What matters is what's in here, and your ability to use that to your fullest potential."

Jacob smiled but wondered how sure of this Bron could be, after only knowing him for a few cycles.

"There is one man who has refused to let light shelter our world," Seran began. "He hasn't only terrorized Cloudia, Jacob. He has terrorized the entire realm, and now he will stop at absolutely nothing until he bests you." Jacob's heart was being crushed, and his nerves made him feel as though he had missed a step and he was tumbling to his doom. "He may possess a lot, and his army may be building, but he doesn't have you. We do, and we have your back. We always will, Jacob."

Jacob paused for a moment, searching Seran to find the strength that he could easily show. "But what if I fail-"

"We're here, gang." Seran cut off Jacob as they reached the bottom floor of Gordonclyff. "Bron, thank you for your help tonight. Will you stand guard in the morning?" Bron nodded at Seran and handed over Caden. The trespasser's face was pale. Jacob couldn't believe that such a young boy could have such hate inside of him.

"For the first time in a long time, Jacob, hope has crept into the hearts of Cloudians. To Tomorrow, Jacob Wesley." Bron extended his forearm.

Effortlessly, Jacob grabbed his in return. "To Tomorrow, Bron."

The group went up and back into the lobby.

Selena Tee was twirling her golden hair in between her long fingernails as she watched the group enter the building again.

Albert was practically sleepwalking at this point, his head resting on Jacob's shoulder. "But it's only one trumnit, Magistra, I promise," he said as Jacob shrugged him off.

"This is where I leave you all," Seran announced. "Anna, Albert, watch over this guy for me. He's kind of important." He shook their arms and then gave Jacob a wink. "We will all be just fine. To Tomorrow." Seran's silver Volans coat turned, and he was gone in a single whoosh.

"Follcane needs the emblem to prevent me from stopping him. Now he has his guard infiltrating Cloudia to find different ways to get in here and attack secretly." Jacob couldn't even wait another day to start discussing it.

"Green eyes, relax," Anna said.

Jacob didn't even pay attention. "If his guard can get through unnoticed, just imagine what he can do. You heard Bron. He is bent on destroying all of Cloudia."

"Relax, man," Albert chimed in. He was waving him off, trying to make Jacob stop all this crazy talk.

"So, now what happens?" Jacob continued feverishly. "Follcane shows up, kidnaps me, tortures me, kills me, and kills everyone else?"

"I don't think Seran will allow that to happen," Anna said, looking frightened as well, but trying to remain optimistic. "Even without you here, Follcane hasn't been able to do anything but kidnap Incendiaries. Seran has been able to protect Cloudia. You saw what he did in there. He is powerful and sharp, and in touch with what needs to get done."

"Yeah, but my presence alone has caused Follcane to want to finish things," Jacob retorted.

"We will fight!" Albert gave a few sloppy movements to try and bring comedic relief to Jacob's nervousness.

Hours later, tired and exhausted, Jacob climbed into bed too tired to think and drifted off into a dark sleep.

Maybe tomorrow held the darkness he feared, and maybe it didn't. All he cared about was resting for now.

# 18

# DIVERSION

The following week, the clouds had shifted to reddish orange, indicating it was the end of their training semester. The group was outside Gordonclyff Tower near the cobblestone walkway of the center.

"How can you guys even think about anything else right now?" Albert was pacing back and forth on the cobblestones, his hand under his chin, rubbing anxiously.

"Relax, little dude. Ya know ya aced everything, guy," Colby flicked a few ice puffs in Albert's direction.

"Yeah, what are ya worried about, getting a 9.9 instead of a 10, Al?" Brandy chuckled and tossed in a few ice puffs of her own. Albert dodged the flurry of ice balls.

"It will be any minute Al, don't worry," Anna said.

It was tough for Jacob to focus. A cold feeling was spreading through him that had nothing to do with the weather or the impending assessment results; a tight obstruction in his chest seemed to be increasing. He knew that the group was used to stories of terrifying villains, but the mere fact that it was so easy for kids his age to sneak in and out of Cloudia made him feel less and less secure. His friends, playing and laughing near him, speaking soft words and cracking jokes about Albert, not shrinking in place and doing everything that they could to hide from the inevitable danger that Follcane would create for them baffled him. He was restless, his leg nervously shaking up and down.

Albert's was only shaking faster because he was anticipating his assessment. "Has anyone received a holomessage yet?" Albert spat out anxiously.

Colby's eyebrows raised at the tiny band on his wrist. Albert jumped over.

"False alarm, just a message from ya mom." He shook his head in Albert's direction and then giggled.

"Watch, I bet I failed Movements," muttered Albert feverishly. "I haven't mastered the double-stomp as well as sir Athene prefers it. And skyracing, I'm a joke, I took too many alphashells to the skull. I thought for sure I aced Cloudian History, but…" Albert began pacing again.

"Albert, shut up! Ya, starting to make me nervous and I don't even care!" barked Brandy. "And when ya get the best grades out of all the elementals…"

"Stop! Don't jinx me, don't jinx me!" said Albert, flailing his arms around hysterically. "I know I've failed everything! My sources will be severely disappointed. I'll be shoveling flycer fecal matter for the rest of my days!"

"Wait, what happens if you fail?" Jacob asked the group, trying to snap out of it.

"Ya get kicked outta Cloudia for good, bro," Colby looked seriously into Jacob's eyes. Jacob's stomach squirmed, regretting the morning trumnits that he had downed so quickly.

"Don't listen to these buffoons, Green Eyes," said Anna complacently. "You get another chance to retake them over the break before next yer. There's usually a few elementals who don't pass, and-"

Anna's words were interrupted by a loud alarm that went off in her lux-band. Albert leaped back, holding his lux-band as steady as could be as he crashed through the group. A bubble jumped up on his holo-screen, flashing the words Level 1 Results.

"Whoa, I got mine, too!" Colby and Brandy shouted at the same time.

"Me too," Anna said, smiling brightly.

Jacob's wrist started flashing shortly after. Albert climbed to his feet quickly. His legs were still trembling, but he tried his fastest to swipe through the screens, looking at each result as it passed his wrist. Jacob crawled slowly to his feet. Anna, Colby, and Brandy were huddled up nearby, too. Jacob swiped through each screen. The first screen displayed the grading system they used:

7-10 Passing Grades 4-6 Retakes 0-3 Repeats

And then came Jacob's results:

Level 1 Results: Jacob Wesley's Performance

Skyracing 10
Movements 8
Elemental Training 7
Weapons 6
Skyzing 3
Cloudian History 5
Total Assessment Score 6.5

Recommendation: Retake Two Cycles from Todi

Jacob swiped the screens several times, his breathing becoming heavier with each slide. This may have changed his mind about Follcane being the terrifying news. He was stuck on the screens for Skyzing and Cloudian History. He was in shock. His perfect 10 in Skyracing and 8 in Movements didn't make him flinch. He felt as though he would struggle in Weapons, and even Skyzing, because he had paid the least attention to those classes, even skipping it accidentally a few times. Mr. Natansis had very little patience for him when he fell asleep in the middle of a lesson, but to fail Cloudian History, only getting a 3? it must have been a wrong score. Maybe his scores were swapped with Buster Nalum's. That had to be it!

He barely lifted his head to look at the others, unsure of what to say. Colby and Brandy were dancing in a circle with their arms entangled. "7s on the dot! Getting through to the next round! Wicked!" they shouted as they left each other's arms, only to return and repeat the same dance.

"How did you do, Anna?" Jacob's voice cracked.

"10s in everything except for two 8s in Skyzing and Skyracing," she said happily. "I expected Skyracing, but it looks like Natansis was super hard for everyone."

"Yeah," Jacob mumbled.

"That's fantastic, Anna!" Albert shouted while flailing his arms.

"Alright, let's hear it, little dude," Colby said.

"Only one 9, and it was in Skyracing." Albert did another leg-kick dance. "I thought I was statistically due for a much lower grade."

"Nicely done, Albert!" Anna patted him on the back. "You probably did the best out of all the elementals."

"Wait a tick, what about Jacob?" Brandy asked.

"Yeah, dude! Ya must have done wicked good in everything," Colby followed.

Jacob was just standing there frozen like he had seen a ghost, and he couldn't shake the feeling. "I... not too great," said Jacob, in a small voice.

"No way, Green Eyes," said Anna, holding up Jacob's wrist abruptly and swiping through his screens for him.

"Oh… ya weren't kidding," Colby said, as he peeked over Anna's shoulders at the results. "Man, what a jerk Natansis is. A 3?! Come on."

"Well, it's not so bad, Jacob. You can retake them over the Decembri Cycle and pass easily." Anna was rubbing his back to make him feel better. The rest of the group nodded and patted him on the back lightly.

Jacob looked back down at the screens above his wrist. They were much worse than he could have ever imagined. Sure, he knew he was in a new world where everything was foreign to him, but he felt like he stood a solid chance of being on the same level as everyone else. He was just starting to get the hang of everything. His stomach was sinking faster than a giant ship. The 5 in Cloudian History was killing him. It was odd, really. Magistra Dayan was so lovely, and he looked up to her. He was the only one who even enjoyed that class. Elementals complained all the time about how boring it was and that they couldn't wait until Movements. He lowered his head again in one last sulking effort to erase the grades from his mind.

The group decided to head out on that note. Reaching the exit, Anna turned to say something, but a flash of red light surrounded by what looked like flames spiraled past their faces. It was an incredible explosion that smacked right into Gordonclyff's walls opposite of them.

# 19

# THE RESCUE

Next, to Selena Tee's desk, the explosion slammed into the wall, sending pebbles of stone all over the ground. Jacob instinctively ducked his head to dodge the blast. After the blast had cleared, he heard a bunch of feet running in the opposite direction. Slowly lifting his head, he found Selena Tee laying on the ground with burn marks on her cheeks and a cloud of smoke evaporating near her forehead. She coughed, indicating that she was okay. He heard screams behind him and turned around.

Behind Jacob were seven smaller individuals who appeared devoid of life. They were holding Albert and Anna, who was flailing and screaming for help. Colby and Brandy slowly got to their feet, too.

"They took Al and Anna!" Jacob shouted, and then leaned forward to chase after them.

Colby caught Jacob on his Volans collar. "Dude, wait!"

"For what? They have our friends, come on!" Jacob shouted and tried to get free of Colby's grip. "I'm going through to Athene's room, and I expect you two to come with me." Jacob nodded towards Colby and Brandy, who seemed to think they were going to get away without being a part of this plan.

"But Jacob-" Brandy began.

"NO BUTS!" Jacob shouted. "You want to live in a world that's covered in clouds, or one that's burning in fire? Do you want to enjoy flerry trumnits for the rest of your life, Brandy? You think skyracing will still exist if Follcane gets through? I've only been here barely a yer, and all of you have known about this your entire life, yet it seems like I'm the only one who cares. We need to stop Follcane and his army, and we have to get our friends back. You want to live long enough to see me become the Light One, or do you want to die young because you're scared? Who cares about assessments or Magistras or prophecies? This is our life, Cloudia's life, and unfortunately for us, it will be up to us to save it. We have to go after them now. I know where they are going, and we have to go now. I'm sorry, but I'll never join Follcane. I won't allow myself to be kidnapped like the other elementals were before. I'm going with or without you, but I have to go now."

Jacob was huffing and puffing. It was almost like he was an Incendiary; the way smoke was shooting out from his ears and nostrils.

Colby and Brandy paused for a moment, stared at each other, and then they clunked their heads and their forearms together. Jacob was right, and he knew that they knew it, too. "We're with you," they said firmly, at the same time.

"Good," Jacob said. "Now, let's go get our friends back." Jacob started to run off.

"But wait," Brandy said. "Shouldn't we tell Seran?"

"Yeah, it may pay off to have the best Cloudian on our side. No offense, dude," Colby said. "At least leave a note to alert him, or something?"

Jacob pondered for a moment but then came to his senses. "That's a good idea." Jacob opened up his holoband and was trying his best to figure out how to send the message. He had never done it before and was struggling with sifting through the 3D screens above his wrist.

"Here, let me do it!" Brandy shouted and took Jacob's arm. She swiped through and finally sent a holomessage that said, "We're in trouble, meet at the..." she turned to Jacob, looking for the answer.

"Sixth floor," he said firmly. The message was sent, and Jacob darted off. "Follow me."

Two cleaning coordinators gave them an odd look as they walked by, but they remained quiet and went back to check the rooms.

It was dark in the tower that night. Everyone was mostly in bed since they were the only elementals out past curfew.

"Hey, what are you guys still doing up?" Brian Saunders had clumsily stepped into the conversation.

Jacob's patience was running thin, but he knew that they had to remain steady. "Uh, Brian, we're just playing Holosees, it's a new game that just came out. We'll see ya later." Jacob said, attempting to shoo him away.

This didn't work, as Brian just remained next to Colby, staring at them suspiciously. "Oh, cool! Any chance I can join? I've been super bored since the assessments finished and all of Timber is just hanging outside. I don't get much sleep. I usually sleepwalk through the night, and Selena has to point me back to bed. Hey, where is she? I don't see her by her desk."

Jacob peeked back over at the desk and remembered that she was on the ground. They couldn't waste any more time. Any tick now, Seran would receive the note discussing their plan and potentially blow it up. Even worse, Follcane could be sneaking in through the Underportal and their friends could be dead. "Brian, we are busy, please leave," Jacob shouted, but too impatient to make up excuses. He led the others past Brian and towards the platforms.

"I guess no one wants to be my friend, not even the Light One." Brian put his hands in his Volans pockets and walked very somberly back up the hall.

"Man, I thought he'd never leave. I thought we would have to tie him up or something," Colby said.

"Yeah, that was close," Brandy said.

Jacob was staring at Brian's purple dreads as he walked away. They were swishing back and forth. Jacob felt bad; he knew what it was like to be an outcast. It had been a long while since the days of Ms. Larrier and Tommy's wedgies, but he felt for Brian. Reluctantly going against everything his gut was shouting at him, he spoke up. "Brian, wait!"

Brian turned around instantly and dashed towards Jacob, almost falling several times, of course.

"Jake, what are ya doing?" Colby asked.

"Yeah Jake, he will get us all killed," Brandy followed.

"The more, the merrier. The better chance we'll have against the Dark One," Jacob said briskly.

Colby and Brandy lowered their heads but didn't have a choice.

It may have been a mistake, but Jacob wanted to do for Brian what Nyx had done for him, even if it was the last nice thing he would ever do again. On the platform ride up to the sixth floor, Jacob caught Brian up on the plan.

"So, we're going to face Follcane and his guard ourselves?" Brian asked, panicking now that he understood the mission he was partaking in.

"You in or out, Dread Head?" Colby asked firmly.

"I thought this was a good idea, Jacob, but bringing him was a mistake, man," Brandy tried to plead with Jacob.

"Brian it's going to be scary, but I need you to be fearless right now. Can you do that?" Jacob put out his hand. Brian gave him the Cloudian greeting, gulped, and nodded. "Okay, glad to have you. We don't have any time to waste now. We need to get going."

The group reached the cold and mysterious sixth floor. Jacob paused for a moment. He noticed six red rings and burned marks all over the glass case in front of them.

"Well, this is how they have been sneaking into Cloudia," Colby said, his knees beginning to tremble. The staircase was dark, and they didn't have a light to guide them. "Jacob, dude, check it out," Colby said in a low whisper.

"What is that stuff?" Brian peeked over Brandy's shoulder to see a glittering gold substance sparkling along the cracks in the floor.

"It looks like there's a ton of grailum around here," Jacob said while tracing the walls with his fingers.

"What's grailum?" Brian was still trying to catch up to the rest of the group.

"Boogeyman powder," Brandy said, and then chuckled to herself.

"This is no laughing manner, Brandy." Jacob gave her a glare that looked like it would turn Brandy into stone. "We don't know too much about it, Brian, but we have found it all over Gordonclyff and the Underportal entrance. I have a feeling it's tied into the Incendiaries that were captured, and maybe even Follcane."

Moments later, the group found themselves in front of a mysterious door. "This is it." Jacob halted their movements with his arms. The siblings looked at each other with bewildered faces. Brian edged over Jacob's shoulder nervously.

"Lux Aparte," Jacob said, raising his right hand with his lux-bands flashing brightly. Darkness was clouded with light that radiated from the center of his hand like a small ball twisting towards the bronze door.

Floor six disappeared, and in front of them, there was a greenlit room with gears spinning on the ceiling.

Kneeling across the room was a crimson-cloaked figure, whispering something to himself.

"Hey!" Jacob called. Spiked red hair bolted forwards leaving a trail of fire behind. Jacob chased after him. The group reluctantly pursued behind. "Get back here!" Jacob growled, reaching out to try and stop the blazing figure.

"Jake!" Brandy screamed.

"That's Jasper Collins," Jacob said. "One of the Incendiaries that Follcane kidnapped."

Jasper Collins was skyzing out of platform and up through a tunnel in the wall that was barely big enough to fit any of them. Jacob and the Johnstons barreled through, struggling to keep up. On the other side of the wind tunnel was the training gymnasium for Movements. That is where they found Jasper, who was standing still, with jars of darklights in each hand.

Jacob and the others stopped short only a few feet away from him. "Put the jars down, Jasper," Jacob hissed from across the room.

"Take one more step, Light One, and these little creatures' lights go out for good." A fire started to rise behind Jasper, blue flames coiling upward like mini tornadoes. "And you can call me Zar Fume."

The flames took a circular approach, creating a ring around the group. Stuck with no way out, Jacob whispered something to Colby. Brandy tensed up, catching wind of it, too. Brian shielded himself, crouching near the ground.

"Oh, isn't that delightful? A little huddle!" Jasper yelled.

Jacob smiled and peeked over his shoulder at Colby, who nodded softly while clicking on his lux-bands. "I'd watch your grip, Jasper," Jacob said.

"The only thing you need to worry about-"

"NOW!" Jacob yelled. "Lux Evannnnnnuuuuuuscent!" Jacob waved both arms in the air. The light disappeared from everything in the room, even the jars holding the darklights.

"Fanum Metalllllllliiiiiii!" Brandy and Colby belted out, sending silver tin ropes flying from their arms, snapping right in Jasper's face, cold-clocking him straight to the ground. Then, the siblings' ropes wrapped around him like a mummy, and the two pulled him towards the group. The lights came back on, and Brandy and Colby stood over him, smirking. Jasper was tied with his hands behind his back. Solid steel ropes intertwined around his body. Struggling did nothing.

"Clever trick, but there's nothing you can do," Zar Fume smiled, with a drop of blood trickling down from his lips. "It's only a matter of time now."

"Shut up!" Colby couldn't help himself and punched Jasper in the face. Then he waved his hand in the air, trying to wipe away the pain. Brian even let out a giggle this time. "Always wanted to do that," Colby said.

"Where's Athene?" Jacob asked, kneeling beside Jasper.

"Who?" Jasper coldly asked.

"Soriun Athene, the man whose office you're sitting in." Jacob grabbed Jasper by the collar of his Volans coat.

"Got me confused with someone else?" Jasper asked.

Jacob stood, confused, and Colby pressed forward, trying to force his way at Jasper Collins again.

"Relax, Colby," Jacob said, shoving him back towards his sister.

"He's not worth two broken hands, Colbs," Brandy said, leaning forward.

"How do you know about the darklights? How did you know how to get in here?" Jacob continued his questions, hoping to get anything he could out of him.

"If I told you that, you'd lose your marbles. We don't want the Light One to go losing his marbles, now," Zar Fume continued.

"When is he coming? I know you know. Where are my friends being taken?!" Jacob got closer, holding Zar Fume against the wall of the office. Zar Fume looked down, and then up again at Jacob. Jacob's eyebrows tightened, trying to search for an answer he could muster from the intimidating interrogation he believed he was conducting.

"See you soon, Light One." In a flash of black smoke, Zar Fume vanished clean out of sight, and Jacob was left looking like he was holding an invisible collar.

"What happened?!" Brian squeaked.

"Yeah, where'd he go?" Brandy cried.

"I don't know. There's nothing left of him." Jacob checked the small office inside the gymnasium. Old textbooks and papers were scattered everywhere.

"Hey Jake, check these out." Colby was holding a few pieces of crumpled paper written with blue and silver ink.

Seran,

I'm close. I've been through the Underportal and into Shei'El, but no sight of Follcane. I've seen his army, the guard. One boy was ordering them around and giving speeches. I'm not sure who he is, but from what I can tell, he's starting to delegate to them. His ranks are growing. I'm onto Forrestine and will be back next cycle.

Regards,
S.U. Athene

"I don't get it, though. These are letters from Athene to Seran stating that his findings are bringing nothing," Jacob said.

"This means Athene is working for the PPA, too," Colby said. "Good to know he's on our side. Dude is sketchy."

"That's relieving news," Brandy said sarcastically. "And Jasper, or Zar Fume, whatever his name is, had no idea who he was."

"Right." Brian patted her on the back. She wiped off the handprint that Brian left behind.

"So, why are they sneaking into his office, then?" Jacob began looking around again for an answer that might jump out from the shelves of Athene's cold office.

"I have no idea, but do ya smell that?" Colby whispered. Jacob paused, putting the roll of paper on the ground.

"Smell what?" Brandy was like a hound dog, sniffing around to see what Colby was talking about. "I smell it, too. It's fire!"

"Fire?!" Jacob questioned.

They looked down and felt the ground start to heat up. A moment later, the floorboards fell from underneath their feet. Darkness fell upon them, with a sparkle of red from an explosion. The group went tumbling down a rough surface which felt like a slide, with daggers piercing their limbs as they fell through the building. As they were tumbling, they came across nails and other shards that dug into their skin. Finally, after a long tumble, their bodies slammed into the floor and they felt their bones ache. Luckily, something had prevented them from hitting the ground too hard.

"Oh, man," Brandy moaned, trying to get up.

"My forehead, my ribs, and my back," Colby began. "Jake, it's killing me."

"The tumble was too much. I can't feel my feet." Brian was shaking his legs and trying to regain feeling in them.

Jacob stood up and tried to crack his potentially broken back into place. "Where are we?" he asked, facing the group.

However, the purple streams of flowing water and the trail of grailum answered his question for him. "We're right back underground. It's the Underportal."

Jacob turned back to face the group, but something was off. Their faces had become pale, and their legs began trembling. In the background, he could hear mumbling and grumbling.

"What's the matter, you guys? What is it?"

A ball of light fluttered through the Underportal. Jacob turned around to face this mysterious sight. It wasn't a freaked-out Seran or even a giddy Nyx. It was something else, something cold and lifeless. He felt an odd sensation climb up his spine as the figure stood in front of him, a hooded cloak slipping off its head.

# 20

# SILAS FOLLCANE

Several feet from Jacob's face was a man with dark burnt skin like ash, his face held together by a tight metal mask. Swiveling down his body was a dark crimson Volans cloak with giant holes. Its edges were burnt. He folded his hands behind his back, his dark red eyes giving him a sinister look. His vacant eyes remained fixated on Jacob, completely ignoring the two Johnstons who stood trembling behind Jacob, fear taking over their bodies. They put their hands on Jacob's shoulders, bracing for the peril that Follcane would bring.

Follcane slowly inched forward, leaving traces of ash behind him. "Well," he said, in a raspy, chilling voice. "How nice of you to join us. The hero, the Light One, the chosen protector, Jacob Wesley."

Jacob felt a spider crawling up through his stomach and into his throat, but this was a spider full of nerves. He began to speak softly. "You're him, you're-"

"Silas Follcane. A pleasure to meet me?" Follcane asked sarcastically.

Laughter echoed throughout the room. Jacob noticed that five reddish orange-cloaked figures were standing behind Follcane with their hands wrapped around the necks of Albert and Anna, who were struggling to get up.

"Do ya know who ya talking to?!" Colby shouted. "Yeah, this is Jacob-"

"Igggggniisssss Remitionis!" Follcane spat out, and instantly, Colby and Brandy were tossed against nearby walls, collapsing like dominos.

"Brian, no!" Jacob tried to cut him off, but it was too late; Brian charged forward and was sent barreling towards the stone wall. He fell to the ground, piling onto the others. Their bodies were laying on the floor, crushed and lifeless.

Follcane winked creepily at Jacob. Jacob tried to rush forward to attend to the Johnstons, but Follcane waved his right arm in a cyclical motion, freezing Jacob into a coerced statue. The invisible pull holding him in place was too strong to break. Follcane turned his head eerily towards the group, laughing nefariously before turning his crimson eyes back to Jacob. "Careful, boy. You may have skyracing speed, but you're in dark territory now. It isn't polite for a guest to strike their host. Don't fear, though; you'll be able to put those outstanding amperes to the test soon enough."

Jacob felt worse than he'd ever felt before. With no Seran or Bron in sight, and his friends all knocked out, it was inevitable that their Light One would fail. In his solitude, the lonely feeling that had finally disappeared all those cycles ago rushed back to smack him in the face. The Kendall Drive Orphanage was nothing compared to this.

"But the Underportal… it was closed," Jacob mumbled to himself.

"Closed? Ha! I am not bound by your silly technology, Jacob Wesley. Your fearless leader isn't as smart as you think." Follcane had heard him under his breath somehow.

Jacob remembered that Seran had disabled the Underportal when they had caught one of Follcane's Zars. Bracing for his life, he could only listen to Follcane who now began to pace back and forth across the marble floor, taunting Jacob with every step. After a moment his wild eyes widened into an evil stare.

"My Zars were only stalled temporarily, but being me has its privileges. Let's get this straight, boy. I am the boogeyman in everyone's nightmare. I torture dreams and souls. No amount of darklights or Underportal or grailum will ever stop me from taking what I want. Tonight, I take the one thing that puts the clouds back in the sky. Tonight, I finish what I started with your pitiful prophecy nonsense. Tonight, I finish you. No more prophecy. No more Light One."

Jacob nervously twitched as Follcane turned back to face him. His skin looked severely burned. Only one of his eyes could be seen, and it was just enough to send a shriveling sensation down Jacob's spine. Follcane's right arm raised, and he stretched his thin fingers out before closing them into a fist. Flames sprouted out of nowhere, circling them and creating an arena of fire. Jacob knew his death was soon to follow, and now, any chance of last-minute help was closed off by the fiery blockade of doom.

"Do you think you're so special, Jacob Wesley?" His breath rasped with disdain. "Just like your mother, you're so naïve. You think the world is made of good. You think people can be saved. Well, I'll tell you something… my father, he couldn't be saved. Who was there to stand up and save him?"

Follcane pointed at Jacob with such force that wind blew past his face, almost knocking him out of his frozen pose. "He was deemed insane, helpless… beyond saving. He lost my mother, but he still had me. That didn't matter, did it? It didn't matter that he still had a child. She left him and ruined him. She ruined the work he did. She ruined the man he was and took him away from me!"

Follcane lifted his arm maniacally and let out a streak of hot, piercing fire, setting the Underportal ablaze. "Now, it's time to finish the work he started. It's time to seek out revenge on what your people did to him. Your world thought my father was so dangerous? I could destroy more of you with my little finger than my father could ever dream of doing. It's a shame you won't live long enough for the Great Skyrace. I would have loved to have seen you struggle a bit more."

As Follcane paced around the circle, Jacob spotted something shiny on the ground nearby. *That's it!* Jacob shouted inside. It was the Jewel of Futura, gorgeous in its splendor, resting near his foot. Jasper, or Zar Fume, whatever his name was, must have left it in Athene's room when he disappeared.

"And to think that measly Seran Keerinus sent that oaf Bron to look for me. Well, a possessed flycer was waiting for him." Follcane continued addressing the group, pacing around Jacob.

Jacob was trying with all his might to break the invisible chains that held him in place. *The jewel is only inches away.* "Have you no compassion?" Jacob was mustering all the courage he could, trying to distract Follcane.

"Me? Have compassion?" Ignoring Jacob's comment, Follcane faced his Zars again, and they erupted into laughter. "Do you have any idea how easy it's been to sneak into your tower and recruit my Zars?" Follcane whipped his neck around, turning his head towards Jacob. "The lack of security in this dump of a city is quite amusing. And the most precious one of all is allowed to walk the grounds at night only to be captured by me, your feared Dark One. It's not just sad, it's pathetic."

Jacob did not take kindly to the words Follcane was using to describe his home.

"Now, you're in for a treat, Jacob Wesley." Again, Follcane's skinny fingers twisted in front of the crowd of admirers. "And to think that this boy here is the one to end my revenge. Oh, he's prophesized to defeat me… me, the Dark One!" As the harsh words left his mouth, the surrounding Zars continued their maniacal laughter, but Follcane didn't move. He didn't even laugh. His cold, crimson eyes were burning right into Jacob's. He slowly crept forward until he was within inches of Jacob's face. The smell of burning ash consumed Jacob's nose. Fear turned to red-hot anger and Jacob wanted nothing more than to end Follcane right there. Follcane's scarred face passed by Jacob's left cheek. The cold from his metal mask brushed against Jacob's skin. "You evaded me once, boy," Follcane whispered in his right ear. "Don't think it will happen again. Pity, you'll never get to meet your mother."

Jacob winced. Heat began to brew inside of him. His eyebrows arched at the mention of his mother.

"Oh, didn't you know your selfish mother is still alive? Well... barely alive." Follcane lifted his head from Jacob's cheek, laughing deeply. "Now, boy, there's one thing that I require, and I believe you know what it is," Follcane recited, pacing back and forth, taunting Jacob. "And no, Seran isn't here to save you. He's too busy lurking around your protective agency. I'll be long gone with you and the jewel by the time he figures it out."

Jacob was trying to stall as much as he could until Seran figured out where he was and showed up. "I know where the jewel is," Jacob mumbled.

Follcane stopped pacing and halted his steps. "And where is it?" asked Follcane, who now stood as still as Jacob did. "I knew you'd have it. Seran is too frightened of me, you know. Leave it to him to trust the Light One with the most precious emblem in all of Cloudia." Follcane edged closer, sizing Jacob up and down as if searching for it. "I'll ask one more time, where... is... it?" He could feel the heat from the flames burning the hairs off the back of his neck. This didn't stop Follcane from continuing his taunt. "Silly, isn't it? The man who so famously escaped the Dark One isn't here to see the city lose its most prophesized hero." Follcane inched closer. "I've been watching you, Jacob... a lot more than you think. As admirable as your powers are, your insipid refusal to do what's right brings you low. Top of your class, winning in skyracing, becoming the youngest Electro. Why waste such talent?"

"Jealous?" The bit of courage that Jacob had been reserving leaped from his mouth before he could catch it.

Follcane let out a slow and methodical laughter. "You know, Jacob, the most sought-after joy in life isn't happiness, but true power, and those who have the most of it are the ones who take it." Follcane cracked his neck. "And I intend to take that sacred emblem either by gift or by force. There's no reason to be jealous of a little boy who's been handed everything."

Follcane released his grip on Jacob, who collapsed to the floor after the invisible chains had been removed from his feet. Taking advantage of the moment, Jacob kicked the emblem closer. He still struggled, but not nearly as much as before.

"Where is it, boy? Only one last chance."

*Somehow, I need to get the emblem on, blast Follcane, and rescue my friends. Maybe I can send a holomessage so Seran can see where I am?* Jacob tried to reach for any possible out.

Terrifying darkness came into Follcane's face. "Such a shame. You could have been great as one of my Zars, perhaps even the best of the group. But now you're just letting all those amperes go to waste." Follcane kneeled next to Jacob and brought his face against Jacob's nose again. His breath smelled like old newspapers.

Here goes nothing. One last thought swept through his mind before Jacob's foot swept through the emblem's silver chain and kicked up it into his hand. He closed his eyes and just caught the edge of the jewel.

"Don't move a muscle!" Jacob demanded.

Follcane froze in place as if to mock Jacob's request. "Or what?" Follcane laughed.

"Or this."

Jacob threw the emblem around his neck. The Jewel of Futura tightened on his chest, and a burst of energy filled his veins. A gust of wind blew the cloaked figures to their knees. He could feel the energy sprinting up his spine and out of his throat. Jacob's eyes burned brighter than they had ever before. The light was emitting from his lids like waves of sunshine. He saw Follcane shielding his face with his arm.

"He's been hiding it!" Follcane shouted. "No matter, the boy is showing his full hand of cards."

Follcane retreated a few steps as Jacob lowered to the ground with his arms outstretched, feeling stronger than ever. His lux-bands clicked on and started spinning wildly with immense energy.

"Pathetic," Follcane whispered. "And certainly not worthy of me. Let's see just how much power he has. Get him, Zars."

Standing still in the center of the fire ring, Jacob awaited the four cloaked figures approaching with red and blue flames spiraling towards him. "NE, NE!" Jacob shouted, deflecting the attack with his left arm. It was coming very naturally to him. Fear escaped Jacob as confidence swam in. The cloaked figures jumped into his circle as Follcane fled the scene to observe. One of the figures to the left tried a double-stomp-swipe, and Jacob quickly dodged the attack while swiping a cloaked figure to the right with his foot, who was sent spinning onto the ground and out of the flames.

"Destroy this miscreant!" Follcane yelled impatiently.

"Visor Firestorm!" one of the cloaked figures shouted, and a rope of fire flung in Jacob's direction.

"Electro Toss!" Jacob rebutted, catching the rope and tossing the figure like a rag doll into the flames. He dodged and blocked another attack while delivering two sharp knees to the stomachs of the two remaining figures, and then took a hold of their hands incredibly tight. He shoved the figures off him and stared at Follcane with his eyes burning deep into his soul, feelings of vengeance stewing in his heart.

Follcane was applauding the show he had put on. He even leaned forward, bowing as well. "Impressive, I must say, even if they were all young anyway."

The Zars could barely stand, but still manage to retreat behind Follcane.

"Leave now, Follcane," Jacob spat confidently from across the room. "While you still can." He started to pace forward in Follcane's direction, confidently locking eyes with him, peering into his cold, empty darkness. There was a silver aura rotating around him like a clear forcefield.

"Oh, we're not done just yet, boy." Follcane tiptoed forward.

"Then fight me!" Jacob demanded, his knuckles braced, fists clenched, and standing with his arms locked in the fighting pose that Athene had taught him during Movements training.

"Be careful what you wish for." Follcane folded his arms and took a step forward. He lifted his cloak to the right and cracked his neck. "Oh, how I have waited for this moment."

Jacob was standing still, awaiting the battle that Follcane had promised.

"Prepare to meet your fate, and say goodbye to your poor excuse for a life," Follcane said, with hatred and a hint of excitement. "Now, why don't we all see what you are truly made of? Enjoy your last breaths, Jacob Wesley."

The taunt from Follcane barely affected Jacob who stood confidently still as he embraced the surrounding energy around him. *The Electro Blast,* he thought to himself. This was the most appropriate time to use it and he only had a small window to use it.

"Don't worry. Soon, you'll be reunited with your arrogant father," Follcane maniacally laughed.

"SHUT UP!" Jacob screamed at the top of his lungs, letting out a loud wind that collapsed the room and even made a few bricks fall from the walls nearby. The purple rivers that were flowing around them rushed into jets of water that rained down over both Jacob and Follcane.

"Enough!" Follcane shouted. "It's time for you to die!"

Jacob barely got to blink before red flames went spiraling by his head nearly, ripping off his ears. As he spotted them, a searing pain blasted through the pit of his stomach. Follcane's fist was leaving Jacob's gut, and a knee connected with his chin right after. He could have sworn that his jaw and his brain had become detached from his head. Reeling backwards, he barely kept his balance. The pain made him scream more loudly than he had ever screamed in his life. He could barely stand, let alone open his eyes. Follcane was nowhere to be found, only a dark fog remained in his place.

Turning to his right, he was met with red beady eyes. The next thing Jacob felt was a sharp pain through the small of his back, and within a tick, his face got slammed against the cold, wet floor. Turning over, he felt like his spine was about to fall out of his body.

"Was that a smart move? Asking me to engage in combat? Now I finish the prophecy once and for all!"

Jacob could feel the wind from Follcane's scream. Jacob tried to stand, mustering any courage he had. Unfortunately, it was short-lived, as flames pressed against his chest, crushing him to the ground once again. Smoke evaporated from Jacob's body. The next thing he knew, his feet had left the ground, and the only thing holding him in place was Follcane's cold, rock solid hands clutching Jacob's neck like it was a baseball bat.

"This is it, boy! Remember this day, Cloudia!" Follcane was yelling at the ceiling. "The day your hero, Jacob Wesley, became nothing more than a fictional story."

Jacob could feel the Follcane squeeze and tighten his grip. Every last breath poured out of his own lungs.

"Mertooommmmmmmm…"

Jacob heard the beginning of the death blast that he read about in the restricted commands section of his Electro training textbook.

"JACOB, NO!"

His attention was diverted, as, to his surprise, Seran was standing what felt like a football field's length away.

"Ahhh, the great escape artist finally makes his appearance. You're too late this time!" Follcane grinned and turned back to Jacob. "Flll…"

"NO!" Follcane's words stopped as soon as Jacob screamed instinctively, "ELECTRO BLAST!"

The grip around Jacob's neck loosened as a beautiful ball of electricity formed in the palms of his hands. Like a jolt of lightning, it crashed against Follcane's chest, sending him spiraling through the air. In the distance, Seran stood in place, stunned. Wasting no time, Jacob rushed through the air and grabbed Follcane's stomach, followed by another "ELECTRO BLAST!" which sent a blue electric spiral of energy upwards, blasting the burnt Dark One again. It smashed him against the ceiling, and then he fell, limp, to the ground.

Jacob rose to his feet and approached his fallen enemy. Follcane was laying in front of Jacob and appeared to be severely injured by the blast. Seran remained still, shocked at the sight that he had witnessed.

Follcane began to speak, but Jacob didn't let him. He performed a quick swipe-double-stomp, knocking Follcane's grasping hands away. Then, he held his palm out towards Follcane's face. Follcane was wheezing and coughing as the smoke cleared away from his limp body.

"Now you know that I am the Light One-"

Before Jacob could finish, he felt a gust of wind crack into his chest, which sent him spiraling through the air and onto the ground. He could barely see Seran's silver hair waving in front of him.

"ELECTRO FLARE!" Seran shouted, and a green ray shot out from the palm of his hand. The Underportal suddenly started spinning again.

"Lucky boy. Lucky move. I'll be back. You may have won tonight, but the war is far from over. Your ashes are inevitably going to be mine." Follcane moved his hands in the air and yelled as loud as he could before sending a flaming red ball to the top of the ceiling. The ceiling instantaneously collapsed, turning dust and rocks into a pile of rubble on the floor.

Limping, Follcane waved over to the remaining fallen Zars and retreated through the Underportal just before it collapsed and bent inward. The metal holding the transferring platform broke, sending balls of white light forward, along with thousands of tiny grailum specs. The walls started to cave in.

Jacob saw a glimmer of light shining from Seran as he approached him, but Jacob was bleeding from his chest, and his eyes started to quiver.

Darkness overcame him, cold black darkness. Then his eyes finally closed.

# 21

# EXTRA CREDIT

When Jacob came to, he was met with a strange but familiar freckled face surrounded by orange curls. "Looks like he's awake, hee-hee, ta!" Jacob heard Nyx's excited voice ring in his ears.

"Take a step back, you clown, and make way for the caregiver." Bron pushed Nyx out of the way as a beautiful short-haired brunette woman with lux-shades on approached Jacob's bedside with what looked like a wet towel.

Nyx and Bron strutted away, while Nyx was humming, "The Light One's okay, tee-hee, ha-ha, he ousted the Dark One, we're free, ta ta!" all the way back down a row of cream-colored beds that were hovering in place.

"Feeling better?" the caregiver asked, in a soft voice that soothed Jacob's ears.

"Slightly. Feels like a knife is sticking out of my back, and brick is stuck to my forehead."

The nurse bent over Jacob and patted his forehead with the towel. He felt a creamy substance instantly take the pain away.

Jacob saw the caregiver's nametag. It read, "Heidi Egan".

"Wait, you're-"

"Albert's Mom, yes. They sent me in to tend to you specifically. Makes sense, with you being the Light One and all. Albert's told me a lot about you."

"Well-"

"Thank you for taking care of him, and for being his friend, Jacob. Albert doesn't have many back home. Now, rub this towel on your head and back twice a day for the next week. You'll feel better in no time."

"Thank you." Jacob was delighted to meet Albert's Mom for the first time, but he was even more relieved that someone was tending to him.

"My pleasure. You have one last visitor waiting to speak with you."

Seran's silvery dark hair came into Jacob's view. And just like that, with a smile, Mrs. Egan was out of sight.

"Sir, first let me say I'm sorry for not clueing you in and letting you know our plan. I just couldn't risk anyone stopping me. I- I hope you understand."

"I was young once too, Jacob," Seran began. "I would be lying if I said I never disobeyed someone." That made Jacob feel a bit better, and he smiled while attempting to sit up in his bed. Seran turned to him, patting Jacob on the shoulder. "That being said, what you did was extremely stupid, and you nearly got yourself kidnapped - or even worse, killed."

"I'm sorry, sir," Jacob said, his cheeks bright red with embarrassment.

"Well, let's just say that having the emblem around your neck makes it even. The whole hero thing is making its rounds throughout Cloudia. You've become the hero we all knew you were. That's two successful attempts at dodging Silas Follcane. Except this time, you actually fought the man."

Jacob barely could retell the scene. At this point, it was all just hazy memories and flames. "Where are my friends, sir? They were all-"

"They are fine, after attending to you," Seran interrupted. "Mrs. Egan is making her rounds to her son first and then the rest. Just bumps and bruises for most of them. You took it the worst, broken back and several concussions. Good thing she does wonders in here."

Jacob almost fainted again at the phrase "broken back." Sweat began to drip from his forehead.

"It seems Ms. Friendly has taken a strong liking to you, Jacob. She's been pacing back and forth by your bed for the past few dis. She's distraught." The news of Anna's concern made him ease back into the bed a bit, his back still aching. "It was a close call with Follcane, but surely it won't be the last. We can expect him to make several attempts to retrieve the Jewel of Futura, and you, again."

"Sir, Follcane... he had Electro powers too. I'm sure of it."

"Yes. Follcane was a former student of Athene's teachings. He's more powerful than any other Electro. His amperes were slightly over 800 at the time. It seems Follcane is letting slip some of his magic tricks already. Luckily for us, you are just a bit more powerful than he anticipated." Seran confidently winked at Jacob. "From the looks of it, he's got a nice little limp to remember you by now, too. That Electro Blast was impressive."

"I injured him, that's right!" Jacob's smiled. "I- I- I got him? I mean, I had no choice, but I never imagined I would be able to complete the move. I failed several times in Athene's class," Jacob explained.

"The display of bravery you showed was quite special, especially for someone your age. Don't focus too much on the deed that was done, though. You have much training to do. It will take much more to stop him next time."

Jacob sat back in his bed and rubbed his forehead, taking in the realization that he had barely left a scratch on Follcane.

"You'll get over it soon enough. Unfortunately, throughout this war, a lot of deaths will happen until one side wins."

"One side wins?"

"Yes, this will be a war for the pursuit of power. Power is the root of all evil, and the thirst for it can be your greatest downfall. It's simple. Either Follcane wins, or he loses. And the key to the outcome is you."

Nothing at this point could shock Jacob after learning that he had actually put up a fight against the darkest villain that Cloudia had ever faced, but nevertheless, this responsibility was not something that he necessarily wanted. "Sir, do you think Follcane will come back soon?" Jacob asked, worried.

"I'm not sure, Jacob, but I can tell you he most likely will continue to build his guard of Zars in preparation. I think he underestimated you, and we have to maintain that advantage. It won't be long before he decides to challenge you again, and we want to make sure you are fully ready for such a battle."

Jacob lowered his head in agreement, which hurt him a bit, as he was still ailing from the fight. "Follcane mentioned something else. Something about my mother. I have this weird feeling inside of me like she's alive, but I can't explain it."

Jacob could see Seran's smile change slightly to a firm look. He scratched the back of his head and put his arm under his chin in thought. "The state your mother was left was uncertain. By the time I arrived, she was gone." As Seran spoke, Jacob noticed an odd air about him, as if he wasn't completely telling the truth, but he knew better than to inquire.

"And my father? I'm confused as to where my father is in all of this. No one seems to know, and it's odd that Follcane mentioned him."

"That's something that I'm afraid is unknown, as well. We only knew of your birth from the prophecy, which doesn't speak of your actual parents; who they are or where they come from. The prophecy speaks of the date and place you were to be born. The details are rather vague, and we spent many cycles trying to decipher the meaning behind all of it. It's an interesting book, I'll tell you. It sure has thrown the PPA for a loop. This world was drowning in negativity before we got our hands on that book. We were yearning for something to believe in, and then it fell into our lap."

"Fell in your lap? I thought someone in Cloudia wrote it."

"Someone did, but not someone from Cloudia," Seran stated.

Jacob was becoming more and more puzzled by their discussion. "Then who?"

"Hmm, we aren't too sure. To be honest, it just arrived one day through the Underportal. Bron discovered it. Ever since, we've been reading it. We've believed in it. It's what saved this world before your arrival, the hope and faith that something would protect us." Seran smiled and winked, and Jacob felt warmth overtake him.

"Seran? Last question."

"Anything, Jacob. It's quite alright."

"The orphanage, Kendall Drive. Why did you leave me there? That place is awful. Ms. Larrier was extremely cruel to me." Jacob put firmly.

Seran let out a deep sigh of reaction to Jacob's words. "Trust me, Jacob, it was never my or anyone in the PPA's intention to put you in harm's way. We needed to find an area to send you where Follcane and his guard would never be tempted to look for you. Griffin was our best chance. The trace on your amperes stopped right on that street so that no one could detect you, not even us. Luckily for us, we had Nyx to watch over you as you got older. I am very sorry that you were mistreated, and that it was a terrible home to live in."

Jacob smiled a bit, feeling a sense of forgiveness. Just as he was getting comfortable, his back ached again, and he held onto it to try and stop the pain.

"Why don't you get some rest now, Jacob? You've been through enough. Besides, you have barely had any sleep, and you're going to need it."

"For what?"

"There is still much left to do."

"But sir, I failed the Level One Assessment, I can't even go to the next tier of training."

"Be that as it may, a test does not determine the life that lives in your body. I'm sure you'll pass it on the retake." Seran turned to leave, dragging his Volans coat behind him.

"Seran?" Jacob called after him.

"Yes, Jacob?"

Jacob waved his hand forward, careful not to hurt himself. "To Tomorrow."

"To Tomorrow to you, Jacob."

The following day, Jacob was still feeling woozy, so with the assistance of his friends, he made his way up the platform towards the beautiful auditorium. His aching shoulder and barely-attached head kept him from getting a good seat in the floating bleachers. The crowd sat covered in darkness as a blue strobe light faded away. Cloaked figures were waving the different elemental groups into their rightful sections. The examination scores were showing on the large holographic screen in the center of the auditorium. Jacob staggered a bit and heaved a sigh of disappointment when he again saw his grade low grade next to a picture of himself.

Below and to the right of the cheering Incendiaries sat Buster, bumping fists and then foreheads with Probus. There was one remaining seat in the Electro section which with the assistance of the Johnstons he was able to take. Suddenly, two strobe lights fluttered throughout the room and a skyzing Magistra Dayan took the stage.

"The first yer of Elemental Academy is complete!" Magistra Dayan shouted cheerfully. "And quite the yer it has been, wouldn't you say? Assessments have been totaled, skyracing has commenced, and we have witnessed some of the highest scores ever in our elemental training. I hope all of you enjoyed learning about your amperes as much as I did." Dayan winked and smiled in Jacob's direction, and then she raised her arms in the air enthusiastically.

"As you can see, the scores behind me reflect the top performances from our first yer elemental groups. In third position, representing the Hydros with a 9.3 is Anna Friendly. In second position, representing the Incendiaries, with a 9.4 is Buster Nalum." Cheers and stomping feet flooded the auditorium. Buster stood up and bowed toward Magistra Dayan before turning to sneer in Jacob's direction.

"In first position, with an incredible 9.8, representing the Hydros is Albert Egan!" When his score flashed on the screen, thunderous applause struck the room. Magistra Dayan bowed to him from the center. He waved back in her direction gleefully.

"Very well. Great job to the three of you," said Magistra Dayan. "Now, as you know, a few of you didn't pass this yer, but that's okay. Decembri session will allow you to retake your first assessment."

"Excuse me for a moment, Magistra." The cheers came to a screeching halt and silence fell upon the room. Dark silver strands of hair crept out from one of the cloaked figures as Seran emerged onto the center stage. The Magistra smiled, nodded, and left the stage so that Seran could take her place. He stood firmly with his hands folded behind his back.

"Thank you, Alexandria," said Seran. "It's no longer a surprise to all of you that our hero has now returned to Cloudia and is sitting among you…"

Jacob turned beet red, blushing even worse than when Anna grabbed his hand.

"It was surprising to us all that he became the youngest Electro ever to grace the Academy of Gordonclyff."

The Johnston siblings jumped out of their seats with loud yells that almost knocked over Brian Saunders.

"He's the Light One, and he rescued all of us!" Brian stood up as well, a little wobbly, bringing his hands together to cheer on Jacob.

"Was it a surprise to you when he went on to finish a cool first place in one of the most thrilling skyrace trials we have ever seen?"

Anna and Albert jumped up this time, cheering and pointing in his direction. Jacob held up a limp hand to acknowledge his friends. An amazing feeling started to swell inside of him.

"Perhaps the biggest surprise of all was when he showed a sensational amount of bravery by standing up to the Dark One known as Silas Follcane."

A wave of silence swept the room. Jacob's friends slowly retook their seats, anticipating the next few words. The rest of the auditorium uttered shock and turned their heads in Jacob's direction. Seran began to pace silently in the center of the room, the lights falling upon his feet, and then back up to his face.

"It takes a great amount of strength to carry the incredible burden of being the Light One," said Seran, smiling at Jacob. "To join a world you know nothing of, and then find out that you are here to save that world from a terrible and dangerous force." Seran stopped in front of Jacob and his smile disappeared. "Even though it shouldn't, it surprised me to witness the power that Jacob Wesley holds. He defeated Follcane a week ago. He stood in front of him, didn't back down, and overpowered him until Follcane fled the scene."

The auditorium was quiet enough to hear a darklight buzz by. No one was cheering, no one was standing, and no one was blinking. They were all sitting, shocked and awestruck by the words Seran was speaking. Jacob couldn't help but notice Buster and Probus standing with a look of disgust that made it seem like they had eaten chamenions again.

"This score, in my opinion, doesn't represent the anomaly of an elemental that sits before me." His hands waved off the score of 6.5/10 that displayed next to Jacob's name. He raised both of his hands in unison, summoning electricity from his fingertips. A beautiful yellow ball of electricity sprouted from his hands and smashed into the holoscreen. "I'd say he earned a little extra credit!"

Seran sent another wave of blue electricity smashing into the holoscreen and forcing the score to change to an 8/10. The auditorium erupted with roaring cheers and powerful stomps. The tower felt like it was shaking as Jacob began to beam. He was overwhelmed with such incredible joy. His friends bolted over to him quicker than Ezekial Addams and lifted him into the air. Seran nodded in Jacob's direction before heading off the platform and out of sight. Everyone was throwing their hands up in excitement and joy for him.

He was hoisted above Colby's head and carried throughout Gordonclyff Tower that night in celebration of his new passing score.

After the assessment review, things calmed down a bit. The end of the yer brought the end of Elemental Academy. After going a thousand miles an hour this past yer, Jacob enjoyed the calming dis ahead of him. From skyracing lessons to Movements and Donumdans, and finally facing the Dark One in an epic battle, Jacob had accomplished more in one yer than he had in his entire life.

The next di, his legs still felt like noodles, and his arms were barely holding on by the strings. The cobblestone street was still frozen over outside, and all the elementals were out and about, skyzing around while tossing ice puffs and snow at one another.

Walking by Gordonclyff Tower was a giant hologram of Magistra Dayan who was saluting and applauding the elementals. "To Timber, To Metallum, To Hydro, To Incendiary, To Electro!"

Although feeling broken and hurt, his mind was as stable and strong as he could ever hope for. Unfortunately, for all the good that had happened, Buster and Probus hadn't been banned from the school, but that would probably be pushing his luck. On his way over to his group of friends, Buster scoffed at him and whizzed an ice puff past his face. Jacob didn't have the energy even to entertain that nonsense. Nearby, Colby was chasing Brandy, sliding around on one of the ice slides.

"You're gonna get an ice puff to the dome, B!" Colby taunted Brandy with a wrapped-up ball of fluffy silver snow.

"You'll have to try and catch me first, Colbs," she shouted back.

Albert was practicing some celebration that involved flailing his arms in a swinging motion. Anna had to duck out of his way multiple times to avoid being caught by a rogue fist. Jacob realized that this was the first time he was going to be speaking to them since the battle. The excitement began to bubble like a stew inside his belly.

"Hey, guys," Jacob said, anxiously strolling up to the group.

"Jake!" Colby shouted, stumbling to the ground.

"Hey, Green Eyes," Anna said bashfully.

"Hey, Jake. How ya feeling, dude?" Brandy called from behind Colby.

Albert wasted no time in running up and hugging Jacob immediately.

"I'm okay, I guess. It's been a rough few days. My back was sore, and I broke my right arm, as you can tell." Anna looked worried.

"You're a true hero, Jacob! I can't wait to tell my sources about you rescuing us from Follcane and his Zars." Albert was leaping with joy.

"Truly scary down there. Don't remember much, to be honest, Jacob," Colby said, rubbing his arm.

"Yeah, getting kidnapped and teased by all those brainwashed Incendiaries wasn't too fun," Albert said, finally letting go of Jacob.

"Next thing we knew, Seran, Nyx, and Bron were carrying us out to see Al's Mom back in Gordonclyff tower," Anna spoke up.

"Did anyone get to see what Seran did?" Jacob asked. They shook their heads.

"But what I would have given to see ya up against Follcane! Man, that must have been awesome!" Colby shouted. Jacob smiled and winced, holding his ribs tenderly.

"But what about the Underportal and the grailum and the four-" Albert began.

"Let's worry about it later, Al," Anna giggled. "I think it's time we finally start celebrating, instead of worrying." She put her arm around him and Albert as Colby and Brandy joined them. Their Volans coats all swished in the wind as they stood there, soaking in the moment of not having to worry about Follcane attacking or breaking into Cloudia. Jacob knew in the pit of his stomach that this battle was far from over, but it reassured him to bask in the moment of temporary freedom.

"So, what are you guys doing until the next level of training?" Albert asked.

Colby and Brandy answered at the same time, "skyracing!" The group laughed.

"I'll be shopping at High Corner most of the break with mom and dad. Lyndsey is bragging about her boots, and she's getting the next Magenta Freezes for the rest of the cold term." Anna twirled her hair.

"My sources will be back in H-Twenty, so I guess I won't be hanging out," Albert gloomily replied.

"You'll be with me, Al," Jacob said, with a wide smile. "We have some training to do!" Albert jumped for joy, and Jacob wobbled a bit.

The sun passed through the clouds.

"Even the mighty Light One, Jacob Wesley, has to babysit sometimes!" Colby said, skyzing away.

Albert chased after him as the wind blew some of the ice off the stony platform. Jacob, his belly full of laughter, could not be happier than in that moment, with all his new friends. He took great pride in spending time with Albert, even if it was babysitting him, as Colby had said.

Jacob waved goodbye as the siblings, along with Anna, hopped on the giant Airz Taxi and headed back to their home. Jacob gave them the Cloudian greeting, and followed Albert back towards Gordonclyff, looking forward to what came next.

"To Tomorrow!" they all shouted.

Printed in the United States
By Bookmasters